Seek the Fair Land

Walter Macken, author and dramatist, died in April 1967 in his native
Galway at the age of fifty-one. At seventeen he began writing plays
and also joined the Galway Gaelic Theatre (the now celebrated
Taibhdhearc) as an actor. In 1936 he married and moved to London
for two years, returning to become actor-manager-director of the
Gaelic Theatre for nine years, during which time he produced many
successful translations of plays by Ibsen, Shaw, O'Casey, Capek and
Shakespeare. To enable him to have more time for playwriting, he
moved to the Abbey Theatre in Dublin. Macken acted on the London
stage, on Broadway, and also took a leading part in the film of
Brendan Behan's *The Quare Fellow*. Many of his plays have been
published, and of his novels the first two, *I Am Alone* (1948) and *Rain
on the Wind* (1949), were initially banned in Ireland. Several other
novels followed including *The Bogman*, which first appeared in 1952,
and the historical trilogy on Ireland, *Seek the Fair Land*, *The Silent
People* and *The Scorching Wind*. *Brown Lord of the Mountain* was
published a month before his death.

Walter Macken

Seek the Fair Land

Pan Books

First published 1959 by Macmillan
First published by Pan Books 1962
This edition published 1988 by Pan Books
an imprint of Pan Macmillan Ltd
Pan Macmillan, 20 New Wharf Road, London N1 9RR
Basingstoke and Oxford
Associated companies throughout the world
www.panmacmillan.com

ISBN 0 330 30327 9

29 28 27 26 25 24 23 22 21 20

A CIP catalogue record for this book is available from
the British Library.

Printed and bound in Great Britain by
Mackays of Chatham plc, Chatham, Kent

HISTORICAL NOTE

When Murdoc and Dominick meet in Chapter One, Drogheda
is invested by Irish insurgent forces who rose in rebellion in
1641 against, among other things, (a) the forcible plantation of
Ulster by Scots and English; (b) the Act of Supremacy, where-
by to be a judge, lawyer or government official required an
oath that the King of England was Head of the Church – an
impossible oath for Catholics; (c) the Act of Uniformity, where-
by Catholics could be fined or imprisoned for not attending
Protestant services; (d) the militant anti-Catholic attitude of
the Parliament in England who were already in opposition to
King Charles and determined to remove all Catholic land-
owners, Irish and Anglo-Irish, from their estates.

By Chapter Two, Cromwell is investing Drogheda with his
Ironsides, King Charles has been executed, and Irish and
Anglo-Irish, Catholic and Protestant, are partly united in a
last despairing effort to avert a terrible destruction by a gloomy
and pitiless enemy.

In the event the whole of the country was to be reduced
for the first time; the remnants of the powers of the Gaelic chieftains to be shattered for ever; the Brehon laws by which they
lived to be finally abolished; Gaelic judges and bardic poets to
sink into poverty and virtual oblivion; all Irishmen to be deprived of their possessions unless they took the Oath of Abjuration, which was an oath of apostasy. So, deprived of their leaders
by apostasy or exile, the fate of the nation was to be left in
the hands of the little men, who over the centuries and almost
from scratch were to build a new nation, tenaciously, slowly,
and indomitably, sustained by their hunted priests who 'cried
to God' in 'wood and bower and attic tower on mountain side
and bleak sea-shore'.

Seek the fair land
that is over the brow of the hill.

FROM AN IRISH PROVERB

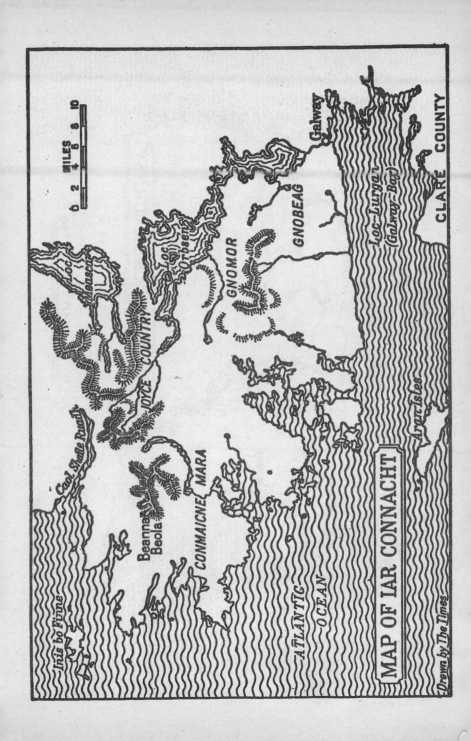

MAP OF IAR CONNACHT

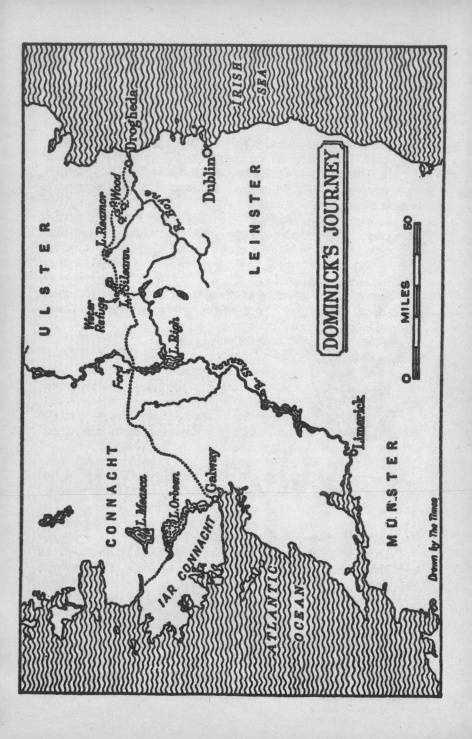

CHAPTER ONE

THE MOON shone fitfully through the clouds. It was piercingly cold. The waters of the Boyne carried slabs of ice towards the sea. The heights outside the walls, beyond the Mill Mount, were covered with a white hoar frost, so that they seemed to be part of the fortifications.

The men moved cautiously through the orchard, putting each canvas-covered foot carefully on the frozen ground, their weapons gripped tightly in their hands, almost five hundred little white clouds rising from their mouths each time they breathed. The path through the orchard wasn't large enough for their numbers as more of them came in through the small blind door. There they scattered out, merging with the gaunt, leafless, black, distorted fruit trees.

The iron gate of the orchard was open too.

They poured through that now, more quickly. They all found it hard to believe that they were walking in the town itself; that by all the rights of war they had the whole place at their mercy.

They stood in an unorganized bunch outside the wall of the orchard looking at the buildings all around them silhouetted against the night sky. They didn't like the buildings.

Murdoc didn't like them. He was used to the wide sky, trees and open plains, or the deep woods. Hundreds of buildings one on top of another appalled him. Now, he thought, we should turn to the left and, taking the garrison of the ports guarding the St James's Gate in the back, wipe them out, and let the besiegers come flooding in.

He moved in that direction. He could see the gleam of an arch that led into the street of St James in front of the towers guarding the gate. But he was on his own. The mass of men had moved to the right towards the quays and the salt workings near the river. He shrugged his huge shoulders and followed after them. They will make for the bridge, he thought, and get into the north town. But then what about the soldiers behind us? They can take us in the rear. It is more important to get a gate open first. That was the trouble: nobody had believed in this foray, nobody had believed that there would be a little orchard door between the main gate and the river left open at a certain hour. It was only a chance. It might have been a trap. So about five hundred curious adventurers had taken the bait. And now they were in, and there was nobody to lead them. This was the place for the Great Chieftain himself to be, Murdoc thought with a sneer, instead of preening himself miles from the walls.

He hurried after the bulk of the men.

There was plenty of room for them at the south quays. They all stood there like *cabógs* gazing at the water of the Boyne pushing past below, ferrying blocks of ice like white fairy boats. Then they looked across the river where the town rose behind the ramparts of the built-up walls and the Maiden Tower. She was a queer maiden, Murdoc thought. They could see the wooden steeple of St Peter's gleaming dully in the moonlight, and the houses climbing the steep hills on the far side looked like weary, burthened, back-bent men.

And then a terrible thing happened.

From the throats of the men gathered at the quays there arose a great shout. It was a primitive shout of joy, of victory, just a good shout from being in an advantageous position. It's the reason we never win wars, damn them to hell, Murdoc thought savagely. Like boys playing at soldiers. What kind of a people are we at all?

He shouted. He had a powerful voice.

'To the bridge, you fools!' he roared. 'To the bridge!'

There was a silence for a moment after his cry, as if the town was holding its breath, and then there came the sounds of a trumpet call, and clang of steel, a musket shot, and the tolling of a steeple bell.

Murdoc turned and ran right, through the narrow street that backed on the ramparts of the river, and the rest of them followed him, shouting, shouting, damn them, in case people didn't know they were there now.

They came into the wide market-place in front of the bridge, swivelled on their running legs there like horses, and then charged across the open maw of the bridge towards the tall tower on the opposite side. Too late, too late, because a thick body of pikemen, half-dressed, sleepy-eyed, but startled into quick awaking, were plunging towards them from under the arch. The two unorganized bodies of men met in the centre of

8

the bridge and soon the sound of cold steel could be heard entering into warm bodies. There were shouts and groans.

Murdoc, hitting aside the pikes aimed at his body and trying unavailingly to sink the head of his own into the chest of the man opposing him, was cursing the Great Chieftain. Where is the powder and ball, Great Chieftain? Where are decent long handles for our pikes, dear Chieftain? The pike handles were too short. They had cut them themselves in the woods from ash and birch and willow, but they were too short, and as the long pikes of their opponents felt for their chests and their eyes and their brains, they started to fall back across the bridge. Then Murdoc hurled his pike as if it was a spear at the man who was harassing him. It went soughing into his chest, and as he fell Murdoc caught his long pike, reversed it and shouting, shouting, started to beat around him with it.

The men behind him rallied, and pikes flew through the air like arrows.

The men before them fell, but as they did so they disclosed behind them the kneeling musketeers. There was just time to see them before the heavy volley sounded, and the smoke-cloud arose, and all around him Murdoc heard the men falling, and screaming as they fell. A ball plucked the heavy cap from his own head. As they wavered another line of musketeers came through and knelt, and behind them Murdoc could see the white-shirted man on the black horse, waving a sword. He threw himself flat as the next volley sounded, then he rose and ran back and he ran fast and now he had a sword in his hand. The bridge was littered with the bodies of men, groaning or silent. There wasn't much time. The garrison was now facing them on the other side too. Murdoc cleaved his way through them with the sword. Behind them again the muskets sounded. You could hear the balls ploughing their way into men's backs, and then they stopped since some of their own had fallen. Murdoc cleaved his way, got past the mouth of the bridge and then, being blocked by the mass of shouting men there, turned right and ran down a narrow lane. Some of the others, the main bulk of them, had turned left, running and fighting their way back towards the orchard.

He was grinding his teeth. Like rats, he thought, like rats, and not through their being good, but we being bad. Useless. By now they could have been raping this town. We had it like a rotten apple.

9

He kept going left and ran into what must be St John's Street. There were four armed men running up it. Murdoc ran towards them, a tall towering figure, his teeth white in the middle of a black beard. He was roaring like the devil out of hell, they said. He nearly decapitated one man, backswiped with the sword at another, and then was through them. The first archway on his right he went into, hoping it wasn't a close. It wasn't. It led into a rabbit warren of lanes; all small stone houses or mud-walled ones with thatch. He had an idea. The poorer the quarter the surer you were that they were Irish. He paused to listen.

There was great uproar over to the right of him. That would be the men getting back through the orchard door. Some of them would never get through the door. They would be like himself; cornered inevitably and just having to fight until he died.

He cut through another narrow lane. It was dark in these lanes. Not a light shone anywhere. How would a man know where he might find a friend? If only he could run to a copse. If only it was in the open air. These places smelled to his nostrils of foetid things, discarded sewage, and rotten fish. He closed his lungs on them, got into another laneway, and as he ran past a stone house that must be backing on the river, he saw a gleam of light through a wooden shutter.

He stopped. He went back. He felt the door. It was a heavy oak door, low, soundly built, studded, iron-clad. Was it too good to be Irish?

He knocked at it with the hilt of his sword.

He spoke urgently, penetratingly, in Irish. 'If you are an O or a Mac, for the love of Our Lady, open the door!'

He listened, his ear close to the wood. He thought he heard a whisper of movement.

He spoke again.

'If you are an O or a Mac, for the love of St. Patrick open the door!'

He heard the iron bolts inside being drawn. The test was true then.

The door opened. It was black inside, the light he had seen was doused. He stumbled on the step as a hand reached out and pulled him in and then the door closed behind him. He could hear the bolts being shot home. He stood there helplessly in impenetrable blackness, feeling like shouting. Listening closely.

Maybe ne would get a knife in the back.

He straightened his back at the thought, gripped his sword very tightly. He heard a rumbling as if of some heavy thing being moved, and then something being opened. Then he felt a hand on his arm and heard a soft voice at his ear. 'Come,' said the voice in Irish. 'Watch your feet. Climb down steps when I put your feet on them. Eight until you get below. Stay there. Don't make any sound.'

He was led, like a blind man, a few paces. Then he felt the hand leaving his arm and holding his foot, shifting it. He felt a step under it and stood on that, then felt for one below, found that and started to walk down. It was really black. He bent in a futile effort to see and cracked his forehead. He didn't shout or groan. 'Best of men,' said the voice above him, and then Murdoc's feet felt rock and he stood there. Above him he heard the flap closing and then the sound of a heavy thing moving over it. Murdoc sat on the ground. Stone flags they were. He welcomed them. They felt cool to his hot body.

He sat there, the sword gripped between his knees, and then he heard the hammering, muffled but unmistakable, on the door above.

That's the way to die, he thought, squealing in a sewer. It brought him to his feet. He could smell strange things all around him, spices and leather. He felt around with his hand until he discovered the steps. He mounted them softly, until his head was stopped. He put pressure on the flap. It was immovable. He listened.

He could hear the bolts going back. The floor above his head thundered as heavy boots walked on it. An authoritative voice was speaking in English. 'Vermin. Introduced by a traitor. Is this the way we are repaid for our kindness? We will find the one who opened the door and send him to hell without a limb whole on him.'

That soft voice again. 'And you would be right too, Mister Ledwick.'

'This fellow was seen coming this way. Two corpses behind him in the street. We will scour and flush the whole Irish quarter until we find him, and we will hang the people protecting him, without mercy.'

'You would be right too, Mister Ledwick. We were sleeping. We heard the shouting and the shooting. There is just the place up the steps. My wife and little girl are there, that's all '

II

'Go and look,' said the other voice. The heavy feet moved on the floor above.

'Don't wake the child if you can,' said the soft voice. Funny the authority of that soft voice. It quietened the military tramping a little.

'You have a good name,' the other said. 'You have kept it clean in the town, and your lady was a Bolton. Which man among the Irish would do a thing like this? You know them. Which of them would do a thing like this?'

'Any of them, with enough courage,' said the soft voice.

'Does it require courage to be a traitor?' the other one shouted rhetorically. 'You want to take care!'

'Irish or English, they are all one to me,' the soft voice insisted. 'Whatever a man is, he has to eat, smoke, and be shod. Beyond that I have only a scientific interest in them.'

'You read too many books,' the other shouted. 'As a citizen of the town it is your duty to expose treachery.'

'I'm not a citizen,' said the other. 'I'm a servitor.'

'You don't talk like one,' said the other with heavy humour. 'Find the man who opened the door and you will be a freeman the next morning.'

'A freeman with a severed throat,' said the voice. 'That would be pleasant. It could be written on my gravestone.'

Oddly enough, Murdoc thought, the other fellow laughed. He shouldn't be laughing, Murdoc thought, he should be looking for a cellar. The other feet tramped across the floor again. He heard the door closing and the heavy bolts being shot. There was peace then. He didn't hear the soft-voiced one's feet on the floor. He must be walking like a cat or else he wore no shoes. He was consumed with curiosity. What kind of a fellow was this to remain so calm in the midst of such bloody events? He must be an old greybeard, to have lived so long with an attitude like this. Suddenly he shivered. He went down the steps again. He felt icy cold. The sweat had frozen on his skin. His fingers were almost stuck to the hilt of the sword. He freed them and stretched them.

Then he heard the rumbling over his head, the cover of the cellar was thrown back and he was looking into a rectangle of candlelight.

'Come up, mighty warrior of Eireann,' said the voice in Irish then, 'until we have a look at you.'

Murdoc, inclined to anger, started to mount the steps.

CHAPTER TWO

MURDOC ROSE out of the hole in the ground like a giant out of a bottle. He was a huge man. His hair was long and his beard was long and hair and beard were as black as basalt rock. He wore a coat of rough yellow-brown home-spun cloth and a thick leather belt around his waist that held two knives, a sword-scabbard, and a heavy pistol. His legs were covered with trousers of the same cloth. His canvas-covered feet and the ends of the trousers were tied around with rough hemp rope. He smelled of sweat and the smoky oil of untreated wool. He also smelled of pine trees and open spaces, and the man facing him had to look up at him.

'You are very big,' he said gravely.

Murdoc laughed. Now I know why that other curmudgeon laughed too, he thought.

The man facing him with the thick candle in his hand was slight and small, with almost yellow hair, a thin face, extraordinary light blue eyes, and a mouth that turned up at the corners. He wore knee-breeches of fairly good cloth and a white linen shirt, open at the neck. He was well made, all the same, Murdoc thought. The wiry kind. The deceptive kind. He also wore heavy shoes that should have made sound, and that hadn't, so he supposed he must walk like a cat.

'I thank you for giving me *dídean*,' said Murdoc.

'All Irishmen are entitled to shelter,' said the other. 'If I didn't give it to you, the next man would, but fortunately for you, you knocked at the only house on this side with a cellar.'

'Who are you?' Murdoc asked.

'I am Dominick MacMahon,' said the man. He's young, Murdoc was thinking. Early twenty. Isn't he very young to be so settled?

'I am Murdoc O'Flaherty,' he said then. 'I owe you my life.'

'You owe me nothing,' said Dominick. 'If you were a dog I would have done the same. In fact I'd prefer to do it for a dog than a soldier.'

'What kind of an Irishman are you at all, with a name like that?' Murdoc was mad. 'Did you know a great man with your

13

name died on the ice of the river a few weeks ago? Were you related to him?'

'I might have been, on the wrong side,' said Dominick.

'Where is your blood?' Murdoc asked.

'It's in my veins,' said Dominick, 'and that's where it's going to stay.' He looked at the furious eyes of the other. 'And you better not spill it now,' he said, 'or you'll have no chance of getting free.'

Damn him to hell, Murdoc thought as he laughed. A blooming laugh. Then he looked with panic at the shutter which had betrayed the light before. It wouldn't do so any more. The crack was covered with a strip of cloth. The other's eyes were twinkling.

'Hindsight,' he said, 'and the walls are thick. Come to the other room with me. It might be warmer there.' He started to climb the wooden ladder that led to the floor above. Murdoc looked around before he followed him. Bales and barrels. Elusive smells. Foreign ones. The heavy thing over the flap of the cellar was a sort of rough table with shelves in it for holding cloth. Then the light went out of it as Dominick's candle went with him to the room above.

Murdoc mounted the ladder.

He emerged into a more brightly lighted room, and a little warmer. There was a raised place over in the far corner covered with blankets. He could see the straw under the blankets. There was a girl sitting up in this bed looking at him. The sight of her made Murdoc hold his breath. Dominick's candle was revealing her. Black, black, curly hair and brown eyes and a white skin. The eyes looking closely at him.

'She should be living in the west,' said Murdoc, 'riding a little horse with her hair on the breeze. She is wasted in this rich land.'

Dominick laughed. Why did I say that? Murdoc wondered.

'The big soldier is paying you a compliment, Eibhlin,' said Dominick then.

'Thank you,' said Eibhlin.

'It's true,' said Murdoc. 'Only good people should live in the west land. Strong people, good-looking people. All these rich land places. No good. That's why I said it.'

'Why are you here so, man?' she asked him.

'Anywhere I can get at them, I will go,' he said. 'If we kill enough of them there won't be any of them left and then we will have this land to ourselves again.'

'In other words, you just want to fight,' said Dominick. 'Sit on the stool near the fire. You notice there is no fire. That's your Phelim O'Neill. There's no food. Until tomorrow. The ships got through yesterday. But we will give you something to drink.'

'That O'Neill,' said Murdoc, spitting in the dead ashes of the fireplace. 'A cock on a dungpit, crowing and crawing and scratching. The siege is lost, I tell you that. If it had been Rory O'More. But it wasn't. It's that other one. If it had been Eoghan Ruadh. But it might be yet. Then we can fight all over again.'

'Fight, fight, fight,' said Dominick, handing him a pewter tankard. 'What in the name of God would you do if there was no more fighting? Would you set up straw men in a field and start fighting them?'

Murdoc drank. The spirit was very fiery. It nearly made him cough. It was good to feel it ripping its red-hot way to his belly.

'How did you marry a man like that?' Murdoc asked Eibhlin. 'An Irishman with a noble name serving a crowd of lickspittles in a walled town when he should be out abroad in the fields and the woods with a horse under him and the rest of his clan at his back.'

'Too many of his people did that,' she said. 'Go and look at my baby,' she said then imperiously, pointing to the bottom of the bed.

He rose and lumbered over to where her finger was pointing. There was a basket there. A little girl was sleeping. She just fitted the basket. One pudgy arm was thrown back. She was the living spit of her mother, black curly hair. Murdoc chuckled. He straightened to look at them. Dominick was looking at the sleeping child. His face was soft. Eibhlin was looking at Dominick. A terrible black gloom came over the heart of Murdoc as he looked at the three of them. Not that he hadn't children of his own, wherever they were, and women, not wives. He couldn't see his children in the womb, which was where he would have to, since he never stayed long enough to see them any other way.

'I know,' he said. 'But one day ...'

'One day that never comes,' said Dominick. 'I know that. Up in the north we were many. We were planted and so we resisted the planting. Until I was sixteen. Fighting, fighting,

15

living like animals in the woods. Who had I left then? Nobody, nobody at all. All gone. Every single soul gone. Only me. I came into the walls. I'm going to stay in the walls. Let them rise or fall. I'm going to be me and my family, and I'm going to survive. All of us are going to survive.'

'You poor innocent man,' said Murdoc. 'There is worse coming to the towns. Men have told me, who have smelled the wind. There is a new power rising in England. The others will be only lambs compared to them. Listen. Leave the town. Remember I told you this. I tell you, go and seek the mountains. You hear that. No man is really free until he has the Beanna Beola at his back. Then you are free. No man can come at you but you see him. Take off when this is over. Listen to me. Oh, man, seek out the fair land under the Beanna Beola, and you will be free and you will survive.'

'Why can't you do that, then?' Eibhlin asked him.

'You see me,' he said, 'what am I? I'm a soldier. I like to fight. I like to be what I am, but always this is a dream. Some day I will go back.'

'You go back and leave us alone,' said Dominick. 'What are their wars to us? We are here, and we will stay here, let the English take the town or the Irish take the town, the little men will always be there, working away, rebuilding what is destroyed. They want us. They need us. They can't get on without us. We will be all right as long as we let them fight over our heads. Will you go now? They'll come back again.'

'How will I go?' Murdoc asked. 'Could I get over the walls?'

'No,' said Dominick. 'They will be well watched. Can you swim?'

'I can,' said Murdoc.

'Then swim you will have to,' said Dominick. 'Put this in your breast.' He handed him a small stone jar. 'It will keep you warm.'

'I owe you my life,' said Murdoc.

Dominick laughed.

'It's not worth much,' he said. 'It won't be long-lasting, I can see.'

Murdoc laughed too.

'May God befriend you,' he said, 'and give you happiness.'

'And you too, Murdoc,' said Eibhlin. She held out her hand to him. He took it in his own huge paw, a bloodstained one, he saw now. They both looked at it. Then he saw her eyes on his coat. That was bloodstained too.

'I don't want to smell blood on Dominick,' she said.

'I hope you never have to, Eibhlin,' he said. 'We will meet again under the Beanna Beola, with the help of God.'

'I hope Our Lady brings you safe away,' she said.

'Come now,' said Dominick, 'soon it will be getting light and it will be too late.'

Murdoc looked around the room before he followed him down the ladder. It was a happy room. There were gleaming copper pots on the wall, and over the bed there were shelves holding heavy bound books. These made Murdoc shake his head.

'They are the things that made a slave out of a MacMahon, I'll wager,' he said, pointing to them.

Eibhlin laughed. She had a deep bubbling laugh. It was the last sound of her that Murdoc heard before he went down the ladder after Dominick.

'Where now, friend?' he asked.

'Into the cellar,' said Dominick, going down. Murdoc followed him. It was a small cellar. It was damp. It was filled with barrels and bales. Dominick left the candle on a barrel and cleared a space near the river side of the wall. He leaned there and pulled and a deep heavy stone came out of the wall as if it was on oiled runners, as it was.

'It will be a tight fit for you,' said Dominick, 'but it's your only way. The tide is in the estuary. It will carry you up the river. When you are free of the walls you can get on the bank.'

'Why is this here?' Murdoc asked.

'I'm Irishman enough not to want to pay tolls,' said Dominick.

Murdoc chuckled.

'I'm glad we came inside the wall, even if we failed, so that I met you,' he said. 'I'll remember you for sure. God be with you!'

He held out his hand. Dominick shook it.

'The God of war will probably look after you,' he said.

Murdoc got on the floor and started to put his legs through the aperture. Then he levered himself backwards with his hands. The sword scraped the stone and he paused. It seemed to make a loud noise.

'Easy now,' the soft voice of Dominick whispered in his ear.

He had the candle. 'You'll find your feet in the tide when you stretch your arms. Let yourself in gently and it will sail you away. Come back again, Murdoc, in better times and we will talk to you.'

'I'll see you in the fair land of the Beanna Beola,' said Murdoc and then he was gone.

Dominick listened closely. He could barely hear the splash that Murdoc made as he let himself into the freezing water. Then he pushed back the stone into its position, piled the bales around it, climbed the ladder to the room above and said to Eibhlin : 'Our big slob of a soldier is safe away.'

'He was a nice man,' said Eibhlin.

'For a soldier,' said Dominick, and they both laughed.

Swimming with one hand, Murdoc felt for the brandy jar with the other. If you thought of how cold it is you would die, he said to himself. He drank all the jar contained, and let it sink empty and gurgling into the water, then he used two hands to swim, keeping close to the quayed walls. The time seemed endless to him until the quays petered out and he smelled the decayed rushes on the river bank. He hauled his way into them and scrabbled his way to safety through the mud and stones.

Then sitting in the mud he looked back at the town lying smugly under the waning moon and he said :

'May the luck rise with you, Drogheda.'

CHAPTER THREE

AT FOUR of the clock on the eleventh of September the first breach appeared in the wall to the east of St Mary's Convent.

Dominick was at the third breastwork where it joined the breastwork that curved to cover the towers behind the Duleek Gate.

St Mary's Church was almost in ruins, the broken stones of its steeple had served to make part of the breastwork where he now stood. The whole south of the town was wreathed in smoke, and in places flames which were quickly put out.

It was a demented moment as the heavy wall opened its chink of light and then burst apart as if it had been hit by the fist of a giant. Through the great crack appearing you could see the cannon belching flame from the Bevrack Mount outside, and the whole area black with the movement of men and animals – like ants they were, covering every hill and mound – and twinkling lights were appearing at the muzzles of muskets, and a harvest sun was gleaming benignly from the fittings of guns and weapons and stores. When he was on the Mill Mount before, he had seen the hosts of besieging men, and behind them the fields waving with golden grain, all but the great avenues trampled through the hearts of the cornfields.

The breach in the wall was suddenly filled with men. You could see their mouths open in their black faces as they came through and were shot down, and then hacked to pieces by the horsemen who converged on them through the opening in the breastwork.

Dominick's bow went twing, not twang as it should have done if it were even a long bow, or quonk if it were a crossbow. What am I doing here, shooting at men's throats with the short Irish bow that excited the curiosity of Spenser so long ago? Weren't all governing people the same? Don't arm the common people, and then when the great emergency arises bring them to the armoury and hand out weapons that have been stored there for a hundred years. When it was too late. He remembered the long evenings in the butts outside Tooting Tower. He was good with the bow. The butts were a relic of the days when the men were forced under penalty to practise the bow. But what use was the bow now against all the metal that was beating the town as flat as an oat-cake on an iron griddle; or taking the bodies of men apart and spreading them to the four corners of the world?

Twing, and this time he saw one landing deep in the throat of a man. His head was thrown back. Scarlet started to flow on to his russet tunic before he fell.

Then the opening was wreathed with smoke again as the guns outside, aiming half-pound bullets at the horses, found their mark and the horses screamed and threshed with agony as their blood flowed, and the footmen slipped on it, and the tall Colonel who had been commanding the horsemen fell with half of his chest shot away, exposed, black, and terrible.

The friars were on the breastworks, about six of them. They had nearly built the breastworks themselves with their bare hands. Black-faced, courageous, appealing, encouraging, shouting. The man he really knew, Father Sebastian, a very big man with a thin face, his robes tucked into his girdle, waving his arms, calling, building, appearing through the smoke.

It cannot last, Dominick thought. They are too many. They can afford to die. But we are not all common men. Our people in here cannot afford to die. They have great possessions. They will want to live on. What is it to me if Englishmen kill other Englishmen, because that is what it amounts to. Because it is my town. Because I have a house here and because my wife Eibhlin is here and my daughter Mary Ann and my son Peter. It's more than that too. He had been to Dublin since Cromwell had taken it. By sea in the small boat, for provisions. He had heard the hatred. Smelt it. He had seen the tall Puritan divine down on his knees addressing the troops with his arms held wide:

I beg on my hands and knees that you go against them now while the hands and hearts of our soldiers are hot, and to you, my soldiers, I say briefly: Cursed is he that shall do the work of the Lord negligently: Cursed is he that holds back his sword from blood; yes, cursed be he that makes not his sword stark drunk with Irish blood, that makes them not heaps upon heaps, and their cursed country a dwelling place for dragons, an astonishment to the nations. Let no eye look for pity, nor a hand be spared that does pity and spare them, and accursed be the man that curses them not bitterly from the depths of his heart.

He was a gaunt man with a black hat, very tall and thin, and Dominick wanted to laugh at him, but he stopped as the forest of swords were raised in the air, with a great shout, and he and his companion melted away through the noisome filthy backways of the city and his blood ran cold at the calling behind him. That was in August. He got back in time to draw his ancient bow and quiver of arrows before the self-same soldiers and the self-same divine sat down before the walls, and prayed to their odd God to help them.

The banks of a river can only hold a certain amount of flood water: the sea can be only partly contained by buttresses and quays until it is stirred by a mighty wind and unleashes its power.

Now, almost it seemed in a moment, the breastworks were overwhelmed, overturned, and saturated with blood as a sea of men and horses and guns came through the breaches in the wall; a flood of cursing, psalm-singing, shouting men, cleaving and shooting, dying and killing.

Dominick was swept away, in the rip-tide of men that retreated in a mass, many of them facing towards their slaughterers to hold them for a moment as the others got away. Some men just threw down their weapons and ran. Dominick was caught in the edge of the tide. His mind was clear. He wanted to work free to get down to St John's Street and through it to the Irish quarter and his home. But he couldn't do it. The press of men swept fast and inexorable like the tide to the square in front of the bridge and then over it, to become packed in the middle so that for a moment no man could move, hardly a sword-arm could be raised. Balls from the guns slew them and they remained standing though dead in the press. And then it caved in, almost it seemed again like the magic move of a jester, and Dominick and the others were beyond the Maiden's Tower, and all the others, their destroyers, were breathing on the far side of the bridge, while drums beat Quarter and trumpets, frightened ones, called shrilly to be spared.

The cause of it walked almost to the centre of the bridge, and faced his enemies.

He was a middling-sized man, with long grizzled grey hair.

21

He carried a naked sword in his hand. He wore a damask tunic and velvet breeches and a highly polished long boot on one leg. His other leg had long ago been shot away above the knee and he wore a wooden leg on it, the wood blackened and polished and burnished until it rivalled the sheen of his leather boot. A coloured feather swept back from his hat and waved in the gentle September breeze.

Calmly and deliberately he walked to the centre of the bridge, almost seeming to avoid the corpses of his soldiers without seeing them or listening to the screams of wounded men. He stood there in the centre of the bridge, alone, in complete command of himself. A thin sunburned face, an aristocratic cast of countenance, Sir Arthur Aston, Bart, of Aston Sutton near Cheshire, veteran of Lithuania, of Poland, of the wars of Gustavus Adolphus, Sergeant-Major-General of the Royal Army, commander of the dragoons at Edgehill, former Governor of Reading and Oxford, and now Governor of this town which he was ordered to burn and evacuate, which order he had refused. What was he thinking about now, Dominick wondered, as he faced the black man on the black horse on the other side of the bridge, a pale-faced black man, squat, with flat features and an inscrutable countenance. Aston was like a yellowhammer facing crows, a colourful, fearless bird.

Dominick always remembered the silence that reigned then for a short time. He could hear the screams of the gulls fighting for the offal in the river that shuddered as it wound its way through these few hundred yards of town where it was soiled and dirtied until it met farther out the clean sand of the seashore.

There were birds singing in the trees too.

'I beg you for quarter, sir, for me and my men and the town of Drogheda,' the clipped, incisive, emotionless voice said, as if he was inviting him to feast in the Tholsel. The other just stood staring at him. There was an officer close to his saddle. He bent his head and spoke to him. This officer nodded, and showed his teeth. He was blood-bespattered, powder-begrimed.

'You will get quarter when you lay down your arms,' this man said as he advanced with his sword in his hand. The blade of the sword was still bright with blood, so short a time it was taking.

The man with the wooden leg hesitated, reversed his sword and held out the hilt to the approaching officer. Behind him all

22

the men guarding the towers of the bridge, and the soldiers clustered half way up the steep hill to St Peter's, threw down their arms. The sound clattered, clattered, clattered on the cobblestones like a noise echoing in the hills, and on top of that Dominick shouted, and it sounded over the clattering of the surrender: 'No!' Just one expletive which he couldn't explain and it seemed that it was like a battle-cry.

The officer had reached Aston; he took his sword. There were four troopers at his back. He bent down swiftly, caught Aston by the wooden leg and upended him. As he fell one of the troopers slashed with a knife and the wooden leg came free in the hand of the officer. He raised it and crashed the heavy end of it on the head of the man who was elbow-leaning on the ground, the leather straps, that had attached it, coiling around his arm like snakes. Everyone there heard the crunch of the blow, and saw Aston die, with his brains spattering the cobbles of the bridge; saw all this in a moment of incredible horror, that even in the midst of savage wars a man could die like that, like vermin crushed by a stick, like a snake, like a rat, like anything but a human being, and the defenders knew in a terrible moment of time what was in store for them if this was the way their aristocratic leader died, and they bent frantically for their discarded weapons as in a tide of black, russet, and brown vengeance, Cromwell and his soldiers came after them with horse and gun and sword.

The hill behind was very steep. It gave them half a chance as the hooves of the horses of the enemy slithered on the blood-wet cobblestones.

Past the Tholsel Dominick ran, across the mouth of West Street, and found beside him a house whose walls showed gaping holes from the bombardment. This was the north side of the town where the wealthy people lived, where the loot would be rich. They were wooden houses, covered on the outside with lath and plaster, the upper stories projecting over the lower; leaded window-panes. The inside was a shambles where the heavy balls had hit home, and from which the people had fled, probably to the sanctuary of St Peter's Church on the top of the hill.

Dominick didn't stay below. He climbed the narrow wooden staircase that wound to the top of the house and he sought the attic and found it. He didn't have to find a way out to the roof, the bombardment had taken away half of the roof. He dragged himself through and crouched on the rough-hewn slates, sliding down them into the gully between two roofs. It would be the only way to get home, he had thought. Get to the river across the roofs and maybe then a quick dive into the river. What shelter could there be in the streets? He raised his head to look. He remembered one time when the river had flooded the lower reaches of the town where he had then been living. How the water had come through under the door and then spread its way over the floor seeking every level to fill itself in. That was the way it was below now as the victorious army slashed its way up towards St Peter's, spread in side-waves through all the streets, and for the first time the screams of women rose in the air, and Dominick shivered. Be careful, Eibhlin. Get into the cellar. He had the cellar prepared, covering all eventualities, in his desire to survive. It was a good cellar. Even now, walking on the flap of it, you wouldn't know it existed. He had bound it underneath so that there was no hollow sound and he had provisioned it.

He turned to look at St Peter's.

So wonderful on Sunday morning. Was it only days ago? It seemed so long. An amazing upsurging of the people had taken place and they had reclaimed their church, which had been taken from them in the years when the Defender of the Faith had driven them from their churches and their chapels and their monasteries; at last it had come back, for so short a time, and once again the incense had reached to its roof and the rich vestments gleamed in the sunlight that burst through the windows, and the great candles once again lighted the altars and the chant of the sung Mass was wonderful to hear, sending shivers up the back and bringing tears to the eyes of the most hardened as they sung the responses loud and clear with a great wealth of optimism. And in a place of honour at the foot of the altar had been the English gentleman with the wooden leg. His fate was the fate that was to befall the lot of them. His end was the end of their dreams, his death was the death of their brief flickering hopes.

The way to the church was littered with the dead, freshly killed, so that their blood was actual rivulets flowing down the hill. The doors of the church were closed and it was surrounded and for a moment there was a pause in the screaming and the shouting and the shooting and the clash of arms, and, muffled on the air, from the inside of the church Dominick

24

heard the voices of the people singing. They were singing *Gloria in Excelsis Deo*, and then the guns shot in the door and the army flooded into the church, beating one another to get in, and at the same moment the wooden steeple caught fire and blazed, and seemed to become a prolonged scream. He saw the people running out of the narrow doors below it and being butchered.

Once it had been a stone steeple. They boasted of their steeple that it was the highest one in the world, and then the Lord had sent a great wind that knocked it down. That was nearly a hundred years ago. That quieted their boasting, so they built it anew and they built it of wood, and now it was acting as a pyre for the people who sought its shelter.

He dropped his head and his aching eyes. He raised them thereafter very infrequently. He didn't want to look. He could imagine what was going on inside the church as the singing became weaker and weaker. Once he saw a woman in a deep red brocade gown running from the front of the church, her long hair flowing. And one of them followed her and caught her hair and swung his sword and waved her decapitated head in his hand. That was a swift death. And he saw one of them come out wearing the vestments of a priest over his blood-stained clothes, and he mounted a horse and they brought a statue of Our Lady and tied it to the horse's tail and he galloped the horse in the church square and down the hill, through the corpses; and the head of the statue bumped and bumped on the cobbles and the corpses, until it broke and rolled away and the soldier, laughing like a maniac in his torn lace and chasuble, raced across the bridge to the cheers of those who were resting from their work.

Thereafter he looked no more. He buried his head in his arms. Something happened to him that he didn't believe possible there. He slept. He didn't know for how long. He thought he would never be able to sleep again. But he did. He was startled to awareness by the tremendous roar. He saw the church outlined in a great red flash of flame and rubble. And then the rubble settled and the church was a ruin, without a roof, its walls caved in, just one strong wall standing alone. Like an enormous headstone for the dead. It would need no inscription anyhow, he thought. That one ought to be written the minds of men.

A soft darkness had descended on the town, but there would

be a moon to relieve the darkness. That was a terrible thought. Because there was no silence in the town. None at all. He shut out the sounds he was hearing. He didn't want to identify them. He stirred himself from his position. He was stiff. He was still carrying his useless bow. He wondered if he would leave it. He didn't. He took it with him.

He scaled the roof he was on towards the back. He saw the roof of another house built into the back of this one about ten feet below him. He dropped on the top of that, his legs straddling the slope. There was a short row of them going down towards the west gate. He climbed and jumped his way down a line of them until he came to a gap where a street stopped him. It was empty at the moment. From all the houses around there were terrible sounds emerging. He dropped and leaned against the wall, and flattened himself against it as running steps turned towards the place where he was. It was almost too dark to see. But it was a young girl. He saw her teeth and the whites of her eyes. Her bodice was torn down to her waist. She was running silently but she had no hope in her. There was one of them following her. He was roaring. He was laughing. And as he passed, Dominick leaned out and slipped the bowstring over his head and twisted, once, twice, three times. The soldier stopped, and gurgled and fell to his knees. His fingers were scraping at his neck. Dominick got him between his knees and kept twisting until he stopped moving. The girl was gone. Where would she go? There was only one end for her.

He turned the soldier over and unbuckled the straps of his breastplate. He put his arms through it and pulled it as tight as he could at the back. Then he took the man's helmet and put it on. It was noisome, feeling the leather of it wet with sweat, smelling of somebody else. He was a trooper, this one, and he wore long boots. Dominick stripped him of them and donned them. These were warm with sweat too and smelled, but he donned them, and took a fallen sword, and left the man there and staggered into the West Street and down towards the Tholsel and under the arch of the Maiden Tower and he went across the bridge staggering and muttering. Mostly he kept his eyes closed. He didn't want to hear. He turned down St John's Street and when he was half way down he cut out of it and into the alleys and backways towards his home. He thought oddly then of Murdoc. So long ago. Eight years ago that was, that Murdoc would have been a fugitive down these back places as he himself was now. But it wasn't the silent street that Murdoc had found. This street was full of terrible things now, with several of the thatched houses blazing and screams and the movements of people and the sound of shots, as the soldiers drank, raped, and shot, and almost outside his own door Dominick stumbled over the body of the woman.

He opened his eyes then.

He knew before he got to his knees beside her. O God, no, I beg, he said as he got to his knees, but his prayer was in vain, because Eibhlin was lying there on the street, her face to the sky, her black curly hair loosed and lying in the dust. Her breast and stomach had been pierced again and again with the blade of a heavy sword. Her eyes were open. He put his hands on them. He felt her face. It was warm, only cooling. If I had only been a little earlier, just a little earlier, just a little bit. He could see her face in the light of the fires and the ascending moon. Maybe it wasn't she at all. But it was. Her nose turned up a bit at the tip. Calm she seemed, almost a smile on her face, the small teeth showing. They hadn't done anything else to her, only killed her. But what did they do to my children?

He turned. The door of his house, the heavy open door, was gaping on battered hinges. He went over to it. Inside it was wrecked, mutilated, it was torn apart. He looked for the bodies of his children. It was dark, but if they had been there he would have seen them. He ran at the ladder to the room above. That was torn apart too, but his children weren't there. Did they kill them and throw them away? He ran down to the place below and he leaned on the flap of the cellar. 'Mary Ann! Oh, Mary Ann,' he called down through one of the cracks, and held his breath, and then a voice came almost into his ear.

'Oh, Daddy,' said the voice, 'little Peter got out the door and Mammy ran after him, and a man hit him, and hit Mammy, but he ran back and I got him and there's blood on his head and I put a cloth on it and he's down here, and oh, Daddy, where's Mammy, and I'm glad you're home.'

Her breathless way.

He didn't have time to weep. He whispered, 'Stay there, Man, you stay there. I will come back.'

'Oh, hurry, Daddy, hurry,' she said.

Then he rose and went out to Eibhlin.

Because he knew what he was going to do. He would put her

27

where she would want to be, on the highest part of this town, and then, well, then he would see, to kill and kill and die or what, he didn't know.

He knelt beside her. He put his arms under her body. He had raised her so that her head was resting on his shoulder, struggling into his as she often did, her hair silky on his cheek. Then he saw the feet of the soldier beside him.

'I killed her,' the voice said. He looked up. A young face looking down at them, hardly down on the cheeks, flaxen-haired.

'They said it was right. That they were only animals. Un-civilized, like.'

He had a thick voice. He had big teeth, thick loose lips. But his eyes were soft and blue,. and a little bewildered. Dominick wondered at himself. What was happening?

'I never killed a woman before. But she is the same as an English woman. She is the same as they are at home. She was a pretty woman. They said it was right. But I don't know. I came back to see her. I hit a kid on the head too. Just a little kid. He had fair hair. They're the same as our own. It is right to do this? It's all right to do it, isn't it? They're only like animals, isn't that all?'

Dominick rose to his feet. She was quite light. She still smelt like Eibhlin.

'That's all, friend,' he said. 'Just animals. Just pretty animals.' He started to walk away from him.

'And papists too,' the other called after him. 'That's what they said. It makes it all right. It's the Lord's work, isn't it?'

'Whatever way you look at it, it's the Lord's work,' said Dominick. 'If He didn't want it to happen, it wouldn't happen. Carry on the good work, friend.'

Then he walked away with his burden.

'Oh, you pretty, pretty papist,' he said to her as he bent his head and put his face against her cheek. Her cheek was turning cold. Like the time when they would walk outside the walls by the river, and her cheek would be cold then too, as he pressed his face to it, kissing her neck, making her gurgle. 'You're the prettiest papist of them all,' he said.

He carried her into St John's Street, and into the market-place and across the bridge and at the Tholsel he turned into St Lawrence Street and from that he climbed the hill towards St Peter's from the back way, and he got in there by the grave-

28

stones and the headstones, until he came to the one he needed, a great flat stone raised on four pillars about three feet off the ground, and leaving her gently on the grass, he crawled under this great stone and started to excavate the earth there with his hands. It was soft earth. It came easy.

And he could have been alone, in this town, in this place. He heard nothing, he saw nothing. He didn't care for anything, as he dug away at the earth with his hands.

CHAPTER FOUR

HE KNELT there at the stone, his head resting on his arms. He felt absolutely nothing. He should have been baying at the mocking harvest moon, like an anguished dog. Here was a thought! One time he had a little black and brown mongrel dog. It was affectionate. It was in the street one day and it had been run over by the wheel of a drayman's cart. It took a few days to die. And when it died they wept. About a dog. Now he had no tears, no weeping. His heart felt empty. He had no desire to die, no desire to live. It would be quite simple to find death. There were over ten thousand men in the town who would be pleased to show it to him.

He felt as if he was walking blindly in a tunnel, with no light to be seen in it, stumbling and hitting himself from one side to the other, unmindful of the bruising; the only niggle of light that remained to him was the picture of two children, who in some way belonged to him, hiding in a cellar under the floors of a raped and desecrated house.

He got to his feet and started to walk away, blindly, falling over grave-mounds, bumping into headstones. He was conscious of nothing except desolation, if this numbness of the mind could be called desolation, and yet when he neared the iron gate that led out of the churchyard, and he heard the movement and the groan, he fell crouched, his hand feeling for the sword that he no longer carried. That is just instinctive, that gesture, he thought as he rose to his feet again and walked towards the movement. It was dim enough in here near the wall, but light enough to see the dark bulk lying behind a gravestone. He approached it. It was the body of a man, a supine body that had raised itself on an arm. He looked over the stone. All the side of the man's face was covered with dried blood and fresh oozing blood from a sword slash on the left side of the head. Part of the scalp was hanging down over his ear.

It took him a few moments to recognize the broad shoulders that made the head look small, the big hand rising to hold the side of the wounded head. It was Father Sebastian. He had seen him before at the breastworks with his habit tucked into his girdle. He had retreated with the people to the church. He had probably conducted the singing as they died.

He saw the whites of his eyes as the priest looked up at him. There was no fear appearing in them, just resignation as he saw a Cromwellian soldier looking down at him. Dominick got on one knee in front of him.

'Father,' he said, 'I'm not who you think.'

'Won't you kill me?' the priest asked.

Dominick put his hand in under the breastplate, caught hold of his linen shirt and tore it. He kept pulling at it until a substantial piece came away in his hand. He folded it, gently eased back the flap of the torn scalp and tied the piece of linen around the priest's head.

'Friend,' the priest said.

'We'll have to go,' said Dominick. 'We can't stay here.'

'Where will we go?' the priest asked.

'We'll go home,' Dominick said.

'If that's the will of God,' said the priest.

'Can you stand?' Dominick asked.

'I can try,' said the priest.

Dominick helped him to his feet. He was very shaky on his legs. He leaned against a tombstone.

'My strength is drained away,' he said. 'Why am I here? I was in the church. I saw the sword falling.'

'We'll go through the town,' said Dominick. 'If we die we will die.'

'No man can kill us,' the priest said, 'if it's against God's will.'

'We might be better dead,' said Dominick.

He was tearing at the lower part of the priest's habit, so that what remained looked like a tunic held at the waist by a leather belt, with coarse narrow-fitting breeches below. He pulled the sandals off his feet. He could have been a wounded soldier divested of his accoutrements for ease of movement. Dominick didn't care. He did all this as if he was somebody else, his brain moving his hands to actions in which he had not the least interest.

'We will go now,' he said, putting his right arm around the priest's waist. 'Lean on me.'

'God bless you, Dominick,' said the priest. 'Dominick Mac-Mahon who lives in the lane of the Irish behind St John's

Street. "Our enemies encompass us about. They fall on us in their myriads. There is no escape." '

'So be it,' said Dominick.

He led out of the gate. The priest was a heavy man. He stumbled as he walked.

'Listen to the sounds of the town, dear God,' the priest said, 'and tell us what we have done to You.'

'Don't listen,' said Dominick. 'Just don't listen.'

How can the moon shine, he wondered? Why can't dark clouds cover it? Wouldn't you think the moon would be so sad that it couldn't look down, here on this night; this pin-point on the map of the universe? Was it because it saw a great space of the world, and in other places people were laughing and making love and dancing harvest dances and singing and there was so much happiness in those places that the moon could be complacent about this one spot on the face of the earth?

They walked slowly through soldiers and horse-droppings and blood and unlicensed terror. It was the licence that saved them perhaps, men being told that all was theirs, people and places, maidens and virgins and widows and the soft flesh of infants, the gold and silver and precious things and food and wine and furnishings, so that very little men felt as great as God with all these things under their hands to do with as they willed. What an opportunity for man to throw off all the habiliments of civilization and conscience, knowing that what you were doing was right, that your commander had ordered you to do so, that everyone was doing it, and that no matter what you did, you were pleasing God?

They walked down the hill.

Everywhere God's work was going on. Indescribable. The dregs of tattered souls. Who had time to pay attention to a soldier who was foolish enough to take time out from the rape and the slaughter to help a wounded comrade? Nobody. And that saved them for the time. Even crossing the bridge where they were tying people back to back, despite their screams, their pleadings, their soiling of themselves through abject fear, and hoisting them and throwing them into the tide-swollen waters of the Boyne, on which the moon was beaming benignly.

'Oh, no, Lord, no!' the priest was saying. He could hear the screaming, the terrible fear-ridden pleading that would reduce any man's stomach to jelly; that and the screams that were drowned in gurglings, and loud laughter and the encouraging of the spectators, shouting down over the bridge. 'Swim for it, you filthy fishes, swim for it,' and the sound of here and there a discharged musket.

Dominick's teeth were clenched so tightly that his jaw was sore as they walked away from the river. 'It would be easy to die,' was what he said. The priest was dry sobbing. Dominick had a very tight grip on him until they were well past the bridge.

It was only as they came nearer to his own street that his desire to live survived, perhaps because he thought they had no hope at all of getting this far and they had. Even if it was only a respite from their eventual end, because it was clear now that the whole intention was that there should be no witnesses left alive to Drogheda. And when there are no witnesses, isn't every man innocent? You have his word, and his word is good indeed.

His short street was empty. The hurricane had passed through it, the great cleansing wind, the sword of the Lord.

He got to his door, and over the step, past the drunken doorway. The priest fell to his knees near the counter and supported himself on his hands. Dominick eased up the flap of the cellar.

'Man,' he called. If only she were a man now, he would need her. That was young Peter, when he started to talk. He couldn't get his tongue around Mary Ann. He held his breath. Perhaps they had found the cellar. 'Yes, Daddy,' he heard her whisper. 'I'm glad you came home to us. Peter is raving, so he is.'

'All right, love,' said Dominick, 'keep away from the steps. We are coming down.'

He raised the priest to his feet and practically lifted him down, swung him free and let him drop. Then he came down after him, carefully closing and bolting the cellar flap. Then he went down the steps, walking very carefully, went blindly to the niche where the candles were, struck the flint, got the spark, and shortly the cellar was flooded with the dim yellow light. Dominick went on his knees beside his son.

Man had him lying on straw in the corner. His four-year-old face was flushed, his flaxen hair was wet.

Man said: 'I washed the cut on him, Daddy. It was bleeding awful.'

He looked at her. A competent little girl in a red kirtle. Very

33

black hair all curled and very black eyelashes. Her eyes were wide and her red lips held out from her teeth, with her head on one side. Always that way. Intense.

'Oh, Man,' said Dominick and took her into his arms.

'Why are you wearing that thing, Daddy?' she asked. 'It's hurting me.'

He freed her. Just as well. He divested himself of the breastplate and the helmet. His torn shirt hung around him awkwardly. He pushed it into his breeches. Then he looked at his son again. He raised the cloth that was covering the wound in his head. He had been hit with the flat of the sword. Otherwise he would be dead. But there was a gaping cut in his scalp, and as he pressed the skull gently Dominick could feel it depressing under his fingers. The boy muttered and moved his legs.

'Oh, Pedro, Pedro,' said Dominick, calling him.

The eyes opened for a moment to look at him, but closed again. No words came from the childish lips, just a sort of wuff sound.

'He's been at that, Daddy. Wasn't he bold to run out on the street? Mammy told him not to. Where's Mammy gone, Daddy?'

'She's with friends, Man,' said Dominick. 'She can't come now. We'll meet her again.'

He was searching the shelves. He found the basket and took the shoemaker's thread from it and a sharp needle. He took the bung off the small barrel of whisky and dipped the thread and used some of the whisky to bathe the cut on Peter's head. Then gently, very gently, he eased the needle into the scalp one, two, three, four, five times, and drew the edges of the wound together. The sweat was running down all over his body when he tied the knot. He rubbed it away from his forehead, and then tearing more from his shirt, and wetting that too with whisky, he wrapped it around the boy's head and covered his hot body with cloth which he cut from the bolt of frieze.

'Who's that man, Daddy?' Man asked him.

'Listen, Man,' he said. 'You sit here by Pedro. Here's a cloth. When he sweats rub this on his forehead. Will you do that?'

'I will, Daddy,' she said, and sat obediently by the side of her brother. Looking at her and Peter was nearly breaking Dominick's heart. Only he wasn't being given time for heartbreak. It had been arranged that way.

34

He went over to the priest, who was leaning against the steps, his head rising and falling. He was in pain. His lips were moving. Dominick placed the back of his hand against his cheek. It was hot.

'Father! Father!' he called.

The priest's eyes focused on him.

'Yes,' he said.

'I will have to stitch your wound,' said Dominick. 'It will hurt you. Will you drink a lot of brandy? That might kill the pain.'

'A little brandy, Dominick, not a lot,' said the priest. 'You won't hurt me now. I am gone beyond hurt.'

Dominick filled a small pewter tankard from the cask. He put it into his hand. He helped him to raise it to his lips. The priest drank a little of it.

'You have good brandy, Dominick,' he said.

'That's because it came in without paying toll,' said Dominick.

The priest laughed weakly. He had strong white teeth. His lips were pale.

'Do what you have to do now,' he said.

Dominick unwound the piece of his bloodstained shirt. He had a dreadful reluctance to do what had to be done. What is the use, his mind was asking him. Won't we all be dead anyhow in a short time? Just a little time for diligent search and they will find us here.

But he drank some of the brandy himself and then set to and sewed up the priest's head, thinking that it was like sewing a large piece of leather, and wondering at the coincidence of Father Sebastian and Peter having somewhat similar wounds, only the priest's skull was intact, and wondering at himself, how he could be doing all this as calmly as a tailor sewing at a bench. The priest winced very little, even when the alcohol went deep into his wound first, and afterwards the needle. He believes in God now, Dominick thought, and he is offering up his suffering. Little use that is. If God was listening what had happened would never have happened. He would have saved the women and children at least. He would have sent his angels with flaming swords to protect them. They could not have been destroyed.

It was done. He put the priest lying down on the straw and covered him with his expensive cloth. The priest sighed very

35

deeply and closed his eyes, and over their heads the tramping and the noise began.

Man came to him and he held her in his arms. He sat on the stone floor leaning his back against a barrel, and wrapped her in cloth.

'I'm afraid,' she said, listening.

'Don't be afraid,' he said. 'Go to sleep, Man. Just go to sleep. Don't be afraid. Here's your Daddy.'

She snuggled deeply into him. He kept one hand over her free ear. He didn't blow out the candle. He looked at the propped floor over his head. It was padded and lined with canvas and straw. He could hear the shouting and the laughter and the heavy feet. They were going to sleep. Their work for one day was over. Tomorrow would be another day. They wanted rest so that they could rise refreshed to commence on more of the Lord's work. He was surprised how cool he felt. How calm.

Now what am I going to do, he wondered? A sick and wounded boy and a sick and wounded and almost helpless priest, and my beloved daughter.

All the gates would be guarded, all the walls patrolled. The country for miles around by this time would have been laid bare and the very field-mice would be cowering in terror. So what way out have I, dear Lord, if there is a lord of us all, kinder and more decent than earthly ones.

And he set himself to think, the warm body of his daughter in his arms, her small, sweet breath an inspiration on his cheek.

CHAPTER FIVE

HE EASED the stone back a few inches and sweet fresh air blew into the cellar as well as chinks of daylight. He tried to judge what time of the day it would be from the quality of the light. He'd say well after midday. Immediately he had awakened from his troubled and restless dreams and night-mares, he had closed his mind. It was almost automatic, like a shutter coming down on it.

The candle had burned away. He lighted another one and then went to look at his son. He was lying on his back, one arm thrown across the form of his sleeping sister. Dominick felt his cheek. It was quite cool. Eibhlin often said that about them, that children could get things that would kill an adult and throw them off. Man's sleep was untroubled. Her cheeks were flushed, but from a healthy flush.

He sat down for a moment and looked at them.

You are mine, he thought. You are all I have left, and I'm going to see that you are left. You are going to survive. I don't know how yet but you are going to survive. He listened. There was no noise now from the house above. He had heard various noises during the night and the morning, but there was nothing to be heard now. He knew what he was going to do. At least he knew what he was going to try to do. There was only one way.

He went over to the priest.

His face was very pale and haggard. He had a clean-shaven face like Dominick's own, but now it wanted to be shaved, a blue-black beard was sprouting on his jaws. It emphasized his paleness and made him look like the illustration of a saint after a tortured death.

He shook him gently.

'Father! Father!' he said.

He saw the eyes opening. There was blankness in them. They looked at Dominick and then they filled with a look of pain, not physical but mental, and for a moment Dominick's heart raced as his mind turned over the events of yesterday, sicken-ingly, and then he tightened his jaws.

37

'How do you feel?' he asked.

The priest put a hand up to feel his bandaged head. He didn't wince as his fingers pressed there. His hand was large, with long fingers, a useful hand. He struggled up on to an elbow.

'I am alive, Dominick,' he said.

'Have some wine,' Dominick said. 'And there is a little oaten bread.' He had it ready for him. The priest pulled himself up farther, his back against a barrel. He took the tankard of wine. He sipped it, tasted it, swallowed it.

'God bless you,' he said. 'What are you going to do?'

'We will have to leave the town,' said Dominick.

'How?' the priest asked.

'There is only one way,' said Dominick. 'By the river. How well are you? Will you be able to help?'

'I'll see,' said the priest.

He helped himself to his feet, Dominick squatting and watching him critically. He took a few steps.

'I'll be able to help,' said the priest. 'I think you can rely on me.'

Dominick thought so too. He was assessing in his mind how much he would be able to ask from him.

'Daddy,' said the voice of Man. There was fright in it. He was over beside her in a moment.

'Yes, my love,' he said.

She put her arms about his neck. She hugged him.

'Why are we here, Daddy?' she asked.

'It's an adventure, Man,' said Dominick, 'like in a story.'

'Peter is awake too,' she said.

His heart contracted. He looked at Peter. The eyes were open widely, blue eyes. They were looking at him.

He put his hand on the boy's face.

'Hello, Pedro,' he said, 'and how are you?'

Pedro's lips moved, but no sound came out of them.

'Hello, Mary Ann,' said the priest. He was kneeling beside Dominick.

She went shy, a finger going into her mouth.

'You remember me, Mary Ann,' he said softly. 'Who made the world?'

'God made the world,' said Mary Ann, 'and you're Father Sebastian. I wouldn't know you with the funny cap you have.'

He smiled.

'You're welcome to our house,' she said.

'Thank you, Mary Ann,' he said gravely.

'You fell, Pedro,' said Dominick, 'and you hurt your head.'

The child's hand was up feeling the cloth wrapped around his hair.

'Over there beside the steps,' said Dominick deliberately, 'you'll find bread in a bowl. Go on over and eat it, Pedro.'

The priest moved. Dominick held him back with his hand.

'Go on, Pedro,' he said, 'over by the steps.' Because the child had only moved a hand. That was all. And he could hear. But could he walk?

In a moment, Peter considered what he had been ordered to do. He turned over, he was still such a child, and started to crawl; then he rose, tripped over the sort of dress he wore, righted himself with the adroitness of long practice and walked towards the steps, firmly.

Dominick released his pent-up breath.

'They hit him with a sword,' he said quietly to the priest. 'His skull is hurt.'

He followed him. He had the bowls prepared, of the bread soaked in wine. Peter was diligently poking in the bowl with his fingers. Dominick sat beside him and fed it into his mouth, looking anxiously at him. The child chewed slowly, as if it was an effort, and then carefully swallowed and would have said 'More' but no sound came from his lips. Dominick fed him more.

'Yours is ready too, Mary Ann,' he said.

She came over and sat down beside him and started feeding delicately from the wooden bowl.

The priest sat beside Dominick. He ate some bread and washed it down with a mouthful of wine.

'How, Dominick?' he asked.

'I'll have to go and look for a boat,' said Dominick. 'I can't go down the river. All the ships are there. I'll have to go up river. It will be a very small boat. There are only two hours in which we can do it. Before the moon comes up and while the tide is flowing. We have to be on the water before it starts to ebb, or we are lost. That's the only way. I will go and I will come back. If I don't come back you will know that I am dead.'

'You will come back,' said the priest.

'How do you know?' Dominick asked.

'First because you are determined to come back,' said the priest. 'And second because God wants us to live.'

'Let's leave God out of it,' said Dominick. His voice was hard. 'If we get free we will try and get across the country to the mountains. In the siege of '41 we sheltered a man. His name was Murdoc. He came from over there. He talked a lot, but I remember one thing he said about the fair land in the mountains where you could see your enemies and where you could be free. That's where we are going, where we can be free, free.'

'Freedom is in your own heart,' said the priest.

'Father,' said Dominick, 'I am under a strain. Don't talk to me about things like that. Promise that, or I won't be able to go on with it. These hands and these legs and this brain of mine are going to get us free. Don't hold me back.'

'I won't hold you back,' said the priest.

'We can take very little with us,' said Dominick. 'We will have to load our bodies with the things that will be necessary. I don't know how long it will take us to get across. It might be years. The whole land will be torn apart. But we will get there. And we will survive.'

'Where is your wife?' the priest asked.

Dominick looked at him. His face was ravaged. He rubbed his hands through his hair, clenched his teeth. Then he got hold of himself.

'She is ... she is with neighbours,' he said, as he cast a glance at Man, who heard things when she wasn't supposed to hear them. But the priest understood. He had seen it all in Dominick's eyes. So that was why, he thought. Poor Dominick!

'I will have to chance going up above,' said Dominick. 'There are things up there that we cannot do without, if they haven't found them. The children must be quiet.'

'They will be quiet,' said the priest.

Dominick walked up the steps. He listened. Raised the flap, looked, went swiftly out, and closed the flap all in one movement. He listened again. Then he moved towards the steps to the upstairs room. He regarded the chaos of downstairs indifferently. There was nothing left whole. The place was like a privy.

He went up the steps slowly. It was empty. His books were on the floor. Nearly every leaf of them had been torn. They had used them to light a fire. Only the heavy calf bindings remained of the book of the Gospels. He went over to the dais where they had slept. He bent his head to the spot where she had slept, but there was no scent of her remaining. Only the smell of leather and sweat, and of the rough men who like birds had soiled the place with their droppings. He closed his nostrils, pulled back the straw and lifted the stone under the palliasse. He took the canvas bag out of it. Its contents had been added to over a long period, and what had they been added to for, he wondered. But in the times ahead it might be useful. The meanest of men would sell himself for money.

He didn't look at the place any more. It was dead for him. It didn't belong to him. Things without people are as dead as the dead. It takes people to make them appear to breathe and live and have quality.

He stopped half way down the steps as the horse hooves clattered in the street outside.

They didn't stop, so he went on. The shouts and screams from outside left him indifferent too.

He called at the crack and when he heard the bolts being pulled back, he went down. He shot the bolts again after him.

The priest was breathing hard. The effort of climbing and unbolting had left him almost exhausted. I can't rely too much on him, Dominick thought coldly.

He got his needle and thread and cloth, which he cut with a knife, and he started to sew together a belt that would go around his waist. The priest was leaning back again. Peter had finished his bowl and was holding it with one fat fist, and beating it with another.

'Pedro is not talking at all,' said Man.

'He will,' said Dominick. 'It's as well that he doesn't talk now.'

'Father Sebastian must be tired,' said Man. 'He's going to sleep again.'

'Ssh,' said Dominick, 'sit down now and be quiet.'

'Will you tell me a story?' Man asked.

'I will,' said Dominick, and told her the story of the Prince who rescued the lady from the dragon. Man enjoyed it. She questioned him all the way through it. She accepted nothing. Only once did she ask him when is Mammy coming home.

Dominick held a board over the flame of the candle and each time the black soot formed he rubbed it on his body. His fair hair was tied back. He had his face blackened and most of his shoulders and his arms. He wore breeches and black stockings on his legs and nothing more. The two children were asleep on the straw. Father Sebastian rubbed the soot on the parts where Dominick couldn't reach. His rubbing was feeble enough. His arm got tired very quickly, and his breathing came fast. He thought how deceptive Dominick was in his clothes, what a powerful muscular body he possessed. He felt the strength of him and hoped that his closed mind would open.

Dominick said: 'That's enough. I'll go now. When I come back you will hear me. Stay close to the stone. Douse the light of the candle. When I call, send out Peter to me and then Man, and then the bundle, and after that come through yourself. Will you be able to do all that?'

'I will,' said Father Sebastian.

'We won't have a lot of time,' said Dominick.

'You can rely on me,' said Father Sebastian.

'Good,' said Dominick. He blew out the candle. He went over to where the stone was, feeling his way. He pulled it back. His judgement was good. It was as black outside as the inside of an evil heart. He backed out.

'God bless you,' he heard the voice of Father Sebastian whispering. Then he let himself down until he felt the water tugging at his legs and he dropped noiselessly into the water. The tide was flowing. Just starting to flow, so he let himself go along with it, his hands holding on to the slimy stones not yet covered. It was really dark. He couldn't see even the bulk of the town. The water gurgling in his ears kept him from hearing anything. The houses that backed on the river had privies. They would be over his head. They also dumped offal and unwanted things into the river so that the sea would scour them away. He didn't want to get into the middle of the flood. There the river would be running, and it was hard to swim in it.

Very slowly his eyes became accustomed to the blackness as the tide swept him slowly up and up. He knew he was free of the walls when his hand was no longer touching the stones, and his nostrils filled with the smell of autumn rushes and mud and silt. As the river narrowed he found he had to swim ever harder as the tide weakened. But it was not as bad as he thought it would be. It was better to have the tide weak now in order to have it strong when he wanted it. He knew the river and the way it wound, very well. That was his business, a man who had been intent on by-passing the toll laws of the town and spreading his wares where no questions would be asked. The knowledge was useful to him now.

Less than a mile on, he came into the sandy reach where the river wound. He rested there, before pulling himself up. He felt the stones under his bare feet and the grass and he walked towards the dimly outlined buildings of the fishing village.

His long journey was in vain.

Not a house intact. The roofs had been set on fire. All that remained of them were gaunt blackened sticks and an overpowering smell of burnt straw and wood. His hands felt bodies too. He didn't stop to look at them, to peer closely and try and recognize a well-known face that might have joked and laughed at him. Once his hand touched the naked flesh of a woman. Here too. He wondered how many people had got away. A river was a treacherous place for escape. You could be tracked along the banks, but some of them would have got away. Some of them.

He went back to the river. He walked four hundred yards down from it, into the four acres of rushes. He knew his way through, walking in the soft tilth, sinking up to his knees, and extracting his foot before it went too deep, and he came to the cleared space where they left the coracles.

There were three coracles there. So all of them had not got away. Was he to thank God that some of them had been killed so that he could have a boat?

What use questions like that? They were round coracles, cowhide stretched over willow, birch, and larch branches. They were difficult to manage if you didn't know how. He knew how. He had so little time and he had a good way to go against the stream. He sat into one, freed it and paddled out through the rushes, to the faint gleam of water where the river was.

Out there the tide was flowing faster and he was swept around and around in his boat until his legs found purchase against the batons, and using the sweep he made headway against the tide. This time he travelled in the very middle of the river where the stream would help him before it was overwhelmed. There was a gleam of light in the eastern sky. Don't come up yet, he beseeched the moon. It was somewhere there.

He could see the bulk of the town faintly, lights and reflected gleams. It was just a town for him, his mind told him, no name, no nature, no attachment. It was just a place he was leaving.

It was difficult. He had a hard time getting the unwieldy craft to the south side of the river when he had crept into the blackness of the wall bordering it. When he was a little way in, he grabbed for the stones still remaining over the tide, held the rope of the coracle in his hand, got out of the boat and started to walk and scramble down along. The tide took the boat. He had the rope over his shoulder. It was cutting into it. He found it hard to walk. The stones were very slippery, but his right hand gripped the top ones that were dry.

He was pleased to come to the iron hook. He pulled the boat close, tied the rope. Then he put his head in the aperture and called: 'Father! Father!' There was no sound in reply. They have been found, was his thought. Oh, they have been found! And then as he was about to mount and crawl he heard the voice of the priest. 'All right, Dominick.'

He closed his eyes and dropped his head. He was trembling.

'Here's one,' said the voice.

Dominick reached and found Peter's legs pushed out to him. He sought greater purchase for his feet as he held him. 'Ssh,' he said in his ear as he hauled the boat close and placed him into it. Peter made no sound.

'No talk, no talk, Man,' he said into her ear as her body came to him. She said 'Ssh', that was all, and then he carefully placed her beside her brother. He took the two bundles as they came, and put them into the boat which was now pressing painfully into his legs as it was being swept upstream by the tide.

'Now, Father,' he said.

This was the worst part. If it was only himself they could be away. What did a priest know about round coracles?

The bulky body came through the aperture. He pulled the boat around as well as he could.

'Careful, careful,' he whispered, guiding the legs of the priest as they felt for the boat. If he leaned his weight on the side it would topple. But the priest surprised him. He curled one foot inside the edge and twitched it, and the boat swung around and as it swung the priest stepped right into the middle of it and sat. It balanced.

Dominick paused for a moment before he freed the rope. He

wondered if he would reach in and pull out the stone. He decided he wouldn't. Let them wonder. Let them see it. Let the thought strike them that after all there might be a witness. Then he pulled the boat towards him with his foot, stepped into it on the end opposite the priest, freed the rope and let it go.

They were swept into the middle of the stream. He didn't want to use the paddle. His feet were high in the air, resting on a bundle and on the body of Man, hitting the knees of the priest. If he used a paddle it might flash, it might make a noise.

The boat swirled and swirled and then remained steady in the middle of the tide, and then went up with it, carried on it, and they were free from the town and approaching the first bend, when the great swollen yellow moon arose for a magnified look at the slaughtered town.

CHAPTER SIX

HE WORMED his way through the tall stalks of wheat. There was no wind. The only sound he could hear was the lowing of unmilked cattle. The sun was sinking, beginning to colour the clouds on the horizon. The vault of the sky was coloured a misty blue.

He had had a change of mind. He had landed on the north bank of the river that morning instead of the south. It was an instinct in him that said, go to the land where the sword has already fallen lest in fleeing it falls on your neck. He wondered if he had been right, if they would not have been safer to go south and escape before the army converged on it. Looking north now from his height, he could see that the hill on which he lay was ringed with smoke, as if he was encircled with signal fires. The smoke rose in tall columns to the sky like black and grey marble pillars supporting the vault of heaven. Who could have believed that destruction would have come to this land so fast! It was a pleasant smiling land of gently rounded hills and wooded slopes, as fertile as a healthy woman. The soil was deep and it was rich, and it reared great cattle and crops. Its wealth was in itself and that was why it was so desirable to men who didn't possess it. To be safe you must own nothing, you must possess nothing.

He heard the sound of the approaching horses below him and looked down towards the river. From here as it looped below his hill he could have leaped into the water of it. On each side it was open and shelved to beaches of golden sand, and even in the middle it was very shallow and made music for itself as it sang its way over the gravel and the small stones. The approaches on either side were built of *toghers*, wooden hurdles laid on the soft ground to absorb the passage of hooves and occasional wheels. The band of horsemen came from the south. There were about twenty of them in a troop. They splashed across the river and dismounted on the other side. Their faces were smoke-begrimed. Their tunics were stained. They removed their helmets and pegged the horses. They took

46

food from their saddle-bags and squatted on the ground free of the *toghers* and started to chew. He could hear their voices. His stomach tightened at the sound of the almost unintelligible English they spoke. They were clean-shaven, needing shaves. Some of them went to the water of the river and scooped water into their faces. Some of them relieved themselves into the river, standing there talking to one another as they did so, laughing.

The Colonel sat apart. He didn't dismount. He stayed on his horse. His eyes moved steadily over all the landscape around him, searching the hillock where Dominick rested. He had a flat face with bunched muscles at the side of his jaws. Dominick could see the muscles bulging tightly as he chewed.

His hands were dirty. Such was the clarity of the late day.

Dominick stiffened as he saw the figures coming towards the ford. They came very slowly from the north. They saw the troopers and they still kept coming. A woman, a tall woman. Her hair was uncovered. It was long hair falling on her shoulders. There were grey ashes on her black hair. Her face was smoke-begrimed, the long woollen dress she wore was dirty with soot. She was carrying a bundle in her hand, possessions wrapped in what had once been a black cloak. There were three children with her. One was a boy of about twelve. His black hair was matted. He wore a coarse tunic and torn breeches. His legs were bare and brown and dirty. His face was dirty. His prominent teeth seemed startlingly white in his face. There were two girls, small ones, about ten years of age. They walked one each side of the woman, holding on to her dress with grimy hands. One was very fair-haired. Her face was dirtied, as was the face of the other little one. They are walking to death, Dominick thought. It was pathetic. He could see the improvisations that had been made. The dirt applied to the faces was too regular; the clothes were obviously wrong. He wanted to stand up and scream at them 'Go back! Go back!' like the heather bird.

They came on. Some of the soldiers came close to the road, one of them unsheathing a sword, and still eating. He looked to the Colonel. The eyes of the Colonel were regarding them. They passed by under the muzzle of his horse, as if they didn't see him. The hand of the woman didn't even tighten on her bundle. The soldier was waiting for the Colonel's nod. He didn't nod.

The strange little party walked into the water of the river. The water came almost to their knees. Dominick could see the water darkening the bottom of their clothes. The boy stumbled once and fell forward. He saved himself with his hands but the water had wet all the front of him. The two soldiers near him laughed. That was all. They crossed the ford and walked out on the other side.

Only Dominick could see what happened then when a turn hid them from the ford. The way the woman looked back, one hand up to her heart, her dull-looking, stupid-looking face now transformed, and then she gathered the three children, spoke to them, and they ran off the rough path, through a copse of low sallies, and ran and ran across a broad cleared space towards an oak wood on the far hill. Could I do that? Dominick wondered. It's something to know. Look like nothing. Look dirty and deprived, like nothing, and you might get away with it. But how about if you were a man? Even if you drooled and were dirty and put on the face of a fool would you get away with it?

The next one came riding towards the ford. He was a good stout man on a black horse. He had a red face. His saddle-bags were new and they were full. He was dressed sedately in brown clothes and good white linen. He was a little worried. There was a slight frown between his eyes. Behind him there came another horse. His good lady was obviously mounted on it. Her white face was reddened from the sun. She wore a dress of red damask and a black woollen cloak lined with scarlet. A middle-aged servant walked beside the master's horse. He was a thin-faced man with a hat set firmly across his forehead. And a young maid-servant walked by the side of the lady, holding on to her stirrup. She was young and plump, this maid, and she was fair. She wore a black cloak and a brown dress and her hair was uncovered.

The man wasn't terribly nervous. He looked at the gathered soldiers. He easily picked out the Colonel, who sat staring at him, still chewing slowly at his food like a great black and russet bullock. The man drew his horse close to him.

'Ah, Colonel,' he said. 'I am Master Gantley. I am the owner of the manse at Monasterboice. Your brave soldiers have taken possession of it in the name of the Parliament. I know justice will be done to me when these dreadful wars are over. The Colonel gave me protection which I was to present to whoever stopped me. It grants me protection to get to Dublin. I wouldn't have come this way but I was told to avoid Drogheda, which would have been an easier road. I hope you will be pleased to grant me the facilities which your other friends have given me up to this.'

'Show,' said the Colonel, holding out his free hand.

'Oh, yes,' said Master Gantley, 'I have it right here.' He put his hand into the breast of his coat and took out a sheet of vellum. It was good vellum. You could almost tell his circumstances from listening to the sound of its dull rustling. 'I hailed with delight the knowledge that you were coming over here, Colonel. It is the only way that peace can be established in this savage land, so that we can sleep in our beds, not looking over our shoulders, waiting for them to fall on us from the woods.'

The Colonel was reading the protection, still chewing.

'This is Mistress Gantley,' the man went on. 'She is so upset by the events of the past few years, but even if we are temporarily dispossessed, she knows that it is in a good cause.'

'Hold it up to your breast,' the Colonel said, handing back the protection.

'What? What?' Master Gantley asked, slightly bewildered.

'Just hold it over your heart,' said the Colonel.

The soldiers had gathered around the group. They were grinning.

'Like this?' Master Gantley asked, still slightly bewildered. He held the opened vellum sheet until it covered the left side of the breast of his coat. He looked down to see if he was doing what he was told and probably never even knew what killed him. The Colonel drew his pistol and shot and a hole appeared in the dead centre of the paper. It was black and then just before Master Gantley fell from his horse Dominick saw that it was stained red.

'Why,' said the Colonel, 'he was wrong. It didn't protect him at all.'

It just took a count of ten to kill the servant, who died with his mouth in a rounded O as a soldier's sword went right through his chest and came out on the other side. Mistress Gantley died quickly too. She still had a look of pathetic horror on her face as they cut her head off when they pulled her from the horse.

Dominick pulled away as they started to tear the clothes off the fair maid, who was now screaming. She would be pleasured

49

before she died for all her screaming No, No, in a schoolgirlish prim sort of English way.

Now I know, Dominick thought. It took all that to make me know. On yourself alone does safety depend. Not on being disguised, not on protection which can be bought but is not worth the paper it is written on. And if they were such cannibals as to eat their own, what would they do to those who were not their own? It was the soft evening that deceived him, the misty blue sky. I will never again be deceived by misty blue skies.

He moved very cautiously. The thing is that you must never be caught unawares. There is no need to be caught if all your senses are awake. Master Gantley had been cute. He disguised his Irish people, or what remained of them, and sent them ahead of him to draw the fire, or to see what would become of them. It was clear now as if Dominick had been there when they planned it. And the decoys were safe while the real geese died.

He cleared the patch of wheat and scanned the open field before he crossed it, and even then he didn't cross directly but wound his way through hollow and copse until he could hear the noise of the stream where it ran over stones, through the grove of the tall beeches, on its winding way to the Boyne. He said in his mind: Never again stop at a place where the noise of a river can dull your hearing.

It was proved to him when he edged his way over the steep bank and looked down below. The sun was slanting through the trees and dappling the hollow near the stream on the far bank. There the priest was sitting, cross-legged, his face to the sun, his eyes blinking to its glare, his face still startlingly white under his three-day growth of beard. Was it only three days? The tonsure on his head was less pronounced. Anyhow its round line was broken by the jagged patch of sewn scalp, which they had decided to expose to the air and the sun. Man was sitting at one side of him, her arms resting on his leg, and Peter at the other, playing with wet pebbles. The priest was talking. He was saying:

'Yes, Man. You have seen in the big window of the church how the shaft of sunlight shines through the great panes and colours the floor. Why can't a pane of glass, which is solid, stop the beam of the sun? It should be able to. A stone wall can stop the beams. Glass is a pure substance; a purified material.

That was Our Lady. She was a purified material too and the Holy Ghost could penetrate her like the sunbeams through a pane of glass.'

'Bang!' shouted Dominick in a loud voice.

Man buried her head in the priest's lap. He grasped her tightly. Peter dropped his pebbles and ran like a rabbit on all fours until he was behind the body of the priest.

'You see,' said Dominick. 'You could be dead. I told you not to come out of the trees. Don't you know that they are all around you? How do you know what minute they are going to fall on you? Did we escape from Drogheda to die spitted like rabbits by a drinking-place?'

He was angry with the priest. He was angry with himself for being angry. He stood erect and leaped from his eminence right across the stream to land on his feet beside them.

'I'm sorry, Dominick,' the priest said. 'It was so pleasant in the sun.'

'From now on, keep out of the sun,' said Dominick, 'if you want to live.'

'You frightened me, Daddy,' said Man.

'I wanted to frighten you, Man,' said Dominick. 'You must always be frightened until we are free. And do what your Daddy tells you.'

'They are only children,' said the priest. 'It was easy for me to lead them astray. I'm sorry.'

He was looking at Dominick with his great calm eyes, which seemed to have become sunken into his head. Dominick couldn't look into his eyes. He didn't want to. He didn't understand the antagonism he felt. He was loaded with a burden of a wounded priest. He felt that if he was on his own he could travel faster and travel safer.

'You look too much like a priest,' he said. 'If we meet them there will be no hope when you look like a priest. We will stop at the first place possible and change your clothes.'

'Are we not going south?' the priest asked.

'Suppose,' said Dominick, 'that you could choose between going where a fire had already burned and going where a fire might follow you, where would you go?'

'I would go to the burned-out land,' said the priest.

'So we are going north,' said Dominick. 'I remember a little of the land since the time before I went to live inside the walls. There are two places. First we must reach the wood of Coillcree and then if we are still alive we will head for a safe place I know between Loc Sileann and Loc Reamore. If it is still the same, we can hide there for the winter, and maybe after that the storm will be past.'

'Do whatever you think is best,' said the priest. 'Soon I will be of more help to you.'

'We will move now,' said Dominick. 'There is a village about four miles away. We'll have to get through it before dark. We will lie up beyond it and after that we will have to travel at night. Are you tired, Man? Can you walk a little more?'

'I'm not tired, Daddy,' said Man.

'You're a good girl,' said Dominick. He walked into the trees to where their possessions were stacked. He buckled a short sword over his shoulder, so that it rested between his shoulder-blades and he could draw it by putting his hand behind his head. Then he tied the two bundles by their necks and wore them around his neck. He turned to look back. The priest was having trouble getting to his feet. Man was helping him up, pulling at his hand. He was smiling.

'Hurry, hurry,' said Dominick impatiently and frowned as the smile was wiped off the face of the priest. 'Come on, Peter,' he said. Peter looked at him and walked towards him. The patch on his fair head looked black and ugly, but he had no fever and he could walk. He came to Dominick holding out his hand. Dominick took it. 'You are not tired, Pedro?' he asked. The boy shook his head. Dominick felt tears of anger in his eyes. What kind of a cruel God could let things like that happen to little children? 'Come on, son,' he said then, and walked through the trees. He heard the feet of the priest and Man on the fallen leaves.

The sun was almost setting when they cautiously came into the clearing before the village. They had been guided to it by a dying pillar of smoke. The pretty stream where they had rested some miles down flowed through the village and had turned the small wheel of the mill near the church. Dominick remembered the place. He had been there two or three times.

The church was a simple thatched one with stone walls. There had been just six mud-walled thatched houses, one of which was a sort of rude inn. Nothing remained. The thatch of the church with its wooden supports succumbed to the fire. It was just four blackened walls. The cottages had disintegrated as if they had been blown up by gunpowder. The stone mill was still there, the wheel turning. You could hear the stones grinding with a dull rumble. There were several corpses lying in front of the houses.

Dominick walked towards them. There was no sound at all to be heard except the grinding of the stones.

He thought, all this doesn't matter. Just that there are dead people and they wear clothes and the priest must get clothes. That's all that matters, because they are dead and they are well out of it. There were only three bodies, one a young man and the other two old men. So pray that the rest had fled before the holocaust. Except there in front of the church where a long beam of limestone had been inserted in the stones over the door so that it could carry a small bell. There was a rope tied around this stone and the body of a man was hanging from it, his feet about two steps off the ground. You could distinguish the black and white habit of a friar, rent and torn. Unminding, Dominick walked towards him. The dying sun made a long shadow from the improvised gallows. The body was swaying. You could see the deep cuts around the ankles and the mutilation of the face and the palms of the hands which were turned outwards as if in display. He had been dragged behind a horse before he was hanged, Dominick saw. He hoped that he had died before that.

He heard the thump in the dust and turned. The priest was kneeling on the ground, his face upturned. Man was looking up too. Why can't I shake off this impassivity? Dominick wondered. Am I mad? He walked away and over towards the body of the young man. He was a strong young man. He had died fighting. There was a blood-stained cudgel near his hand. Well, he's dead, Dominick thought. He won't miss his clothes. Then he pulled away from him in distaste. He couldn't do it.

'Come on, Man,' he called. 'Come on, Peter. Let us get away from here. Come on! Come on!' There was an evening breeze arising from the clear day. It was rustling the corn in the surrounding fields. The blackbirds were stirring in the bushes. He walked past them. 'Come on!' he called again, heading towards the stream.

'Loan me your knife, Dominick,' he heard the priest call then.

Dominick turned.

'Let the dead bury the dead,' he said. 'Me and my children are getting away from here. Do you want us to die too?'

53

The priest was standing.

'Of your mercy loan me the knife,' he said.

'We will leave you,' said Dominick. 'Don't forget. We will leave you. We are going to survive. They will be back.'

'God go with you,' said the priest and turned away. He started to pile some flat stones near the body of the hanging friar.

Dominick walked off towards the stream. Then he turned.

Man and Peter were looking after him. She was holding Peter's hand.

'Come on, Man,' he said.

She didn't move. Just looking at him.

He walked back a few paces to her.

'You are to come when your daddy says so, Man,' he told her.

She dropped her head.

'Come on, Man,' he said.

She slowly came towards him. Peter walked with her. Both their heads were lowered. Little children, like that. He watched them walk past him and followed after them. The stream here was fordable. He went across first, and then dropping his load he turned to help them across. He only looked once towards the church. The priest had got his stones high enough and was pulling at the knot sunk into the neck of the dead friar. 'Oh, God! God!' Dominick shouted. He clenched his teeth. He dug the heel of his shoe into the soft ground, and then he went back across the stream. 'Wait here! Wait here!' he said to them.

His movements were quick, almost savage.

He handed the knife to the priest, who didn't look at him, and when the rope was cut and the body freed he let it slide into his arms and walked with it beside the church where the crude tombstones were. He had to do it all himself. Father Sebastian just didn't have the strength for it. What did he have to do? He had to dig and dig, until his clothes were soaked in sweat, a wide, shallow grave in the soft earth, where they buried four people. He resented every inch of it. Every bit of it. All the time listening with half of his mind to all the sounds of the evening. Ready to flee, or hide or run, shepherding his charges. But the priest would have to shift for himself in that case.

They patted the earth, and only then the priest went for the children and brought them back and he knelt on the earth with one of them each side of him and he prayed in Latin.

Dominick didn't kneel. Not he. He was smelling the scent of new-turned earth, and the scent of the dead, and he felt as if all his nerves were open to a chill wind, blowing on them so that it was all he could do to save himself from trembling to death.

'Hurry! Hurry! Hurry!' he finally ground out, almost in agony, and the priest blessed himself and rose to his feet.

'We are ready to go now,' he said.

'Well, come, come, come,' said Dominick.

'That's the glory of anonymous death,' said the priest as he walked. 'Nobody will ever know. There will never be a name in the book of martyrs. Just a soft turn of the earth, that won't be known to the generations that follow after. I had nearly forgotten that I was a priest.'

Dominick said: 'I wish I could forget it.'

'You won't have to suffer me much longer,' the priest said.

'All I want to do is to hurry,' said Dominick. 'That's all I want to do. If we stay in one place long enough, they will find us. That's all I want you to understand. I want to live. I want my children to live. If it would be glory for you to die, it wouldn't be for us. That's all I want you to understand.'

'I understand, Dominick,' said the priest. He bent and lifted Peter into his arms. 'I am stronger now. I will be of more help to you.'

Dominick went to the stream and crossed it and started to burden himself with his possessions.

CHAPTER SEVEN

DOMINICK MOVED carefully through the trees. In the open spaces the frost was still on the ground. A breaking twig under the foot was like the sound of a discharged pistol. But very few twigs broke under his feet. The wood mainly consisted of giant oak trees and beeches with an under-scrub of stunted willows and thorn trees, some of them so enveloped in briars that they had formed themselves into thick and almost impenetrable thickets. It was an easy place to hide and an easy place to dodge, but now the cold wind was whipping the leaves off the trees and soon most of them would be bare. It was time to move.

There were three dead rabbits tied to his belt. He held the bow which he had fashioned himself in his hand. His old skill with it was coming back to him. In fact if he stopped to think about it, it would seem to him that his life had taken up where he had left it off when he was sixteen; that there had been no interval of comparatively civilized living. All this furtive living was what he had been used to, and he carried out its rules now as if he had never abandoned them. He never crossed a clearing without looking very closely and listening for the scolding of a disturbed bird or the sound of a breaking branch. He never stood still unless he had the thick bole of a tree to his back. He did this almost mechanically. He knew there was safety in it, but he despised the necessity for it.

He came to the thicket that disguised their existence. He pulled away the opening to it and crawled inside, closing the opening after him. He paused, crouched in there, and looked over his head. He could see more of the sky. Soon the long fronds of the blackberries would be brown and dying and the thin choked branches of the bushes would be naked. It wouldn't be cover much longer for man or animals.

He broke through on the other side. Here there was a fall of ten feet to the narrow clearing below. He listened and then dropped. He made no sound. It was a pleasant little place. The height of it was made by two great granite rocks leaning on each other to form an arch. The opening in the arch was naturally covered by trailing woodbine vines and thick ivy. To the left of it, a trickle of water poured and dropped to the stream that ran away down a hill towards the pool below. He listened. He thought he could hear Man's voice. He detached the rabbits from his belt and hung them on a tree branch. He went into the arch. He could enter standing. There was a beam of light coming from above at the one spot where the two stones did not touch. It was like a skylight in a town house. When it rained the rain came in there, but it had been doing it for so long that it fell straight into a rock pool that its falling had created over the centuries, overflowed and ran out on the sloping rock floor. At each side of the pool there were fresh rushes covering the stone where they slept. Natural shelves in the rocks held their belongings.

Dominick looked at them.

A lifetime and that's what they were – a handful of possessions: a change of clothes for them all, which he had fashioned himself with a knife and a needle. Utilitarian things, two knives, an axe, a saw, wooden bowls, pewter tankards. He didn't have time or space to take much from their home. Meal and wine and a little brandy, all coming slowly to an end. It was all right for Sebastian to say God would provide. He believed in that. Dominick had to plan for it. It was just as well to have light possessions. There was a long road ahead of them now before they found their winter shelter, and the less they had to carry the safer they would be.

He left the shelter. Outside, he sniffed the air. The light wind brought to his nostrils the fragrant scent of burning wood. He broke through the trees surrounding the little clearing and walked towards the smell of the smoke.

He went very carefully. He had drilled this into the priest – never if at all possible to use the same way twice. Walk a path and then avoid it until no trace of the former passage remained. His whole body told him that it was time to leave the woods. Sometimes a normal sound would make him stand still and the hair would rise on his head, like a dog or a wolf, he thought grimly.

They had separated their living-places from the cooking-place. It was tedious, but it was worth while. It had proved to be safe so far. The cooking-place was in an open clearing. You could hear enemies coming and you could be away before they breached through to find nothing but a smoking fire.

He crouched now and scrutinized it. The fire had been freshly lighted. It wasn't making much smoke. That was good. On one side of the fire he could see the iron griddle resting on flat stones under which the red twigs from the fire would go. The priest had been about to cook something. And then he had vanished. Why? He couldn't have heard Dominick's approach.

'You're dead,' said his voice, and the point of a stick was poked into Dominick's back. Dominick nearly impaled himself on the stick as he jumped. Then he rested his head on his arms for a moment before he turned.

The priest was regarding him, head on one side.

'I'm learning, Dominick?' he asked anxiously.

Dominick laughed. He couldn't help it.

'Learning too well,' he said. 'How did you spot me?'

'A blackbird told me,' Father Sebastian said.

Dominick remembered hearing the bird and chided himself.

'You were cooking?' he asked.

'Yes,' said the priest. 'Something important.' He walked past Dominick towards the fire. Dominick followed him.

'Look at me!' he called then.

The priest stopped and turned to face him.

Dominick looked at him closely. His face had lost the terrible pallor. He wore a neat brown beard clipped close. His hair was much longer. It was combed back from a high broad forehead. All you could see of the head scar was the angry red crescent on his temple. For the rest he wore a coarse woollen shirt and heavy trousers stopping short at the shins. He wore patched heavy shoes on his feet. Dominick shook his head.

'You look well,' he said; 'but although you shouldn't you still look different from ordinary people.'

Father Sebastian laughed.

'If only I could tell you how differently I feel,' he said. He looked at Dominick, but the affection he felt for him didn't show on his face. If he himself didn't look the part, Dominick did. His chest, arms, and legs, all his exposed parts, were browned by the sun and the weather, and his fair hair, tied with a ribbon, was white on the top from the sun and white at the sides from suffering. It seemed to the priest that, even since he had come to know him, deep lines had been chiselled in his face. Dominick kept himself clean-shaven.

'You are fit enough now,' Dominick said. 'Do you feel that you can travel?'

'I can carry the world on my back now,' said the priest, raising his arms to the sky. 'Every time you get tired, that is.'

Dominick laughed.

'Am I that serious?' he asked.

'A good thing you are,' said the priest. 'We are alive because you were serious. Now I am strong again, thanks to you.' He turned and went to the fire. Dominick followed him. The priest crouched. He took a wooden bowl from behind a stone. It held a little crushed wheaten meal which he had ground with a pestle in the hollow of a stone. He stirred a little water into it now with a stick and moved it around and around until it was a paste.

'We will have to travel five, six, or maybe even eight miles to get where we are going,' said Dominick.

'When?' the priest asked.

'Maybe tonight,' said Dominick. 'The moon will be with us early tonight.'

'Tomorrow,' said Sebastian, 'I was going to become a real priest again. Outside the wood I said I'd go, and find some parishioners. All the people to baptize, to shrive, to bless, to pray into heaven. It's been a load on me all this time.'

'I've been out there,' said Dominick. 'You wouldn't find a parishioner in a day's journey.'

'Is it that bad?' the priest asked, his face clouding.

'It is bad,' said Dominick. 'It is worse. Over north this morning near Slieveban I came on a house. There was smoke from the fire, but inside there was only the dead. They weren't killed. Their faces were black. There was an evil smell. This was plague, I think. I didn't bury them. I set fire to the house.'

'Lord have mercy on them,' said the priest.

'Another reason for going,' said Dominick. 'I saw more wolves. They were increasing. They have plenty of food, you see. They have been provided for. Now they are used to that kind of food. There is frost in the air. The winter is going to be early. I feel this. We will have to go where there are no wolves and no plague.'

The priest carefully poured a little of the paste on to the hot griddle. It fell in a small round circle and simmered. He poured a bigger one.

'You know what day this is?' he asked.

'Does it matter what day it is?' Dominick asked.

'It's the feast of St Francis,' said the priest. 'I'm going to say

59

my first Mass today. Will you say the responses, Dominick?'

Dominick felt the hardening inside him. He wanted to be curt.

'Maybe you don't know them,' the priest said.

'Yes, I do,' said Dominick involuntarily.

'Ah, thank you,' said the priest.

He turned the two circles on the griddle. They were white.

'Man is going to make her first Communion today too,' said the priest, not looking at Dominick.

'What?' Dominick ejaculated.

'It's time,' said the priest.

'But not like this,' Dominick protested. 'That's for tall churches and music and people singing, and little children with hands joined and gifts and celebrations at home. Eibhlin and I talked about it so often. We...' He stopped dead. For a moment he saw her there, squatting on the ground facing him, chewing a wisp of grass which she would use to rub down the side of his face. About what Man would wear. About how Man would look. All your own remembered joy passed on to your children so that you would grow in them.

'You don't object, Dominick, do you?' the priest asked. 'How do you know what is ahead of us?'

'I know!' said Dominick. 'I know!'

'Will you go and get her so,' the priest said, 'and bring her?'

Dominick wanted to object. He wanted to argue. But he could afford to argue on stronger grounds than this. If Man already knew how could he take it away from her?

'I'll get her,' he said, and he rose and walked away. Father Sebastian looked after him until the trees swallowed him, then he sighed and carefully placed the two hot breads on the silver paten. It had been a silver medal. Father Sebastian had spent long hours beating it with a stone until it stretched itself to its present rough round.

Dominick wondered at himself as he made his way back to the clearing and beyond it to the pool where the children were. I am going around, he thought, like a husk being moved by some sort of clockwork contrivance. All the things I have done, I have done mechanically. Inside I seem to have become deprived of feeling and emotion. This cannot be right. Am I not capable of feeling emotional any more? Am I to go the rest of my life acting on instinct? Isn't that what animals do? Am I an animal?

He stood sheltered behind the trunk of a tree and watched his children.

Man was washing Peter's face.

He was sitting. The dress was pulled up on his bare legs. His legs were fatter than they had been, and brown. He was objecting to Man's washing of his face with a cloth. His eyes were closed and he was sputtering. The pool gurgled and they were both bathed in sunlight that came dappled through the trees.

'It has to be done, Pedro,' Man was saying. 'How can you look at the Lord Jesus with a dirty face?'

Man was shining with cleanliness. Her black curly hair was gleaming. She was wearing an odd dress. The lower part of it was rough wool and the top part of it was white silk. That had come in the bundles wrapped around something else. Now it was the top part of a dress, and even if it was wrinkled it made her look different. What a good little girl she is, he thought. At her age and all the things she is able to do, and she never complains. She is always obedient.

She looked up at his approach. There was a little apprehension in her face.

'You'll have to wear flowers in your hair, Man,' he said.

'Oh, Daddy,' she said, 'you know! Didn't I keep it well secret?'

'Yes,' he said. 'It was a big secret.'

'There are so few flowers in October,' she said.

'I'll get you some,' he said, 'you'll see.' He went back into the wood. In the shelter of the trees he found a few flowers; white and yellow daisies, blue gentians and the purple daisy of Michaelmas. Only a few. He went back and sat by them and, piercing the stems with the point of his knife, he drew one through the other to make a chain.

'Pedro is terrible,' Man said. 'I had a task to wash him. He doesn't like to be washed, Daddy. Why is that?'

'You have to be washed, Pedro,' Dominick said, looking at him. Pedro hung his head. 'Come here, Man,' said Dominick then.

She knelt between his knees. He fixed the chain of flowers in her hair like a crown.

'You have a halo, Man,' he said. The flowers became her.

'I'll inspect them,' she said. She leaned over the pool. She regarded her reflection.

'They look nice, Daddy,' she said, 'but you look a bit dirty too.' Dominick laughed.

'We'll cure that,' he said. He slipped off his shoes and sat with his feet in the stream. He washed them and his bare legs which were dirty from his crawling and scratched with briars.

'Is that better?' he asked.

'There's dirt on your face too,' she replied.

So he washed his face.

'Can't you wear a coat?' she asked. 'This is important.'

Pedro was looking at him sympathetically. Dominick winked at him, sighed and said: 'All right. I'll wear a coat.' He leaned and hefted Peter into his arms and walked to the shelter. He brushed back Peter's damp fair hair and said: 'It's a hard life for men, Pedro. You'll have to get used to it.' Pedro put an arm about his neck and placed his cheek against his father's. Dominick automatically clamped down on his feelings.

The three of them walked towards Father Sebastian's hut. Dominick felt all tightened up wearing a coat. He was so unused to it. Like long ago walking to Mass on Sundays all dressed in your best. He carried Pedro on his shoulder and held Man's hand.

About a hundred yards from the cooking-place Father Sebastian had built a shelter for himself between two big stones. Over the tops of the stones he had fashioned a sloping roof of branches overlaid with rushes. He led a separate existence here. It was the right thing to do. He had recovered his health, wrestled with the blinding head pains that had come to him again and again; built up his strength which had been all but drained away from him with the loss of blood, and on the little writing paper which they had, or the paper they had rescued from ruined places, with the help of his memory and the tattered remnants of the holy books they had found in destroyed churches, he had laboriously set to with a quill and an indigo dye extracted from roots to write out the Holy Office and the Ordinary of the Mass. It had been a difficult task – with his head in the state it was – but he had fled into the wild world with nothing of his own except a rosary and a silver medal. All the canonicals would have to be repaired.

He was vesting himself in the open shelter. The three stood outside and watched him. Dominick was amazed.

From a bit here and a piece there, of their own and what Dominick had found in the destroyed houses of the poor,

Father Sebastian had made for himself a set of vestments. They were surely the strangest set of vestments ever to clothe a priest, but they were all recognizable. The amice was coarse linen. The alb, which had been a white linen covering, barely reached to below his knees. The cincture was a coarse rope used on a wagon. The maniple and stole had been fashioned from his old habit and were decorated with white cloth crosses. The chasuble was sackcloth, simply made with a hole for the head, and it bore the symbol of the cross sewn on from the remains of a white linen shirt. As he donned each one Father Sebastian prayed. The three onlookers remained silent.

By the side of the shelter he had fitted a rough wooden altar. It held a crucifix fashioned from oak, with a figure carved on it. The figure was not well made because Father Sebastian couldn't carve, but it was recognizable. There was a pewter chalice; a sun-whitened handkerchief for a purificator; a stiffened cover of calf wrapped in a small square of silk for a pall; a chalice veil made of the same material, and a burse of the same holding another white handkerchief as a corporal. All these so painstakingly put together – crudely enough because Father Sebastian was not handy with his hands – made Dominick think: He really believes, oh, but he believes indeed! and it made him glad that there was one person in this chaos who held firmly to belief.

Father Sebastian said the Mass. Dominick made the responses automatically, thinking how strange all this was, out in the open air where the birds were singing, and you listening to the sound of the wind in the branches of the trees. How different it was from the last time Mass was said in St Peter's before it was smitten: the choirs and the music and the fervour and the costly vestments. Was it ever reduced to as crude a form as this?

Where the stately bell should ring, Dominick clapped two sticks together, thinking: Is this mummery or what is it? Why is it leaving me cold? Didn't many thousands die because this was what they wanted to deprive them of? And what is it all? Not this. They didn't die for this. Just because they had possessions that other men wanted. That was why they died. The whole world – all the world that they knew – in a day or so was reduced to death and blood spilt on stones and brains dashed out against stones, nothing, nothing, proving that it was nothing when thousands could die less gracefully than animals.

63

It meant nothing at all to Dominick.

Even if the birds seemed to hush themselves at the Consecration and he saw little Man with her hands joined and her eyes fastened on the priest; and even if he could see that something visibly happened to her when the priest laid the crude Host on her small tongue and she had difficulty in swallowing It; seeing her closed eyes and her reverently bent head, he tried to think back to the time when he was her age and what it had meant to him. It had meant a lot, he remembered. Some sort of metamorphosis had taken place inside him then, but Drogheda had forced another change on him which seemed even more powerful.

Just as if he was in a great cathedral, Father Sebastian with his patchwork vestments turned then from his shaky altar and, putting his hands under his chasuble and looking at them from his bright eyes, spoke and said: 'Little flock, God has been good to us. He has permitted us the privilege of this day, in this way. This was like it was in the beginning. We must all start from the beginning. Like Mary Ann. The Gospel of today says – *"And Jesus answering said: I confess to thee, O Father, Lord of Heaven and earth, because thou hast hid these things from the wise and prudent and revealed them to little ones."* Little ones like our dear Mary Ann. You can never forget this day, Mary Ann, not while there is breath in your body. And the Gospel of today also has words for us, the old ones, the weary ones. Listen to it. *"Come to me all you that labour and are burdened and I will refresh you. Take up my yoke upon you and learn of me, because I am meek and humble of heart; and you shall find rest to your souls. For my yoke is sweet and my burden light."* '

Dominick got from his knees at that point and walked away. He couldn't tell why. He didn't resent it. He just had to get away as if he was in a closed room and couldn't breathe, when he wasn't but out in the air where he could breathe and fill his lungs.

Father Sebastian called after him: 'Dominick! Dominick!' Dominick didn't heed him, just to sort of raise an arm without looking back, and to wave it over his head. He walked through the trees and into the cooking-clearing and past that again into the trees, dodging, walking, sometimes breaking into a run, feeling stifled, stripping off his coat and throwing it away from him, tearing his shirt so that it opened down to his waist and he could feel the wind on his body, but it gave him no relief inside at all. He was smothering, so he headed through the trees where the land broke free from the wood and a great meadow stretched away down the hill towards the stream, and when he reached the centre of this great field he could travel no more, but went to his knees and dug his fingers into the grass roots and pawed at them like a dog cleaning its claws, and up from inside of him there welled the most despairing bile that emerged from his twisted mouth in sort-of groaning cries, and out of these there came angry tears that blinded him and so many of them that they seemed to be tears streaming from his pores rather than his eyes. He didn't know how long it lasted, this terrible thing, this water from a well that he had thought was dry. And he was marvelling at it himself, in agony that he didn't know that these things existed in the bottom of his soul; that they seemed to last forever and would never end.

He heard, sensed that the priest was beside him.

He felt the hand on his shoulder and heard the soft voice saying: 'Dominick! Dominick!' and he turned on him then, on one knee and one hand. It made it worse to see tears in the eyes of the priest.

'You never knew her!' he shouted at him. 'What do you know about her? You knew nothing about her. Nobody did. But me. What she was. The wonder of her, that could make a daydream or a wakeful night seem like a tale of fairy enchantment. You don't know love, what it is, how it grows and develops, the depths of it, the height of it.'

'I know,' said Father Sebastian.

'No, you don't,' Dominick shouted. 'You love a dream. Not reality. Here and now. Flesh and blood. Flesh and blood. Sought and found. Real, substantial, wonderful. A haven here and now. Not a heaven which might be but is not seen. I saw it with her. But nobody knows what she was. There's nobody left in the world that I can talk about her to. Nobody on the face of the world. Would God do that? Why? To me and to her? Killing her like that. She was good. She was filled with goodness. She was dedicated to goodness. Why like that? Like a speared pig. Why would God do that? No, it cannot be. We are all just animals. She was as innocent as the babies whose brains they dashed out against a wall. But what had she done? What had they done to deserve death like that? Tell me!'

'They were paying for us,' said Sebastian. 'Innocent blood so that even their executioners might be saved.'

65

'Dung,' said Dominick. 'Just dung. Spare me that. She was mine. I needed her and she was killed like a pig.'

His face was buried in the grass.

'God must have wanted her more than you did,' said Sebastian.

'Don't talk to me,' said Dominick. 'I heard it all before. It's just words, words, words. What is reality? What is meaning? I have a hole in my heart. I am desolate. I can't go on. I will die.'

'Oh, Dominick,' said Father Sebastian, but never went on, because from across the stream came the shouts of men on horseback. Father Sebastian looked. There were about twelve of them. They had seen the two men in the middle of the meadow. They were hallooing, like the huntsmen who chased the stag or the fox or the wolf.

He reached down, pulled Dominick to his feet..

'Dominick,' he said, 'come on, run, or we will surely die.'

'Let us die then,' said Dominick, watching the hunters with swollen eyes.

'Let us die and they will get Man and Peter,' said Father Sebastian. 'What will they do to Man, dear Dominick? Do you want Man's brains dashed out against the trunk of a tree?'

He was pulling at Dominick, hauling at him.

And Dominick started to run, at first mechanically and then seriously, a picture flashing in front of his mind of the little girl in the half silk dress with her eyes closed and a chain of fading flowers on her black curls.

It was up the hill. He was exhausted, but Father Sebastian gave him a start, almost lifting his feet off the ground, tearing the shirt from his back with the strength of his pulling arm.

They didn't look back over their shoulders. They kept their eyes on the trees of the wood and ran for them.

Behind, the horses closed on them, saddle leather creaking, wildly shouting men in the saddles, hurrooing and waving long swords over their heads.

It seemed a very long way to the trees.

It seemed a very short way to death.

CHAPTER EIGHT

THEY REACHED the trees. But here at the edge of the woods the spaces between the trees were wide and there was little scrub, so it seemed as if there was no chance for them.

Dominick had to make a tremendous effort to prevent his arms from rising to cover his head as he ran. He could hear the thunder of the hooves. Almost he could hear the whistling of the horses' breath. From the side of his left eye he could see Father Sebastian running strongly.

No time for tears, Dominick thought. You are allowed no time for weeping. I am a weak man. All the canons that I had created. All the rules of the woods. You mustn't do this and you must do that, and he had done all the things he shouldn't have done, had hurled caution to the winds, and now he was going to die and his children would die with him and the priest he had enticed from the woods with his own weakness.

Suddenly from behind him, and it seemed from all around him, there were shouts and yells, the sound of pistol shots and the heavier sound of muskets being discharged. Instinctively he drew in his shoulderblades expecting to feel a ball tearing into his back. But nothing hit him and when he reached the heavy scrub he didn't dive into it but turned and faced back.

It seemed impossible that it could have happened in so short a time. But twelve soldiers were lying on the ground and twelve horses were standing still, good trained horses. Some of the soldiers were obscured from his sight by the men who were bending over them using their knives efficiently on the wounded. There were about twenty of them. Even now some of them were swinging to the ground from the trees, holding their muskets in their hands. They were all bearded men dressed in odds and ends of clothing, but all tall and all strong and all of them having the bearing of soldiers. They were laughing. They were talking in Irish. One saying to the other: 'Did you see the way...' They were casual about it, stabbing their knives into the ground to clean them.

Dominick looked to his right. Father Sebastian was standing as stock still as he was himself, and then he started to walk towards the men. Dominick followed him.

Out of the confusion a tall man with a fair beard and long hair, dressed in the tunic of a Cromwellian Colonel, came towards them.

'It was little but ye were spitted,' he said. He laughed. He clapped a hand on his thigh. 'We had laid a trail for them. We wanted horses. Then ye became hares for us. It was better that way. Otherwise they might have been more cautious coming into the woods.'

'We thank you for our lives,' said Dominick.

'Thanks are returned to you,' said the man. 'Lives were never cheaper than they are today. You want to be more careful.'

Father Sebastian was going around looking at the dead soldiers.

'You have restored my faith,' said Dominick.

'How so?' the man asked.

'I thought there was no more resistance,' said Dominick. 'I thought we were all left for the scythe.'

'Don't believe that,' the man said. 'We will all have to be dead before that happens. They don't know it but they are making a nation out of us.'

Dominick snorted.

The man regarded him with his head on one side.

'Friend,' he said, 'you are in despair.'

'I was in Drogheda,' said Dominick.

'All right,' said the man. 'Put the name on a flag and carry it over your shoulder. The towns are dead, but they will rise again with new men. The people till the earth and live in the woods. They will always till the earth until it belongs to them again.' He turned and shouted at his men. 'Strip the boots and the weapons,' he called to them, 'and bury them back in the quarry. Throw them on the horses.'

Dominick walked past him. Father Sebastian was kneeling on the ground over a soldier. The soldier had raised himself on an elbow. His helmet had fallen off. Dominick as he saw his face felt cold shivers running up and down his back. He could never forget that face, even though then he had been looking up at it and there was a fog on his mind. A thin-faced, big-toothed, flaxen-haired man. There were blood bubbles coming out of his mouth. Dominick stood looking at him over the priest's shoulder. His hands were clenched.

'This is the one! This is the one!' he shouted. He bent, pulled the man's own sword from his scabbard and raised it high. The tenseness in his voice brought the attention of the others to him. Father Sebastian caught his wrist as the sword point was about to enter the man's stomach.

'Dominick!' said Father Sebastian.

'He's the one,' said Dominick. 'The very one. He told me. I talked to him. Under her breast in and out. He told me. Free my hand!'

Father Sebastian's jaw tightened.

He released his grip on Dominick's wrist.

'There you are, Dominick,' he said. 'Kill him. Slaughter him. He's a dying man. Plunge your sword in his guts. That's the way, Dominick. You have learnt a lot, Dominick.'

Dominick was looking at him with glazed eyes. There was a tense silence in the woods.

'Hurry, Dominick,' the priest shouted. 'In another few moments he might be dead and you won't have the chance. He's your enemy. Kill him. That's what you have been brought up to believe, isn't it? Perish him, Dominick. What are you waiting for? There's not enough blood spilt in the world. Kill him dead, can't you?'

Dominick saw the angry face, the hurt eyes of the priest. The upper part of his face was white under the brown from anger.

He dropped the sword.

'I'm sorry, Father,' he said.

'Father,' said the tall fair man. 'I knew there was something about you. God sent you. You are looking at a band of sinners that never needed confession more in their lives. Up to three weeks ago we had our own priest, but one time he waited to bury the dead and they got him. Father, you will listen to us?'

Father Sebastian looked at Dominick. Dominick was regarding the dying soldier with wide eyes. Then he turned from him.

'I will listen to ye,' he said, 'and tell me who was your priest?'

He walked away with the fair man. The others were stripping the bodies with great dexterity. One man came to Dominick and hauled off the boots of the soldier, unclipped his belt.

'Would you like me to send him off for you?' he asked Dominick.

'Let him lie,' said Dominick. 'He hasn't long.'

He got down on his knees and searched the soldier's pouch. His name was Martin Rokeby. He was a ploughman. He was aged twenty-four years. He was illiterate. There was a paper signed 'Martin Rokeby, his mark'. There were some coins and a gold-plated cross that had been torn from a rosary. Four of the beads, wooden ones with silver cups around them, and a piece of the silver chain. Dominick took the cross and put the other things back. He looked at the dying man.

His face was green-tinged. There were cold beads of sweat on his forehead. His eyes were open. They were blue. They were glazing over. There were bubbles of blood coming over his thick lips.

'Nits make lice,' he said.

Dominick heard the sentence clearly. He bent over and wiped the man's forehead with the sleeve of his shirt.

'Why,' he breathed. 'That's why. You must kill kids. Or they will be goats. And they will creep back, like lice, and take the land again when they have all been killed. Take your sickle and your scythe. But not women too because they are soft. They are the same. Is it right?'

'No, Martin Rokeby,' said Dominick. 'It is not right.'

'That's what I thought.' The words were very thick now in his blood-filled throat. 'It's not right. But why, tell me why, sir? Just tell me why, sir?'

That was all he said. He died. And something happened to Dominick that he didn't believe possible. Tears came to his eyes. Not for himself. He was sick of himself. Not for Eibhlin – he had cried out his heart for her – but for this young, bewildered, foreign soldier dying in a foreign land. Who would ever know what became of him? What he had done was truly the work of the Lord, Who didn't will it, or ordain it but permitted it, for a reason, dear God, because there must be a reason else everything is chaos and there is no past, present, or future.

'Is he gone?' a voice asked him.

'Yes,' said Dominick, 'he's gone.'

'Well, hoist him in a hurry,' the man said. 'My soul is as black as a deep bog and I'll have to get to the priest.'

Dominick took the man's legs and helped the other to hoist him, feet and head hanging, on the horse's back. Then he watched as the man led the horse away.

Dominick walked through the trees. Behind him nothing remained in the clearing of death but broken twigs, blood soaking into the ground, and horse manure. That was all. In a few days the wood would have eliminated all the signs of the brief struggle where a dozen men had been wiped out as if they had never existed. Truly anonymous death.

He found Man and Peter in the priest's shelter. She had folded all the hurriedly discarded vestments and placed them neatly on the makeshift altar. She was sitting there with her arm around her brother. Poor Man!

'Hello,' he said.

'Oh, Daddy,' she said, 'where did you go?'

'Just for a walk, Man,' he said.

'We heard things,' she said. 'We were afraid.'

He sat beside them.

'Don't be afraid, Man,' he said. 'You mustn't be afraid. Your father won't ever run away again.'

'Am I near an angel now, Daddy?' she asked.

'You'll never be nearer, Man,' he said. 'I have a gift for you.'

'You have?' she asked.

'Look,' he said, and held out the cross.

'Oh, it's beautiful,' she said. 'Is it for me? Can I keep it?'

'It's for you and you can keep it,' he said. 'Some day we will get a most beautiful chain for it.'

'We will?' she asked.

'Yes,' he said. 'Just for now, we'll mount it on a cord and put it around your neck.'

'Oh,' she said, and watched him as he mounted it. Peter was looking at all this with wide pleased eyes. He placed it around her neck and tied it at the back. He wondered at how soft and innocent her flesh was as his hard palms touched her shoulders. She put her arms around his neck and hugged him.

'Are you sad because Mammy is lost on us?' she asked him. All Dominick's bones started to scream at the question, but he swallowed and relaxed his muscles.

'Yes, Man,' he said. 'I'm afraid we won't see Mammy any more.'

'Father Sebastian told me that she is much happier,' said Man. 'He said she is spared all the travelling and living in the woods that we do. Isn't that right? Sure Mammy wouldn't like all that, Daddy?' she asked.

'It wouldn't be good for her,' he said.

'So it's as well she is gone,' said Man. 'Don't you believe Father Sebastian?'

'Some of the time,' said Dominick. 'We must go now and get the rabbits and cook them. It's getting late. We'll have to walk more tonight, Man. Will you mind that?'

'Oh no, Daddy,' she said. 'One gets weary in the one place all the time.'

Dominick laughed.

'Oh, Man,' he said. 'One day I'll settle. We'll have a house of our own again.'

'That'll be nice,' said Man.

They went back to their own shelter and Dominick skinned and cleaned the rabbits and cut them up, and they came back and built the fire and spitting the quarters started to cook them.

They were cooked and scenting the air when Dominick heard the breaking twigs. He gathered the two children and swept them behind a tree. I know it's not likely, he thought, but I will never take a chance again.

He waited there until he saw Father Sebastian and the tall fair man coming into the clearing and looking around. Then he went to meet them.

'Ah,' said Father Sebastian, 'Rory wanted to see you.'

'I'd like to address your daughter,' said Rory. 'I hear she had a big day.'

'This is Mary Ann,' said Dominick. 'This is Rory. Rory is a soldier who came in the nick of time, Mary Ann.'

She looked at him. He was very tall. He had clear grey eyes, and he was smiling. She went to meet him. She held out her hand. He bent and took it, and kissed it. Mary Ann laughed.

'That's funny,' she said, 'your beard tickled me.'

'And Peter,' said Dominick, bringing him out by the hand.

Rory gravely shook hands with him.

'On account of the great day,' he said, 'I would be pleased if you would accept a gift from me, Miss MacMahon.'

'Oh!' said Mary Ann.

He reached inside his tunic and brought forth a most beautiful blue and white coloured silk kerchief.

'Oh!' said Mary Ann.

He got on one knee and tied it around her shoulders.

'Oh!' said Man, preening herself. 'Thank you. It's beautiful.'

'It belonged to my lady,' said Rory. 'She would be pleased for you to have it.'

'Oh, I love it,' said Man.

'Now I must leave you,' said Rory. 'You ought to leave too. This place will be unsafe for some time.'

'See what I got, Dominick,' said Father Sebastian. He was holding out a Mass book and a gilt chalice. 'God is good. He had to make a martyr so that I could have them.'

'Thanks for all you have done,' said Dominick.

'Walk back with me,' said Rory. 'I want to talk to you. Goodbye, Miss MacMahon. Could I hope for the pleasure of a kiss?'

'Oh, yes,' said Man, who was rubbing her palms on the silk scarf. She kissed him. He looked sadly at her and at pudgy Peter, and then he walked away with Dominick beside him.

'I wanted your priest to come with us,' he said, 'but he felt that the Lord wanted him with you.'

Dominick tried to think of themselves without the priest. How often he had wished that he was anywhere but with them. Now the thought of being deprived of him would not be good.

'I'm glad,' he said.

'He told me about you,' said Rory. 'There are people worse off than you. They killed my wife too. Unfortunately I had great possessions and they wanted them and no future claimants. So they killed my three children too. They said nits make lice. They killed her first, so she didn't see.'

Dominick's heart was beating madly.

'You take it quietly,' he said.

'I am a soldier,' said Rory. 'I want to live, although there doesn't seem to be any actual reason for living. But you can't live on emotion. That will lead you into death very quickly. You are lucky to have your children. You have something to live for. So don't get emotional. Where are you heading?'

Dominick told him.

'Stay there awhile,' Rory said. 'All the middle south is going to become a great graveyard. The soldiers have been promised the land. They are being issued with scythes and sickles. That will cause starvation, plague, and famine. After that go west.'

'Another soldier told me that too,' said Dominick.

'You will have no alternative in the end,' said Rory. 'God be with you. Don't come any farther.'

'Where are you going?' Dominick asked.

'North, where I belong,' Rory said. 'We will fight there for some time to come. We can't last, not unless we want to be wood soldiers all our lives. Maybe we will have to go away, like the wild geese, across the sea to other lands where they want good soldiers who will fight the English. You stay here. Fight for your children. They will inherit the land. If I had my children, I would dig a burrow in the earth, anything at all, so that they would be there.'

'God be with you,' said Rory.

He looked at Dominick for a moment and then he was gone. Dominick looked after him.

There is a good man, he thought, and he is strong because he has acceptance. He wondered if the fine hand of Father Sebastian was behind the way he had unburdened himself to Dominick. Dominick supposed it was, but he felt no resentment. He went back to his cares.

When they were all packed up and himself and Father Sebastian were loaded with burdens and they were heading out of the woods in the red twilight of that October evening, he watched the two children walking ahead of them in the clearing and he said to Father Sebastian:

'I'd better face it now, Father, I suppose. Pedro is dumb, isn't he?'

Father Sebastian didn't answer for a moment.

'But he has most expressive eyes, Dominick,' he said. 'And he has Man.'

'And me,' said Dominick.

'And me,' said Father Sebastian, and he thumped Dominick on the shoulder with his big hand.

CHAPTER NINE

THE SEAGULL, soaring high in the air, exercising himself from the cold waters of Loc Sileann, looked down from his great height.

He could see the big loc shaping to a point at its south-west corner where rested three other lakes, the one in the centre carrying two smaller ones at each end of it so that the three together looked like a tail added to the bulk of Sileann, and making the whole resemble the ungainly shape of a prehistoric fish. The waters of the lakes glinted in the afternoon sun, and the land all around them was white from the fall of snow. In the curve of the fish's tail there was a wooded valley. The valley itself had been raped of its timber, and even the fall of snow could barely hide the way the earth had been gouged and punished by the hauling of the great logs of oak and pine. This narrow cleared valley was about twenty yards wide and if the seagull had any interest in human affairs he could have noticed the small dot that was a man toiling up the valley towards the height where the tree-cutting had ended.

The seagull, if his eyes were keen enough, could have seen in the shelter of the woods, on the opposite side of this height, the other figure of a man who was quietly stealing from tree to tree in the wake of a thin goat, who moved and munched, moved and munched anything at all green that came his way, discarded branches of pine not yet turned yellow, or searching the ground under the oak where snow had not fallen thickly, to crunch the husks of the acorns that had been left by the wild pigs.

The seagull could have warned, by a shrill cry, the man toiling up the valley, that at each side of him in the woods lean shapes were moving almost parallel to him, three on each side, brown shaggy-coated animals that looked like the great dogs that hunted them, but they weren't dogs and they moved like shadows, soundlessly, and the man was not aware of them.

The seagull may not have liked the look of them. He lifted a wing and coasted back to the blue waters of the lake.

Dominick was on one knee behind a tree, and the arrow was

set in the bow. He edged around the tree. He got the goat into his sight and aimed for his body behind the foreleg. The goat died, on his feet. His narrow mouth made two more crunches and then he just fell over.

Dominick let out his breath and moved towards him. The snow was crisp under his long hide boots. He knelt beside the goat and felt him. He was warm to the touch and he smelt, and he was very thin. But he would do. He extracted the arrow and cleaned it in the snow. It stained the snow a very bright scarlet. The hair of the goat was long.

He heard a sound carried to his ear from in front of him.

He stiffened, listened, and then crouched low, moved through the trees towards the spot where they ended and the sky was coldly coloured. He paused there behind the bole of the largest oak and looked down the valley.

The man trudging up towards him was about a hundred yards away. He wasn't walking strongly. He was walking from side to side as if to ease the climb towards the top. It wasn't a steep climb. If he was strong he could have walked straight up. This man was walking in a zigzag.

Then Dominick froze as he saw the shapes flitting from tree to tree on each side of the man.

He rose and ran, and he shouted, 'At your back! At your back!' He saw the man looking up at him with his mouth open, drawing great breaths into his lungs, and at the same time he saw the wolves as if on a signal converge on the man from each side. Dominick was flying fast down the hill. Move! Move! his mind ordered the man, and the man reacted. He turned to face back and drew a sword from his belt. His arm swung and the first wolf that leapt for him was decapitated. It was a terrible stroke. His falling head still had its teeth bared. Dominick had knelt when he judged the distance right, had fitted the arrow and saw it strike the other leaping one in the throat. The man shouted and ran at the other hesitators. They didn't wait for him. They ran for the trees at each side.

Dominick came down to the man.

As he came close to him he saw that his own size seemed to decrease and the size of the fast-breathing man to increase, so that when he faced him, Dominick, although he had the advantage of the hill, had to look up at him. A thickly bearded black face seeming more black from the white streaks running through it. The man took the soft cloth hat from his ragged hair and wiped sweat off his face. He had a very big chest and an immense hand gripping the dripping sword. The coarse cloth of his clothes made him seem even bigger than he was. But there was strain in his face and his cheeks were gaunt and there were deep shadows under his eyes, but somewhere out of his face Dominick pulled the thought of him as seen before. In frost weather too, by candlelight in a cellar, and in a room with a woman in the bed imperiously pointing to a cradle at the bottom of it, saying, 'Look at my baby.'

'God bless you, Murdoc,' said Dominick.

Murdoc screwed up his eyes, and put his head on one side. He walked to one side of Dominick and walked to the other side of Dominick. His forehead was furrowed. He was still breathing very hard. He saw a long-haired man, fair hair, and a cleanshaven narrow face, low-sized, stocky, confident, with a half smile on his face.

He hit his head with his free hand.

'Why don't I know you, man?' he asked, abusing himself. 'Speak to me again.'

'It is very cold,' said Dominick. 'The town is asleep. Many men are marching through an orchard. There is the sound of clashing pikes, loud hurroos and the clash of arms, and you run into the back ways seeking shelter.'

'Oh, no! Oh, no!' exclaimed Murdoc. 'It couldn't be you.' Holding out his hand, Dominick took it. 'Not again. How many years? So many years. In between the two times. And you do it again. Not that I wouldn't have been able to handle those butchers. Cowardly butchers. You understand that? Oh, let me think. A great name, I said, and you skulking behind walls, not caring. It was Mac, Mac, MacMahon!' he said then in a shout. 'Hah. There's the memory of Murdoc! You got away. I thought of you, and of her, that black-haired woman in the bed that should have been on a mountain in the west. When I heard what they did to it, I mourned for you. I lit a big candle in the church and I got the priest to pray for you. I didn't forget, Dominick MacMahon.'

He squeezed Dominick's hand, almost crunching the bones of it, so pleased to see him, so pleased at his own memories.

'You got away,' he said again.

'I got away,' said Dominick, 'but she didn't get away. She is still there, under a stone.' He marvelled at his own calm now.

'Oh,' said Murdoc. 'That's not right. Oh, sad, sad! And where are you? How did it happen?'

'They say God makes meetings,' said Dominick. 'Meetings are meant. How do I know? We are here. We are sheltered in a very safe spot between the four lakes. We have been there nearly two years. I was hunting meat. I found the meat and then I found you. You will come back with me?'

'Oh, but I will,' said Murdoc. 'I am sapped. I was a man of great strength, but they have reduced me. Maybe I mightn't have been able to kill all those wolves.' He caught the one that Dominick had killed by the tail and raised her up. 'A bitch,' he said. 'She's worth ten pounds. Did you know that? And the fellow that I killed is worth six pounds. Will we gather the heads and go into an Uaimh with them, and collect the bounty?'

That amused him. He laughed.

'Oh, but I am glad to see you, man,' he said. 'For the last half year, I have been like a hunted wolf myself. I was heading west and each time they kept heading me east. I got caught on the wrong side of the Blackwater, but it was fate, man. If I could have crossed the Shannon we would never have met. I will go with you. Lead me on.'

'I'm glad to see you, Murdoc,' said Dominick. 'I haven't forgotten you.'

'How could you, man?' said Murdoc. 'Does any man forget people who owe their lives to him? It's a precious thing.'

They didn't talk, they just wondered as they climbed back up the hill to the dead goat. Dominick caught him by the legs and wore him around his neck, holding him by the hooves. He didn't smell well, but what did it matter? All the time Murdoc was shaking his head and saying: 'Well, well!' and 'Man! Man!' and following Dominick's footsteps in the snow.

They didn't talk. They saved their breaths because both of them moved with caution, their bodies tense, listening. It's a wonder, Dominick thought, that our ears haven't grown as long as the ears of a donkey with all the listening we do.

They came from the wooded place. From this height they could see the evening sun changing the colours of the water of the lakes below them, from blue to red. There were great black lowering clouds rolling up from the north to their right. They were like snow-capped mountains. In all the vast stretch of land below them there was no sign of smoke to be seen, nor the sign of a person. There were people there, somewhere, but no man moved unless he moved as they themselves moved, always in shelter, by thickets and trees and concealing folds in the earth.

Dominick sighed.

He felt the burden of the goat on his shoulders, but it was worth while. He thought of the way it would be greeted.

It took them an hour to get down from the heights into the callows and rushes by the soft lands.

Here Dominick stopped. He dropped the goat and sat on his haunches. 'We will rest awhile,' he said. 'From here it is hard.'

Murdoc sat. He was breathing heavily. Dominick noticed sweat on him.

'I'm an old man,' said Murdoc. 'Before my time. It's only home that will cure me and make me strong. I'll breathe in the mountains. You don't need food. You can eat the air.'

'How long is it since you have been home?' Dominick asked.

Murdoc thought.

'In forty-one,' he said, 'I met you. I had been a year out before that. Eleven years ago. Dear God, I was a young man with fire in me then. Now look at me!'

'You look young enough and strong enough to me still,' said Dominick.

'Ah, but the fire is gone,' said Murdoc. 'I have seen too many sights. I have killed too many men.'

'We'll go now,' said Dominick, looking at the spreading twilight. 'It's a clever place. We have to get in by the light.' He wore the goat again. 'Follow me closely,' he said.

'Lead on, man,' said Murdoc tiredly.

They came to where acres of faded rushes grew on soft ground. Dominick chose a point and stepped into them. Murdoc followed him. His feet sank into the greyish-yellow ooze, and it tried to hold on to them. He had to pull each foot out. It took an effort. Dominick didn't take a straight way through the rushes, but went from side to side, twisting and turning. Murdoc floundered after him, wondering at the light way his feet seemed to rest on the soft ground. It was very hard walking. When Murdoc thought that his heart would burst its way through the wall of his chest, they came to a stretch, a wide stretch, of open water. Dominick waited for him.

'Keep close here,' he said, and seemed to walk out on the

water. Murdoc followed him and felt the firm ground about six inches under the water. Dominick didn't cross here the straight way either. He took a line on the land in front of him and sometimes he went to the right and sometimes he went to the left. The whole place was a maze of rushes and open water, and more rushes and more open water. The sun was gone and the last light was fading from the sky when Murdoc felt solid ground under his feet.

'The worst is over now,' said Dominick. Murdoc guessed they were on a sort of island in the middle of the miles of quaking land. There was a lot of scrub willows and alders, bare of foliage, and stunted forest trees that got little room to expand. In five minutes they came to a fence of hurdles. They went around this and saw the fire. Its light was blocked by the hurdles in front and by the steep rise of overhang behind it. In this overhang there was a big man tending the fire. He looked up at them.

'I found a friend,' said Dominick. 'I got a goat. Here is the goat and this is my friend Murdoc. This is Sebastian. Sebastian came from Drogheda too.' He didn't say Sebastian was a priest.

Sebastian rose and held out his hand. 'Dominick told me of you,' he said.

They could see very little of one another now, just the bones of their faces lighted up by the fire.

'Our fates are entwined,' said Murdoc, shaking his hand. A big hard hand, as rough as his own. 'And where's the little one?'

Dominick laughed.

'Ah, she's no longer little,' he said. 'Come and see her.'

'They are sleeping,' said Sebastian.

'More than one,' said Murdoc, following Dominick away from the fire. Their feet were squelching in the wet boots.

'I have a son, too,' said Dominick.

'You are wealthy,' said Murdoc.

They came to the mound. It was a round mound rising roughly from the surrounding thickets. There was a narrow rectangular stone opening to it. Dominick bent and went in. Murdoc followed him.

It was lighted inside by rushlight, guttering. It was beehive shape. Murdoc had seen them before, built at the time when men were less civilized than they were now – that made him chuckle, that thought – perfectly formed, where saintly men had come to get away from their fellow men. The roof was arched, one stone supporting another, held together by mortar that was still as hard as the day it was put in maybe a thousand years ago. There was a small room above with narrow stone steps up to it. He followed Dominick. Dominick was crouched inside. Murdoc just shoved his head and shoulders through the opening and looked. Dominick held the light high so that Murdoc could see the sleeping girl. Oh, but it brought it all back, the sight of her. There was a fair boy sleeping on the rushes beside her. Dominick pulled the skins more closely around them and came down after Murdoc.

'Out of her mother's mouth, the same spit,' said Murdoc. He was shaking his head. 'She will be her mother,' he said. 'How lucky you are, man! While you have her, you have her mother.'

'Come to the fire and eat,' said Dominick.

Sebastian was already skinning the goat. Dominick indicated a crude wooden seat near the fire. Murdoc sank on it with a sigh. He took off his soaked boots and rubbed his cold feet with his hands and held them out to the fire.

'That's the heat of God,' he said.

Dominick handed him a wooden platter. It held rough oaten bread and a little cold rabbit.

'It's not much, Murdoc,' said Dominick, 'and you will have to drink water.' He handed him a pewter tankard, thinking how sad it was that their wine was all gone. Thinking of the way Sebastian had husbanded the altar wine, using just a fingerful each time to consecrate it for Mass, measuring one twentieth of its small bulk to add the water. Now it was all gone. He could no longer say Mass.

'We will have to leave here soon now,' he said. 'What is the world abroad like, Murdoc?'

'I have never seen a desert,' said Murdoc. 'It is a fertile desert. Can such a thing be?'

'It's man himself that makes the deserts,' said Sebastian. He puzzled Murdoc – his quiet voice, his calm eyes in a thin face. Yet he looked like a ploughman.

'Maybe we should have brought the wolves and eaten them,' he said. 'I've eaten everything else. Not wolf.'

'You killed a wolf?' Sebastian asked.

'Yes,' said Murdoc. 'They wanted to make a meal of me. But Dominick saved me. Two heads. They would be worth sixteen pounds. Equal to the price you'd get for the heads of two and a half priests.'

'Is that the price?' Sebastian asked.

'Six pounds a skull,' said Murdoc. 'That's the price of them. The same as a he-wolf. Who made this bread? It is good bread.'

'Mary Ann made that,' said Dominick. 'She has a light hand with rough materials.'

'Wait until she gets the proper meal,' said Murdoc. 'She will be a treasure. Listen. In one week I walked thirty miles. In all that time, between the Blackwater and here, I haven't seen a single human being. This is as true as God. Houses without smoke, skeletons in fields. A great dead desert, with the land putting forth weeds the size of the empty houses. They have defeated us. They have made us into a blighted land.'

'It's the will of God,' said Sebastian.

'I beg to disagree with you,' said Murdoc. 'I have seen a lot. There are only two conclusions.'

'State them,' said Sebastian.

'There is no God,' said Murdoc, 'or God is on the side of them and we were wrong.'

'You have seen a lot?' Sebastian hazarded.

'Too much,' said Murdoc. 'When Drogheda fell I was in Wexford. There were two men there called Cooke and Bolton. Their names will be remembered. They murdered about ten thousand. This I saw. There were about three hundred women and children praying around the corpses in the square. You have heard of evil things done by the Turks or the Goths or the Huns. They would have spared those, I think, but Cooke didn't. I was dressed as one of them by this and I saw them being killed, every one of them. They didn't leave a sinner alive of them within twenty miles of the place. I was in Clonmel when it fell. I was with Hugh Dubh. And I was in Limerick. I've seen them being locked into churches and the churches set on fire. I've heard them screaming. I've seen commanders holding babies by the leg and knocking their brains out against a stone. Every church in the land is turned into a stable or a brothel. I've seen this. It's a terrible thing. Now if our God had seen all this too, He would have done something about it. But no. All the time it happens. And it is permitted. It doesn't make sense. You get to the point where you can look at these things and say: well, maybe they are right, maybe we are the whore of Babylon and the time has come to destroy us.'

Sebastian had stopped skinning the goat. He let his head rest on the back of his hand. Then he looked up.

'Have you seen nothing with hope at all, Murdoc?' he asked.

'I don't know what hope is now,' said Murdoc.

'Nothing at all that was noble?' Sebastian asked.

'I've seen things that pleased me,' said Murdoc. 'I've seen the soldiers dying in thousands from a very painful black flux. I've often stood over them and watched them dying in agony. Each time I would say: Well, if you had stayed at home, this wouldn't have happened to you. I've been with bands of good men, since Limerick, and we have often trapped a score of them and hanged them from trees. That was pleasing. But is that hope when we can kill a few of them? Isn't it too much? Hasn't Cromwell's God got the edge on us?'

'Have you seen nothing that stirred your heart?' Sebastian asked.

'I don't know,' said Murdoc. 'Last winter I was in the woods. I was looking for honey. And I came to a hollow tree. Do you know what was in that tree?'

'What?' Sebastian asked.

'A woman,' said Murdoc. 'A young girl. She was a nun. She had a black habit on her and a white thing on her head. She must have fled there from them and died. She was lucky. Some nuns didn't get away in time from them. I don't know how long this girl had been there. It must have been a long time, maybe from the winter before. The spiders had woven cobwebs all about her. And there was a look of peace on her face. Her body should have been rotted. But this is strange, it wasn't. And she smelled of honey. There in the woods. It was probably the bees. I buried her under the tree.'

'Doesn't that mean something to you?' Sebastian asked.

'One bud doesn't make spring,' said Murdoc. 'I saw brave things. There was this Bishop of Limerick. Ireton caught him. He condemned him. He gave him a painful death. "I will see you in eight days, Ireton," he said to him, "before the Tribunal of God." You could see Ireton wilting after that. Every day. And he was called. I'd like to think he was in hell, but I don't know. Maybe it's the Bishop that's in hell.'

'You have seen too much, all right, Murdoc,' said Sebastian. 'You have lost hope. You are tired.'

'Yes, I am,' said Murdoc. 'I'm just thinking over things. What cause is there for hope? All our soldiers are gone. In their thousands after Limerick. There are songs in Irish being sung in every land from Holland to Russia, but what does that do? It leaves this land as open as the embrace of an evil woman. From sea to sea. We have been given everything, war, plague, famine, and the sword. We are left without hope. Can you tell me why?'

'Because we were all sinners,' said Sebastian.

Murdoc looked at him, opened his mouth, and laughed. Dominick noticed that Murdoc had lost quite a few of his strong white teeth. He was trying to think back, to visualize the big pulsating warrior he had remembered. Have I changed too? he wondered. All these things that Murdoc is saying, were they in my own mind too?

'You talk like a friar,' said Murdoc. 'That's not reality. Were we worse sinners than the people who are destroying us? Are they saints?'

'The Israelites were chosen by God,' said Sebastian. 'When they sinned they were punished. They were purged by pagans. That is the answer, Murdoc. We will emerge a better people, not today but tomorrow. We will learn to live with sorrow and to laugh at it, but we never will, if we abandon hope. We must believe in God, hope in His mercy and love our enemies.'

'Even while they are cutting our throats, raping our children, hanging our priests, we must love them, is that it?'

'That's it,' said Sebastian.

Murdoc was on his feet.

'No,' he shouted. 'None of that. We were meek. We took them in. We didn't hate enough. We didn't fight enough. We left them an opening in our sides and they infected our blood-stream. We didn't hate enough.'

'We didn't love enough,' said Sebastian.

Dominick thought that Murdoc would hit him. He rose to his feet.

'You are tired, Murdoc,' he said. 'Why don't you rest?'

Murdoc let the breath out of his body.

'Yes, Dominick, that's what's wrong with me. I'm tired. I have seen too much. Maybe I will see clearer when I go home and smell the clean sea. Hah! We will argue again, Sebastian. But I like fighters. Have you ever fought?'

Sebastian considered this.

'Yes, Murdoc,' he said. 'I have fought.'

'Well, you are alive,' said Murdoc.

'That is the will of God too,' said Sebastian.

Murdoc snorted. He followed after Dominick. Dominick showed him where to lie in the cell, gave him the skins to cover him.

'You keep odd company now, Dominick,' Murdoc said. 'Leave this place and come with me. Bring the girl and the boy and come with me to the mountains.'

'No, Murdoc,' said Dominick. 'Not now. I'm tired of the mountains. I'm tired of plains. I'm tired of land. I'm tired of hunting and fishing and living on the edge of starvation. I want the town around me.'

Murdoc laughed.

'Still the same,' he laughed. 'Right, man, go and see the towns. I have seen them. You go and see them. Oh, God, but I'm tired of towns and land and walking. When I am settled down, I will never walk again even if I have to make men carry me on their backs. Oh, man, but I'm tired.' He was stretched and asleep almost before he had finished speaking.

Dominick went back. He stirred up the fire, threw a little more wood on it.

'Murdoc is sick,' said Sebastian.

'It is a sickness that comes on all of us,' said Dominick. 'It is very strange that we should meet again like this.'

'Not very strange,' said Sebastian. 'It was meant that way. There is a reason for it. There is some purpose in it.'

'I hope it is for good,' said Dominick.

'I hope so too,' said Sebastian.

'We will have to leave here,' said Dominick. 'There's no game left. It's getting harder and harder to find them. All the animals are being swept away by the wolves.'

'And soon the people will be. I heard today,' said Sebastian, 'that they are going to shift everyone west of the Shannon. There is going to be the greatest transplantation of all time.'

'There won't be many left to go,' said Dominick. 'At least they will be pushing us in the way we want to go. I want a place where we can stay, and never move.'

'You'll find it, Dominick,' said Sebastian. 'Some day you will find it.'

'God is good,' said Dominick, and the priest looked at him a moment. Dominick met his eyes. They smiled.

CHAPTER TEN

THE RAIN poured steadily from a leaden sky. They stood on a rise and looked down at the town of the ford. Smoke from a few houses was baffled by the low clouds and spread out in a grey haze over the town and the broad river of the Shannon. The river was on their right and they could see where the long lake of Ribh was swollen by it.

Dominick wore a goatskin cloak and held it out from him so that Peter could shelter under it. Mary Ann was sheltering under the bulk of Murdoc.

'Well?' said Murdoc.

'Well?' said Dominick.

Sebastian pointed down below them. From all sides of the compass the small black dots of people were converging on the town.

'My way is with the people,' he said.

'To go with the people you will have to have papers,' said Murdoc. 'Every crossing, every ford, every way there will be soldiers waiting for your papers. The soldiers alone are the judges of life or death, man. If the papers are blotted, they can kill you out of hand, like a chicken for the pot. It is an evil thing to submit your life to a paper that's signed by their hands. Is it a protection?'

'My way is with the people,' said Sebastian.

'From here, the way is known to me, Dominick,' Murdoc said. 'We will cleave our way across Roscommon, over into Muigheo. From there it will be easy. These are men that never surrendered to anyone. The way is hard but it is clear.'

'My children have had it very hard, Murdoc,' said Dominick. He could feel the bones of Peter's face under his hand. The bones were prominent. He saw the eyes of Mary Ann peering at him from under the cover of Murdoc. Her eyes were very big. They were too big. It had been a very hard winter. He had not liked leaving their watery haven, but it had become too hard to find food. Murdoc had foraged. He had never returned empty-handed. Nor had Dominick himself, but their hauls were meagre. All the corn they had scraped from the untended fields had now failed them. They possessed between them and starvation about four oatmeal loaves. 'No, Murdoc,' he said decisively. 'I have to go down to that town.'

'You are foolish,' said Murdoc. 'But off with you. I go the other way. I could never live without a sword at my belt. No man in the world is going to get that off me. It's a sad parting, but I wish ye well. Some day we will meet again. You know the where. I have talked of it many times. You know the way of it.'

'I have a picture in my head of it,' said Dominick.

Murdoc bent down, held Mary Ann in front of him.

'God be with you, my love,' he said. 'Don't forget Murdoc easy, will you?'

Mary Ann shook her head.

'No, Murdoc,' she said. 'We will miss you.'

'That's good,' he said. 'I'll miss you too.'

But Mary Ann wasn't crying, Dominick noticed. Murdoc was changeable. A restless man. Sometimes he would play with Mary Ann and Peter. He would roll on the rushes with them shouting with laughter. That was one moment and the next moment he would be sitting up, sour-faced, a frown between his eyebrows, his fist thumping the ground. Then he would have no time for playing with children. So they were wary of him and his moods. So was Dominick for that matter. In a way he would be glad when they had parted. He thought this and then he thought that it was wrong, because when he was in a good mood, Murdoc was colourful, dramatic, with his eyes lighting up with laughter and excitement, talking about his ancestors, boasting of their deeds, emulating them with movements, and talking of himself and his actions, a giant figure of a man, a big man, small only in the way that he never cared for Sebastian. Sebastian was patient, kind, but inflexible in his views of right and wrong. It came to the point that all Murdoc's explanations were challenges. Sebastian often avoided them, but when he was faced with it, he expressed his views calmly and clearly and Murdoc would shout at him: 'You should have been a friar. You're wound in wool, man.'

So Dominick went close to Murdoc and took his huge hand and squeezed it with both of his own.

'We will miss you, Murdoc,' he said. 'You will take strength from us. But we are little people, and we may escape in under their arms like little people always do. Nobody could mistake you. We will meet again, God willing, and we will laugh over these days.'

'I hope so, Dominick,' said Murdoc, 'I hope so. Beware of yourselves and don't let them hear Sebastian talking or they'll take him for a priest and hang the lot of ye.' He kissed Mary Ann. She rubbed her face. She always did after the feel of his tough whiskers.

He slapped Peter on the back. He slapped Dominick on the back. Then he faced Sebastian. They were of a height, and yet Murdoc looked the bigger man.

'We are going to meet again, Sebastian,' said Murdoc. 'I feel it in here.' Thumping his big chest. 'I don't know if that's good.'

'What's meant will be, Murdoc. You are a good man. Use your sword less and your head more and things will run sweetly for you.'

'The devil with you,' said Murdoc. 'There you go again. You talk in parables. Why can't you use straight sentences like an honest man? Tell me that?'

'It must be because I am crooked, Murdoc,' said Sebastian.

'No,' said Murdoc, 'but you are twisty. My soul to hell if I understand you. But I wouldn't mind you in a fight. And you are a good teacher. That Mary Ann can write better than I can, old as I am. Pray for me, see. You'll do that, I know. I'm what I am and I don't change. You'll see.'

'God be with you, Murdoc,' said Sebastian.

'All to the good, so,' said Murdoc. 'I'm off. Ye're foolish but who am I to change ye? Watch yeerselves. Be cunning. Be dirty. Be ignorant. That's the way ye'll get by. Only the useless ones of the land they let get by. I'm gone.'

He didn't look at them any more. He had no bundles, no possessions, only what he wore and his sword and a piece of oaten bread in his pouch. He went down the hill and headed back the way they had come, to the farther lonely reaches of the Shannon where he could cross in hardship but in comparative peace. He was like a great bear. One that you get fond of. But unpredictable. No cunning in him at all. Then he was gone from their sight.

'I will go down to the town,' said Dominick. 'I will buy what we need. Man always wants gold. Let us find shelter for you first. You wait for me. I will be back.'

'You know what you are doing, Dominick?' said Sebastian.

'I'll get by,' said Dominick. 'They are not killing us much now. That's the sign. Now they are in the market. I was always a good merchant.'

'I see an empty house down there,' said Sebastian. He pointed. It was below near the river. They could see the thatch of it. The cleared space around it was being encroached on by scrub. The thatch was green from decay. No smoke rose from it.

'Come on,' said Dominick. He took off the skins and gave them to Peter and Mary Ann. They walked together under the cover of them.

They approached the house cautiously, breaking their way through the thickets of withered briars. What a change, Dominick thought, remembering back, so long ago when he could freely travel in the country. There would be chickens picking and dogs barking, baring their teeth in front and wagging their tails behind, and a curious woman at the doorway with the well of emptiness on her face until you talked and she knew what you were and she would loosen her face and you could see her warm feelings.

The door was banging drunkenly. The windows were very small and deep and sloping so that while the winds could enter the rain could not.

Sebastian went to the door.

'God bless all in this house,' he said. It was gloomy. Not a lot of light entered. The fireplace was black but no fire burned in it. There was a smell of dampness and decaying straw.

He was about to turn and say, 'It is empty', when he heard the voice. A weak voice coming from the place above the fire. He peered and could see the bundle on the rushes and out of the bundle the movement of a hand. He walked in and over, keeping his body from blocking the light from the door. What light there was shone on the face of the old woman too weak to raise her head. He got on one knee beside her and felt for her hand. It was a hand of mainly skin and bone.

'God bless you,' her voice said, 'and are you a priest?'

Sebastian felt as if he had been hit in the chest. He could see the long straggly white hair and a thin peaked face with sunken eyes surrounded by a million wrinkles.

'How did you know I was a priest?' Sebastian asked, stroking her hand.

She sighed.

'They told me,' she said, 'and they were right.'

'Who told you?' he asked.

'They did,' she said. 'Wasn't God good?'

'Have you no one?' he asked.

'No one now,' she said. 'The sickness took the gradle of them and the soldiers took the rest. Yesterday I could walk and light the bit of fire and cook the gruel. Now it is over.'

'We came looking for shelter,' said Sebastian.

'My house is yours, love,' she said. 'You will listen to me and let me go. You were sent. Don't leave me now.'

'Only for a fraction,' he said to her. He let her hand go. He went to the door. He said to Dominick: 'Bear the rain a minute more,' and then went back to her, taking the makeshift stole from his pocket and putting it around his neck.

Dominick wasn't sure what was going on. He had heard the voices but not what they were saying. There seemed to be a terribly intense silence coming from the inside of the house. He remained unmoving, and so did the children as the rain beat on them and dripped from the thatch. Some time and then Sebastian was back with them.

'Come and meet a great lady,' he said.

They followed him in curiously. They stood there dripping water on to the beaten mud floor. Then after a time they could see her face.

'Children?' she asked.

'This is Mary Ann and Peter,' said Sebastian.

'You are welcome to my house,' she said. 'They will own land one day. We had the desolation.' Mary Ann went close to her and sat on her heels.

'Are you sick?' she asked.

'I was,' said the old woman, 'but soon I will be well. It makes me well to see a young face. You own the world. Now the world belongs to you. God bless you.'

Sebastian had walked out into the rain. Dominick followed him. Sebastian was standing outside with his face to the sky, and tears were mingled on his cheeks with the raindrops. Dominick came close to him.

'Don't,' he said, 'not now. We haven't time. You know that!'

' "With desolation is the whole land desolate," ' Sebastian quoted. ' "Our adversaries are our lords, our enemies are enriched; the enemy has put out his hands to all our desirable things, our persecutors are swifter than the eagles of the air;

they pursue on the mountain and lie in wait for us in the wilderness – we have found no rest; our cities are captured; our gates broken down, our priests sigh; our virgins are in affliction." '

His voice seemed to rebound off the low clouds.

He lowered his head.

'Is that true, Dominick?'

Dominick thought back on all they had suffered, all they had seen, the rich lands turning wild, the desecrated churches, the empty villages. 'It has gone on since the beginning of the world,' he said. 'We are not the first and we won't be the last.'

'Yes,' said Sebastian, 'I saw it all and it meant not as much as it does at this moment on account of the faith of an old dying woman. A little woman. Her name we don't know. But God knows it. And it came to me then, Dominick. There are millions like her. Even if the whole land is reduced still more there will be thousands like her. You see. And there is our salvation. That's where we rise again from her ashes. Do you see?'

'No,' said Dominick, 'I don't see. I feel something. But I don't see it. I'm going down now. I will be back. Maybe I won't be back. If I have my life I will return. If not, you have Mary Ann and Peter.'

'No man could have a better legacy,' said Sebastian.

Then Dominick walked away from him, towards the town, and he didn't look back either.

CHAPTER ELEVEN

T H E D A W N brought no easing of the dreadful rain.

Sebastian stood at the doorway of the house and looked towards the town. There was no sign of Dominick. I won't despair, he thought. Dominick is indestructible. He went back in. He had a fire of sticks burning in the hearth. It was a very open chimney, more of a hole in the roof than a proper chimney. The rain fell sizzling on the damply burning wood. In one corner the children were sleeping under the skins. In the other corner there was a mound where he had buried the old woman. He got a sharp stone now and proceeded to write roughly with it over the head of the grave. The walls were built of limestone rocks loosely put together. Over the mound in the corner he wrote, a stone on a stone:

CATHERINE O KANE, Saint.

'I'm hungry,' said the voice of Mary Ann.

He went over to her. She was sitting up. Peter was awake too, looking at him. Their eyes were too wide, he saw.

'Soon, now, Man,' he said, 'your father will come back to us.' What am I going to do if he doesn't? he wondered. How could a priest on the run rear two children? He would have to continue his journey and find people who would look after them.

'Where is the old woman?' Mary Ann asked.

'She's gone away,' said Sebastian.

'Like Mammy?' Mary Ann asked.

'Yes,' he said.

'She was a nice woman,' said Mary Ann. 'She was holy. Is she in heaven?'

'I'd say so,' said Sebastian.

'It's well for her,' said Mary Ann. 'She won't have to do any more walking like us.'

'Some day, Mary Ann,' said Sebastian, 'your walking will be ended. You'll be sitting down in a nice house spinning wool in front of a great fire.'

'I wish it would hurry up,' said Mary Ann with a sigh. 'Come on, Pedro. Outside morning absolutions.' Sebastian laughed. 'Is there nothing to eat at all?' she asked then.

'No, Mary Ann,' he said. 'Last night was the last. The old lady had nothing in the house at all. Nothing at all.'

'Had she no neighbours?' Mary Ann asked.

'They are all gone,' said Sebastian. 'Cover yourselves going out into the rain.'

They put the skins over their heads and went out. Sebastian searched the house again. It was easy to search. There were a few pieces of crockery, wooden platters, iron pots and griddles, but not a grain of wheat, or a head of oats. He gleaned every corner. How long had the old lady been starving? he wondered. How had she held on to life until their coming? Over the fire there was a kind of loft. He reached and hauled himself up there. It was a boarded-off part of the roof. It had been used as a sleeping-place. Now there was nothing, just the scurrying of mice in the faded rushes. There were woven St Bridget crosses, fixed to the black wooden beams supporting the scraws and straw of the roof.

While he was there, Dominick came into the house from below. He carried a bundle under his arm. He was breathless from running.

He came in the door, and when he saw nobody there he was frightened. He called loudly, almost in a panic, 'Mary Ann! Mary Ann! Peter! Peter!'

'Easy, Dominick. Easy, Dominick,' said Sebastian, putting his head over the loft.

Dominick looked up at him. Sebastian noted the white panic of his eyes. 'They are at their morning absolutions,' said Sebastian.

Dominick just sat on the floor. He was very wet.

'I thought they were gone. I thought they might have been grabbed,' he said.

'God help anybody that touches your children, Dominick,' said Sebastian.

'God help them indeed,' said Dominick. He opened his bundle.

'Look,' he said. Sebastian looked. He saw bread and a filled bottle. Dominick carefully then, out of his pocket, took eggs, one two three four five six eggs. 'Oh,' said Father Sebastian, 'and what's in the bottle?'

'Milk,' said Dominick. They hadn't tasted milk for nearly a year.

'The simple pleasures of the poor,' said Sebastian.

'And this,' said Dominick, taking out of his pocket a rectangle of salted bacon. 'Cook them. I'll get my children.'

He went quickly out of the door, looking for them. He saw them coming towards the house wrapped up. He sat on his heels at the door and waited until they bumped into him. They were surprised. They were glad to see him. He was glad to see them. 'Soon it will be over, Mary Ann,' he said. 'Soon we will find rest, you'll see.'

'I'm happy you're back, Daddy,' said Man. 'We were afraid.'

'I told you not to be afraid,' he said.

'You can't help it sometimes,' said Mary Ann.

'We will go and eat,' said Dominick. 'What would you like for your breakfast, Miss MacMahon? Some milk maybe and an egg or a little bacon and wheaten bread?'

'Oh, no,' said Mary Ann.

'Oh, yes,' said Dominick and brought them in.

They savoured the food, as Dominick half dried himself in front of the fire.

'It is bad in there in the town?' Sebastian asked him.

Dominick thought.

'Not good,' he said. 'But I think we will get away. I met a friend. Oh, a very special friend. I would have been back but there were a lot of things I had to find out, the proper way to manoeuvre, and then I had to search for food. Nobody wants to sell it. Only the gleam of gold could bring it out of them. You want to be careful, Sebastian. It's still death to be a priest. You'll see. So dirty your face and open your mouth and blacken your teeth with a bit of soot, and be dumb. Will you do these things? Are they beneath your dignity?'

'Better to have life alive than dignity dead,' said Sebastian, reaching for the soot. Dominick laughed.

They gathered their belongings. Very diminished now. Which is why, Dominick told himself, we will have to get to town. This is not an excuse to get to a town, he told himself severely. But things must be bought. Necessary things, even if you are seeking a fair land where you will be free from fear. You can't eat grass.

'Don't eat all the food,' he said. 'We will be waiting for a long time. I hope we will be able to get across before nightfall.'

They left the house. Before heading down towards the town

they tried to close the door. They got it almost shut and then blocked it on the outside with a stone.

There was a sort of track all the way down, but it was very slippery now from the rain. Rocks moved under their feet and there were many filled potholes which they could not avoid. But their eyes were on the town. It wasn't a heavily fortified place. The walls were low and not thick, but there were a lot of stone towers and one main gate leading into the town from the east. There were many lines of figures converging on the gate. All of them were in distinct groups, Sebastian saw, as they came close to them. There would be a gentleman on a horse and a lady on a farm cart with maybe children with her there, or grown children walking by their father's stirrups. And behind the family came other families of poorer-dressed people, driving a skinny cow maybe or sometimes even two cows, a few sheep and pigs. The lady and her lord would be wearing once fashionable clothes, or silks or damasks, with woollen cloaks lined with coloured satin. But their journey had soiled their clothes. They were grubby from the rain and the mud or thorn-torn. There were many such families, making Sebastian think: How low have the mighty fallen! When he looked at those groups and then looked at the others, sturdy phlegmatic farmers with heavy bodies and blank faces, trudging with their women and children, carrying their possessions on their backs, he thought: How many of the gentle will be able to revert to being poor or hardworking? He could see the white hands of the ladies. He saw the pain in their faces, but they still hoped. It was like the Exodus, he thought, only in that nearly all had been on the same level starting out. His heart missed a beat as he thought of his own family. What had happened to them? Were they also wanderers or were they peaceably dead? He hoped they were dead.

'Do you feel very sorry for them?' Dominick asked. He had been watching the expressions on Sebastian's face.

'Oh, yes,' said Sebastian.

'Why? Dominick asked. 'Their turn has come. Thirty, forty, fifty, a hundred years ago, they drove out other people. They were the planters then. Now they are the transplanters. The wheel has just turned.'

'They are human beings,' said Sebastian. 'It will be harder on them than on the hard-working men.'

'It will be harder even than they think,' said Dominick. 'They have to leave their castles and their mansions and their broad acres to go to Connacht. They have been promised the same amount of land there. But this is the thing. There isn't enough land to go around. They won't even get what they think they will get. The poor creatures! Look at them. They are still proud. Watch how they scorn the common people. They still think they have those possessions at their backs, when the only real possessions they have are on their backs.'

Sebastian watched. The proud old man on the horse with his white sweeping moustache, and the whip in his hand. If he was held up, he used the whip, without expression, on the backs of the plodding, dirty, soaked people who were holding him up. And worse, Dominick thought, the whipped ones got out of his way.

'Don't be hard, Dominick,' said Sebastian.

'You be dumb, Sebastian,' said Dominick, as they squeezed their way into the throng and approached the gate. Dominick was carrying Mary Ann. Sebastian was carrying Peter.

They were squeezed tightly, and advanced very slowly. Dominick thought how terrible the silence was. Just the shuffle of feet, and the sound of the horses' hooves as the throng was forced upon to let them pass. Just a woman coughing, or a man clearing his throat, and the smell of woollen cloth soaked with rain, smelling like the smoke of a turf fire. And the way that no man's eyes met. Nobody looked or spoke. It's the helpless feeling of shame, he thought. Why haven't we swords in our hands slashing all around us? He had counted the soldiers. There were only about two hundred of them in the town. There were at least two thousand weary transplanters, as docile as driven sheep, making their way in, to be docketed, stamped, certificated, as if they were animals, and sent to their stalls, or else the butcher's block.

He was uneasy with so many people around him. The so-called freedom which they had had for two years, when meeting a person was a miracle, had been good in comparison with now. As they shuffled down the streets of the town, he noticed the houses. Most of them were thatched, one-storey. One or two of them were two-storey lath and plaster with brown wooden beams. But they were no longer homes or shops. They were stables and quarters for horses and men. He had never noticed before how pungent and almost unbearable to the nose could be the droppings of horses. If he ever smelled it again it would for ever bring to his mind the sounds and sight of this town of the ford.

When they had reached the end of one street he could look and see the guarded bridge that led off into Connacht. There were a few people crossing it. They were held up there while the soldiers examined their papers. He watched to see if any of them looked back once they had crossed the bridge. They didn't look back. This seemed strange to him.

His arms were aching from holding Mary Ann. He had to heft her several times. 'Am I too heavy, Daddy?' she whispered once. Why did she whisper? Because nobody was speaking. At the crossing there were soldiers watching. There were some at windows watching. The line of people slowly approached the church.

Here the people joined with the men on horseback and the ladies and children on the carts. The carts and horses were turned off into the churchyard. There were a lot of them. They had to be driven over the graves. The tombstones were knocked and the carvings on some obliterated by the heavy cartwheels. You could hear some of the people sucking in their breaths as the beaten horses, flogged by whips, pulled over the obstacle of a flat stone, and the iron of the wheels screamed.

The approach to the church was up an incline. This is where Sebastian is going to suffer, Dominick thought.

Over the door there had been a statue of Our Lady holding the Infant Jesus in her arms. The statue was still there but both the Lady and the Infant had been beheaded. The beheaded statue looked terrible in its niche. The heavy oak doors of the church had been beaten in with some sort of battering-ram. They lay back, open and burst, hanging on twisted iron hinges. Inside there was light. All the long narrow Gothic windows had been made of stained glass. None of the glass remained. It had been shot out, knocked out, beaten out, all that was left being a little piece of coloured glass here and there gripping tightly to the twisted lead. Up where the main altar had been, long rough tables were stretched across, in three sort of distinct sections. The confessionals had been ripped out at the sides. The slabs of stone on the floor were thick with mud, and even in here there was a prevailing smell of horse droppings. There were armed soldiers all around, pushing with long-handled pikes, chewing tobacco and spitting. They didn't care where their spit landed. They laughed about this. They had bets on some of the spits, where they would land.

Dominick put Mary Ann on her feet and edged his way so that he remained in the centre and they were making their way towards the table in front of the high altar, or where the high altar had been, because none of it remained, except the steps leading up to it, and here where Christ had rested there was a rough table with a man standing up interrogating the people, and two clerks writing, and a man with a hooked nose and a ripe red face, with prominent teeth and red-rimmed eyes, looking and looking, and taking draughts from a bottle and grunting. It was towards this table that they were aiming.

Dominick looked at the standing man. He was handsome. He wore his hair longer than the puritan rules would have it, and a white lace collar over a dark-blue silk coat. He was tall, and his face was lean and his teeth were white. As they got closer they could distinguish the words.

'Sir Nicholas Comyn of Caltra House.' Standing on his toes, Dominick could see that this was the proud gentleman who had used the whip.

'Sir,' Sir Nicholas began.

The red-faced man leaned forward.

'Be silent!' he ordered. Dominick saw that he was sitting on the red plush chair that the Bishop would have used on a visit to this church.

'But Mister Cole . . .'

'Silence!' Mister Cole ordered. 'I am the magistrate, sir. I ask the questions. Now, have you got a Particular?'

The old gentleman reached forward a document.

'Read it, Doyle,' said Mister Cole, taking a drink from the bottle and looking at Sir Nicholas as if he hated him.

The elegant man took the document and read.

'Sir Nicholas Comyn, pale complexion, white hair, indifferent stature, his wife Alison Netterville, otherwise Comyn, with two children, aged twelve and fourteen, one boy, blue eyes, dark hair, and the other a girl. Said Sir Nicholas no proof of Constant Good Affection to Parliament. Acted in the service of the King.'

'But, sir,' Sir Nicholas interrupted, 'at that time the King was the legitimate Government.'

'Silence, sir,' Cole roared, 'or I'm damned if I won't confine you for contempt. You worked with the enemies of the Parliament. Are we too tender with you? Read on!'

'To transplant before the 1st of May under penalty of death. To be provided in the province of Connacht, said land to be assigned by the Commissioners sitting at Athlone, of three hundred and forty acres. With said Comyn four servants, viz. Daniel Barry, tall stature, red beard, bald pate; Thady Cullen, small stature, brown hair, no hair on face; Morgan Cullen, small stature, blind of one eye, no hair on face, and Honour McNamara, middle stature, pale complexion, red hair.'

'And where is your woman and your children and the rest of your people?' Cole asked him.

'Sir,' said Sir Nicholas, 'I wished to avoid the rush. My lady is in delicate health. I thought of your kindness you would grant me the pass to Athlone without interrogating her and my children.'

'Monstrous!' Cole was on his feet. 'Go back! Each one must be brought here to face me. How do I know you are not sheltering a beast of the woods in your pack? Bring them all before me.'

'Sir,' Sir Nicholas was getting desperate, 'I swear there is no priest in our company.'

'Go back! Go back! Bring them before me!' Cole was leaning on the table shouting. Tendons were standing out on his neck.

Now what will the proud man do? Dominick wondered.

The proud man said, 'I thank you, sir. I will find them and bring them before you.' Then he turned and blindly made his way back through the dense crowd. Dominick saw his face. The blankness of defeat, and helplessness. Maybe he is like ourselves after all, he thought, and then edged closer to the table.

The reading went on as they got closer and closer. 'Thomas Eustace, low stature, brown hair, twenty-five years, hath ten hogs, a plough of garrans, two cows, five sheep.

'Ignatius Stacpoole, orphan, aged eleven years, flaxen hair, full face, low stature: Katherine Stacpoole, orphan, sister to the said Ignatius, aged eight years, flaxen hair, full face, having no substance to relieve themselves but desires the benefit of his claim before the Commissioners of Revenue.'

These two made Dominick feel sad. Two young children, holding hands, well dressed one time but not now. What story was behind them? What had happened to all their people? What was to happen to them?

One of three things, he saw.

Pass to Athlone for land assignment by the Commissioners. Pass across the bridge to Connacht, or what they called laughingly, Pass to Bristol.

This was if people had no substance or no claim of substance. Over on the right there was another table to which they were passed. Here there was a tall swarthy man, dressed in black, who always seemed to have a black tube of rolled tobacco in his mouth. Over to confront him went the destitute, always, Dominick noticed, if they were young women or young men. Here this man rose and put his hands on them. He squeezed the breasts of the girls and hit their chests and felt their thighs through their wet clothes. He made the young men take off their coats and he felt their limbs. Some of these were taken through the small door there, and others of them were sent back for a pass for the bridge.

And then Dominick was facing the magistrate, trying to keep his face calm, his mouth open a little, trying to stop himself from spitting into the face of Cole who watched him with red-rimmed eyes.

The elegant Doyle was reading a paper that Dominick handed to him. Where in the world did Dominick get the paper? Sebastian wondered, as he kept his mouth hanging open and looked with a blank vague look at the window over the altar.

'Dominick MacMahon, merchant, fair complexion, middling stature, no hair on face, ordered to transplant from the townland of Drogheda.'

'Drogheda!' Cole shouted. 'Were you in Drogheda, man?'

Dominick looked at him and muttered in Irish: 'I don't understand you.'

'Speak up! Speak up! Speak up!' said Cole.

'The man can't talk English, apparently, your Honour,' said Doyle.

'How can he be a merchant and not talk English?' Cole asked.

Dominick nearly chuckled. A reasonable query, he thought.

'He sold merchandise to the natives, your Honour,' Doyle said.

'He should have been destroyed in Drogheda, ground down there. How did he get away? Ask him?'

'How did you escape from Drogheda?' Doyle asked in Irish.

'We escaped through a hole in the cellar of our house,' said Dominick. 'I got a boat. That's how we got away. We are witnesses of the massacre. We will never forget.'

Sebastian felt his blood go cold. He swallowed. He had to make a terrible effort to keep the horror out of his face.

Doyle said: 'It's hard to understand, your honour, but the fellow apparently wasn't there, when the town was, eh, cleansed.'

'Pity,' said Cole. 'Who's with him?'

'A servant and two children,' said Doyle.

'Pass him into Connacht,' said Cole, tiring of them. 'Hurry up! Hurry up! Who's next? It's time for food. Must I be here for hours?'

Doyle passed the document to one of the clerks. He wrote across the face of it. Dominick took it. Sebastian tried a look at Doyle as they turned. He only got a glimpse of the smoothly shaved side of his face and then he followed Dominick.

When they got outside the church, they saw that the rain had lessened. It was tapering away.

They didn't speak. They walked towards the bridge.

There was just one crowd in front of them getting their papers examined, but there was another test, they saw now. There was a tower each side of the bridge and from each tower there was a man hanging from a block of wood that had been forced out of one of the narrow windows. On the body on the right there was a notice: 'A popish priest', and on the other body there was a notice: 'For sheltering a popish priest'. This was the test. The soldiers were watching each face as they looked at the hanged man. You see, your natural inclination would be to bless yourself and say, The Lord have mercy on the dead. They wanted that. What would they do to you if you did it? Dominick didn't stop and think. He kept his mouth shut, his lips from moving and his hands by his sides, praying that the children would not look up. They didn't. They kept their heads bowed to the rain.

They waited and waited, and they handed the document to the soldier. The soldier looked at him and then at Sebastian.

'Any of you a priest?' he asked.

They didn't answer.

'See what we do with them?' The soldier pointed. They didn't look. 'Go on, look,' he shouted. They looked. Their faces were blank. The men hadn't been killed by hanging. No spine breaking. They had been let down gently so that they strangled to death. 'Come back here,' the soldier went on, 'and that's what'll happen to you. Go on !'

They walked on. The end of the bridge seemed to be a mile away. They walked slowly. Now at least ⍳ know, Dominick thought, why the others didn't look back.

A bit farther on, when they were out of sight of the bridge, Sebastian said : 'Dominick, how in the name of God did you do it?'

'Mister Doyle,' said Dominick, 'the elegant one. He did ⍳t. Could you not recognize a brother in him?'

'Doyle, a brother?' Sebastian asked.

'Yes,' said Dominick, 'he's a Reverend Francis Doyle. He is a Jesuit. Last night I came on him. He was nearing confession at the back of the church. You see, Sebastian, your old lady gave you faith. Then there's the Reverend Francis Doyle to give courage.'

'Alleluia,' said Sebastian.

As if to greet them, the western sun broke through the clouds for a few moments, and sent broad sunbeams slanting to the sodden earth.

CHAPTER TWELVE

THEY STOOD on the rampart overlooking the Ship Quay and
Tom Tarpy declaimed:

'Twice seven high towers defend her lofty walls,
And polished marble decks her splendid halls;
Twice seven her massive gates, o'er which arise
Twice seven strong castles tow'ring to the skies;
Twice seven her bridges, thro' whose arches flow
The silvery tides, majestically slow;
Her ample Church with twice sev'n altars flames,
An heavenly patron every altar claims;
While twice sev'n convents pious anthems raise,
(Sev'n for each sex), to sound Jehovah's praise.'

'In other words,' Tom went on, 'fourteen bulwarks, fourteen
towers, fourteen gates, fourteen tribes and the lot of them
bastards.'

Suddenly it seemed to them as if on a signal, from all around
inside the city, there came a roll of drums, a rolling that went
on and on, while interspersed with the roll of the drums came
the strident call of trumpets, harsh, challenging.

It seemed to Dominick as if the whole of heaven held its
breath for a short time. There were three ships below them
moored to the quays on the high tide. All the sailors and men
bustling and shouting around them stopped what they were
doing and listened. In the city itself the clatter of horses'
hooves, the grinding of the cart-wheels on the cobbles of the
main streets, the chattering of people in the four markets,
ceased. Even the soldier near them, sitting on the carriage of
the culverin, lowered the bottle from his lips and listened.
Dominick felt the hair on the back of his neck rising. He had
been in the city for some weeks. It shouldn't have meant anything to him, but for a moment he could appreciate the terror
that struck at the heart of the people. Every Saturday without
fail at this time in the morning the drums rolled and the
trumpets called. He could appreciate their feeling that the last

trumpet call at the end of the world would be the reality of which this was the foretaste.

Almost as suddenly as they began, the drums and the trumpets ceased and people took up their work and their talk again, talking louder and working faster as if to shut out the meaning of the rolling drums.

From where they stood on the rampart Dominick could see the towers and castles, the landmarks of the walled town he had come to know. To the south of them reared the Lion's Tower, the Tower of the Great Gate with the clock on it, and the Shoemaker's Tower. To the north of them he could see the Tower of St Nicholas' Church, behind it the towers of Athy's Castle and the French Castle, and straight in front of them beyond the masts of the three-masted barges, he could see the rise of Martin's Mill, set behind Blake's Castle, and the three great fortified towers of the Bridge Gate. It was strong-looking, formidable, great towers rising inside great walls, and yet it seemed to him as if the trumpet calls had made all the whole town shrink a little. It could have been the June mists rising and fading from the kiss of the sun.

'Bastards,' Tom Tarpy repeated, 'proud lovers of Christ and haters of the Irish, but they are paying for it now, the poor devils, they are paying for it now.'

The soldier approached them with the empty bottle. He was wiping his mouth on his sleeve. He was a big uncouth fellow with strong hairy wrists emerging from tunic sleeves that were too short for him.

'Better go home, Tom,' he said, 'and get your tribute ready, or they'll take the clothes off your back.'

'All right, you great filthy ape, you scouring of dung,' said Tom in Irish, taking the bottle from him. 'Thanks, Jake. I'll do that. It's only the officers that get the tribute, hah? What do they do with it all? Four hundred pounds a month is nice money! Where does it all go to, Jake, tell me that?'

'The common soldier doesn't see much of it, anyhow,' said Jake. 'I can tell you that.'

'Why should you get anything when you can take what you want?' Tom asked.

'All I want now is to get home,' said Jake. 'You listen. I'm sick of this bloody country, I am. I'm sick of what I see. I don't want to be here. I want to be in the hop-fields now, and in the great places where the apples are hard, and the cider is good, and the ale is good. Not hogwash, not fancy Spanish wines. I want to go home, Tom, that's what I want to do. I fight. That's good. But not afterwards, when the officers are making hay for themselves and we have to look at the hate in the faces of the people.'

'That's a long speech, Jake,' said Tom. 'I don't hate you.'

'You're a fool if you don't,' said Jake. 'You should. Get a sword and strike around you. Do something. Don't be waiting to be slaughtered or sent away like those poor baskets. What kind of a war is that? What have soldiers got to do with things like that?'

He was looking down below him at the quays. There were two gates, the Strand Gate near them and the Ould Quay Gate farther back, and through the two gates now from Earl's Street and Quay Street marched two lines of people, shepherded by soldiers with pikes. They were manacled wrist to wrist. They were very silent. There were young boys and older boys and young girls and older girls. Most of them were bare-footed, or had rags or canvas tied around their feet. Their clothes were ragged, soiled. There were woollen clothes and linen and what had once been silk dresses. There were girls with fair hair and brown hair and black hair. Their faces were dirty. Some of them were barely covered; some of them were holding their clothes in front with their free hand so that they would not be exposed.

There were older men, some of them white-haired, some of them tonsured. These men were manacled separately, hands behind their backs. You could see they were priests. One or two of them were dressed in the tattered habits of their orders, the rest were dressed in torn civilian clothes, which somehow looked terribly incongruous on them. They were all brought to stand in front of the gangway going up to the middle ship. Dominick found he was holding his breath, that his hands were grasping the stone under them until he could feel it biting into his palms.

Because one pair he noticed. They were tied but they still held hands. He had seen them before, in the terrible church at the town of the ford. He could hear the reading in his ears: Ignatius Stacpoole, orphan, aged eleven years, flaxen hair, full face, low stature; Katherine Stacpoole, orphan, sister to the said Ignatius, aged eight years, flaxen hair, full face, having no substance. He remembered them all right. They had got a pass to

Athlone, and now here they were on a pass to Bristol. Only since he came here had he recalled the terrible fate that awaited any sinner who got the pass to Bristol.

'What's it for?' Jake was asking. 'Kill them! That's easier. Send them off to the Barbadoes. Why? So that Coote gets his share of the slave money. Every week I see them being shipped out. You know what will become of them? What do they do with the children? The young girls? What has happened to us? Do we believe in God? They are people, like ourselves. They could laugh and sing.'

They weren't singing now. Because suddenly some of the women started wailing, as the first few mounted the gang-planks and were herded to the holds where they climbed down ladders into the dark deeps of the ship. The women started screaming and crying. The men with them tried to hush them. They weren't all the poor and the destitute. You could see intelligent foreheads, slim hands, and the priests started to chant and hymn. Their song rose gently like the mists rising off the river, but it seemed to drive their captors into a frenzy. They used the handles of the pikes on shoulders and backs, and then Dominick saw the swarthy man, who had been there at the town of the ford too, with the rolled tobacco unlighted in his mouth. The man with the black hat. He was there now, too, but he wasn't beating his captives. He was striking out at his soldiers. He was a big man and his blows were effective. 'No, no, no!' he was shouting in his Bristol accent. But he wasn't trying to save them from blows for their own sake. He was like a cattle dealer who wanted his wares to be delivered to the market without blemish. The price would be higher.

From practice, almost as soon as it started, the flock of white slaves were battened under the hatches, and the cries and hymns came very muffled from below. The soldiers talked to one another and walked off and stood on the quay as the sailors went to their jobs, loosened sail, threw off ropes, and the ship moved into the pull of the tide and slowly and majestic-ally and beautifully pulled out into the middle of the estuary and with a nice gentle wind behind her sailed out into the bay with the sun behind her shining on the waters, heading a long way across the Atlantic to the romantic islands of the Bar-badoes, where the sun always shone, where there were lonely gentlemen getting a little tired of black women and half-breeds; where it was hoped that this present brood of indigent and

106

papist people would, with the grace of God, be made into obedient, compliant people, almost English and Protestant.

'What has God to do with it?' Jake asked. 'That's what I want to know. It's all a matter of money. Somebody buys them at ten pounds a head and sells them for about fifty. If they do that to them, how do we know that some day they won't do it to ourselves?'

Dominick was looking at him. There was sweat pouring down the soldier's face. He remembered the other one, who was asking questions too, almost until the moment he died. He looked at Tom. Tom was an enormous fat man, wearing a heavy linen shirt with the sleeves pulled up on it. He had a big head, two chins of rolling flesh. His arms were enormous. His dark curly hair was pitted with grey. It took a fantastic amount of cloth to go around his great belly. He was gripping the stone too and his face was held up to the sky and his teeth were grinding.

'Why do they go like sheep?' he said then. 'Why couldn't they turn on them and make them kill them? Why like sheep? Not me. Not me, I tell you. I would die and I would take some of them with me on the way. I would grind their faces on the flagstones. I would smash them to pulp, like crushed black-berries.'

He hit his hand on the stone. It made a loud smack.

'They want to live,' said Dominick. 'They want to survive.'

'Oh, God,' said Tom.

'Thanks for the bottle, Tom,' said Jake, handing the empty one back to him. 'I will pay you tonight.'

'You're half human,' said Tom, taking it. 'We'd make an Irishman of you if you were here long enough.'

'I'll be here long enough,' said Jake, 'if the plague doesn't get me, or if I'm not knifed of an evening in the Red Earl's Lane.'

'No man can live for ever,' said Tom. 'Come on, Dominick.'

He walked off the rampart, on to the cobbled walk towards the steps that led down to the Ship Quay. Dominick followed him. He felt sad. He felt, after all, it is better to be out in the open. Murdoc was right about that.

The seagulls were screaming over the river. The quay was crowded with people. Some of the soldiers and carriers were sitting on the barrels. There was a smell of fish and spilt wine and the fresh scouring sea. Dominick walked behind Tom, feel-ing as if he had a warhorse breaking a way through for him.

They stood for a moment in the middle of the first quay. At the quay across from them, where the slave ship had loaded, he again noticed the swarthy man standing. He was squat and powerful-looking, and had big jowls working away chewing at the cylinder of black rolled tobacco. There was a soldier standing beside him. Presumably the man was ticking off in his mind how much the departing ship would bring him, hoping that too many of them wouldn't die before they reached their destination. Whatever he was thinking about was interrupted. From a cleared space behind where the carriers were sitting and lolling and spitting there came a heavy round wine-cask that rolled down the incline towards where the swarthy one was standing. Silence descended over the quays. The cask rolled and rolled while hundreds of eyes watched it and then it caught the dark one just behind the knees. He threw up his hands. There was nothing he could do to save himself. He went head first into the tide. He disappeared in the water and the cask fell after him and then popped up again like a cork, dancing joyfully. All one could see of the man was the curious flat black hat he had worn, with a coloured ribbon around it, that sailed off on the ebbing tide.

And then the man's head emerged from the water. He had a gleaming bald head. All around his pate the long black hair was lank. His mouth was open. He shouted. There was a dreadful look of fear and panic in his face before the tide pulled him under again, dragging him inexorably in the wake of his departing ship.

He couldn't swim.

Not a soul moved. There was dead silence on the quay. He came up again farther down the estuary and he shouted. If he could see them, he must have been panic-stricken at the cold impersonal glances of the onlookers. They were looking at him even as they would look at a drowning rat. Dominick could see this.

He couldn't help what happened then. He kicked his way out of his heavy shoes, ran in his stockinged feet to the side of the ship near him, vaulted over the wooden side of it, ran across its holystoned decks, mounted the rail on the other side and jumped into the sea just ahead of where he judged the man to be.

He found him, away down, and gripped his clothes and rose to feel the air on his face. Fortunately the man was half drowned. All the same he waved his arms, so Dominick hit him on the temple with his closed fist. Hit him with anger and frustration and annoyance at his own actions. The man went fairly limp. Dominick saw the side of the ship sliding past him, the current of the conquering river bringing him closer to it. He scrabbed at the side of it with a free hand and found no grip, and then a heavy rope hit him in the face and he grabbed that. He saw the tobacco-chewing faces above, hairy faces with coloured woollen caps on their heads. They threw another rope. He fixed it under the arms of the man as best he could. They pulled him free from the water like a wet cask. It must have been an accident that when they had him almost up they let the rope free again, so that he entered the water with a splash. This revived him. He shouted when he came free this time. So they hauled him all the way, and Dominick, catching his breath, swarmed up the rope and stood dripping on the deck.

The man was on the deck. He was leaning on an elbow. He was being sick. The circle of sailors was looking curiously at Dominick.

'Why did you do a thing like that?' one asked.

Dominick didn't answer. How could he? He took off his shirt and began to wring the water out of it. The swarthy one was a bit better now. He struggled to his feet grasping the rail. Nobody helped him. He turned then and looked at the blank faces regarding him. His eyes shifted, moved to the face of Dominick, a thin face framed with long wet fair hair.

'Friend,' said he.

Dominick had sea water in his mouth. He gathered it and spat it out. Then he walked away. The man called after him, 'Friend,' but Dominick didn't regard him. He leaped on to the quay, worked his feet into his shoes and still wringing his shirt joined Tom Tarpy. Tom was looking at him curiously. Dominick dropped his eyes. He couldn't do anything else. 'Come on,' said Tom and walked towards the Strand Gate. Dominick followed after him. As they neared the gate, he was conscious of the group of carriers to the left from where the cask had come rolling. From that group, so soft as to be all the more offensive, a very dirty word was thrown at him, in Irish. He stopped and looked, his jaws tight. They were regarding him blankly but storing up the memory of him. Tom turned. 'No more of that,' he said. 'He's my friend.' Tom looked at them and then walked on. They came through the gate into the horse market. There were a lot of horses. Most of them were panniered, having woven baskets on each side of them, carrying turf, firewood, some vegetables or bags of uncrushed meal. It was a packed place, but there was little loud talk. He knew that feeling well now, the lack of talk, the fear that was everywhere. But men had to live, to sell what they could and hope for the best.

Tom walked through the market elbowing his way rudely, slapping a horse on the flanks to get it out of the way. When he got through the market, he walked into Earl's Street, and near the ruins of the De Burgo castle, turned left into Red Earl's Lane. Past the castle there were rows of two-storey houses, built of limestone like most of the others. At a door here, Tom shot a bolt and walked down steps to the tavern.

Light came into the place from two half-circular windows on the street. There were shelves with the light glinting off bottles, saffron-coloured jars, barrels. Here Tom faced him.

'Why?' he asked. 'In the name of God why? They have been trying to injure that fellow for a year. You know what he is?'

'You knew it was going to happen?' Dominick asked. 'Was that why we were on the rampart, giving Jake a drink?'

'What made you do it?' Tom asked.

'I wish I knew,' said Dominick. Suddenly he felt angry. 'But of course I know. It's that Sebastian. That's who it was. Just as if he was there beside me, whispering into my ear. You haven't been with Sebastian as long as I have. He sort of grows on you. He doesn't say anything, but he impels his ideas into your brain, without saying anything. You know Sebastian.'

'Yes,' said Tom. 'You accept everything. Even if you are being turned into a slave. You accept that. That's God's will. If everyone went on that way where would the world be, will you tell me that?'

Dominick's anger drained away.

'I don't know,' he said. 'Maybe we'd be all better off to accept things as they befall. Maybe then there would be none of this cruelty.'

'Yes, but the trouble is,' said Tom, 'that you have to get the other fellow thinking that way too. If you don't you will be wiped out. You shouldn't have done that. Hell was waiting for that fellow.'

'What's his name?' Dominick asked.

'I don't know,' said Tom. 'I wouldn't pronounce it. Wouldn't it be like dung on the tongue?' He went behind the counter. 'Here's some clothes for you. They're rough, but they'll be better than your own. You want to see Coote, don't you? Well, you can carry the tribute. You want to see the lowest form of life outside of privy beetles, don't you? Well, come and see Coote. Where's that Sebastian now?'

'I don't know,' said Dominick, taking off his breeches. 'He took the children with him. They are good for deceit, he said. How could any man suspect a priest with a child in each hand?'

'He takes too many chances, he won't survive,' said Tom. 'But he might as well. Sometimes it might be better to be dead than alive. There seems to be no hope for us, dammit, no hope.'

'There is always hope,' said Dominick.

'You come and see Coote,' said Tom, 'and you'll see what I mean.'

Dominick pulled on the coarse breeches and the canvas shirt. He tied the breeches with a piece of rope. Tom handed him a rough hat. 'Wear this,' he said. 'It'll dim the bright look of you. And keep your mouth shut, and your eyes open.'

When he was ready, Tom hefted a big jar on his shoulder and they went out into the lane again. He shot the heavy bolt on the door. They walked in the dust of the lane. When it rained it was like a swamp. They emerged into the street of the quays and then turned right, over the Crosse Street, and into the welter and confusion that was Market Street.

'Now for the Lord President of Connacht,' said Tom, grunting.

CHAPTER THIRTEEN

A V-SHAPED block of buildings with its base resting on the Crosse Street, and pointing straight up to the big arch of the Great Gate Tower, held on each side of it the packed market-place. There were stalls and baskets. It was mainly country women, dressed ungainly in heavy wool and frieze, who offered eggs and butter and vegetables for sale. There were pedlars with ribbons and pins and little dolls and furbelows that women wear, their portable stalls hung around their necks. There was a lot of colour in the market-place, a lot of shouting, and a lot of smells, not all of them nice, just the whiff passing of the spiced little cakes and sweet titbits of the vendors. Dominick noticed that it was mainly the poorer people who were buying and selling. There was no sign of silk or fine worsted or lace or clean white linen.

And all the time Tom was talking. It was a good town, he was saying, even if it was owned by the tribes and very few men could get a wedge in with them. But even if they were proud tyrants and monopolizers they built the town and made it big and wealthy, so that little men could live in it and make a living and bring up their families, and have enough to fill their bellies, and to look to a future. Now it was gone. It would never be the same again, never. The present people would do all they could to destroy it. Weren't they at war with the world as well? So no more Spanish ships, no more French ships. What could get in now would be carried in a pucaun and leave space over for ten men.

So, farewell to the marble halls. Their owners were fled and the marble was defaced with the hooves of horses and the depredations of the soldiers. All the people flocking in from the north, south, east, and west, bringing nothing with them but the clothes on their backs, and as the great mansions were emptied they crept into them, ten, twenty to a room, living in squalor, dulling the polish of the marble, soiling the bedrooms where great ladies once lolled on satin sheets and listened to songs sung by gay blades in silk pantaloons.

He was angry, pushing his way through the throng, a deceptively tall man who looked short owing to his great bulk. Dominick was following him, listening and using his eyes, watching brown-faced country girls, their beauty hidden under the weight of wool and the heavy scarfs around their heads and faces. Old women with lined brave faces, as if they had been carved out of the solid earth, the people who had learned to put up with things, to accept things, so that they would survive and leave generations after them who would also survive, mounting in numbers and resolution. That's it, he thought, Sebastian is right. It's a matter of patience. Take the blows, if they kill you, leave two of you afterwards to make more to survive, who will live patiently and absorb by sheer patience the people who were killing them yesterday, so that later they, the killers, will in future generations be killed by fresh killers, will die out and the ones who took what the Lord sent will of necessity be the victors. Why did he see this so clearly, looking at the faces of the country people?

'Don't be destitute, but be poor,' that's what Tom was saying. 'Have nothing to give away, but enough to remain alive. That's the plot. If you are destitute you will end up in the Barbadoes, and if you are poor they can't take anything away from you, not even your life.' Funny that they should have both been thinking on the same lines walking through the market-place. Because, he supposed, that's where the real people are in the world, in the market-places, the small people who cannot flee; who must put up with what is happening to them, of necessity.

There was a great crowd around the Market Cross in front of St Nicholas' Church.

The sellers here were different. The sellers were soldiers. There was one soldier doing all the offering. He was a big man with very white teeth. The whole place was well surrounded with people. He was holding up things for sale, crying, 'What am I bid for this? What am I bid for this? Do I hear sixpence? Do I hear one shilling?' Few of the people around him understood what he was saying, but they knew what he was offering. There were brass candlesticks, and china vases, and brass ornaments, and decorated combs.

'They have scraped them of all their money,' Tom told him. 'Now they are down to the bones.' Dominick had watched the Saturday collections. They would raid the big house, with the people, father, mother, children, looking shabbier as each week passed, saying: 'We cannot pay the tribute today. Give us until next week and we will pay all.' That was the permit to the soldiers to enter the great houses, to search them from floor to cellar. The soldiers enjoyed it. If there was no money they took kind. You would see them emerging with a beautifully carved table or a set of chairs, or huge damask hangings, or pewter tankards, or silver tankards, or oil paintings. Oh, they enjoyed the raids all right. But worse than that, Dominick thought, were the onlookers on the street outside the houses, poor people, who watched their once wealthy neighbours being reduced to this. Some of them took pleasure in it, you could see that, and many a back room, many a noisome tenement place, was decorated with a brass-bound mirror or a foreign comb or a painted fan.

'They are not that badly off, you watch,' Tom was saying. 'Some of them have it salted down somewhere like herrings in a barrel. They have bought their way from this town half way over Connacht – castles, mansions, and broad acres, for the rainy day. They won't be separated from them. If they have to save them by changing their religion, by becoming apostates, they themselves won't do that, but they'll make the lunatics of the family turn. They will dart and twist, but they will survive. Don't mistake that.'

'The choice of the day,' the soldier was saying. 'Look at this, ladies. Why not decorate your smelly bodies with this poem in silk?' He was holding up a silk gown, light blue in colour with red roses imprinted over the blue. 'Warm,' he said, 'warm,' holding it up to his coarse face. 'Still warm from the body of a beautiful girl.' His soldiers laughed. 'And warmer still are these,' bending down and bringing up in his other hand very fine linen underwear. 'Hot from the owner,' he shouted, holding them up. There was a laugh from the crowd. They didn't know what he was saying, but underwear in any age would make a sinner laugh. 'Scilling!' a voice called from the crowd. 'Oh, no,' he said, 'make it two scillings, three scillings, four scillings, five scillings. The pretty lady wouldn't pay the tribute, so we had to strip her with our own hands.'

'Come on,' said Tom. And Dominick followed him. Now he felt fierce, mad with anger, burning with hate.

'Sometimes you don't feel it's worth it,' Tom was saying. 'Sometimes you feel like hitting back, but if you do that how will you survive? I am a man in the middle. I am the owner of a tavern. My father before me owned it and his father before

114

him, back for five generations. So, by fair means and a few crooked means, I have become a man in the middle. And that's a dangerous place to be sometimes. The rich ones clap me on the back and talk of Good Tom; and the poor clap me on the back and owe me money for drink. A man in the middle, and a man now in the middle of High Middle Street. Here, you take this now.'

Dominick took the yellow jar and put it on his shoulder. They were at the four corners where High Middle Street, Little Gate Street, Great Gate Street and Skinner's Street met, and on the other side from them Lynch's Castle loomed, a grey stone building, rising to four storeys with a pointed roof, topped by a flag that waved invitingly in the hot breeze. There were soldiers guarding each side of it, with crossed pikes, holding the entrance. They crossed the street towards them. The street had been paved, but it was now rutted from wheels and sharp hooves and neglect.

The soldiers didn't move.

'You know me,' said Tom. 'I would be obliged if you wouldn't let me in. Then the Lord President of Connacht wouldn't get his weekly brandy and I would be saved that much.'

They pulled back the pikes.

'Pass, friend,' one said, grinning. Tom went in and Dominick followed him, his head lowered.

The two soldiers looked after them and they exchanged a remark and laughed.

At the same time, on the west side of the river, on the road leading from the castle of Rahune, into the suburbs of Fathai Beg, crossing the Balls Bridge river and entering the rough approach between the thatched houses towards the drawbridge of the west bridge fortifications that pointed like a blunt arrow to the wild lands from where they had come, twelve horsemen moved towards the town at a slow jogtrot.

They were very big men riding small horses. But the small horses, the *capaillini*, were very sturdy, and they had proudly shaped heads. They had long tails, some fawn-coloured, some very white-coloured and some jet black. Their manes were the same colours as their tails, but their bodies were a mixture of fawn or light-grey or dark-grey or brown and black. They were well-fed horses with slim legs.

They needed to be well fed to carry the men on their backs.

Even in the heat they wore brown short cloaks, with the hoods thrown back, tied around their necks with leather thongs. They wore linen shirts dyed saffron. Some of them were bare to the elbow, some of them right to the shoulder, and their arms for the most part were brown and hairy and leaping with muscle as they gripped the rope reins leading to the leather bridle of the small horses. They sat on no saddles. Their hair was long. Most of them were black-haired, but some of them were brown and one or two of them very fair. Their long hair wasn't neat. It was tangled, and some of them had it tied back behind their ears. But all of them had one thing in common, the thick drooping Irish moustache, the forbidden *crombheal*, which they wore, blatantly, luxuriously, and fiercely.

The man at the head of them was the only grey one. His hair was black and well streaked with grey. His eyebrows were thick, and the caverned eyes under them were quick and darting, and missed nothing on the way. The belts holding up their Irish trousers held swords in scabbards, and there were knives in their belts resting in highly decorated sheaths.

They saw few people on the way. The ones they did meet looked curiously at them, and almost fearfully.

They drew up in a tight bunch in front of the drawbridge of the fortification and the leading man looked coldly at the two soldiers who barred their way.

'Who are you?' the soldier asked. 'What do you want?' He was gripping his musket tightly.

'Tell your leader,' said the man in a rich deep voice, in clear English, 'that O'Flaherty has come to see the President of Connacht.'

The soldier looked at him, then said to a companion, 'Back, Jack, and tell the Colonel.'

He stayed there while the other went. He looked from one to the other of them. He met black, brown, blue, and green eyes, all having one thing in common, that they hated the sight of him. The soldier was nervous. He shuffled his feet. He was glad to hear the firm step of the Colonel behind him.

'Well, now,' said the Colonel. 'You want to see Sir Charles Coote.'

'No,' said O'Flaherty, 'he wants to see me.'

'Ho,' said the Colonel, 'hair-splitting.'

'Better than skull-splitting,' said O'Flaherty sardonically.

'You are armed,' said the Colonel.

116

'Swords could be no match for muskets and culverins,' said O'Flaherty.

'All right,' said the Colonel. 'I will take you to Sir Charles.'

He turned and walked briskly.

The horsemen clattered across the wooden bridge, inside the fortifications on Giant's Hill. Here the Colonel mounted a horse, a very beautiful black horse, who would make two of any of the little horses, but the others looked at him, and one of them spat. He was a war horse, a big heavy bastard, they thought, who would sink to his withers in the bogs of the mountains and be food for the grey crows.

The Colonel waved his hand at them and·set off and they followed him through the first tower on the bridge. O'Flaherty could see the ships at the quays on his right, and away up on his left the wicker salmon traps. There were men in small black boats up there with poles in their hands. On the bridge itself were fishermen with tridents, which they were preparing to drop from the height of the bridge on to the shallow waters where the salmon would rest after their struggle from the sea. The fishermen looked blankly at the cortège. They mounted the steps and went through the leaves of the middle tower, the hooves of the little horses very sure on the stone steps going up and coming down. Then they went through the third tower, O'Flaherty wondering and thinking how hard it would be to take this town; seeing the looming towers and the thick walls. But greater places than this had been taken before. Not that he wanted to take it. They could have it for themselves, now that he had what he wanted. He would do a lot to hold on to what he had now.

The Colonel cursed and lashed out with a whip as they came through the jam of the sea-fish market inside the third tower. There was a terrible smell of fish, fresh, salted, decayed, and on the point of decay. It was all women who sold the fish, big handsome women, peculiarly dressed. These were the women of the Claddagh, selling the catches of their men who would be lolling now on the green in the warm sun.

They passed from fish to the smell of meat near the Shambles where the butchers carved and gouged and tore at the skinned animals with hooks and knives. The Shambles was not full. The meat was scarce but becoming a bit more free after the dearth of last year's famine.

Through the market-place they forced their way, the people

looking at them, even the soldiers holding the auction becoming silent to watch the curious cavalcade. O'Flaherty looked at the faces of the people. He could pick out the townspeople by the look of shut-off fear and dislike that appeared there when they saw the saffron-shirted men. They had had cause to fear the O'Flahertys for many long years before this. The dislike and fear were inherent in them. He snorted, as he thought how puerile their fear was, and a far worse than the O'Flaherty here now.

The Colonel dismounted outside the castle.

'Will you dismiss your men?' he asked.

'My men, all but one, come with me,' said O'Flaherty. 'Why? Are you afraid?'

The Colonel was scornful.

'If that's the way the Lord President wants it,' he said.

'That's the way he is going to get it,' said O'Flaherty.

He dismounted. His men dismounted. One man gathered the reins of the little horses and walked them around the corner of Skinner's Street where they would not be in the way of the crowds. He held them there, leaning against the wall, spitting occasionally in the dust, while the Colonel entered the castle gate, O'Flaherty followed the Colonel, and his men followed O'Flaherty. They seemed to fill the entire hall before the door into the great room opened before them.

There was a guardroom just before the door. When Dominick followed Tom in here it was occupied by a few lounging soldiers and three men. They were restless men. One of them was white-haired with delicate features. He walked with his hands clasped behind him, his blue eyes darting a glance as they came in.

'You too, Tom?' this man said.

'Yes,' said Tom.

'Is your brandy tribute not running short?' he asked.

'Every well has a bottom,' said Tom.

A short dark-haired stocky man laughed. He was well dressed. He looked well fed. His hands were hairy but they bore no signs of hard work.

'Who will reach the bottom first?' this one asked.

'I will,' said a young fair-haired man standing beside him. 'Some monsters are insatiable, like the gods of the Incas. Coote is like that. His belly is unfillable.'

Said Tom to Dominick in Irish in a low voice, 'The white one is Richard Blake, the squat one is Oliver French, and the young one is Martin Browne. Isn't it low the high are becoming?'

The door opened. A small man with severe black clothes on him stood there. His puritan haircut was destroyed by the way his hair curled. He had long eyelashes, a small mouth. He was delicately built, like a young woman. His gestures were feminine, like his walk. He stood aside and gestured them past him. Dominick followed the other four. He noticed as he passed that the young man was highly scented.

They stopped dead, just inside the door, because a very strange scene confronted them in the great hall. Right at the back there was a large fireplace of polished black and green marble. Out from this there was a table of black oak, carved. The walls all around were lined with soldiers, and behind the table sat a lounging man, dressed in black.

His hands were very big, but very white. His hair was black and his face was very white. His eyes were intelligent and close-set, his nose big and bony, his mouth small with narrow lips. The cropped hair showed ears that were small and set close to his skull.

But it wasn't the sight of the Lord President that made them stand still It was the sight in the fireplace. Two long-handled pikes had been lashed together to make a great X, and a young woman was tied to this X by wrists and ankles. She wore no clothes. Whatever covering she had was provided by her long black hair which she had been able to shake over her shoulder by swift jerky movements of her head. Coote was watching their faces. The soldiers were watching their faces. They laughed. They saw the eyes of the tall white-haired man flick as if he had got a blow in the face from a switch. They saw the eyes of the dark squat one goggle. Dominick saw the back of Tom's neck turn fiery red. For himself he couldn't look quickly enough at the face of a man who could set a scene like this. The man spoke.

'You may approach, gentlemen,' he said. They walked towards the table. Now Dominick understood why Tom was one of the party. A sort of subtle blow at the pride of the great ones, that even in paying their tribute they should have to do it in the company of a tavern-keeper and his assistant. Dominick felt that each man would have gladly killed Coote, if the odds were even. That was it, if the odds were even, if none of them wanted to survive. And didn't he know it?

As they got closer, he saw that the very white skin of Coote was oozing moisture, which he was constantly wiping away with a linen handkerchief. Each time he put up his hand to wipe his unpleasant skin, Dominick could see that his fingernails were long and dirty.

'You have come in due time, Richard,' Coote said to the tall man. The tall man was counting out guineas on the table from a leather bag.

'It can't last much longer, Coote,' he said. 'You are coming near the end of my resources.'

'Don't say that, Richard,' Coote said. 'I have noticed the ones who squeal most manage to come back longest.'

'If they don't come back,' said Richard, 'their houses and properties are confiscated.'

'Correction, sir,' said the little black fellow who was standing by Coote counting the money and ticking it off on a sheet of paper with a quill, 'they are not confiscated. They revert to the Parliament for non-payment of taxes.'

'It's robbery either way,' said Richard.

'Please, Blake,' said Coote, 'be careful with your words. They could be taken as a reflection on the Lord Protector and where would you end up then? You might end up tied to a fireplace like your friend young Mrs Walter Dorsi.'

He was challenging Blake to make a remark about her. Blake's eyes didn't shift from his.

'What unspeakable crime would a Christian have to commit, Coote, to be degraded in a way only you could devise?'

He is courageous, Dominick thought, but where does that go? It doesn't let the girl go free. He could look at the girl. He could admire her composure. She could be in her early twenties. She had dark eyebrows, and widely spaced eyes, over a thin sensitive nose with flared nostrils. Her eyes were calm. They were avoiding the looks of no man. He didn't think that any man could look at her and not drop his eyes from the calm look of hers.

'She refused tribute,' said Coote, 'and referred in malodorous terms to the personal appearance of the Lord Protector, a crime for which we all pray that the Lord will forgive her.'

He was grinning. His teeth were big and yellow-stained. He looked to Dominick like a man with a disease of the liver. Was that why he was such a man, or was his nature devised for the times?

'Now that you have won your effect,' said Blake, 'isn't it possible for you to display a spark of human decency and let her go?'

'No,' said Coote. He banged his hand on the table. 'And you be careful, Blake. It is unusual for me to warn twice. I have done it with you. There will be no third.'

'Have I permission to retire?' Blake said.

'No, you haven't,' said Coote. 'You can step back until you get permission to go, and feast your old eyes on the punishment of heretics.'

'Here, here, Coote,' said French, paying the guineas on the table. 'You have me nearly broken, dammit. How can we survive? If you don't take it easy, there will be nothing left.'

'Next,' said Coote.

Young Browne put down no money.

'I have come to the end,' he said.

'You know what that means?' Coote asked.

'I know,' said Browne, 'but I'd prefer it that way. At least I won't have to see you every week.'

'It's a game cock, hah,' said Coote. Dominick saw how he enjoyed himself. 'Can you see all your nice apartments being raped by the common soldiery, Browne? And the inmates? Do we have to expose your intimate possessions for sale in the public market-place? We'll do it. Mistress Dorsi's most intimate things are at this moment on the block.'

Dominick had a flash in his mind of the blue silk dress with the red roses. He wondered if he would kill Coote. He had no weapon. Could he snatch a weapon from a soldier and have him killed before he himself was killed? Was it his duty to die? There it was again. Was it his duty? So Mistress Dorsi would remain tied and exposed at a marble fireplace because none of them had the real courage. He understood a little now of the sheeplike way in which the men and women had boarded the slave ship.

'You'll suffer, Browne,' said Coote. 'You have offended me and the Lord Protector, whose laws are designed for your own good, inspired by God.'

'I have made my choice,' said Browne.

'The good Tom,' said Coote. 'How faithful you are, dear Tom!'

'Here it is,' said Tom. He reached back and took the jar from Dominick's hands. 'You wanted it, but by all that's holy, just when I was going to hand it to you, didn't the great thing slip out of my hands and fall on the marble floor like this, and break into bits?'

Dominick held his breath, for Tom had taken the jar and broken it deliberately at his feet. The bits of crock flew and the room was pervaded with the smell of brandy. Tom's neck was still red. He was glaring at Coote. If he had something in his hand he might have killed Coote. But why didn't he hit him with the crock, Dominick wondered, that might have done it? But he didn't. None of them were willing to do it. They had all made gestures, and he could see from Coote's cold grin that he liked people to make gestures.

Coote shook his head.

'I'm afraid that crock will have to be replaced with six more, Tom,' he said.

'There aren't six more,' said Tom; 'there aren't five or four or three or two or one. There are no more.'

'Then,' said Coote, 'the soldiers will have to search for them.'

At that moment the doors were flung back and it seemed as if the empty part of the room was filled with giants. They all turned. Dominick found it hard to believe that he was looking at Murdoc. He recognized him at once behind the fierce moustache. He saw his eyes going to Coote and then to the girl at the marble fireplace, and then he approached Coote and the table with his ten tall men behind him, as the harried voice of the Colonel was shouting, 'O'Flaherty, Lord President.' The men in front of the table fell back as he drew near.

But Murdoc's approach was unorthodox. He thrust a great hand across the table and instead of taking the Lord President's hand he grabbed him by the tunic and lifted him straight out of his chair into the air and swung him around, so that his legs were dangling off the floor, and with the other hand he held a dagger so that the great white chin was resting on the point of it. It looked as if it had been practised. Murdoc's men turned outward in a semicircle from him where he held Coote and their swords were free. All around them after the first shock of amazement the soldiers had cocked muskets and come forward or the long pikes were lowered.

'You die, Lord President,' said Murdoc, 'before a shot can be discharged.'

He was looking into the yellow eyes so near his own. For a few seconds of time a frightening look had appeared in them. That's his weakness, Murdoc thought, he is afraid of death, but then as the eyes became cold, and lost their dreadful emptiness, he thought, but he is not afraid to die.

'Don't move,' Coote said, into the tenseness.

'The girl goes free,' said Murdoc.

'The girl goes free,' agreed Coote.

Murdoc spoke to one of his men, in Irish. 'Free her,' he said, 'and help her, and when she knows what she wants to do, bring me word.'

A big fellow with a fierce black moustache detached himself from Murdoc's group and went up to the girl. He drew a knife and severed her bonds, freed himself of the brown cloak and wrapped it around her. He held her arm. She tottered for a few paces, and then she walked with him. She didn't look at Coote as she passed. She didn't turn on him and spit at him. She showed great control. She walked beside the big man and then they were gone.

Murdoc said to Coote: 'I'll let you go, that's easy. What happens then? Are we killed? Before we die, we will kill a lot of men, including you. If that's the way you want it, say so and I'll cut your throat now and save us the trouble later.'

'You will not be killed,' said Coote. 'You have my word.'

'From what I hear, it's not up to much,' said Murdoc, lowering him to the ground but still keeping a grip of him. 'But I suppose it will have to do.' He was grinning. To his surprise, he found the yellow teeth grinning back at him. Coote was taller than he had thought. It's a wonder he was taken by surprise. It wouldn't be usual for him to be taken by surprise. He loosed his grip of him.

'You sent for me, Coote,' he said. 'I came.' Coote kept looking at him.

'It was kind of you,' he said, with delicate sarcasm. 'Everyone else get out of this room. Percy, get everyone else out of here, except myself and my friend.'

Percy was wringing his hands. 'Oh, sir! Oh, sir, this violence,' he was saying.

'Percy!' said Coote.

Percy fluttered. 'Please, please, clear the room for the Lord President.'

Slowly the soldiers drew back. Percy approached the others.

'Gentlemen! Gentlemen, if you will,' he implored by gesture. Blake, French, and Browne turned and walked out the door. They didn't look back. Tom followed them, and Dominick followed Tom. He was laughing inside. It wasn't funny, but he was laughing. It could only be Murdoc, he thought. Only Murdoc.

The room was cleared. The door was closed. Coote went back and sat behind his desk. He was brave all right, Murdoc thought.

'You are not afraid?' he asked.

'I am not afraid,' said Coote.

'Not even of hell?' Murdoc asked.

'No,' said Coote. 'Your uncle died. You have taken over his possessions.'

'In trust for his three sons who have fled,' said Murdoc.

'If you want to be the chief, in fact, you can,' said Coote, 'if you will acknowledge the Crown. I beg your pardon, I mean the Parliament. Are you willing to do this, publicly?'

'I might,' said Murdoc.

'You have no choice,' said Coote. 'If you don't I will wipe you out. I may seem a weak man to you in this situation, but I'm not weak. I can do what I want to do.'

'Tell me, Coote,' Murdoc asked, 'about the girl? Have you no pity in you at all?'

'Pity,' said Coote, 'is like a small hole in a dam holding back a great body of water. Unless it is plugged the whole collapses. No. I have no pity. You know, I like you, O'Flaherty. I think we could be friends.'

Murdoc laughed. He spoke a verse in Irish. 'What does that mean?' Coote asked.

Murdoc said:

> '"With one of the English race, no friendship make.
> Shouldst thou, destruction will thee overtake.
> He'll lie in wait to ruin thee when he can;
> Such is the friendship of an Englishman."

'Is that true, Coote?'

'Isn't it only time will tell?' Coote asked.

Murdoc looked closely at him.

'A lot of our feathers are the same,' he said. 'We will talk.'

'Our talk will be good,' Coote said, 'but first we will walk. Alone.'

He strode towards the door. The guard-room was crowded. They made way for him. Percy, about to attach himself again like a tick on the body of a dog, went to follow.

'No, Percy,' said Coote. 'You will look after good Tom and that other young man, young Mister Browne. See that they are inconvenienced.'

'That has already been seen to, sir,' said Percy, smirking.

He walked into the sunlight. Murdoc's men were on the other side of the street. They were watching.

'Stay there!' Murdoc ordered them loudly in Irish, 'I walk with the black dog for a little. I will be back.'

Then he matched step with Coote as they walked towards the Great Gate Tower.

CHAPTER FOURTEEN

THEY WALKED along the crowded street, and through the Great Tower and into the fortifications, and over the draw-bridge into the Green.

Where they went they brought silence, except for the clash of arms from the soldiers, who stood rigidly until they passed. Murdoc noticed the blank look that came over the faces of the people. He knew what were the feelings behind that blankness. He watched the unconcerned features of the Lord President. They came onto the Green. It had once been a fair place where the gentlemen disported themselves at jousting, the bowls and the archery butts, under the glances of the ladies in silk and satin. It had been a gay place in Murdoc's memory when he was young and had travelled to the town with his father, and when, even then, they had been forced to sleep outside the walls in the Bull Inn near the Great Gate.

Now the Green was nothing. In wet days the grass had been turned into yellow mud by the horses of the soldiers. They were still bivouacking there, and it looked dirty and smelled dirty. The Bull Inn was just walls blackened from the fire that had destroyed it. The New Market-place was crowded, but a great hush descended on it as they walked by, a great silence, and they turned their steps to climb the hill of the King's Way, the Bohermor. Here were the south suburbs, lines of houses on each side of the wide road, most of them thatched and most of them wanting roofs or walls since the siege. Each side was crowded with people, who silently watched them pass.

Coote was wiping moisture from his bulging forehead, but it wasn't the sweat of fear.

'You are not afraid to walk among the people?' Murdoc asked. He was wondering why. Was Coote trying to show him what a brave man he was?

'No,' said Coote, putting a handkerchief to his nose to spare it from the smells that were rising from all around them.

'What is to prevent one of those people burying a *scian* in you?' Murdoc asked. 'Does that upset you?'

'No,' said Coote. 'They are a spineless people. If one of them

126

did acquire the courage, I would die happy thinking of what my soldiers would do to them, to all of them. It would be a very famous massacre.'

Murdoc looked at him. He almost believed him.

Then they stood under the gallows.

They were doubled now, Murdoc saw. One on each side. There were clients occupying both.

'You have added to the amenities of the suburbs,' he said.

Coote turned to the one on the left.

'I want you to meet your uncle,' he said.

Murdoc knew he was looking at him; knew now the reason for the walk. He kept his features unmoving as he looked at the hanging man.

He could hardly be distinguished as a man, just a skeleton with tattered weathered clothes which had once been good.

'This is your uncle, Colonel Edmond,' said Coote. 'He was a murderer. He assaulted the castle of Tromragh in Clare and killed the owner, a good Christian, Mister Peter Ward. He met his just deserts at the desire of the people.'

'He didn't kill anyone,' said Murdoc, still looking up.

'His followers did,' said Coote.

'If one were to be hanged for the deeds of followers,' said Murdoc, 'there wouldn't be enough gallows in the world to hang you all. No, Coote. He hanged because he was on the losing side. But for the grace of Cromwell's God, you would be there, not he.'

'Any man in this province can end up there,' said Coote.

'I understand the lesson,' said Murdoc, looking at him, wondering what patience was given to him not to take this man in front of him and tear him apart with his bare hands, pull off his head and his limbs and throw them to the four corners of the world. 'Tell me something. For the last ten years you have been responsible for the deaths of more people than any man alive apart from your master. How does it feel, Coote?'

'Let us return,' said Coote.

They retraced their steps. Murdoc found that his mouth was dry. He gathered spittle on his tongue and spat it on the dust.

'I am an obedient servant,' said Coote. 'And when you talk of people, to you they may be people, but not to me. To me they are an uncivilized race of brutes. If you move into a jungle to bring it to order, to reduce it to cultivation so that it will bring forth fruit instead of weeds, you must first destroy the animals, the wild beasts of the forest. In your heart you must know as well as I that most of them are better off dead. What have they to give to life? What have they to give to civilization? They talk with the tongue of monkeys and act like apes. If they refuse to be tamed, to be cultivated, it is necessary to kill them and train their young.'

'Do you really believe this?' Murdoc asked.

Coote stopped and looked at him.

'I do,' he said. 'In years to come it will be seen how right I am. Cruelty is essential for the advance of civilization. You must do what is to be done and you must do it unflinchingly.'

Murdoc looked at the pale yellow eyes. They were serious.

'There are no chinks at all in you,' said Murdoc.

'Some day, where these gallows now stand,' said Coote, 'the descendants of this same people will erect a monument to my memory. Coote of Connacht will be remembered for ever.'

'I have only one wish for you,' said Murdoc.

'Yes?' Coote inquired.

'How long is a moment?' Murdoc asked. 'A moment can last for a long time, almost the length of eternity. When you come to die, Coote, I wish you a long moment so that all the dead beasts can rise up and pass before your eyes, every one of them.'

'I will die easy,' said Coote. 'I will die in the bosom of the Lord. I have that assurance from the pen of the Lord Protector himself.' He spoke sardonically. He walked on. His hands were clasped behind his back.

'So you have possessed yourself of the lands of Edmond in Rinnmhil,' he said. 'I will assure you of them, but I warn you that they can be taken away again in the same way as they were given. I want a loyal man there. I need a loyal man there.'

'They may be taken away again, man,' said Murdoc. 'That is true, but they can only be taken away again at great expense. I'm telling you that so that you will know.'

They walked past the market and into the fortifications and through the bridge and down the Great Gate Street, and Murdoc was thinking: The only weakness he has is that fear of death, and Coote was thinking: His weakness is possession. From what he had heard of Murdoc, he knew that he had never had anything much. Now he would have something. It would be interesting to find out how far he would go, or the things he would do, in order to hold on to it.

He stopped in front of the castle. He held out his white hand.

Murdoc looked at it. He was conscious of the men of his band behind him watching, of the people who walked the streets standing still and watching. Murdoc took the moist flabby white hand in his own for a moment. Oddly, Coote's eyes were anxious. That's because, Murdoc thought, he has no friend, he never had a friend, he never will have a friend; and because he was Irish and soft, he felt a momentary pang of pity for this powerful man, a great soldier, a pitilessly efficient administrator, enriched beyond all knowledge by his depredations, a man without mercy or honour, confident, sure, despising the weaknesses of the human beings who came within his orbit; and as their hands touched, the brown, hard, heavily muscled hand of the soldier and the white moist hand of the baronet, for a moment each mind was shocked with a fleeting vision. Our destinies are bound. As if this had happened before somewhere in the past, or maybe in the future, for good or bad that they were bound, a tingle of subconscious knowledge that made them widen their eyes and look closely at one another, and that for a moment made Murdoc's breath come fast.

Then their hands dropped and it was gone, whatever it was.

Coote said: 'You and your men may walk the streets and drink in the taverns until nightfall. I would remind you that there is still a byelaw which says no O or Mac may strut or swagger in the streets of Galway. So now I suspend the byelaw. If you discomfort the citizens, that is their luck. At nightfall your men will leave the town and go outside the walls. You will come to a banquet with the gentlemen of the town who hate you and your name and everything you stand for. They will welcome you. Tomorrow morning you will swear fealty. And another thing. You will keep away from young Mrs Walter Dorsi. You understand that. Her punishment is only suspended.'

He turned and walked into the door of the castle.

Murdoc looked after him.

Who won? he wondered. He hoped it was himself but he was beginning to doubt it. All the same, the whole game was not out of his hands yet.

He walked to his men.

'Morogh Dubh,' he addressed the dark one who had taken the girl away. 'What of the girl?'

'She is brave,' said Morogh Dubh, 'but what chance is there for her? He will get his hands on her again.'

'Has she no suggestions?' Murdoc asked.

'She said that there is a place underground from her house that leads to the churchyard,' said Morogh.

'A clever girl too,' said Murdoc. 'When it is dark go back to her. In the meantime, go out of the little gate and to the Wood Quay. Ask for a man named Davie O'Fowda. He is the master of the boatmen. Tell him O'Flaherty will want a boat at night-fall.'

'I'll do that,' said Morogh.

'Listen, the rest of you,' said Murdoc. 'There is a relative of ours swinging outside on the gallows. At nightfall you must leave the town. You will take down our relative and find a priest and have him buried in holy ground. Now we will go and drink and plan.'

They mounted their little horses and under the sour gaze of the citizens they clattered down Skinner's Street.

Tom was glum.

Dominick mostly took pleasure out of walking on the main street, passing the shops and smelling their trade from them, the chandler's, and the baker's, and the malthouse, and the tavern and the spice shop which brought you a whiff of strange and far-off foreign lands.

Before they reached the market-place they turned down Shoemaker's Lane into the Middle Street.

'Why couldn't we do that?' asked Tom. 'Aren't we spineless people? It had to be that Irishman.'

'You are Irish too,' said Dominick.

'Not like these wild ones,' said Tom. 'Didn't he shame us, high and low alike?'

'Why?' Dominick asked.

'If we did what he did.'

'You would be dead,' said Dominick.

'Yes, but Coote would be dead too,' said Tom.

'If Coote was killed what would happen to the town?' Dominick asked.

'It would be swamped in a bath of blood,' said Tom.

'You know that, I know that, and Coote knows that. That's why he appears to be unafraid. The big fellow has the courage of recklessness. He could do it. Maybe it wasn't so reckless. Maybe he is useful to Coote. Maybe he could do a thing like that knowing that he would get away with it. In these days, Tom, it's the heroes who live and the cowards who die.'

'All the same, we should have done something real,' said Tom. He sighed. 'It might be better to be dead, anyhow, than to watch what's going on.'

'I don't want to die,' said Dominick. 'There was a time when I didn't mind, but not now. I like the feel of the hot sun on my face and the smell of fish and horses and dust and sweat.'

'All I smell is fear,' said Tom, 'my own fear and the fear of people around me. Nothing will ever be the same again. There was courage here. For nine months we held out against them. Nine months, and all the time the frightened ones were sneaking away in ships, some this month and some the next month. That was a good time. All men were friends. All men were equal in their resolution. But after the betrayal and the surrender, then it changed. It was bad then. It's not good now.'

'It will be good again too,' said Dominick.

'Not in my time, boy, not in my time,' said Tom.

They cut across to Earl's Street, passing the Fish Shambles, and Dominick was remembering Murdoc. How he would see him and walk up on him if he could and tap him on the shoulder and surprise him. He would have to search out Sebastian too and tell him, and Mary Ann, that Murdoc was in town, and if that was what they decided that there was hope for the future. Life had been kind enough to them since they came here. A golden coin slipped to the soldier checking their passes at the main gate had got twenty-four days stamped on it instead of twenty-four hours.

They entered the tavern. Tom was grumbling. 'Fine doings,' he was saying. 'What am I going to do now? I won't get free of it. Coote never forgets.'

'Have you got more brandy?' Dominick asked.

'I have seven kegs of it,' said Tom, 'but I'm damned if he's going to lay a lip on a drip of it.'

'It might be better to submit,' said Dominick, who had recovered his wet clothes and was squeezing the last drop of water out of them.

'I'd breach the casks and empty them into the privy first,'

said Tom, 'every last drop of them. Then let him do what he will.'

'No price is too high at the moment to pay for peace, Tom,' said Dominick, 'Pay for your gesture, that is all you can do.'

Tom was shifting casks, moving kegs, muttering away to himself, when they suddenly heard the clatter of feet outside, and the opening was darkened by the forms of three men, two of them soldiers, who came blinking in out of the sun-bathed street.

Dominick recognized the man. His name was Marcus Lynch Fitzthomas. He was one of the two sheriffs. All men spat when he passed by. So far he was the only one who had really gone over. He had publicly made the Oath of Abjuration, discarding his religion, all he had believed in, for the moment of power. His reward was to become a sheriff, but watching him Dominick had thought that the reward did not make up for the loss. He had seen him flinching at every spit, reacting to the soft name-calling coming from a group of men gathered at a street corner when he passed by. He was clean-shaven with brown hair that was going grey. He made nervous gestures with his hands and his body, and always his hand was on his sword, and his eyes had become redshot from looking over his shoulder.

'Tarpy,' he said in a high voice, that broke occasionally, 'you have offended the Lord President, and the Government of this country in his body. You have been ordered to produce six kegs of brandy as tribute. Where is it? Or do we have to search for it and find it out?'

Tom was red-faced. He was tightly gripping the handle of the keg in his hand.

'You dungpit!' he said. 'You misbegotten son of a pig. You should never have been born. Submit to conquerors, all right, you filth, but to you born with a name that was good, until you smaddered it, you quaking perverted apostate!' And he gathered a spit in his mouth and accurately threw it with his heavy lips into the face of the sheriff.

Things happened very suddenly.

One of the soldiers near the sheriff shouted, 'Here, you black devil!' He drew his sword and moved towards the red-faced tavern-keeper.

Dominick saw the spittle flowing down the face of the man, and the soldier drawing the sword, and then Tom's hand that held the jar rising and falling and hitting the soldier a great and skull-shattering blow on the side of the head; but before he could move, the other soldier had drawn a pistol and fired, and the small place was filled with the smoke of gunpowder, and he saw the ball hitting the great expanse of Tom's chest, moving the linen like a sudden swift breeze, and then he saw the quick spurt of scarlet starting to spread and he saw the great body about to fall, and it hadn't reached the floor when his own hand had found the dagger in the belt of the soldier who had used the pistol, had drawn it and driven it deep with a cry of anger, and then he knew that he was standing in the smoke-filled room holding a stained dagger, looking across at the man who was wiping the spittle from his face with the side of his hand. They looked at one another and then the sheriff, his face white, his limbs quaking, turned and ran out and tried to call with a croaking voice, and couldn't, and Dominick heard his steps running and running on the road, and he thought, Poor Tom, and then he thought of himself and of how little time he would have now, and that the problem of what he was going to do was finally solved for him, and he went over and got on his knee beside the great bulk of the tavern-keeper.

'Tom,' he said, 'Tom,' but the man was dying and nearly dead. Almost in seconds, it seemed, the death-look of green had spread over his broad face. His eyes were clouding.

'See,' he said. 'See. Not accept. Sebastian to pray. Hear that. My goods to the poor. Hurry. Lord have mercy on me.' Just that and he was dead. Dominick had so little time. It wouldn't take long for the apostate to get to the nearest band of soldiers. He just folded the great hands across the bloody breast, and grabbed his clothes. He still had the dagger. He decided to keep it. He went into the lane. The light was blinding. The lane was filled with people who had heard the report of the pistol. At doors, at windows, some standing in the street.

He looked at them.

'They killed Tom,' he shouted. 'He left you his possessions. Get them. They are yours.'

He ran right towards the horse-market. As he ran he saw them flooding like a troop of ants into the tavern. When he got to the corner near the horse-market he turned back to look. They were coming out of the place swiftly with barrels and casks and kegs and precious bottles. Good, he thought, good! The place would be as bare as a bald pate by the time the others got back. Why should that please him? He didn't know, just that it would be right if when they came back that tavern would hold nothing but the four walls and the body of the man who had been the soul of it, the lively, kindly, dramatic, sensitive, soul of it, and by stripping it bare they would be giving him a sort of Viking's funeral.

He slowed down going through the horse-market. Running men are marked in towns. He hid the dagger under his wet clothes, holding it in his hand. He wouldn't be taken, he decided. If he was taken he knew what his end would be. He had seen the swinging rotten corpses outside-near the Green. He walked up Earl's Street, past the Fish Shambles into the New Tower Street.

The arch leading into the Poor Clares Lane seemed a mile away to him, but he forced himself to walk slowly, diverting his mind, thinking that he would always associate this place with grey arches. The houses were built in front of courtyards with the groups of buildings in a square. There might be a garden in the courtyard, or a fountain if it was a courtyard of the rich. There might be an orchard, or it might just be paved if it was the place of a merchant who stored his goods. But there were blind arches and open arches, low-sized arches, and they might hold ornamental front doors if they were mansions, or iron gates, or be blank-faced if they led into lanes as this one did. He saw it coming closer and closer, and he stopped and went into the Poor Clares Lane. It was a narrow lane with tall three-storey houses on each side of it. The fourth door down was his. It was the tenement of Margaret Coocke, candlemaker, and he prayed with all his heart that the lodgings would contain Sebastian and his children. He went in the narrow passage, but when he came to the stairs he ran up them, not pausing until he came to their room and threw open the door.

CHAPTER FIFTEEN

HE LEANED against the door and looked at them. He found that his limbs were shaking.

Sebastian was sitting on the floor with the children one on each side of him. He was writing on a slate with a thin piece of stone. The westering sun was shining through the leaded panes of the window. The space where they sat was bathed in sunshine. Dominick saw the three faces looking at him. He kept his features as blank as he could.

'Where did you get the funny clothes, Daddy?' Mary asked.

She rose and came towards him. He left the door and sat on a stool. He was glad of the support it gave him.

She didn't wait for an answer. She came between his knees. He put his hands around her. He thought: Mary Anne is growing up. Sitting, he had to look up into her eyes.

'We did fifty-two confessions, four death-beds, three marriages and fourteen baptisms this morning,' she said proudly.

He heard Sebastian laughing.

'That's great,' said Dominick. 'Now do something for me, Man.'

'What?' she asked.

'Go down and watch Mrs Coocke making candles,' he said, 'and bring Pedro with you.'

'Secrets?' she asked.

'Yes,' he said.

'All right, Daddy,' she said. 'Come on, Pedro.'

'Pedro is going to be a great Latin scholar,' said Sebastian.

'Is that so, Pedro?' Dominick asked as Pedro came towards him. His eyes were shining, Dominick saw. He was pleased with the praise. He nodded. Why, he is growing too, Dominick thought. My children are growing on me and I have no time to sit and watch them grow. He ruffled his fair hair. 'Good man,' he said. 'We'll call you.'

They left. The door closed behind them. Sebastian was sitting crosslegged on the floor looking at him. Sebastian looked well. His beard was close trimmed. His body under the rough clothes was thin but lithe.

'What's wrong?' he asked.

'Tom Tarpy is dead,' said Dominick. 'They killed him. And I killed his killer, so we will have to go.'

He threw the dagger on the floor. Sebastian looked at it.

'Why did they kill Tom?' Sebastian asked.

Dominick told him about it. He threw the wet clothes from him and walked around like an animal. His nerves felt raw. He wanted to cry over Tom. But he had no time. Other times he had thought that: There's no time for tears.

'So he died over brandy,' said Sebastian.

'No, no, not that,' said Dominick.

'He lost his temper,' said Sebastian. 'There was no need for him to die.'

Dominick shouted.

'There's a time in every man's life when he must die,' he said. 'You have to choose. In times like these. It was gone past bearing for him.'

'Not if he had faith,' said Sebastian, 'and practised the virtues of his faith.'

'Can a man submit for ever?' Dominick asked.

'Yes, he can,' said Sebastian. 'Where did I learn that? From you. From the beginning. From your will to survive. Isn't what Tom did against all the principles you have been preaching?'

'This is different,' said Dominick. 'If you had seen what he had seen, felt the things he felt, even you would have had to make a gesture. And I liked him. He was my friend. And I'm sorry he is dead and I want to weep for him and I have no time.'

'You will meet him again,' said Sebastian calmly. 'This is not the end.'

'Pray for him,' said Dominick.

'I will,' said Sebastian. 'He was a good man. I'm sorry he died like this. He was a good neighbour. He will be sorely missed.'

'So now we must go,' said Dominick.

'You must go, Dominick,' said Sebastian. 'Not I.'

Dominick stood still.

'Not you?' he said.

'This is my place now,' said Sebastian. 'There are so few priests. In the whole town there are only four. All the rest are gone. Dead or imprisoned or transported. I cannot leave here now.'

'But they'll get you too,' said Dominick. 'They'll flush you out. Come with us. There are people back there who will need you too.'

'The people here need me more,' said Sebastian. 'Dear Dominick, I am giving you your freedom. For many years you have been travelling with Sebastian on your back, like the old man of the sea. Now it will end. You will travel on your own and you will travel faster and farther.'

Dominick thought over this, looking into Sebastian's eyes. Thought of the times he had wished that he was on his own, when Sebastian was wounded and almost helpless. When they would be ready for a new move and there would be no Sebastian to be found. He would be burying the dead or tending the sick, or baptizing the young, always, it would seem, at the wrong time or in the hour of greatest danger. Yes, indeed, Dominick had often thought of him as a burden and had wished that he could be freed from him. Now he was being freed from him. He saw the smile in the eyes of the priest. He sat on the floor beside him.

'Some burdens become light with the wearing of them,' Dominick said. 'Maybe, sometimes, even sweet.'

There was silence between them.

'Thanks, Dominick,' said Sebastian. 'My thanks.'

'We'll find it hard to be without you,' said Dominick. 'Won't you come?'

The priest shook his head. His fingers were rubbing out the Latin words on the slate.

'No, Dominick,' he said. 'I would like to. Maybe that is why I have to stay.'

Dominick thought over it.

'We will have to move fast,' he said. 'All the gates will be guarded. They will start to search every house in the town. The sheriff knows my face.'

'What will you do?' Sebastian asked.

'I will call and see Murdoc,' said Dominick.

'Murdoc!' said Sebastian, surprised. 'Is Murdoc in the camp of the enemy?'

So Dominick told him about Murdoc. 'I am sure he will be of help,' said Dominick. 'I helped him once, I remember. There's something odd about it. All that time he was talking about his mountains, at the back of my mind, where he had planted it, was the sight of a house with a hill at the back of it. It must give a man confidence to have a mountain at his back. As if he could draw strength from it, fight for it. I don't know. I will have to see him. I have much to do. Would you get our things together, Sebastian, such as they are? The children will help you. I must go. The time is running out. I feel cold winds at the back of my neck. I don't want to decorate their gallows for them.'

'God forbid, Dominick,' said Sebastian. 'I will gather your pieces. Do what you have to do.'

Dominick went down the stairs into the long room where the fat bubbled in vats and the many candle-moulds, with the strings of them tied to beams over the vats, were being filled by the children from the long-handled spoons.

Mrs Coocke was standing over the vats, a vast woman, her face red, sweat pouring from under her kerchief. She was a laughing woman with white teeth. She always said that if she was boiled down herself she would make about forty-eight dozen good stout candles.

She greeted him. As he said, 'God bless the work,' the sweat started to pour off himself. The smell of the boiling fat was overpowering.

'Go up again now, Man,' he said to the child. 'Sebastian is putting our things away. Go and help him. Bring Pedro.'

'Are we leaving again, Daddy?' she asked, her eyes wide, and he thought, disappointed.

'Yes, Man,' he said. 'This will be the last, I promise. This time we will land and we will remain unmoving for ever and ever.'

'I hope so,' she said.

'Put on your worst clothes,' he said. 'Do the same for Pedro. Don't be too clean.'

'Are we in trouble again, Daddy?' she asked.

'Yes,' he said, 'and hard trouble to get out of. All right?'

'All right,' she said with a sigh. 'Come on, Pedro. I must say, it's not easy to lead a quiet life with you, Daddy.'

Mrs Coocke was looking at him inquiringly, one hand on her hip, the other stirring at the hot fat.

'Tom Tarpy is killed,' he told her.

She blessed herself. 'Oh, the monsters,' she said.

'I have to leave,' he said. 'I don't know how yet. But I want to thank you for your kindness to us. For taking us in. I won't forget.'

'Ach,' she said.

'Sebastian will be staying,' he said.

'Thank God for that,' she said.

'There will be searches,' he said. 'They'll find out everything in the end. When they come here tell them the truth, that we were here and that we are gone. But watch out for Sebastian. Look after him. They will catch him. He's not too careful. He puts all his trust in the Lord and he's right, but one needs a little cunning as well.'

'I'll keep him on the mark,' she said. 'I'll watch him.'

'God bless you,' he said.

And then he left her. He threw away the woollen hat. They had seen him in that. He walked out into the lane with his head bare. He took off the coat too and just walked in his shirt and breeches. He stood outside in the lane for a moment and thought. He had seen the horses in Skinner's Street. He knew there was an inn in that street too. He wondered if he would find him there. He thought it might be likely. He walked up New Tower Street into the junction of Pludd Street and Skinner's Street where the cow-market was. It was fairly filled with animals now. There was a bellowing in it, and it smelled, but there were a lot of people and he liked that. The market extended almost half way up Skinner's Street and he was just one of many hundreds as he pushed his way through them. He was very pleased when he broke free of them to see the twelve little horses held by one man outside the inn.

There were steps down to the interior. It was thick with the smell of tobacco smoke, and the smell of spilt wine and ale, and sweating men, and it was loud with the rough voices. He stood inside until his eyes became accustomed to the gloom. Then he saw Murdoc at the long table. He was hacking meat from a joint in front of him with his knife, loading it into his mouth and washing it down with great gulps from a pewter tankard. His men seemed very big in the low-ceilinged room. One or two of them were sitting on casks with girls sitting on their legs, laughing. There were a few of the local people there, but they were crowded into the corners. Everyone seemed to be talking at once.

Dominick walked through them. He got around behind Murdoc. Then he put his hand on his shoulder and bent to say into his ear: 'God bless the work, Murdoc.'

He knew Murdoc was going to shout out his name, so he got on one knee beside him and pressed his arm with his hand.

Murdoc strangled the shout in his throat and turned to look at him. He laughed, then he threw back his head and let a shout out of him, 'Ya-huh-hoo!' Murdoc roared. It brought all their eyes to him. So he cut another piece of meat and put it into his mouth, and drank from the tankard, and one of his men let out another shout and then they went back to their work; all except the men near Murdoc who fixed their eyes on the face of the man who was kneeling beside their leader.

'Speak easy, friend,' said Murdoc, then, in Irish, 'because the walls have ears.'

'I'm in trouble, Murdoc,' said Dominick. 'Bad trouble.'

'That's very good, I'm glad to hear it,' said Murdoc.

He felt Dominick's surprise. He chuckled.

'I might be able to help you,' he explained. 'There is a lot of help from me coming to you. That's why I'm glad.'

'You remember all the talk about the fair land?' Murdoc asked.

'How could I forget?' said Murdoc. 'I meant it. And now I'm in it again myself and it looks better than ever.'

'I am oppressed by the walls of the towns,' said Dominick.

'I knew it would happen,' said Murdoc. 'No true man can carry the things on his back.'

'But now I must get away,' said Dominick. 'Very fast. They are looking for me.'

'You can't come with us,' said Murdoc. 'My friend Coote trusts me but not far. His eyes will stretch after me. You would be noticed. Can you get out of town on your own, outside the walls?'

Dominick thought, his head resting on his arm.

'Yes,' he said definitely, 'I can.'

'Hear that, Morogh Dubh?' Murdoc asked the big black fellow.

'I hear,' said the black man. 'It will answer.'

'Two in one,' said Murdoc, 'and I know this small man. He always does what he sets out to do. There could be none better. Listen, my friend, when you get outside the walls, go to the Wood Quay and ask for a man named Davie O'Fowda.'

'Yes,' said Dominick.

'He will fix you with a boat,' said Murdoc. 'After that you are on your own. Take to the lake. About thirty miles north-west, to the very end and tip of it, into a great valley among the mountains. You can't go wrong. All the time you will see the mountains becking their heads at you. All right?'

Dominick thought.

'All right,' he said.

'See that fellow, Morogh Dubh. He never says yes straight away. He thinks first, and you can be sure it will be done. You could go by sea but that is too dangerous. They have patrol boats, and it's an unfriendly shore. By land you would have to pass through too many enemies. We had to fight our own way through at times. So take the long lake. It might take you four days, maybe more, depending on the winds. Someone will be waiting in the valley for you. There is a river out of it. Keep going until you can go no longer. Wait there. Go now. We have talked too long. They will have the eye on you. My heart is glad that I will be seeing you soon. We will talk a book full when we meet.'

Then he reached with his hand and pushed at Dominick's shoulder. Dominick sprawled on the soiled floor.

'Go to hell, you bloody beggar,' said Murdoc in English, shouting. 'Go and look for scraps at an English table. Be off with you!' He aimed a blow at him with his fist. Dominick crawled out of reach and got to his feet.

'You saffron Irish bastard!' he said viciously.

Morogh Dubh rose with a roar and made for him. Dominick scurried away like a rat, across the floor and out of the door. The customers in the inn laughed heartily.

'He's away then,' said Morogh, coming back.

Murdoc was laughing. 'Man, but he is in for a surprise,' said he. 'I'd love to be there to see it. Go and see O'Fowda, Morogh. Tell him about this man. Let him put him away until night. Truly God sent him at the right time, so we will be doing two good turns at once.'

Dominick's mind was working away at his problems. He had the pattern of freedom there. He hadn't a lot of time. He could get over the walls by nightfall, but with two children that might be dangerous, and it might also be too late. So he would have to leave boldly and openly by the light of day. There was only one way to do that.

He pushed his way through the cow-market in Pludd Street. Away at the end of it he could see that the other markets were breaking up. People with horses and cattle were driving away from the squares, and heading towards the gates.

He walked down slowly. He fumbled under his shirt and reached his fingers into his pouch and got the golden sovereign in his hand. He continued rubbing the coin against the cloth of his shirt and his breeches. Gold was always better when it shone. He came into Earl's Street and as he passed the lane he turned and looked down. It was empty, except for a lot of soldiers who were crowding around the door of Tom's tavern. Tom wouldn't be buried. Even dead they would hang him in chains. He lost himself among the crowd in the horse-market, and walked through looking for a likely face.

It is difficult to read the faces of the people. They would have animated faces talking to a friend, with laughter wrinkles crinkling the sides of their eyes. But if they saw you noticing them, the blinds would come down on their faces. Most of the horses had panniers, baskets slung on each side of them, in which the produce had been carried, wood or turf for burning, or cabbage or vegetables, or bags of grain. There were old men and young men and middle-aged men, some with beards and some with moustaches and some of them clean-shaven and some of them needing shaves. How would you find one you could trust, even for money? He was getting a bit desperate as he wandered among them, listening to conversations dying whenever he came too close.

He was over near the walls and the stone steps leading to the ramparts when he felt the hand on his shoulder and heard the voice saying: 'MacMahon.' Instinctively he felt for his belt, and his mind was working on the problem, how he would turn with a sweep of his arm, and a kick with his foot, to topple his arrester, and then he would run through the horses, under their bellies, and he would reach the Strand Gate, run on to the quays and back in the Ould Gate into Quay Street until he would get lost in the Shambles.

'They are looking for you,' said the voice. He turned. A small man, smaller even than he, with ferrety eyes and bandy legs. He lived in the lane. He was badly dressed. He always seemed to be shaking his shoulders as if he was being tormented with fleas. Perhaps he was. 'Tailor,' he said, 'you shortened my life by five years.'

'You have a right to be frightened,' said Tailor. 'They searched the lane like they were looking for gold.'

'Do they know my name?' Dominick asked.

'Not yet,' said the tailor. He chuckled suddenly. 'Man, we

142

cleaned out Tom's place. It was scoured like the white sand on the sea shore afore they kem. You missed though. You failed there.'

'How? How?' Dominick asked.

'The one you knifed, you missed him,' said Tailor. 'He got away on his own legs.'

'Not dead?' Dominick asked. 'Not dead?'

'No,' said Tailor. 'A bad miss. But they'll hang you just the same.' Dominick didn't care. He felt relief flooding over him. Why? Because Sebastian hadn't said: 'Well done, Dominick. It's great that you killed a man for no reason except that he killed one man who had already killed another man.'

'Tailor, dear,' said Dominick, 'find me a man who will rent me his horse and his baskets and his clothes. Do you know one here?'

'Ho-ho,' said Tailor, 'I see. Of course I do. Come, we will look and find the very man. For money he would rent out his grandmother to a sailor.' He walked away from Dominick. He passed through the people. For Tailor they would smile and laugh, Dominick noticed.

In the middle of the crowd they came on a squat man with a four-day-old grey-black beard. He was chewing tobacco. His teeth were stained yellow. He had very heavy eyebrows and small sparkling eyes under them. Tailor clapped him on the back. He didn't knock a stir out of him. He was wearing heavy frieze clothes, with short Irish trousers and his big feet bare. 'Peadar,' said Tailor to him in Irish, 'is your day good and how the devil are you?'

'Oh, Tailor,' said Peadar, 'I'm not well. I'm racked with pains of many descriptions, and if you are looking for the money I owe you for cutting this cloth, believe me I will pay you next market day. Things are bad. The weather is awful. Nothing is growing. And the price they give for turf wouldn't pay for the trouble of cutting and saving it.'

'Calm down,' said the tailor. 'I'm not after you yet. You see my friend here?' The shrewd blue eyes looked him over. 'Aye,' he said. 'I see him for whatever good that will do me.' Then he looked down at Dominick's hand, where the golden sovereign was catching the winking lights of the sun. 'A grand man,' he said. 'A decent citizen as anyone can see, and who do I have to murder?'

'The loan of your horse,' said Dominick, 'and the loan of

143

your clothes, all of which will be returned to you in a couple of hours.'

'That's a lot of money,' said Peadar. 'It would buy both the horse and the clothes all over, and you are willing to give that just for the loan of them? Are you straight in the head?'

'I think so,' said Dominick.

'The black dogs want him,' said the tailor.

'In that case,' said Peadar, 'what's stopping us?' He started to take off his coat.

'No,' said Dominick, 'for God's sake. We'll go over here where we will not be seen.'

He went over towards the Strand Gate where many bales and barrels were piled high. They clambered over some of those until they came on a cleared space where only the tops of their heads would be visible. 'Now,' he said, and proceeded to take off his clothes. Peadar threw off his, while the tailor kept a lookout. There was no word spoken. Dominick donned Peadar's clothes with distaste. They smelled of him and his sweat, but Dominick's would be the same to him.

'They're a tight fit for me,' said Peadar.

'You can give them to your children,' said Dominick.

'You mean you don't want them back as well?' asked Peadar. He was amazed at such waste. Dominick thought of a time before when he had changed clothes too, long long ago, with a man he had killed. He clenched his jaws as the thought came to him. He handed over the gold. Peadar tested it and found it good, and looked at Dominick with wonder, shaking his head. He put it away. 'It will be a good winter,' he said.

They walked back again to the crowd. There were a few heads turned to look at them. Peadar in the unusual garments drew a few wide eyes, but he just grinned and spat and walked to his horse. The baskets were on the ground. He raised them and fixed them to the pegs of the pannier on the horse's back.

'Be good with him, now,' he said. 'He's a good horse.'

'Is a man called Davie O'Fowda known to you?' Dominick asked.

'He's the fourth cousin of my grandmother's people,' said Peadar.

'Watch for him near the Little Gate,' said Dominick. 'He will come back with your horse and your clothes. And you have my thanks. You have saved my life.'

'Very few lives are worth a golden sovereign,' said Peadar,

'but if you are caught I'll say you stole my horse and my clothes. Will that be unkind for you?'

'If I'm caught,' said Dominick with a tight smile, 'it will matter little what you say about me.'

'God speed you, so,' said Peadar. Dominick went to the horse's head and 'ck-ck-cked' and the horse moved. The tailor went with him as far as the Fish Shambles.

'I wish you luck,' he said. 'If you ever come back, you will be welcome with us in the lane. Poor Tom. We will have to wake him. He made his own funeral. We'll be as drunk as lords for three days and nights. They got no decent description of you except from the poor creature who turned. Some said you were six foot with black hair and some that you were only four foot with grey hair. Everyone had a different name on you. So they should be confused for a few hours.'

'God bless you,' said Dominick, and parted from him. Dominick kept his head down, his pace slow, and the awkward shapeless woollen hat pulled down over his eyes until he came to the arch of his own lane. He guided the horse through here, having some trouble with the baskets, then he tied the rope of the horse to a bar outside the door and went in to greet his family.

CHAPTER SIXTEEN

DOMINICK PUSHED the last blanket-wrapped bundle into the basket; took a last hitch at the belly-band rope around the horse, said, 'Now we are ready!' Then he looked around for the others. 'Peter!' he called. 'Come and let me look at you.'

Peter came from the tail end of the horse and stood there looking at his father with his head on one side. They had rubbed a little soot into his fair hair and streaked his face. The shirt he wore was tattered, and the patched breeches tied with a piece of rope. Since he had been in his bare feet for some time, his legs were brown and dusty. 'You're fine, fine,' he said.

Then he looked at his daughter. She was poorly clad, but it wasn't that which gave him a kick in the heart, but the sight of the tears pouring down her face. Man, he thought, the girl who never cried, the little girl who had had thousands of occasions for tears in the last few years. He wanted to be soft with her, to get on his knees in the dust and take her in his arms. But he couldn't. Time was too precious.

'Hurry up!' he said. 'What are you crying for now? This is no time.'

'I'm not crying,' she said. She had to make her mouth crooked to say the words at all.

'Well, you must be sweating so,' he said, and then saw Sebastian standing behind her. He looked at him. Ah, so he thought. Sebastian had been her mother. All those years. Now that he came to think of it, she had been more in Sebastian's company than she had been in his. Sebastian looked a bit stricken, too, for one who was able to control his features so well. He stood just behind her.

'Keep up your writing, Man,' he said. 'I put a slate in the bundle.'

She nodded.

'And keep after the Latin grammar, Peter,' he said. 'That's your weakest part.' Peter didn't look at him either. He was patting the hairy side of the horse's face, rubbing the back of his hand along it and then his palm. The horse was placid. He

146

was a brown horse. One hoof, pointed, rested tiredly on the dust.

'And keep after the catechisms,' said Sebastian. 'It's more important really than the Latin. You hear, Man?' She nodded. 'And if you come on groups of heathens out there who don't know their catechisms you make them learn it. You'll do that?'

She nodded again, with her face averted.

Sebastian got on his knees behind her then and put his hands on her arms, and his head near her kerchief-covered one.

'Don't cry, Man,' he said. 'We'll meet again. You'll see. You and Pedro can be my missionaries until I come.' Then he looked up at Dominick.

'God be with you, Dominick,' he said.

Dominick tightened his jaw muscles. He often noticed that before. Just let one person go soft and everybody was infected. And God knows there wasn't time for that.

'And you too,' he said. 'Well, we better be going. If we don't go now, it will be too late.'

'You better go,' said Sebastian. 'Mistress Coocke said she had too many moulds to fill to see ye further off.'

Probably filling them with tears, Dominick thought grimly. Women were all the same. She had become terribly fond of the children, and why wouldn't she? They were good ones. But she was as soft as her own fat, anyhow.

'Oh,' said Dominick, 'I forgot to tell you. The man I killed isn't dead at all.'

Sebastian thought over that. And then he laughed, rubbing his forefinger under his nose. 'God bless you, Dominick,' he said. 'If I am laughing at the way you put it, my heart is light for you.'

'I knew that would please you,' said Dominick grimly. 'Maybe he's dead since, but they saw him walking.'

'If he's dead, he's not walking,' said Sebastian. 'Look, Dominick, never again, don't ever kill again. There's too much killing.'

'I'll remember,' said Dominick. 'You know the way if you look long enough at a certain thing, and then turn your eyes to the sky, you transfer the image.'

'Yes,' said Sebastian.

'Well, that's the way you have me now,' said Dominick. 'There will be a million Sebastians surrounding me. We will

147

miss you, but that's only natural. You have been with us a long time. Give anyone time enough and they will grow on you. Isn't that true?'

'That's true,' said Sebastian.

Look, be a bit careful,' he said. 'Your head is worth six pounds to anyone who wants to sell you. And six pounds is a lot of money. It only means being careful, that's all. The Lord God expects you to be a bit cunning as well as reckless. You'll watch it, hah?'

'I'll be careful, Dominick,' said Sebastian.

'Well, what are we waiting for so?' said Dominick. 'We're off now at last and with God's help we will get free.'

'You will get free,' said Sebastian.

Dominick slapped the horse on the flank and he set off, holding the lead rope in his hand. Mary Ann was walking beside him, and he could see Peter's brown legs on the other side. He got to the arch and manoeuvred the horse until the baskets came free. They came into New Tower Street and walked towards Pludd Street and the cow-market. It had thinned out a lot. Streams of people were making up Skinner's Street. He joined with them. All the time he was thinking: How many real friends does a person make in the course of a lifetime? What is a friend? Is there in the world a person who will really be your friend, who will give of himself to you every time you are in need, so that you can do the same for him, constant, unremitting friendship, with no selfish motive? Does such a thing exist at all? That's why it was hard parting from Sebastian. Sebastian was only motivated by love. If Sebastian was called on to give his life to save you, he would do that, and he would do it with a smile. That was why it was hard leaving him. He glanced down at his daughter, at her face under the soiled kerchief. Her face was wet.

'Man,' he said, bending down to her, 'if you don't dry your face and blow your nose, I'm going to get angry. We have to save our lives.'

She nodded her head. She obeyed him. She wiped her cheeks with her palms. In streaked them with dirt. That was good. She dabbed her sleeve at her nose. As they came to the four corners near the castle, the tension started to tighten in his stomach.

Here the walking people, loaded with baskets or leading horses, divided into three ways. Some of them went up Great Gate Street to the way out there; some of them turned left

down High Middle Street which would bring them over the
bridge and into the west suburbs, and the rest went straight
across into Little Gate Street. The streets were narrow and the
houses were tall, and the declining sun was shut off so that the
streets were in shade. He felt depressed as they passed the fresh
fish market, with its live eels squirming in the water tanks, the
huge pike smelling already in the hot sun, all except the salted
pike, some of which were strung and hung on poles.

Past the market he could see the opening of Little Gate. It
was crowded with soldiers, and even half way down the street
he could feel the backlash of the hold-up.

In a way it would be as well to be found. You would die, but
however painful the death it could only last a short time and
then it would be over. Ever since he could remember, except
for the few blissful years in Drogheda, he had been running
from something. Running from clans who were at war with his
own clans, or running from clans which his clan had raided for
cattle, and sometimes women. Fighting the new settlers, fighting
the old settlers, living in woods and bogs. For a few short years
only he had known the happiness of being static, just staying
in one place with the person you loved, with no threats hanging over your head that you couldn't avoid by the use of your
intellect. I'm so damn tired of running away, he thought. If this
is going to be the end of the running away, I would be pleased
– until he thought of the children. His Man would be almost
ripe enough to go to the Barbadoes. That was a pleasant
thought. See Man in the Barbadoes. See Pedro, poor dumb intelligent Pedro, slaving in sugar fields with his body scarred with
the lash of the leather whips. That was a pleasant thought.

They were examining passes.

He knew that would happen, but he also knew that the only
people permitted into the town without passes were the sellers
of produce, like Peadar. There was a lot of shouting at the Gate.
A lot of arguing. Some of the better classes were protesting
against the brutal examinations of their persons, shouting out
their names, being pushed to one side or shoved over the
bridge, or sent back into the town with an escort who didn't
treat them delicately. Dominick bent down to the ground and
got dust in his sweat-soaked palm and rubbed it on his face. His
clean-shaven features might look too good. He pulled the cap
farther over his eyes.

'Well, who are you? Are these your kids? What have you in

the baskets? What were you selling?'

Dominick answered him in a blaze of Irish. He gesticulated with his dirty hands. He screwed up his eyes. He spat out the words. They had to be real in case the people around him might betray him. He was Peadar O'Cualain. He was from out the road beyond the lake. He brought turf and fuel to the market. He bought a few things at the market himself, like old clothes and shoes and bits of butter and things and spades for the digging of the land and a little meal and a few bits of bread and fish and things.

They poked at his baskets with a pike. Just to be sure that there was no man hiding in them. If there had been there would have been blood dripping in the dust. He had thought of that too, that he was a small man and he could have gone out of the gates hiding in a basket. He almost turned pale at the thought now.

He kept talking, talking and gesticulating, gesticulating, and he was across the wooden bridge and on the road and heading right towards the Wood Quay before he realized that he was through and free, and he could stop talking. His knees felt weak, and his mouth was dry. He stopped and rubbed the soft muzzle of the horse. The horse liked it. I'm getting too old now, he thought, for these sort of adventures.

'Are we safe now, Daddy?' Mary Ann was asking him.

'No,' he said. 'Not yet. Let us go on.'

He moved on with the horse.

'Where are we going?' she asked.

'Way, way, far off,' he said, 'where we can build a stout house and rest for ever and fear no man.'

'Do we have to walk again?' she asked.

'No, no walking much, Man,' he said. 'We will get a boat.'

They were walking by the Little Bridge river that swept around the walls, under the tower of the Little Gate that joined the main flow at the South Milinn. There were houses on their left, closely packed, most of them thatched, some of them mud built, some of them stout built, quite a few of them tall two-storey houses. Many of them were destroyed since the siege. They had been taken over by the people pouring into Connacht from across the Shannon, waiting until they were assigned their portion of land or tenancies which had been promised them when they had been forced out of the other three corners of Ireland. Most of them would never be settled. There wasn't enough to go around. It was called the Lord's Suburb, because some of the houses were occupied by a Lord and a Lady and a Sir and a Lady and there was said to be a viscountess and her son living in one of the ruined rooms. It was a place of poverty, crowded with miserable people, helpless because they had never used their hands, deprived of their servants and their wealth, reduced to possessing only what was on their back, each day going into the town to wave their pieces of official paper in the faces of the grinning magistrates. Their children were playing in the roadways, looking incongruous in their shabby good clothes. They crossed the wooden hurdles over the Abbey stream. He could see the buildings of the abbey on his left. The tall tower was half destroyed. The rest of it was used for stabling horses; for an overflow from the town gaol; for a courthouse.

Ahead of them where the Deig Nua divided from the Little Bridge River he saw the bustling of the Wood Quay.

It was a very hot day. Even now that the sun was heading towards the west sea, it was hot. The heavy clothes he was wearing were making him break out into rivers of sweat.

There was apparent confusion at the quay. Some of the turf boats were still unloading. There were mounds of brown turf piled along the way, and the baskets of the patient horses were being loaded. The eel fishers were using hand nets to draw their wriggling catch and pack them into the wooden water-butts. Some country people were getting into boats and pulling out into the main river. Old women heavily dressed and red-faced and clumsy with their baskets, and their young ones lithe and playful, drawing curses from their parents as they rocked the light wooden boats.

Dominick walked close and looked for O'Fowda. He should be easy to mark. A master boatman is a man who is in charge and gives orders. He gave the rope to Mary Ann and went closer to the quay. It was a short quay, built up of large loose limestone blocks, unmortared, but cunningly fitted. He was conscious of the lack of noise from feet. All of them, including himself, were in their bare feet. He listened to the scratching noise that hardened soles made on the warm stones.

A stout barrel-chested man with brown hair and a big face. That would be O'Fowda. He was ordering here, shouting there. But he walked with authority. He'd kick a boy in the backside, butt a horse in the belly to get him out of the way.

Then he was standing on the quay with his hands on his hips looking down at a boat which had just arrived. There were two men in it, and they were loaded with wooden logs, which they proceeded to throw up on the quay. They were freshly cut and Dominick smelled them, willow and ash and birch and scrub oak. They smelled as if they were living. They brought to his mind the cool shade of the woodlands, crackling branches under his feet. Funny, but this was the moment he knew that he was finished with towns for ever. This scent of the fresh things, not of sewers, and men's leavings and flesh putrefying on gallows; stale smells were the smells of towns; everything you smelled was at second hand, already on the point of decay, and the smells of fear which was a worse thing.

'Murdoc sent me,' he said, standing behind O'Fowda.

The man didn't move. He kept talking down to the two men in the boat.

'Late you are,' he was saying. 'You'll have us until dark here, so ye will.'

'How could we help it?' one man asked. 'Isn't the night young?'

'Come next week this time and you'll stay on the water,' he said. Then he turned to Dominick. 'Well, man, have you the horse ready?' he asked. 'Where is the horse?'

'Over here,' said Dominick, walking back.

'We'll get him and bring him over,' said O'Fowda. He walked beside Dominick. He was holding his arm.

'I have to change these clothes,' said Dominick, noticing now that there were several soldiers walking here and there on the quay, looking, probing. His heart sank again. 'They must be got back to Peadar O'Cualain. He says you know him, and the horse too.'

'What delayed you?' O'Fowda was shouting at him. 'Bring the horse and get the baskets loaded. They are on to you already,' he said in a lower voice. 'You can't get away from here now. They are looking at every boat that goes or comes.'

'What's the best thing to do?' Dominick asked. He felt helpless. He felt sorry that he hadn't made his own plans. It was always difficult when you had to rely on others. But what could he do now?

'Take the horse,' O'Fowda was saying. 'Go back a bit. Cross the drawbridge and go down by the houses towards the Sickeen bogs. You'll see two paths leading into the big rushes. Take the second path.' They were standing beside the horse now. O'Fowda was looking at the loaded baskets. 'Oh God,' he said. 'You can unload the baskets down there by the rushes and send the horse back. Stay there then. Don't move out of it. We'll get to you when it's dark.'

He stood back.

'Can I help it if the bloody wood boat is late from Annagh?' he said. 'I have to stay here. If you don't want to, take your horse and get out of here,' Dominick muttered at him.

'Go on! Go on! Go home to your wife. She'll be glad to see you if she hasn't another man with her, and then she won't be glad to see you.' He laughed. He walked back shouting, towards the men in the wood boat. 'Now see the trouble you are causing,' he shouted. 'Is there no peace to be found with you? Wouldn't it be better for the lot of us if your damn boat was at the bottom of the lake?'

Dominick had turned back the way he had come. Not too fast. He wanted to get upon the horse's back and beat him into speed. They crossed the wooden hurdles over the river and then turned left and went over the drawbridge. The hooves of the horse sounded hollow. They were far from the Little Gate, but on their right the Lion's Tower rose and the armed men up there were leaning and looking down at them. When they reached the first houses, he skirted them and turned sharply left and breathed again when the bulk of houses cut off the sight of the soldiers on the tower. Beside him, Mary Ann padded on, uncomplaining now. He reached and laid his hand on her head. In five minutes he was free of the houses. They were walking on a rough bridle path on fairly hard ground. Then the ground became softer, and in spots they sank to their shins in black-yellow mud. The rushes were rustling in the heat wind, and he could smell the river. He couldn't see it. But the two great groups of rushes were distinct. The path climbed away while another hardly discernible went left. He climbed and for some time they were on hard ground and he could see the river out to his left, broad and soft-flowing and shimmering bluely in the hazed sunshine. Then they went into the soft parts again, and when he came to the second great acreage of rushes and found the narrow trail that went through them, winding on the little hard ground that remained, he took it, and went up, sending the children to walk ahead of them. The rushes were tall. The tops of them were waving over their heads. After about three hundred yards of rushes they could look out at the river, at the boats that were being rowed away towards the sun. At this point there was a beach of hard yellow gravel. He started to take the bundles out of the baskets.

'Mary Ann,' he said then, 'are you brave?'

Mary Ann looked at him.

'It depends on what I have to do, Daddy,' she said.

He laughed at her.

'Would you be able to lead the horse back to the quay?' he asked.

She considered it.

'I think so,' she said.

'Go slow,' he said. 'Just go there with the horse. Leave him there, and then walk away and come back here. Could you do that?'

'I can do it,' she said.

There were so many things that could happen! He put them out of his mind. This was the only way. He opened one of the bundles and took out his own clothes. He used the horse for a shelter and changed into them. They were lighter than the other sweat-soaked ones. Those he put into the basket. He turned the horse back the way they had come.

'All right, Man,' he said. He kept his voice casual. This was something she could have been doing every day in the week. 'Don't be too long. But don't look as if you were hurrying. All right?'

'All right, Daddy,' she said. Then she 'ck-ck-cked' at the horse, hauled at the rope and he followed her quietly.

Dominick waited and listened until he could hear no more of them and then he sat on the bundle, and put his arm about his son who was looking at him inquiringly.

'She'll be fine, Pedro,' he said. 'Man will be safe. You'll see.' I better be right, he thought grimly. I better be right.

CHAPTER SEVENTEEN

THE SUN went down. They couldn't see its end because on the other side of the river the land rose a little. But they saw its death in the sky all around them. The smooth water became multi-coloured, and in the middle where the current broke the smooth flow the change of light and colour was dazzling. The birds started their night calling, and from upstream two wild duck came whistling down towards them, splashed the water near them and swam into the rushes. The drake quacked twice, contentedly, and then settled down.

Dominick felt Peter's worry, now and then saw the white of his eyes as he raised them to look at his father's face.

She will be all right, he told himself. They couldn't have associated her with him so quickly. It would take them time to find out his name and the fact that there were two children with him. Whatever delayed her had to be good.

'You know Man,' he said to Peter. 'She gets talking to people.' So she did too, even to the wrong kind of people, that was the trouble. If a person was friendly to her, Man would be friendly to him, soldier or sailor. She would even talk to Coote if he was friendly to her. At this thought, Dominick broke out in a cold sweat. 'Wait,' he said then. 'I will go back a little and see if there is sign of her.'

He raised himself. His limbs were stiff. He walked through the path in the rushes, cautiously emerged from them and climbed to the high ground. He looked. He could see the bulk of the town, a dark mass against the green sky. He could see the heads and shoulders of the patrolling sentries on the walls where the dark bulk of buildings behind them did not make them vanish. He could see the gleam on the waters of the many streams that were swallowed by the fortifications and the mills. But there was no sign of the little girl. He wondered if he would go back in and find her. That would be foolish. It would mean three of them separated and he thought how Peter might feel if he was caught. No, for once have faith in goodness, in the name of God, he told himself. He went back to Peter.

'The boatman may have held her for a reason,' he said to Peter. That was a sensible idea, if it was true. 'When he brings the boat he will bring Mary Ann.'

He held on to that thought. It was sensible. He thought of Tom Tarpy. Such a big jolly happy man. Ah, they said, but you should have seen him before the troubles came on us. Death was very fleet. One second you were here, and the next your mind was standing in front of a different judge from the ones provided here. Be merciful, Lord, to Tom, he thought. He was hurt at the things that were happening all around him. Tom's soul was tired of iniquity, he thought. But weren't we all the same way? It was such an easy time to die. It took very little to find death now. A shouted word of defiance, a miscalculated spit, an overheard conversation, a look from the sides of the eye. Little things like that invited death with willing dispensers on every side only too pleased to give it to you. Had it always been like this, he wondered, that one race could so despise another race, that they regarded it as an actual virtue to kill them as if they were vermin? His mind flitted back over his gleanings of history. It was all there. It had happened before. He supposed it would keep on happening until the end of the world. Just because people wouldn't love. What? Love Coote? That's right. The physical look of him, the evil eyes, the white moist flesh. You have to hate what he stands for and what he means, but you have to try to love him. No! That's impossible. But that's the answer according to Sebastian. Could Sebastian do it, if it was put to him to save his life, or lose his life?

He felt Peter's hand pulling at his knee. He looked. It was much darker now. He had to bend low against the light remaining on the horizon.

He strained his ears. He could hear nothing, but he could see after his eyes became adjusted a shapeless-looking thing that was making its way across. Very silently. He saw it reach the centre of the stream and the current took it so that it went off course, and then he heard a splash or two and saw it settling back and heading almost in a line towards their position. He got to his feet.

As it came nearer he could hear the slight slap of the wave against the bow. He could only see the oarsman. There was nothing else to be seen, just the thick bulk of a man, leaning forward and pulling back again. He felt his mouth going dry with anxiety. If Mary Ann wasn't in the boat, he would have to go and find her. There could be no other way of it.

Ten yards from the little beach the oarsman rested. He whistled. It sounded exactly like a querulous water-hen. Dominick chirped awkwardly in reply and the boat moved in towards him. Dominick caught the bow and pulled it on to the beach.

'I have a present for you,' said the voice of O'Fowda. Dominick's heart settled, and he saw the figure rising from almost under O'Fowda's feet.

'Mary Ann, my love,' he said, and caught her arms. Just as he noticed that the arms seemed a little too well fleshed for Mary Ann, he heard his daughter giggling and rising from behind the other.

'You nearly kissed Mrs Dorsi, Daddy,' she said. He released the arms. Mary Ann climbed out of the boat and splashed to the beach.

'Where were you? What happened to you? Why did you frighten us?' he asked Mary Ann, trying to sort out his bewilderment.

'I was with Mrs O'Fowda in her house,' said Mary Ann. 'I was eating until I was stuffed. She had little cakes, with real sugar on them. Here, Pedro, I brought you one or two. Sugar is sweet. I never ate it before.'

'You didn't know I was going with you?' he heard the strange voice say. She had a deep voice with music in it.

'No,' he answered. Going with us? A woman? Am I to be burdened again, he wondered? Is there no rest even in fleeing?

'Murdoc should have told you,' he heard her say. 'I thought he told you.' He remembered Murdoc talking to Morogh. Laughing behind the talk. So like Murdoc.

O'Fowda was standing beside him.

'You better go now,' he said. 'I can only give you an hour. Then I will have to tell them that there is a boat gone. That way I can cover myself. It will take them a few hours to get ready. That gives you three or four hours' headstart. It's all I can do for you.'

'You have done a lot for us,' said Dominick. 'I won't forget.'

'Just help somebody else,' said O'Fowda, 'that needs it. If we all did that, it would be a free land. Here's a chart. It's rough but it will show you the way. Watch yourself. They will

157

follow you. Three men rowing are twice as fast as one man. You want to remember that. Don't be caught in the open.' Dominick felt the piece of parchment in his hand. He put it inside his shirt. 'God be with you, Mrs Dorsi,' he said. 'I'd like to see Coote's face when he finds you are gone. It's worth the risk.'

'Thanks, Davie,' she said. 'Some day I will be back. I will remember.'

'Goodbye, Mary Ann,' said he to her. 'Some day when all is quiet we will hope to see you.'

Dominick was pushing his bundles into the boat, arranging them in the bow and the stern. It wasn't a long boat, but it was broad. There was only a middle seat near the oars. It was a heavy wooden boat, pitch-caulked.

'When you leave here creep over to the land on the east shore,' O'Fowda was saying to Dominick. 'Up all along by Tiroilean. The moon is coming up. When you pass the old castle you can go into the middle of the river. When you come out of the river into the wide way of the lake, head east until you come to the narrow places and beyond that to the great woods. You will have to get that far before morning if you want to be safe.'

Dominick caught his hand and squeezed it. It was a broad hand, well calloused. The woman was sitting on the bundles, and Mary Ann was beside her. Dominick pushed the boat out and Peter climbed into the bow and sank there out of sight. Then Dominick stepped in, sat and raised the oars and O'Fowda leaned and pushed and the boat was free on the water.

Dominick turned the bow of the boat upstream. He could just distinguish O'Fowda, a squat, powerful figure with an arm raised in the air, and then he had merged with the rushes and was gone. The oars felt awkward in his hands. His hands were not very big. The handles of the oars were thick and rough. He pulled the boat over towards the shore and then started to move along by it.

'What is your name?' he heard the woman asking him.

'My name is Dominick MacMahon,' he said.

'You are from the North,' she said.

'I am from all over,' he said. 'From the four corners.'

There was a strain on his arms already from rowing against the stream. Over to his left the moon was high in the sky, but it shone on the water beyond them and left this side of the river in shadow. He saw the town now with the river running into it and curving around the walls. And he saw the light of it for a little longer, torches that seemed to be moving magically of their own accord, and then they came to a bend of the river with the bulk of the destroyed castle near them, standing starkly with the moon looking in through one window of it as they passed, and then there was nothing to see except the sky and the water and he glided the boat out into the centre of the stream, and bent his back and was less cautious about the sound the oars might make.

He was conscious of his own ineptitude, his ignorance of these waters and the inevitability of pursuit.

'Mrs O'Fowda has a sort of moustache, Daddy,' Mary Ann was saying. 'And she is fat and big and she cries at the least thing, but she is very loving and I hope we meet with her again. Did you like the sugar cakes, Pedro?'

Pedro answered by thumping the boards of the boat three times. That was an emphatic affirmative.

'I smell fish,' said Mary Ann.

Dominick heard Mrs Dorsi laughing. He could see the blur of her face and the shine of her white teeth.

'That's me, Mary Ann,' she said.

'You are talking too much maybe, Man,' said Dominick.

'Oh, but I never had such adventures, Daddy,' said Mary Ann. 'If I don't talk, I'll burst. I smell fish and sort of honey. Is that you too, Mrs Dorsi? Why do you smell of fish?'

'I'm wearing a fisherwoman's clothes,' said Mrs Dorsi. 'That's how I got away.'

'Are you fleeing too, like us?' Mary Ann asked. 'We're used to it. We're always at it. When I grow up and get married I'm going to marry nobody unless he stays in the one place all the time.'

Dominick put back his head and laughed heartily. He had to stop rowing for a few strokes.

'God bless you, Mary Ann,' he said then.

'And what's the smell of honey, Mrs Dorsi?' she asked.

'You must call me Columba,' said Mrs Dorsi.

'Is that your name?' she asked.

'Yes,' said Mrs Dorsi. 'The honey smell is the last of a French perfume, Mary Ann. The very last. There will be no more.'

'How did you get away?' Dominick asked her.

'They put a guard on the house,' she said. 'But there is a

passage from the house to the graveyard near the church. I went that way. I changed clothes with a fisherwoman from the Claddagh. She liked the change. She gave me a round basket with fish. I walked over the bridge with the rest of the women.'

'I went with Davie, Daddy,' said Mary Ann. 'We rowed from the quay across the river and Mrs Dor – Columba was waiting there on the shore. And you should have seen Mrs O'Fowda crying because I was going. She said I should have been in bed.'

'Do you know Murdoc?' Columba asked him.

'I do,' he said.

'He's a very brave man,' she said.

'He's a very reckless man,' Dominick said.

'What's in a name?' she asked. 'It's such a wonderful thing to see a brave man. I thought there were no more left at all. I'm tired of cowards. I thought there was no man in the world left who would be brave. Then I saw him.'

'You saw him being brave?' Dominick asked. He couldn't say that he had seen her. She wouldn't remember his face from the hall, he thought. He had that hat over his eyes and the clothes Tom had given him.

'Yes,' she said. 'I . . .' She stopped then. She could hardly go on and tell him the position she had been in. 'I saw him being brave.'

'Where are your people?' he asked her.

'Over the sea,' she said. 'All of them. They went before the siege. Also my husband. My husband is not a brave man. I wouldn't go. I wouldn't go. I despise cowards. You have to stay and fight. Stay and fight, not run away.'

'You are running away now,' he pointed out gently.

'This is different,' she said. 'Coote wants my house. Now he can have it. But I will be breathing freedom. You know where Murdoc lives? Have you been there?'

'No,' said Dominick.

'I have seen it once long ago,' she said. 'It is near the mountains. There will be free people there. Like Murdoc. They won't be afraid. They will fight, and laugh and say what they like in the open air and they won't be looking over their shoulders to see if anybody is listening to them. Isn't that true?'

'I hope it is true,' said Dominick.

'He stood like a mountain,' she said, 'with his legs spread, and he laughed in the face of death. He is a great man. I had begun to believe that there were none left.'

The boat shuddered and jolted them and came to a stop. It had run up on a muddy bank. Dominick freed an oar and pushed it off again.

'I will have to keep my mind on my work,' he said.

She took the hint.

'Put your head on my shoulder, Mary Ann,' she said, 'and go to sleep.'

He was pulling away at the oars again. Blisters had formed on his palms near the butts of his fingers and had broken open. When he grasped the oars now he could feel the fluid bursting out of them. It was like a sharp knife being drawn across his palms. They made him wince. Soft hands, he thought. A few weeks in a town and your hands are as soft as a woman's.

'There's a forest of stars in the sky,' said Mary Ann. 'Is mother like a star, Daddy?' Mary Ann, he thought, as he gasped, always she could hit you in the chest when you didn't expect it.

'Yes,' he said, 'like a star.'

'Well, it's not cold anyhow,' said Mary Ann. 'It's a good job we hadn't to flee in the winter.'

'Shush,' he said, 'try and sleep.'

He felt desolate as he pulled away in this winding alien river. It was wide and deep. From each side of it he could smell the rush-lands, a pungent acrid smell of decay and growth. He was like a wisp blown by the wind, resting nowhere, happy nowhere. He wondered if he could ever rest again; if he would ever be happy again. He thought that his only chance of happiness would come from seeing that his children were happy

The muscles of his back were aching. Already? With many more hours of rowing so that they might find safety. The moon was shining directly on his face.

The woman looked at him. She felt the soft breath of the sleeping girl on her cheek. Remembered how long a time ago it was that you could just fall asleep as if you had been hit on the head.

She liked the look of the man's face. It was a thin face. You could see all the bones of it, a well-shaped head, with the hair tied close to it, rising from a strong neck. But there were sorrow lines on his face. She could see that, the pucker between his eyes and the way his eyebrows slanted down.

'Your wife is dead?' she asked softly.

'My wife is dead,' he answered.

It silenced her, the finality with which it came from him, as if it was dragged from way down in him. She thought: Suppose I was dead and somebody had asked my husband, Walter. Would he be able to answer like that? Her lips curled in disdain. Then she thought of the great figure of Murdoc standing facing Coote in that hall. His one encompassing glance at her tied there at the fireplace. And she knew. Even before he did, she knew that he was going to do it. Her heart had started a slow pound. She wasn't surprised at his actions. She just knew. His strong grim laughing face was implanted for ever on her memory. She wanted to see him again. She didn't care what she had to go through as long as she could see him again.

All Dominick could see of her was the white blur of her face as she turned it into the shadow of the boat. She was asleep, her face close to Mary Ann's. He felt with his hand behind on Peter's shoulder and then to his face. His eyes were closed.

Dominick dug in his feet and squeezed his hands on the oars and pulled away.

He remembered about coming to the place where the river and the lake met. He had trouble getting through it. There were many shallow places, but he guessed his way by the rushes and broke into an expanse where a great sheet of water lay basking under the moonlight. It looked very big and very frightening. But there was no wind and the way was smooth and he headed into it.

He consulted the rough chart when he was about half way across, and he prayed that the moon and its light would stay with him. He rowed for many hours, until his hands were two gaping aches. He came out of the wide water into the narrow places where black rocks poked up their ugly sharp heads over the water, and where many of them lurked just under the water. But there had been a lot of rain before the fine, and the water was high and covered most of them well. He twisted and wound through these narrow places with his heart in his mouth as he watched the moon getting bigger and bigger and lower and lower in the sky, but the luck was with him because just as the moon departed, right behind him a narrow band of dawn-light appeared in the sky and in front of the light he saw the black of the trees, a grand comforting black band of trees stretching for many miles along the shore, and he headed for those across a very wide bay, and was almost too tired to rejoice when the keel of the boat grated on the soft shingle.

CHAPTER EIGHTEEN

HE AWOKE with a start. The sun had cleared the tops of the trees and was shining in his eyes. He didn't think that was why he awoke. He listened. Away from over the water, he thought he heard a sound. He couldn't identify it. He sat up on his bed of pine needles and threw off the blanket. He stood and he groaned, as the muscles in his back screamed for him.

They were in a sheltered bay. The arm on his left poked out into the lake and cut off his vision of the narrows. He looked at the other blanket-covered forms. He would leave them for the moment. Judging by the height of the sun he could have been asleep only for about two hours.

He looked around him. They were sheltered in a belt of tall pine trees. Some of them were straight and some of them were contorted. Closely planted as they were, most of the lower branches had died. He picked the tallest one and started to climb. He groaned as his aching muscles revolted. The weeping resin from the bark stuck to his hands uncomfortably. The open blisters of his palms didn't like the sting of the resin.

He came to the part of the tree where the branches were green and strong. He swung around the trunk so that he would not be visible from the water. The needles were sharp and stuck into him. When he was as high as he could go he parted some of the green branches and looked.

He saw two boats and they were very near to him, particularly the one on the left which was searching along by the shore. They were two long boats, each having six oars, with three men rowing and armed soldiers sitting in the stern. He heard voices now and the dull clump of the oars on the greased row-locks.

He came down from the tree fast, keeping on the hidden side of it. He thought how lucky they were. Another fifteen minutes and they would have been caught. Even now they weren't out of danger.

He bent over the woman. 'Wake up,' he said. His hand was hovering ready to clap it over her mouth. The dark eyes looked at him blankly and then recognition dawned in them. 'They are close,' he said. 'Get up and go back farther into the wood with the children.'

She nodded her head, threw off the blanket, and for the first time he could look at her in the light. Her black shining hair was tied in plaits. One of them had come loose. She had a good forehead, a curved nose, a wide face, and a strong chin. She didn't show fear in her eyes. You could rely on her. Her hands were small and soft, he could see, the hands of a non-worker, but they looked capable. When she stood he thought she looked odd in the thick clothes, as if she was dressed for a part which didn't belong to her. Indeed he could smell the fish, he thought, mixed with pine needles.

He was shaking Mary Ann awake. So used to being in trouble, Mary Ann awoke alert and prepared. He told her.

'All right, Daddy,' she philosophically. 'I'll get Pedro.'

He went back to the boat. It was a heavy boat. You'd want three men to pull it up on the shore. He decided not to try. He took the oars out of it and threw them on the shore. Then he pushed the boat out and jumped into it as it went into deep water. He could see the bottom. It was about six feet deep. He balanced himself on the boat and then walked on the freeboard. It went under water. He kept standing there until the side went under the water and the lake started to pour into it. It took a long time to fill. He kept standing there until it swamped and sank under him. A few strokes took him to the shore.

He shook himself like a dog. Their belongings were piled under a tree. He didn't remove them. He took the blankets and threw them over them, and then covered the blankets with old tree branches and the young growing ferns and green alder branches which he hastily tore from their stems. He looked around once more and then went into the wood carrying the oars. Farther in he hid them in the scrub. He whistled softly and heard Mary Ann's low call. He found them deeper in the trees. They were crouching behind a briar thicket in an open part of the wood.

'Listen,' he said, 'We should be safe. If they come in and find anything, I will attract their attention. While they are chasing me you three go back farther into the wood, as far as you can go, and when you come out of the wood keep going until you meet people, a house. They tell me all the people on the shores are true. All right?'

165

'We'll see,' the woman said.

'You'll see nothing,' he said. 'You'll do what you're told.'

He saw her lips tightening.

'I'm not thinking of me,' he said. 'I'm not thinking of you either. I'm thinking of my children.'

'All right,' she said. 'We'll run.'

He lay flat. He could see their little bay. The water was blue. There was already heat in the sun.

He saw the bow of the boat come across the point. He could hear the voices. The boat turned in towards the shore. They went right along by it keeping about ten yards off. If they had seen the boat? If they had been sleeping there? If anything? It didn't really matter. There was no use bothering your brain with ifs. The soldiers could have seen the sunken boat, he was sure, if they were looking down. They didn't see it. They circled the bay and went out of sight again. He could see the other boat now over on the far side skirting the small islands on the opposite shore.

'What do we do now?' the woman asked.

'We do nothing,' Dominick said. 'We stay here and wait until the boats come back again.' They wouldn't go much farther. They would know there was just one man to row, since it was a single-handed craft. They would know damn well how far one man could travel in the time since the boat had been reported gone. They would go another few miles and then return and give every little bay and beach a thorough searching on the way back to the town.

'I'm going to sleep,' he said. 'I need sleep. Call me when they come back.'

He rested his cheek on the back of his hands. He relaxed his body and he slept.

The woman watched him. She could only see the back of his head. He wore no shirt. His body was still wet from the water. His breeches were beginning to steam in the sun.

'Your father is a brave man,' she said to Mary Ann.

'He's very useful,' said Mary Ann, 'but he rushes around a lot.'

'How long has he been rushing around now?' she asked.

'Oh, ever since I can remember,' said Mary Ann. 'Ever since they cut Peter's head and Mammy died. Show Columba your scar, Pedro.'

Pedro was quite pleased to show his scar. He lifted back his long fair hair. She put her hand on his head. He was smiling at her.

'Who did that to you?' she asked.

'He doesn't talk,' said Mary Ann. 'Since he got that, he doesn't talk any more.'

'Doesn't talk any more?' Columba asked.

Peter was smiling at her. He nodded his head.

'Daddy says it's just as well,' said Mary Ann. 'He says I talk enough for two.' Columba laughed, but it was rueful. You think you have troubles, she thought, until you hear about other people's troubles.

'Tell me more about what you remember,' she said.

Mary Ann was only too pleased to tell her. Mary Ann loved to talk, and Pedro loved to listen. So she talked, and talked, while her father slept and their enemies scoured the bays on the blue water and sweated like pigs under the hot sun, and searched in vain.

It was early morning. The sun was bright already. The sky was clear and blue. There was a healthy south-west wind that ruffled the water, so that low waves sparkled in the sunlight.

Dominick walked the shore. He had floated a line and walked against the waves. The weighted board out from him travelled like a leaky ship, plodding and lopsided, but it made the three roughly fashioned flies hop on the tops of the waves, he thought, like three drunken old ladies doing a dance. He had to laugh at the thought. The shore he walked on was rough with round rocks and sometimes spiky ones biting into his bare feet. He heard Peter behind him hitting his hands three times off his thigh. He looked at him. The boy caught his eyes and pointed west.

Dominick paused in his walking and looked. Ahead of them he could see the land on each side beginning to rise to the low hills until eight or ten miles away they met at a conjunction of real tall ones with tapering peaks, their tops pale blue against a deep blue sky. The narrowing lake down there seemed to be a finger pointing at them.

'That's where we are going, Pedro,' he said. 'Right down there. Right into the middle of the big fellows.'

Pedro clapped his thigh four times.

Dominick laughed, started to walk, and then the pull on the line almost cut his hand in two. He looked. One of his flies had gone and the board was soughing and weaving sullenly. Peter was jumping up and down on the stones clapping his hands.

Dominick started to pull the line towards him. He could see the golden gleam of the struggling fish as he came into the shallower water. He pointed then, and Peter plunged in until the water was to his knees. Dominick kept the strain on the fish and eased him in until he was in front of Peter. Peter crouched, his palms held together, then suddenly darted them down and scooped with them, and much water and a still struggling fish came out of the lake and hit Dominick in the face. The fish rebounded off him. He shouted, startled, but had enough good sense, although half-blinded with the water, to bend down, catch the fish by the tail and throw him farther up on the shore. He was a good fish. He had a small head and a fat body, and he was beautifully speckled with a deep golden sheen on his belly.

Pedro was still in the water. He was laughing. He was bending his body up and down. Dominick spluttered again, a bit exaggerated for his benefit, shook his fist at him, and then freeing the fish from the hook hit his head on a stone until his struggling ended. He held him up. 'Look, Pedro,' he said, 'isn't he lovely?' Pedro looked at him and started to come ashore rubbing his stomach. The line was twisted into a million tangles. Dominick freed it and floated it again and had hardly walked six yards when another trout struck him. Pedro gleefully took to the water again, but before he could scoop this one, Dominick, trusting to the strength of his home-made tackle, switched him on to the shore where the fish floundered most ignominiously. This was a good fish too but it wasn't as heavy as the first one.

'It will do for the ladies,' said Dominick. 'They have delicate appetites.' He won another silent laugh from his son, who, while Dominick gathered and rolled his line around the board, stuck a forked branch through the gills of the fish. They set off back from the shore. They had to break their way through thick alder bushes, willow, and beech scrub before they came into the peace of the woods, where tall, branchless trees reared high over their heads. The ground was like a thick carpet with the long years of fallen leaves and pine needles and rotted branches, with short green grass, smothered in the shade, and wide stretches of a tiny purple-blossomed flower. It was very peaceful, Dominick thought, and for the first time for a long while his heart was light. He had climbed a tree earlier in the morning and on that great body of water, with its many tree-covered islands, he had seen no sign of a boat or smoke, or a single human being. The island was large, but it held no humans, no animals. It seemed to be just a sanctuary for birds, who were scolding them since they landed last night, and very daring in their approach. Because there is no human being near us, therefore we can relax and afford to be happy, he thought. What a terrible reflection! Where man is, there you have to be afraid again; you have to be on your guard constantly. Why couldn't we be like the birds, who fly and search for food, and go to sleep and wake up and start the day over again? That must have been the way man was meant to live too. Like the birds, is it? Then how about their fear? Fear of hawks, or eagles, or rats, or bigger birds? Enough of that now, stick to your first thought, and hold on to your happiness.

Peter had run ahead of him as they laboured up a steep incline. He had reached the top and was standing there waving the fish whose still fresh colours flashed in the sun. Then he was gone and Dominick plodded after him.

He reached the top of the incline and looked below. There was a natural sandy bay down there, sheltered by trees. There was an oval-shaped beach of white sand. The water was glassy calm because the wind was shut off from it. The sun was higher than the trees now, and shone blindingly on the sand. He could see Mary Ann standing up with her hands behind her back and the woman squatting down blowing at a smoking fire, and Peter flying towards them with a fish waving over his head. The red skirt of the woman made a splash of brilliant colour on the sand. For a moment as he paused, he thought, if she were Eibhlin, she would turn and come walking towards me, or even running, and there would be true happiness then to look into his eyes and watch her laughter. Then he sighed and put the thought out of his head and came down to them.

The woman was on her knees, blowing at the wood fire. Her cheeks were red from her efforts, and her forehead and chin were black with wood ashes. She looked very exasperated.

'It's no good, Daddy,' said Mary Ann. 'I'm afraid she's useless.' But the woman was determined.

'I'm going to light this cursed fire,' she said, 'if I have to blow myself inside out.'

'But if you never lit a fire in your life,' Mary Ann asked in a maddeningly reasonable way, 'how are you going to light this one? I'm hungry.'

Suddenly the woman sat back on her heels and started laughing. Her eyes were closed, her throat was working.

'She's right,' she said then. 'May the devil blast it. You do it, Dominick.' She lay back on the sand. Dominick bent over the ill-assorted sticks and started to rearrange them.

'What's a gentlewoman, Daddy?' Mary Ann asked him.

Dominick thought over that one. He answered between puffs that brought the greedy yellow flames licking at the wood.

'A gentlewoman,' he said, 'is a woman who is gentle, who learns to have good manners, to be courteous to others, to be kind to servants.'

'But she doesn't do any work, that's it,' said Mary Ann. 'Columba is a gentlewoman, she says. Can you sew, Columba?'

'Not very well, Mary Ann,' she answered.

'Can you gut a rabbit?' asked Mary Ann.

'Certainly not, how horrible!' said Columba.

'You can't grind corn or bake a cake or sew a cut or make a dress or put leather on a shoe, lots of other things you can't do. What's the use of being a gentlewoman?'

'You have a fearful daughter,' said Columba.

'She's like a nauseating purgative,' agreed Dominick.

'Gentlewomen decorate the world, Mary Ann,' said Columba. 'When their husbands come home tired from work or war, they are there to greet them with soft hands and rustling silk garments and sweetly smelling flesh. They are there to titillate their tired palates with tasty dishes made from ingredients brought from far-off lands.'

'But they don't even cook the dainty dishes,' said Mary Ann.

'Certainly not,' said Columba. 'That's what servants are for. Would you keep a dog and bark yourself? Wouldn't you like to be a gentlewoman, Mary Ann?'

'And do nothing all day, except wait for a man to come home? What would you be doing while you were waiting?'

'My goodness,' said Columba, 'millions of things: polishing your fingernails, bathing, studying a little Latin, a little Greek, reading a little literature, visiting friends or having them visit you, using the switch on the backside of a lazy maid, finding out things about your neighbours, walking on the green, watching young men at bowling or jousting, or letting them hold your hand for a little as they picked up your fallen handkerchief, listening to love songs on the lute in the evenings. My dear Mary Ann, the day is far too short for the doings of a gentlewoman.'

'It's no wonder you can't light a fire,' said Mary Ann. 'That's all I can say. It seems to me that gentlewomen are just no use.'

'Talking about gutting, Man,' said Dominick, 'how about cleaning the fish?'

'All right, Daddy,' said Mary Ann, picking them up and walking towards the water. Peter took a knife from his belt and followed her. Mary Ann turned on the way. Mary Ann would always turn on the way, Dominick thought with a grin. 'I just don't want to be a gentlewoman,' she said.

'You won't,' Dominick shouted at her. 'Never fear.'

Columba leaned on her elbows.

'As she stands now,' said Columba, 'Mary Ann knows far more than I do. Did you long for war to come?'

'God forbid,' said Dominick.

'I did,' she said. 'I was so bored. Mary Ann is right, you know. Times I would just be fit to burst with the things I was doing. They were nothing, nothing. War was excitement, the siege was an excitement.'

'Did you love your husband?' Dominick asked.

'No, I did not,' she said. 'It was a business arrangement. Something to do with my father's ships and Walter's connections in France or Spain or somewhere. When you belong to the tribes they have you married before you are born.'

'You are a spirited young woman,' he said. 'You could revolt.'

'No,' she said. 'They have you conditioned. Besides, no one else attracted me. They all seemed to be out of the same mould, smelling of ships or spices or tobacco or wine. That's all they had in their veins, commerce and profits and guilds and watery blood and pride. I tell you Murdoc was the first man I ever saw in my whole life.'

'No man is perfect,' he said. 'Remember that.'

'Who wants perfection?' she asked scornfully. 'It's so boring.'

'Listen,' he said. 'This is not an adventure we are engaged in. It is real.'

'That's why I like it,' she said. 'I like to feel that I am in

171

danger. I like to feel the people around me are in danger. Doesn't it add a little spice to life?'

'I thought you got too much of the spices,' he said.

She laughed.

'I don't know what I want,' she said. 'I was spoiled. I don't know. I never felt I was living. I never thought the people around me were anything but – well, puppet people. Somebody was always pulling somebody else on a string.'

'What you are going into now,' he said, 'is real. It's more real than you think. It's something you have never been reared for. This life that you will have to live now will be against all the principles of your upbringing.'

'Welcome! Welcome! Welcome!' she said, her hands held clenched to her breast.

He said no more.

It was still pleasant. They ate the fish with their fingers. The flesh of the fish was pink and it tasted good. Later they raised and launched the boat and set out on the long pull towards the mountains.

Dominick's muscles were no longer hurting. His hands had hardened. He could row and look around him without the breath being tight in his chest. The wind was on their right, so if anything it assisted the pulling of the boat. They were jolly. Mary Ann sang a song in her thin treble voice, and Columba sang too in a husky throaty way. They were odd songs. They were in English. Mary Ann said they were pale songs, all about lovers and things. They lacked blood, Mary Ann said. Columba said Mary Ann's Irish songs were too sad for a bright day. Behind him Dominick would hear Peter thumping the side of the boat with the flat of his hand to indicate something that moved him to joy. He would look around then. One time, when they had left the real width of the lake and were going up the narrow place towards the gap between the hills, on rocky land built high out of the water they saw a great stag, an Irish deer. They passed under him, looking up at him towering on his peak. They could see the white under his neck and down into his chest. He remained there unmoving until they called and whistled and hurrooed, and finally he moved away disdainfully, leaving the high prominence bare and lonely. Dominick was sorry they had sent him away.

As they moved farther down, they came where there were mountains on each side of them. The ones on the left were bare and bleak and rocky, lonely-looking and frightening. Their slopes were wooded below, and high over their gleaming rocky heads on two occasions they saw the eagles soaring with ease. On the right of them the mountains were more verdant, green almost all the way to the tops of them, with patches of deep woods, dark green splotches on their sides, and grazing mountain sheep peppered all over them as if somebody had shaken them from a blanket.

No house to be seen. No sign of a human being. No smoke rising to the sky. It was very lonely. And yet Dominick had the feeling that they were being watched, that every mountain peak had a pair of eyes, every crevice in the hills, all the deep gullies cut into the sides of the mountain like black wounds.

And they felt small in their little boat on the water in this immensity, alien intruders in a place that had been here before man, would be here when he was gone, and could only be conquered by a cataclysm.

They passed the ruins of a castle on an island. Once it had towered to the sky, but it had been unroofed and its battlements destroyed, and its stones thrown down, and through the slotted windows you could see the black burned beams and baulks and indeed smell its destruction as you passed by.

Acres and acres of rushes opened before them and they worked their way through these until they were on the gently flowing depths of a broad river. It twisted and wound lazily with the mountains towering over their heads, closing them in and then opening up again as it meandered into a great valley, where its deeps gave way to shallows of yellow piled gravel and rocks. Some parts of it they barely scraped by, and finally they had to stop where the river became a stream, a bare trickle of water, and their heavy sturdy boat could go no more. So Dominick landed on a gravel bed and held the boat steady while the rest of them alighted.

They were on a heather-covered shore, with stretches of low alder bushes kept dwarfed by the winds that would sweep down the valley. Ahead of them a blunt hill rose towering and black as if to bar any further progress.

It seemed to them as they stood there, lonely and lost, that there hadn't been a sinner place foot on this piece of ground since the beginning of time, when right in front of them from a low rise emerged the head and shoulders of a man and another one and another one and another one and then many of them, and then they stood tall, and they were very tall, they looked like giants standing on their hill regarding the strangers, and they were armed men and they weren't Murdoc's men and there were no pleasant looks on their faces and no greetings in their armed hands.

We are back with the people again, Dominick thought resignedly, as he watched their leader approach menacingly.

CHAPTER NINETEEN

HE WAS a very big man. He was half naked. He wore trousers and soft cowhide boots of untanned leather. They had been cut from the hide of a red and white cow. The hair was not worn off them yet. He had a mop of brown curly hair and a fair generous moustache. He wore a knife in his belt as well as a sword. His arms were huge. They were burnt by the sun like his chest and the muscles were leaping in them. He had a good square face. It could contain kindness, Dominick thought, as he watched him coming towards them, and then the rhyme came into his head about 'Beware of that man though he be your brother whose hair and moustache differ in colour', and he couldn't help it. He had to laugh.

If he had discharged a musket he couldn't have had a greater effect. The man stopped still and furrows gathered between his eyes, and his lips tightened over big white teeth.

'What do you find to laugh at, little man?' he asked in Irish. He had a deep voice rumbling from his chest.

I can hardly tell him why, Dominick thought. It's too subtle even for myself.

'I laugh,' he said, 'at the sight of big men like you over-powering a few small people like us. It would only take one of you.'

'You are a foreigner?' the man asked.

'If being born and living in your own country is being a foreigner,' said Dominick, 'I'm a foreigner. I'm an Irishman.'

'Irish, English, what's the difference? Did you get permission to come into this land?'

'Are you of Murdoc O'Flaherty?' Dominick asked. The man paused and then spat. 'I see you are not,' conceded Dominick. 'Well, he invited us into this land.'

'He has a right to invite you into his own land, maybe,' said the man, 'but this is our land. This is the country of the Joyces. You were not invited here.'

'Are the Joyces such savages,' asked Dominick, getting a little angry, 'that they menace every fellow countryman that passes through their land?'

'The Joyces are not savages,' the other said. 'They are a civilized race who know what belongs to them and intend to keep it that way. There are too many people creeping into the land of the Joyces like wolves and taking possession of what doesn't belong to them. What clan are you of?'

'I'm of the Clan of Ireland,' said Dominick.

'Be more particular,' the other said, sliding a sword from its scabbard and waving it suggestively.

'My name is MacMahon,' said Dominick.

'A fairly evil name,' said the other. 'We have heard of many of that tribe who came raiding into us from the north.'

'Wake up,' said Dominick. 'We are in the seventeenth century. There is a black cloud over our land. It encompasses the whole lot of us. It doesn't just wave over the Joyces or the MacMahons. It is over the whole land. That's what makes us brothers. That's what should make us one clan, not a bunch of uncivilized cattle-raiders.'

'This is our land,' said the other. He was becoming heated too. 'And we intend to hold it against all comers, every stone and blade of grass in it. We've seen it happen. Drive them into Connacht at whose expense, ask me? At our expense. To take what belongs to us. They can come, you hear, but they are not going to stay. They'll go the way they came. You came on our river, without permission. Do you know the penalty for that?'

'No,' said Dominick. 'Please tell me.'

'We kill the males and ravish the females,' he said. His eyes moved past Dominick to where Columba stood holding Mary Ann's hand.

'And do you roast the children on spits,' Dominick asked, 'to see if they have Irish fat in them? You listen to me! We have travelled a long way. It has been to us like walking on the way to Calvary, only we thought that at the end there would be no cross, but peace from the hands of our fellow countrymen. We expected nothing from the beasts of Cromwell, and we got nothing. We expected more from our own kind, but how were we to know that they were as bad as the others? Civilized. You're not civilized. If you had a tail you'd be swinging off a tree. Do you hear that?'

Columba held her breath. He wants to get us killed, she thought. Has he gone mad? He looked mad. His legs were spread. His face was red. There were sparks coming out of his eyes.

176

The big man looked at him for a moment, then he turned his head and addressed his fellows behind him. He saw they were grinning. He grinned himself.

'He wants to dance,' he said to them, 'the little cock wants to dance.'

He turned back to Dominick. Suddenly the sword swung.

It went around his head. It described a parabola of light in the sunshine. It nearly cut the hair on the top of Dominick's head, so close it came, and Dominick didn't flinch, and then the man roared: 'Now, dance,' and the sword swung low. Dominick in the split second before he acted knew that if he didn't act his legs would be severed at the knees, because he thought no swordsman could halt the swing of the heavy sword in time.

So he jumped.

There was a loud laugh from the Joyce men, but then as soon as he jumped Dominick ran, and butted his man in the belly with his head. That knocked the sword from his hand and the wind from his body; and as his hands reached to cover his belly, Dominick took a grip of his arms, fell on his back, stuck his feet into the injured belly, levered with his legs, and the man, big and tall as he was, went flying over his head to land with a back-breaking thump on the bank of the river.

Dominick was up and reaching for the sword almost as soon as he hit the ground. He got his hand to the hilt of it, but before he could raise it he felt the point of a knife pricking at his neck. He stayed still.

And then from behind them there came a deep voice from the other side of the river.

'Use the knife, Traolac, and you die.'

Dominick felt the point lifting, and turned his head. Morogh Dubh was standing there. His hands were on his hips, but there were about ten men behind him who didn't have their hands on their hips. Two of them had muskets and they were taking aim.

Dominick rose slowly. Traolac released the grip he had on him. What's wrong with me? Dominick wondered. Why did I do a thing like that? Why did I lose my temper? I could have talked my way out of trouble easy enough. He went over to his children. They were frightened. The eyes of the woman were frightened too.

'I'm sorry,' he said to them. 'I'm sorry.'

Peter took his hand. Held on to it. Dominick was trembling. He turned to Morogh.

'Thank you for coming in time,' he said.

'Have they injured any of you?' Morogh asked.

'No,' said Dominick, 'only our feelings.'

'They can be repaired,' said Morogh. 'You did a foolish thing, Diarmuid,' he said to the man who was raising himself from the ground rubbing his spine. 'They have Murdoc's protection. He's not a man to anger.'

Surprisingly, Diarmuid laughed.

'To the devil in hell with Murdoc and his anger,' he said. 'The little man is the one not to anger.' He came over towards Dominick still rubbing his back. 'How did you do that?' he asked. 'It was a brave trick. You must teach it to me. Sure, you knew we were only having a game?'

'Were you?' Dominick asked. 'It seemed very real to me.'

'Maybe it was,' said Diarmuid, 'part of it. You have a nice wife.' He was looking at Columba. His eyes were crinkling. He was smiling. 'It would have been a pleasure to ravish her.' Columba tried to keep her face frozen, but the blood rose in her cheeks. She bit her lip. 'See, she has forgiven our jape,' he went on. 'You must too. They will have a new old saying in the language after today. You'll see. They will say that such a thing or such a person is nearly as good as the little man. Eh?' He held out his hand. Dominick looked at it for a moment. Then he put his own hand into it. The huge one closed on his. But it was a warm clasp and sincere. Isn't that the curse of us, he thought; one minute we are like murderers and the next minute we would charm the birds off the trees?

Diarmuid spread his arms wide.

'So now, Morogh, you see we are all friends again and the MacMahons have licence to walk every inch of the Joyce country without a sinner to say them nay.'

'As long as they have armed men at their backs,' said Morogh grimly.

Diarmuid thought this was funny. He slapped his thigh.

'I don't mind that,' he said, 'if they bring their own food.'

'Bring up the little horses,' said Morogh to one of his men. 'You are getting careless too, Diarmuid,' he said. 'Eleven of us came within a birdshot of you and you had no guard out.'

Diarmuid spread his arms wide.

'The Joyces are civilized people,' he said, 'and not only that but they are filled with trusting good nature. Why should they set out guards against their friends from Rin Mhil?'

Morogh grunted.

The man had brought up two of the grey horses. 'Tie your bundles on to one of them,' Morogh said to Dominick.

Dominick went into the stream and started to unload the boat.

Diarmuid was full of charm now. He bent in front of Mary Ann.

'Did we frighten you?' he asked

'Yes,' said Mary Ann.

'We didn't mean to,' he said. 'What's your name?'

'Mary Ann,' she said. 'You nearly killed my daddy.'

'Excuse me, Mary Ann,' he said, 'your daddy nearly killed me. You must come and see us, and bring your mother.' He was looking at Columba admiringly. She looked straight back at him.

'Unfortunately,' she said in English, 'I am not her mother.'

He was taken aback. 'Oh,' he said, 'you are not the wife of the little man?' The English words were slow on his tongue.

'No,' she said.

'And who are you the wife of?' he asked.

'You wouldn't know,' she said.

'I am wanting a wife,' he said then.

'You will be wanting,' she said. He laughed. She laughed.

'Now,' Morogh called, 'we are ready.'

They crossed the river. There were two free horses. Morogh helped Columba on to one of them, stepped back to see that she could handle him well, and then mounted his own, leaned down and hefted Peter on to the horse behind him. Dominick bent to Mary Ann and mounted her in front of him and the band of horsemen set off across the valley towards a high hill in front of them.

Dominick turned to look.

Diarmuid was standing there still. When he saw Dominick looking he waved his hand. Dominick jerked his head at him. He wasn't going to forgive him that easily. He saw Columba looking too. She got a wave, and she waved back. She was near to Dominick.

He saw the way her eyes were glinting.

'I suppose you enjoyed all that,' he said a trifle sourly. She looked at him.

'Yes, I did,' she said. 'I enjoyed it.'

'I suppose you call that really living,' he said.

'Well, you started it,' she said a trifle indignantly.

Dominick was silent.

'Well, it's true for her, Daddy,' said Mary Ann. 'You los your temper again.'

'Go on up out of that!' said Dominick, digging his bare heel: into the warm sides of the little horse.

CHAPTER TWENTY

THE COUNTRY through which they travelled induced silence in them. They followed the course of the river down the valley, crossing and criss-crossing its shallow bed where it meandered in their way. The horses were very sure-footed and sturdy.

Then their way rose out of the valley between two sets of hills towards a gap that reared high in the air above them. The ground became stony and between the stones it was soft. Sometimes the hooves of the horses went deeply in, almost throwing the riders, and were delicately extracted with a sogging sound. Only where they passed through wooded paths was the ground hard under them and the horses walked eagerly on the pine needles. The sun was shut off from them. The mountains on the left of them reared away tall and black and shadowed, but streams seamed their sides, fell freely, and catching the light flashed occasionally like diamonds glittering under a torch light.

The horses picked their way with great intelligence – more intelligence than he himself could have shown, Dominick thought. Places he would have avoided they moved over freely, and the places that looked good to him, he saw, were truly dangerous. With no saddle under them it took quite an effort of the thighs to hold on as the horse struggled upwards. His was a grey horse. He had a short silvery mane to which Mary Ann held tightly. The woman was riding ahead of him. He could admire her. She was used to horses, he saw. He could see her face as she looked around her. Her eyes were glinting. She drew deep breaths into her lungs. She liked it. She would approve of everything.

For himself, he felt gloomy. The height of the shaded mountains depressed him. They looked lonely and forbidding. He thought of the way the wind would roar down the valleys in the wintertime. He supposed it was only natural to feel depressed now that they were on the last leg of their roaming. The roughly clad men ahead of him and their shouting and calling seemed queer in his eyes and ears. He tried to feel that they were his people and he was theirs, but it was difficult. It would take time to get to know them. It would take time to know how to live with mountains.

Then with a final spurt they got into the gap and the declining sun shone full in their faces.

Here in the gap there were other men sitting as their horses cropped at the coarse grass. They rose and greeted Morogh and his men with shouts. They had three large wolfhounds with them, great dogs almost as tall as the little horses, with shaggy hair, small heads and melancholy eyes. Some of them barked. They had a deep bark, like a sound passing through a tunnel. There were two dead stags lying on the ground.

Dominick looked ahead of him and sucked in his breath. The ground fell away steeply in front of them. It was cut into a gorge in the middle by a river that ran madly from a great height on the right of them. And it ran down and down towards the sea. The sea it was. Unrippled, flaming with colour as the sun prepared to bury itself in it. He could see it pushing its way like a broad thread far into the land between high hills, like a wide river of immense power laced with black seaweed-covered rocks. The finger of sea wound away until the mountain on his right cut it from his sight. Two long blue lakes lay below at their feet. They were backed by two mountain peaks, and beyond the mountains was the wide sea with a big island and a small island and many black unconquerable rocks.

Peter was looking back at him. When he caught his eye he raised his hands over his head and clapped them three times, then he pointed back. Dominick turned. He looked the way they had come. He saw Loc Orbsen, over which they had travelled, spread out like a great blue and green tapestry, with the mountains cupping it at this end, and reaching away into the misty flat lands on the other side. It is a wild and beautiful land this, he thought, and then looking at the big men around them in their coarse clothes, with their rough hair and beards, hairy men, big laughing men with white teeth, he thought: This is the kind of men they have to be in a land like this.

There was a pile of brush and gorse near where the dogs were. They set fire to this from a flint, and it roared and smoked, and since there was no wind it went straight into the sky, and then, after a pause, from the high hill directly opposite them another tall plume rose in the air. So Morogh called and shouted and waved his big arm and the horses set off down the incline, and Dominick had the feeling that if they fell all of them would fall straight down into the long lakes below them. But the brave little horses were as sure as hares and they negotiated rock and bog and loose stones and the knee-high heather on the good lands, until they reached the left lake below and skirted its north shore. Here they were shut off again from the sun by the rearing mountains, but they moved around it and came on solid land where there were the makings of a road kicked out by the sharp hooves of the small mountain sheep, who had black faces and horns and looked curiously at the cavalcade passing them by; no more curiously than their young attendants, who laughed and exchanged rude remarks, or flung a stone at a horse, to be chased by one of Morogh's men, running with flying brown legs into a soft patch of bog where they could not be reached and then sticking out red tongues. Mary Ann didn't approve of them.

The sun was a red fire that had been lost in the sea, and all around them the sky was aflame with its last burning rays, when they came to the end of the wide peninsula and saw ahead of them the cluster of stone and thatched buildings from which smoke was rising, and from which as they came closer the smell of roasting meat came to twist their guts and remind them of their hunger. Here in a sort of courtyard, with many small houses built as wings to a long house in the centre facing south, they dismounted very stiffly and, looking up, Dominick with a deal of pleasure saw the big figure of Murdoc standing in the open square doorway and saw his arms first on his hips and then spread wide as he came towards them.

'Dominick!' he said. 'My friend.' Dominick was looking up at him, marvelling again at how big he was. He wore a linen shirt opened half way down his chest. 'We saw the signal from Garran. The fatted calf is killed and roasting. I knew Coote wouldn't get you. Where is my beloved one?'

He looked around and then strolled towards the small figure of Mary Ann, bent and scooped her into his arms and planted a kiss on the side of her soft face. 'Man,' he said, 'you are the delight of my eyes.'

'Put me down, Murdoc,' said Man, 'you're very hairy.'

Murdoc laughed. All the men laughed. There was a crush in the yard, the smell of horse sweat and man sweat mingled with the smell of fat that was falling on the spit fire and sizzling there. He put her on her feet and bent over Peter.

'Pedro, Pedro,' he said. 'I am pleased to meet with you again. Soon you will be as high as your father, you are growing so.'

Peter was pleased to see him.

Dominick was watching him. He knew Murdoc was glad to see them. He knew that they were welcome, but he knew that the reserve in their welcome was a light in the eyes of Murdoc, and when he had greeted them like that he went over to Columba who was still sitting astride the horse. She was looking at Murdoc. Her eyes were bright. She saw him coming closer to her. From her height she could survey the courtyard. The sky and the mountain behind them seemed coloured a blue purple. In the open ways three great fires were burning. Over two of them oxen were roasting on big spits, and over another one was slung a round iron pot hanging from a great tripod. If you could distinguish smells at all you could smell boiling mutton from that one. The firelight was glinting on the sweating arms of men, on white teeth in laughing bearded faces. It was a wonderful sight for her. It was open, it was real, it wasn't polite at all. It seemed to take her back to some memory that was buried deep in her, something that she had wanted all her life, raw and real with no sweetmeats about it.

He was even better than her memories of him. The tremendous shoulders; the big head with the curling grey-black hair and the square resolute face, with the quirk of the heavy eyebrows that spoke of a touch of recklessness; of hidden fires that could ignite and burn and die again. She knew it would be like this. She felt her heart beating so that it almost suffocated her. He put one hand on the neck of the little horse and the other one on her knee.

'I am glad to see you,' he said, 'I waited hoping that you were safe. You are safe now. What I have is yours.'

She found it hard to talk to him.

He reached his arms and she put her hands on his shoulders. He held her close to him as he helped her down. For a short time her feet were not on the ground. They were so close she wondered if he could feel the pounding of her heart. He smiled at her, finally let her go and said: 'You are welcome, Mrs Walter Dorsi. You are safe here.'

Then she spoke. 'I hope I am not too safe,' she said.

He listened, then he laughed delightedly. He raised his hand and called, 'Sorcha! Marie! Catriona!' From behind him three women came to his call. They were dark girls, two of them, and the other was an older woman with grey hair. In Irish he said to them : 'Look after the woman. Give care to her and the two children. Go with them,' he said to Columba. 'They will look after you. They will take you to my own house. When you are ready we will eat.'

The two girls looked at her. She went with them. The grey-haired woman went over to Dominick, looked at the two children.

'Will they come with me?' she asked.

'Go with the lady,' said Dominick.

'Where will you be, Daddy?' Mary Ann asked.

'I will be with you,' he said, 'when I have spoken to Murdoc.' They went with the woman dutifully.

Murdoc was beside him again, hitting him on the shoulder.

'Isn't it great to see you, Dominick?' he said. 'When we were on the bad rations, I often thought of this day. I owe you a lot I want to repay you. Come with me!'

Dominick walked beside him. They went out of the court-yard and walked into the open, leaving the glaring firelight behind them. They climbed a rocky knoll out there and Murdoc pointed.

'There they are,' he said. 'The Beanna Beola. Some day I said you would have them at your back and you need never fear again. Is that true?'

Dominick looked. About ten miles away from him across a plain hidden in darkness, he could see the sharp bens reaching into the night sky.

'They are for ever anyhow,' said Dominick.

'And so are you,' said Murdoc. 'Did you have trouble getting away? Did Davie see you off? Were you lonely on the Orbsen lake?'

'We got away,' said Dominick. 'There was a fright or two, but not much. It was not lonely on the lake. It was a great peaceful place that crept into your heart.'

'What is the woman like, Dominick?' Murdoc asked. 'She wasn't brought up to things like that. I know them, these women with soft hands and silken dresses. What do they know about life? Tell me.'

'She is a brave woman,' said Dominick. 'She reminds me of you, Murdoc. She is eager for change. She is restless, like you.'

Murdoc laughed.

'That was the old Murdoc,' he said. 'Not any more. I'm

finished with wars and fighting other people's battles. Now I am fighting my own. I'm an old settled gentleman, Dominick, the paterfamilias, the chieftain of my clan, the benevolent despot. My muscles will get soft and my hair will grey and I will be at peace. All this peninsula, from here in the Beanna Beola, is me, and up to the Caol Shaile Ruadh where the river comes out of the Joyce country. This I will rule with peace and justice, and all the men in it. No more history for Murdoc. I'm a new man.'

'It's a great picture, Murdoc,' said Dominick, 'like the picture that a man would paint on a piece of canvas, but it is just as unreal. It is like the real thing, but somehow it's not the same'

'You shrewd cynical devil,' said Murdoc. 'I will prove all this to you. You won't know me. Wasn't I peaceful and quiet with Coote? I cooed to him like a dove. Now I will charm people with my voice and with the good intentions of my heart. Come, let us go back to the feasting. This is a night that will be remembered for ever in Connmaicnemara.'

He ran down the hillock. Dominick was too weary to run down after him, but he felt warm. The welcome of Murdoc was warm.

'Tomorrow,' said Murdoc, 'I will bring you to the spot that I have chosen for you. There you can build your house with a new life and be ever at peace, I promise you. No more raids, alarms, or excursions. You will be my liege man and I will guarantee you peace and prosperity whatever may befall. You believe me, Dominick?' He was holding out his hand. Dominick took it and smiled.

'I believe you, Murdoc,' he said. 'Your intentions are noble. I won't forget.'

'Good,' said Murdoc as he strode back towards the courtyard. There he set up a shout. 'All is well,' he roared at them. 'Commence the feast. Let no man close an eye until the dawn or be damned to him.'

Dominick walked with him into the square opening of the long house. It was a single-storey house built of coarse granite with great skill. It seemed as if it had been set into the ground from eternity. Inside torches were blazing on brackets and thick candles were lighted on the two long oak tables. At the far end of the room there was an elevation with one table stretching the breadth of the house, and at the longer end another table stretching the length of the house. There were rough benches to seat the feasters. On the floor there were spread fresh rushes and there were rush mats hanging on the walls to repel the dampness. In the very centre the roof showed a square opening, and under that a big fire was prepared of turf and timber, and as they entered it was lighted and it flamed and sent dancing shadows of the people on the walls. The place filled with thick smoke for a time and then it was sucked out as the flames roared in the fire. There were many people there. They set up a shout when Murdoc came in. There were barrels set around the walls and the men were dipping into them with wooden bowls and pewter mugs or crock cups. Murdoc headed up towards the top table.

As he went he called a man and he would say: 'This man is Feilim O'Maoilfabhuill, Dominick MacMahon. Feilim is my brehon. He is a just judge.' Dominick couldn't remember all their names, the ollamh O'Canavan, and Mac Giolla Ganain, master of the horse, and Odo O Dubhain who was a gallowglass and a wonder with a battleaxe. There was the poet-ollamh Mac Cille Ceallaigh. There were Ó Connachtain, O Maolcomair, O Allmhurain, O Tuathail, O Faoilean, O hAngli, O Daingean. Oldish men with white whiskers and young men with glittering eyes, big men and small men all smelling of beer or wine or uisge beatha. Some of them looked at him with suspicion, some with friendliness, some with apathy, but he was Murdoc's friend and they welcomed him somehow, however reluctantly, but they asked him no questions. They had their wives with them, or their daughters, dark-haired girls or fair-haired girls, all sunburned with gleaming teeth and bright eyes, well-built women, handsome girls, and all garrulous, because the place was a bedlam of sound. And Murdoc put him sitting beside him at his right hand and slapped his hand on the table and called for meat. And Dominick drank to get the taste of the smoking fire out of his throat, and it was fiery stuff and he coughed after it, but it seemed to bring the scene into perspective.

And he saw Columba coming in the opening, and she had a different dress on her. The Claddagh fisherwoman was left behind, and however she had managed it with her borrowed dress, she looked very different. She looked like a lady (what is a lady?). She was taller in it and her fine rounded shoulders were bare, and her flesh was white and pink and there was powder on her sunburned face. She had her long black waving hair hanging loose with a kind of gold ribbon tied around it at her forehead and then twisted around it as far as it fell on her back, so that the gold ribbon glittered and her black hair shone and she looked very good and her eyes glued themselves to Murdoc's and stayed there. He went to meet her and brought her with him and put her sitting at his left hand, and Dominick felt sad. (Why am I sad? We are here and we are safe. A new life is opening for us. But he thought for a minute that Columba looked like his Eibhlin. Just for a moment, but it couldn't be, because Eibhlin would have eyes only for him.) And Murdoc roared, 'Let the feasting begin.' And all of them sat down and big hot quarters of roasted oxen were laid in front of them that they could cut off pieces with their knives, and there was boiled mutton in a great dish, steaming, and there were sea fish on platters and speckled trout and salmon on platters too, and all the time there were attendants who filled an empty mug the minute the bottom of it appeared.

He looked for his children, thinking of them. He stood up and saw them and sat down, satisfied again. They were at the long table below. There were other children with them and the grey-haired woman was attending them. So he could go back to his eating and drinking. He was doing one because he was hungry and he was doing the other because he was feeling depressed. He couldn't understand this.

The night was always a mystery to him. Not the bits he remembered but the bits he forgot. He was conscious of Murdoc and Columba and they were like two intertwined nerves. He could almost feel their emotions. He could see their pauses as their hands touched when they reached for meat, how reluctant they were to break the touching of themselves.

There was rejoicing too. Men sang long verses of songs. And the poet-ollamh or the ollamh or the medical-ollamh spoke. There were poems and songs, and to his hazing brain the words beat in, that it was all the history of the O'Flahertys. They spoke and sang about the Muinntir Murchadha, the descendants of the kings, of their great chieftains who owned the land of Moy Seola until they were driven out by the De Burgos and carved a better land for themselves from Iar-Connacht – from Loc Orbsen to the sea. There were tales of battles and treachery and blood flowing freely, of the eyes of kings gouged out so that they could not reign; for no maimed king could reign. Murdoc of the Horse and Morogh of the Battleaxe, and long lists of all their sub-chieftains, from old times, so that every man there could see the high station he once owned in the land. It made them fiery. The songs of battle made them rise sometimes and shout at the top of their lungs, great war-cries that had come down to them, and Odo, the man who was great with the axe, leaped to his feet and had a double-headed battleaxe in his hand and he swung it as if it was a feather, until its flashing blades seemed like fire in the light of the torches, and then he fell under it and they laughed. He was drunk.

They were all drunk, including Dominick. Murdoc is trying to make a little kingdom, he thought, with his judges and his teachers and his master of the horse and his master of the battleaxes and his standard-bearer and his poets, and what were they now? The great tribe that had owned Gnomore and Gnobeg and Baile na hInse and Connmaicnemara, with all its seas and islands and inlets and the great lake of Orbsen, was no more. It was split into little petty holdings, poverty-stricken in comparison with the great time; rutted up into little pieces that would be like a pool broken by the throwing of flints into a calm surface.

He was on his feet and Murdoc himself called for a hearing for him. Oh, the things he said. He wanted a toast to the little men who had fallen, he cried, all the little unknown names, the little men with children, and sons of widows dragged to wars that were not of their making so that fat-bellied poets could write about their murderers. How about that, friends? Who destroyed Ireland? The O'Flahertys and the rest of the clans destroyed Ireland. They would rather be raping a woman or stealing a cow than fighting to make their country safe from the invader. Always it was that way. When great men rose up and joined in battle for their freedom, afterwards the victor or the vanquished would have to fight his way back through his own country to get to the safety of his home. Who would write great poems about the little men slaughtered on battle-fields not of their own choosing or making; who died so that their chieftain could have more cattle or more women?

There was a man on his feet coming towards him shaking his fist, shouting 'Sassenach! Sassenach!' And Murdoc was on his feet shouting: 'This man is my friend. He is under my protection. He who lays a hand on him lays a hand on me!'

'I am as good a man as any here,' the little, fiery, drunken Dominick was shouting. 'My people before me were big but they are not free from guilt. It only required us to depart from our own sins and be one people. Who then could have stood against us? Would the pale-faced hypocrites who now raped our land from shore to shore be able to resist us if we were one? But we weren't one. We didn't care what happened across the river or across the lake or across the mountain as long as there were plenty of our own women to rape; plenty of our own children to kill, plenty of our own cattle to run off with, and while we were doing that, killing and slaughtering the humble flower of our nation, we were opening every door to our own destruction. That's why I say : To hell with the O'Flahertys ! To hell with the O'Neills ! To hell with the O'Donnells ! To hell with every tribe that ever rutted and enslaved our land ! That's why I drink to the little splotches of blood where true men died not knowing what they died for, hoping it was for the good . . .'

The place was smothered, engulfed, exploding with sound. Greasy knives were waving in the air. Where it might have ended, who knows, if Dominick's overstuffed stomach and overdrunk brain didn't take that occasion to revolt, and he, red in the face with anger and drink keeled over, slid from the table, and lay like a dead man at Murdoc's feet.

Murdoc was laughing. That was why they became silent and went back to their places.

He bent. He had to get on one knee because he was not too steady himself and he lifted Dominick into his arms and he walked with him towards the door. 'Throw him to the dogs,' he was advised. He shook his head. 'He is a better man than you,' he answered. 'Who knows what food is in his words, even if they are too late?'

He walked with him into the fresh air. It seemed very fresh after the thick foetid atmosphere of the hot box inside. Walked with him outside the courtyard, and towards the hillock where they had viewed the mountains, and he placed him there on the cool stones. And Dominick groaned.

Murdoc felt the presence of Columba beside him. He stood. They could barely see the man stretched at their feet.

'He's a very fiery little man,' said Columba.

Murdoc chuckled.

'He's a very strange man,' he said. 'Sometimes he has the

sense of a philosopher, and at other times he has the rashness of a child. He is a good man. He will be of great benefit to the community.'

'If they don't kill him first,' said Columba.

They won't,' said Murdoc. 'All men admire courage.'

'As I do,' said Columba. 'I have seen a lot of it in the last week, more than in a lifetime.'

He caught her arm.

'You will grow with us too,' he said. 'You will become part of us. Is that so?'

'Yes,' she said. 'I will become part of you.'

And Dominick groaned again, and became partly sensible and wondered if his children were asleep and hoped they hadn't seen their father drinking, because, he thought, groaning again, Mary Ann will give me hell.

CHAPTER TWENTY-ONE

You stand on a rocky plateau with a high mountain at your back and a long small lake at your feet and as you look north you find the heavy mountains of the O'Maille's meeting your gaze, bluely and unflinchingly, with the harbour of Caol Shaile Ruadh at the feet of them. And if you shift your eyes along the winding length of the fjord-like place you will be confronted by the Devil's Mother, the vanguard of the mountains of Partry, who seems to be shaking a club at you. And at your right hand across a great boggy plain the Mamturc mountains are supporting you, and at your back you will be ever conscious of the bens of Beanna Beola. So here, enclosed by five mountain ranges, surely sufficient protection for any man of good will, you can build your house.

For you haven't long. It is June and the sun is shining, but the sun will not always shine and soon autumn will be here and the winds will be cold from the mountains and the sea, and after that the winter will be on top of you and if your house is not built and snug by then you will be surely in trouble.

This is going to be a good house, because this house is going to last for ever. So you knock the trees in the small wood half way up your mountain and you haul them down with the little grey horse you have bought, and first you build a crude shelter against the hill with rough stone walls and a roof of boughs and scraws, and here you sleep when the last light is gone from the sky, and you rise when the first light appears in the sky, and you take time for one meal at the end of the day and one to fortify yourself in the early morning.

You make a platform on wooden runners that will travel easily over the soft lands and you search for limestone. You will find very little of it, but what you find you bring back and you build a kiln and here you burn your stone until it is white and can be beaten into a powder. And you search for marl or dobe clay and from the shore of the lake below you get your sand, and then you start erecting the walls of your house out of what you can quarry : rough granite and the left-overs of the limestone, and slaty sandstone, and this you build on the solid rock under your feet and you bind the thick walls with the mortar you make, and with the help of the little willing horse hauling, and your son guiding the horse and your daughter cooking and foraging and asking questions and criticizing your work, the walls of that house begin to rise. It will be a good long solid house, and what's more it will have a chimney, not like those other places with the hole in the roof, where the rain and the wind can enter and blind your eyes with the blown-back smoke. And the chimney will start one-third of the way from the end gable so that the warmed rocks will throw out heat before and behind it, and when the house is hipped, you trim the great larch beams and light a big fire and scorch them in it so that they will be free from the worms and the beetles of decay.

So you raise your roof and bind cross-beams of scorched wood across the sloping upright ones and then you cut thick deep scraws from the top of the bog and you cover your roof from end to end with the scraws; and having done that, you can move from your crude shelter and take possession of the house, because it is getting late in the year and already the evening winds are cold and when the rain falls it seems always to be driven by a poking wind that searches you out wherever you are to persecute you.

You have had no hand from any man for this. Because you are a stranger in this land, and you talked too freely at one time, there is none to come and help you build your house. Sometimes they will pass by and walk around looking and saying little, particularly that Odo of the battleaxe, who is a huge gaunt man, with an unfriendly face and about eleven children, for each time he comes and fishes the lake below for the white trout or the salmon – for he is the fisherman for Murdoc – he seems to bring a different one with him, and they are all sons, louts and dumb thicks, according to your daughter who likes to be friendly with them, but they shy away from her as if she had a disease. But you get your straw for money, from a man called Awley O'Daigean, who has a place down near Sal Roc where he attends a new planter who has taken a house there near the sea, since no Irishman is permitted to own land or house within one mile of the sea around the whole coastline of Connacht.

So from him you get your wheaten straw. And you arrange it into neat bundles and bit by bit you pierce it into the underlying scraws and then you fashion a net with a wide mesh and you lace that over the whole of your thatch and you tie the net down with ropes to pegs that are jutting from your wall, so that you can say, 'Let the wind blow now, or the rain storm. I have built my house upon a rock and it is only God can shift it.'

Dominick sat on the rung of the crude ladder stuffing mortar near the place where the thatch joined the chimney. He paused for a few minutes to look around him. It was a cold day. He had to wear a coat with the collar of it turned up around his neck, for the wind was keen. The great stretches of bog around him were golden, because the sedge was turning. The wind was riffling it and it looked under the pale sun like miles of gold cloth with a brown background, that would be fit wearing for a king. But it was false because they said when the sedge is gold the belly of the beast is rumbling. That was the time when cattle had to be moved lower down to the grass lands to eat. He saw his daughter now, away down beyond the lake, and Peter with her. They were coming back with the precious cow. He thought the cow would have to be bedded down in the house with them at night soon, because otherwise the hungry wolves coming down from the mountains would get her. Later he would have to build a shelter against the house for her. Then he would have to burn and clear a few acres of ground and prepare it for spring sowing. Also he would have to purchase some sheep, maybe a pig or two, another cow, and his money was low. He thought that by this time next year they would have to live on what they could grow, and maybe that was no bad thing.

He flexed the muscles of his back. He remembered a time when he thought they would never move again. But now they were pliable and strong, and as he sat there on his roof and looked around him he realized that he felt happy. He hadn't had time to think at all, just to do. Now, for the first time for many years, he owned something, something he had built himself with his own strength and ingenuity. Of course even though he had built it it didn't belong to him. He was a holder of it, but, he thought grimly, it would take a good man to put him off it. He was in agreement with Murdoc. He was his tenant. Each year he would pay five pounds or in lieu its value in wheat or rye, grain or meat to be decided by the parties concerned. You could say that for the first time in his life he owned a bit of Ireland, a wild bit to be sure, and one that would take years to put heart into, so that it could be won back from the wilds and made to smile, but that was for the future, because it would smile, and when it did it would surely smile in a fair land.

He waved an arm. Man saw him wave and answered him, and then he set to work again with a sigh.

'I wish,' said Mary Ann as they trudged up the slope after the slowly ambling black cow, 'that there were more people around here that we could talk to. I'm getting tired of talking to just you and Daddy.'

Pedro ran forward on his bare feet, jumped on his hands, sprang from them and landed again on his feet. He beamed at her for approval.

'Anyone can do that,' she said, 'but what good is it? I wish Father Sebastian would come to us. I wonder if he is all right, Pedro.'

Pedro nodded his head vigorously, and then did a cartwheel with arms and legs.

'There is one of the O'Duane boys down with his father today,' she said, looking where the figure of a boy beside the lake was sitting on the rock working on a brown net. 'They're so stupid,' she said. 'They just look at you with their mouths open.' But she closed a bit on the cow and started edging her a little towards the lake.

The boy working at the net watched them approaching from under his eyebrows. He was a gangling boy with tumbling brown hair and bony limbs which when they filled out would make him a physical copy of his father. He had very clear eyes, red lips, and the down on his upper lip and chin was becoming noticeable. He glanced where his father, down at the lake shore, was hammering at a board at the stern of the boat, and then he concentrated on repairing the rents in the net with the brown line. He didn't look up when he felt they were near him.

'God bless the work,' he heard the girl's voice say in Irish, 'and what are you doing?' Such silly questions women always ask, he thought. He didn't answer her. He didn't look up.

'What's your name?' he heard her asking. Let her find out.

'Oh,' said Mary Ann to her brother in English. 'What a stupid boy! He must be the half-wit of the family.'

The boy looked up then, at Peter.

'It must be a terrible affliction for you,' he said, 'to have a one like that around. She doesn't even appear to be a one with any wit.' He said this in Irish. He saw Peter's eyes opening wide with delight. He liked the look of this fair boy. Peter clapped his hands and hopped from foot to foot. He was pleased.

Mary Ann was furious. The blood mounted into her sun-burned cheeks.

'Ignorant boys make ignorant men,' she said in Latin.

'Can a woman milk a cow with the Latin tongue?' the boy asked Peter in Latin. This charmed Peter. He sat on the heather and kicked his legs in the air, trying to clap his bare feet.

'Well, you are no gentleman,' said Mary Ann in English. 'A gentleman would stand in the presence of a lady and bow his head.'

'Do you see any ladies around?' the boy asked Peter. Peter shook his head vigorously. The boy was vastly amused at Peter. His eyes almost disappeared as he smiled. 'What's your name?' he asked Peter.

On this Peter rose to his feet, thought a moment, then joined his hands piously and looked up to the sky acting like a saint. He made a ring motion around his head then with his hand, and looked inquiringly at the boy. The boy was puzzled. 'Have you no tongue?' he asked. Peter showed him a ripe red tongue. They both laughed.

'He can't talk,' said Mary Ann. 'You could see that if you weren't so stupid. He's telling you his name is Peter.'

'Oh,' the boy said. 'I heard of you. You are the dumb one. I saw you when you came the evening of the big feast. My name is Dualta.'

'My name is Mary Ann,' she said, although he hadn't addressed her at all. 'My friends call me Man.'

He looked at her for the first time. She was a dark beauty. She was growing up. Her eyes were still smouldering a little.

'They named you well,' said Dualta. 'You look more like a man than a girl. You are a very rude little girl in fact.'

'If one meets rude people,' said Man, 'one behaves rudely towards them.'

'One does not,' said Dualta. 'One, if one is a Christian, and a lady, is supposed to be kind and forbearing with rude people.'

'It's something of an ordeal,' said Man, 'to be lectured by savages.'

'And are we savages?' he asked.

196

'What else?' she asked. 'Living like primitive people in these wild places. You have no graces. You won't talk to people. You just glower at people as if you hated people. You don't want to be friends with people.'

'You are strangers,' he said. 'Strangers must win friendship. Will you win it with your rude talk? In the last few minutes Peter has made me his friend because he didn't talk at all. Not you. When you are married, if you ever succeed in winning a husband, which I doubt, then your husband would have to beat you.'

'I'd split his skull,' said Mary Ann, 'if he laid a finger on me!'

She said it very ferociously.

Dualta looked at the determined mouth and the chin and the clenched hands and he laughed. So did Peter.

'May God help the poor devil,' he said. 'You'd be like the woman that went to hell.'

'Who was she?' Mary Ann asked.

'She was so terrible a shrew,' said Dualta, 'that her husband prayed the devil would take her, so he did and brought her to hell, and in three days she had all the devils in hell screaming for mercy, so the devil had to take her back again.'

Mary Ann smiled. She felt more friendly with this Dualta. She might have even sat with him and questioned him kindly about his work, but the figure of his father loomed behind them, like a shadow coming over the sun. She saw the face of Dualta closing down as his father spoke.

'Are you ready with the net?' he asked. 'There's no time for idling. If some people can be feckless, you won't be.'

'The net is ready,' said Dualta, rising to his feet.

'Let me look at it,' Odo said, taking it in his hands. Then he looked at the two. 'Has your father no work for you to do?' he asked. 'Is he bringing you up idle, that you can be sauntering in the middle of the day?' They were looking up at him. He was a very tall man. He seemed to be touching the sky with his head.

'My father is pleased with us,' said Mary Ann.

'He is easily pleased,' said Odo. 'Be off with you. The cow will be over the hill. And tell your father to watch his mearing. That I said that. Let his animals graze his own ground and not that of his neighbour. Tell him I said that.'

'Come on, Peter,' said Mary Ann. She turned away. She didn't want to be rude again, and besides she was a bit afraid of this big fellow. When they had walked a little, they looked back. They saw Dualta carrying the net on his shoulder down to the boat.

'I bet that man beats his children,' said Mary Ann. Then she turned away from them and walked on behind the cow. Ahead of her she saw the figure of her father on the roof of the house. The straw of the roof looked fresh and golden in the sunlight. Somehow it seemed to her that their house looked solid, that it seemed part of the earth, as if it had always been there with the dark mountain behind it. She waved and he saw her and waved back at her.

'We have a nice father all the same,' said Mary Ann.

Dominick was thinking the same thing about his children when, looking over the top of the thatch, he saw two people on horses coming galloping over the shoulder of the mountain. He raised himself. They obviously saw his head over the building and they checked their racing horses for a moment to wave at him and then came cantering down towards him. They were both good riders. The little horses flew very sure-footedly over the heather. As they came nearer he could hear the laughter of the woman. He could see her white teeth, so he came down the rough ladder to the ground in front of the house and started to wipe the wet and congealing mortar from his hands on a tuft of heather.

He had hardly done so when they rounded the house and brought the horses rearing to a stop.

'You are welcome,' said Dominick, looking at Murdoc who was dismounting. He didn't help the woman off the horse. She jumped lightly to the ground herself.

'You didn't come near us, Dominick,' said Murdoc, 'so we had to come near you.'

'I was busy,' said Dominick grimly.

'By God, I can see that,' said Murdoc, looking around him. Then he hit him on the shoulder. 'You are here, Dominick, and it would take a lot of gunpowder to shift you.'

Dominick was looking at him. Murdoc was very well dressed. The stuff of his clothes was good and shaped. It was expensive stuff, he saw, and had been fashioned by a tailor. It hadn't been woven by the local weaver nor put together by a handyman. 'You have come a long way, Dominick.'

'So have you, Murdoc,' said Dominick, looking at the clean-

shaven face and the clean hands and the tended hair. He wore
a ring of gold too and a good chain around his neck. 'You are
like a prince.'

Murdoc laughed.

'You hear that, Columba?' he asked. 'Dominick saw me in
harder days. Dominick, now I am a *tiarna*, I'm a chieftain, with
lots of tenants like you to keep me in a style to which I am
unaccustomed.' He laughed.

'Can I see your house, Dominick?' Columba asked.

'It's humble,' said Dominick, leading the way into it, 'and it
is bare.' He kicked the smouldering logs in the open fire-place.

They were looking around. It did look bare. He hadn't yet
mortared the inside of the stones. He had only had time to
fashion one crude table and two stools. He thought how little
either of them knew of the toil and the sweat and the content-
ment he had put into the almost bare place.

'You did it all alone too, Dominick,' said Murdoc.

'I got no help,' said Dominick.

'Did you ever need help?' Murdoc asked. 'Now you will get
time to know people. You'll see. The winter will be with us.
You must come to us again and not get drunk and tell people
what's wrong with them. They will love you, old friend, when
they know you like I do, eh?'

Dominick laughed.

'It's well for man to manage on his own,' he said, thinking
how well Columba looked, as if a new bloom had come upon
her. She wore imported clothes too. He was conscious of the
feeling between them. It was a violent feeling. It was almost
tangible in this small house. When their eyes met, they held
and glowed for a second. He could almost feel their breathless-
ness, saw how they moved instinctively to be close to one
another. He felt a bit disturbed. He felt there was a new
relationship between himself and Murdoc. Murdoc was his
landlord. For them both now, the time they shared their last
meals, and hunted and stalked and starved together, and crept
around in bad clothes, wet clothes, all of them sharing their
fevers and their hopes and their ambitions, all that was something in the past. Murdoc had procured something he wasn't
expecting.

'I'm very afraid, Murdoc,' he said, 'that you will become
respectable.'

'No,' said Murdoc. 'Not me, Dominick. I'll always be a cut-throat, but now I can afford to get somebody else to cut them for me. You are thinking that?'

'No, not that,' said Dominick. 'It's just that the bad days, in looking back at them, seemed to have been good, better than one thought, and impossible to recapture, even if one wanted to. I don't know.'

Murdoc seemed to make an effort to bring his mind clear. He went close to Dominick, put his hand on his shoulder.

'I haven't changed, Dominick,' he said. 'I am always your friend. I owe you much. How could I forget, even if I wanted to? I don't want to. I want you to know I am always there, if ever you need me. I am your friend. There is nothing I wouldn't do for you. This is true.'

Ah, now, Murdoc, Dominick was thinking. Now a touch of patronage has entered into our relationship. Things between us can never be the same again.

'Where's Peter and Mary Ann?' Columba asked.

Dominick went out into the sunlight again. 'They should be coming with the cow now,' he said. He watched his children approaching. He knew without looking back that they had come out of the door behind him, close to each other in the narrow opening. He felt out of the way. What did a stone-built house in the middle of nowhere mean to them? How could he try and explain his pride in it to them, when to them who had been used to better things it was merely the rude shelter of a peasant.

He watched his children. They were good-looking healthy children, not well dressed. I will have to contact a pedlar, he thought, and buy some nice stuff so that they can look good on the Sunday.

'We have visitors,' he called, and stepped aside.

Hello, Peter. Hello, Mary Ann. On the surface things were the same. But they weren't really the same. He knew that from the look of Mary Ann. She was being very polite. She submitted to their caresses but she wasn't carefree. Peter was polite. He could see his own nameless uneasiness in his children's behaviour, and it made him feel a bit better. It made him grin. That is the hazard of life, he thought. They had gained a patron and lost a friend, because after all Murdoc was now an important man, and he was responsible to a lot of people.

'We have to go,' said Murdoc. 'We have a lot of calling to do yet. O-ho, look below, there's the only blot on the landscape.'

He was looking down below them, below the lake, at the gap in the wide valley where you could see the sea. Along the track there that wandered over the rough coast back to Rin Mhil they saw the column of soldiers on horseback. Periodically they patrolled the coastline all the way around, just to show that if you thought you were free you were free only because they said so. 'The black beetles,' said Murdoc. 'Patience and we will have them out of it. One day they won't be there.'

He mounted the little horse.

Dominick held a hand under Columba's foot. She was wearing a high boot of soft flexible leather.

'Well,' said Murdoc. 'There will be a big feast in four week's time for the harvest. It will be a great day and night, Dominick. You will be there. Listen, something else. You remember that Sebastian?'

'Yes,' said Dominick cautiously, 'I do.'

'You are a sly one, Dominick,' said Murdoc. 'You never told me he was a priest. He never told me he was a priest.'

'We never told you he wasn't,' said Dominick.

'Well, they have him now,' said Murdoc.

'What are you saying?' asked Dominick, his heart almost stopping.

'Coote got him,' said Murdoc. 'I saw him. I was there three weeks ago. He passed me on the street. They had his hands tied behind his back. But I knew him. He knew me too. His eyes met mine. He smiled.'

'What did they do to him?' asked Dominick. 'Where did they take him?'

'I don't know,' said Murdoc. 'What does it matter? He won't mind. Won't a fellow like him love to be sacrificed? You remember the arguments we had, eh, Dominick? I should have known.'

Dominick was close to him gripping his leg.

'You must find out, Murdoc,' he said. 'Find out what happened to him. For the love of God.'

'Is he important to you?' Murdoc asked.

'Yes, he is,' said Dominick. 'Do what you can, Murdoc. Somebody will know. Just so that you will find out.'

'I'll try, Dominick,' said Murdoc. 'But listen, friend, the man is a small loss, I tell you. He won't mind what happens to him. Why should you? A soldier expects to die in battle if he is a soldier. In these times a priest expects to die if he is a priest.'

'There's more than that to it,' said Dominick. 'If you never do another thing for me, Murdoc, for the love of God find out.'

Murdoc was almost amused at his intentness.

'All right, Dominick, if he means that much to you, I'll try. Mary Ann, Peter, farewell, until the harvest feast.'

And then they were gone, galloping down towards the lake. He felt Peter's hand in his own then and Mary Ann was holding his other hand.

'Daddy,' said Mary Ann, 'they couldn't have killed Sebastian, sure they couldn't?'

Peter's hand tightened on his. Peter and Sebastian had been very close.

'I don't know, Mary Ann,' he said. 'I don't know. I don't feel anything in here.' He was beating his chest with a mortar-stained clenched fist. 'If they had done anything to him I would have felt it. They can't have. We'll know. We'll know soon. Murdoc will find out for us.'

But Murdoc didn't find out for them.

They found out another way.

CHAPTER TWENTY-TWO

I T W A S a month later that he found out.

He had burnt an acre near the house. He waited until the wind was east and then he set fire to a square of the land. Driven by the wind the fire ate its way furiously and almost frighteningly through the tufts of withered heather and sedge. He himself was on the north side and Peter and Mary Ann on the south side of the square, beating at the fire with wet sacks so that they kept it in line as it flared. In half an hour it had eaten its way through until it was stopped dead at the west end by the rocky bed of the stream that ran down from the mountain.

They were blackened and breathless then, but triumphant, looking at the acre that lay burnt and smouldering and ready for the heart-breaking kiss of the spade.

So here he was, this November day, engaged on digging the last third of his acre. It was hard digging. The ground had been bruised and pressed for centuries and the top of it, for almost a foot deep, was a tough mass of heather roots and sedge roots and wild flower roots and herb roots. It had to be cut into on each side and then hefted out by the lever of the leg and then chopped and hit until it broke and lay open and later on the hard frost would see to the killing and the sifting of it.

Peter was drawing seaweed from the far seashore with the little horse, and up behind him he could see his small flock of sheep grazing the side of the hill. He couldn't miss seeing Mary Ann who was herding them. She was carrying a long-handled pike, in case a wolf should make a sneak attack from the far mountains, and she had tied a yellow cloth on the top of the pike so that it fluttered in the breeze. She had the handle planted in the ground, so if you wanted to know where she was you looked towards the sheep, saw the fluttering flag, and then looking closer you could see her heavily bundled figure under the lee of a rock.

It was midday when Dominick saw a slowly ambling horse coming from the land below in the valley of the two lakes. At first he thought it was Peter, but looking more closely he saw that the horse was carrying a mounted man, not drawing a seaweed-laden sledge. He marvelled at the way living in lonely places made you so curious. A horse and rider passing a mile away; a man and a dog on the slopes of a distant mountain side, a boat on the sea, all gave your mind food for speculation and curiosity. This man wasn't half way to him when he recognized Awley O'Daigean. Awley was a fine fat man, reminding him sometimes with a thrill of sorrow of a rustic edition of Tom Tarpy. He had big jowls, big limbs, and a big heart; a pleasant man of cunning.

He was doing well. He had moved in to serve the planter who had taken the holding and the big house near the sea. He served him well. This man, who was an ex-Colonel, was appreciative of his efforts. He had brought two working people with him from the army, but after a few months of Awley's persuasive treatment the two men in high dudgeon went back the way they had come, and Awley's niece and his fourth cousin took their places. There wasn't a week passed since, that a near relative of Awley's didn't become indispensable to the Colonel. Before he knew where he was, Dominick thought smiling, Awley's Colonel would be wearing an Irish moustache, a saffron shirt; be speaking Irish and calling for a Catholic priest. He speculated if when things quietened down and the whole land was possessed by them, the same procedure wouldn't be duplicated all over the country. It seemed a sly way of getting back your possessions, but at least it meant you didn't have to shed your blood for them.

'The blessing of God on the work!' Awley shouted in his booming voice when he was hundreds of yards away.

Dominick didn't want to bust a gut roaring that distance, so he contented himself by waving, leaning on the handle of the spade, and watching the other's approach.

Finally he came up, and leaned on his belly with great sighs and grunts to dismount from the horse. It seemed to Dominick that the horse was very pleased to get rid of Awley.

'Well, well,' Awley said then. 'Isn't it you that's hard at it, night and day? Man, you're as busy as a tide. I brought you a few salted sea fish and a little bag of sugar for the children.'

'We are grateful to you,' said Dominick, taking the basket from him. Awley searched two or three pockets for the small screw of sugar wrapped preciously in a linen bag.

'Well, God forgive me,' said Awley puffing, 'but I wouldn't

live near that lake below for all the sugar in the world, and that's a fact. Have ye seen him yet?'

'Seen who?' Dominick asked.

'The *each uisge*, the *dobharchu*,' said Awley.

'Who the hell is he?' Dominick asked.

'Oh, wait'll you see him,' said Awley. 'I saw him myself only five years ago or maybe six. I was out with the hound, in the August time. We were looking for a few heather hens for the pot, down along by the heather on the lake. I was walking along by the shore, and kill me if he didn't come out of the water at me, and grab me by the elbow. You never saw such a sight in your life. He had a black shining skin on him, a switch tail without any hair, and he was as big as a greyhound. He had a big long gob on him like a horse, and sharp teeth like needles. I was a gone man, but the dog came after him and bit him on the black backside and he had to let me go and off with him to the depths of the water. Here, I'll show you the marks of the teeth of him in me arm. But I was thinner then, and since I put on weight, damn if the flesh didn't close on the marks. But he's still there, ready to grab you.'

'You weren't drinking that day?' Dominick asked.

'I had a round of *uisge beatha* with me, I'll admit,' said Awley, 'but there wasn't enough of it to overflow a pinhole. I know you don't believe me but that water-horse is there and he's bad stories. My mother-in-law died the day after.'

'You must have loved her,' said Dominick.

'I might have done if it wasn't against nature,' said Awley, 'but the fact is there. I saw, and a person died. I have a message for you.'

'Oh?' said Dominick.

'The Colonel does have visitors sometimes,' said Awley. 'Fellas from the garrison at Cliogan, or off the Island of Death. They bring their men with them. One of these told me this message.'

'For me?' Dominick asked.

'He didn't know,' said Awley. 'He only knew the message. He had been paid to deliver it to someone in the hope it would get to the right quarter. But I guessed. Listen.' He looked around him elaborately. 'They say that the hawks have ears,' he said. 'This is the message: To the little fair man who is a stranger in the tract of Murdoc, from the tall skinny man from Drogheda. Now before I go on, could this be you?'

'This is me,' said Dominick with his heart beating faster.

'I thought it was,' said Awley, with satisfaction. 'Here is the rest of it. On the south shore of the middle lake in the Island of Death there is a tall black stone. I will be there at each full moon. That's all.'

'That's enough,' said Dominick.

'Listen,' said Awley. 'These are dangerous times. It's as well for people not to know too much, because they have ways of squeezing knowledge out of them. So I know nothing.'

'Can I get a boat?' asked Dominick.

'Since they took over the island,' said Awley, 'no boat is permitted near the shore. If caught, death, straight away. They drown them. Even the fishing boats can't put out for fish without permission, and when they get the licence they must fish on certain courses not closer than ten miles. They send boats all around, day and night. It's easier to get into heaven than into that hell.'

'Can I get a boat?' Dominick asked.

'One man can't row a boat,' said Awley. 'It will have to be that way. A boat with a sail won't do.'

'Can you get me a man?' Dominick asked.

'I could get a hundred men,' said Awley, 'but can I trust them?'

'Listen, Awley,' said Dominick, 'if I had to I would swim out there.'

'But you can't swim another one off with you,' said Awley. 'They don't treat them well. They are only skin and bones. You can smell that island when the wind is right.'

'When is the first full moon?' Dominick asked.

'In four days' time,' said Awley.

'Awley,' said Dominick, 'I don't know many people. I am a stranger. Just get me the boat and tell me where it will be left and get me one man, even if he has only one leg. That's all. And for the rest of my life I will pray for you.'

'Oh, God,' Awley sighed, 'the things that are placed on my shoulders. Listen, if there is a boat near Mamore and a man to help you, do you know that it will still take you five hours to go and five hours to come, with only twelve hours of darkness in between? What is the use of you dying as well as the long skinny one?'

'Awley, just get me the boat,' Dominick pleaded.

'I don't know what's happening to me,' said Awley. 'All

right. If no man calls on you before the night, you will have to
leave it for a month. We'll see, and if they get you, cut your
tongue out before they question you, do you hear?' He said
this seriously.

'I'll do that,' said Dominick. 'I'll bring a sharp knife.'

'I'm not a soldier,' said Awley, going to his horse. 'I don't like
blood. I don't like being hurt. I just want to be happy. Look out
for the water-horse. Remember I warned you about him.'

'I'll keep an eye on him,' said Dominick, helping him on to
the horse's back.

Awley looked at the sky.

'It looks like there's wind in it. You better pray for no wind.
The wind will wipe you out.' He turned the horse's head.

'God bless you, Awley,' said Dominick.

Awley snorted, and dug his heels into the horse's side and
Dominick watched him until he could see him no more, and
found that he was as tense already as if he was on the sea, with
weary waiting ahead of him.

'God be inside with you,' Dualta said, standing at the door.

Dominick whirled from the fire.

Dualta saw Mary Ann over at the table mixing flour for a
cake. He bowed to her, his eyes twinkling. 'I see you well, most
noble fair lady,' he said, and winked at Peter who was smiling
at him. Peter was writing on a slate.

'God be with you too,' said Dominick. 'Won't you come in
and take our welcome?'

'Awley sent me,' said Dualta.

Dominick was dismayed.

Good God, he thought, I asked for a man and he sent me a
boy. The boy's eyes were steady on his own. He could almost
read his thought. 'I am taller than yourself,' said Dualta, 'and I
know the sea, and we are stealing my father's boat.'

Dominick took a second look at him. Calm eyes and a strong
chin, and big spatulate hands, with promise of power in them.

'I didn't mean to belittle you with my thoughts,' he said.
'You are probably better than I would be at the sea.'

'I know it,' said Dualta. 'The time is short. We should be at
the shore by dark.'

Dominick pulled on a cloak that was drying near the fire. He
hadn't told them yet. He wouldn't tell them now either.

'Mary Ann,' he said. 'I will be gone for the night. I hope to be back by first light.' She was disturbed.

'Where are you going?' she asked.

'Some place important,' he said. 'It's better that you don't know. But keep the fire up and gruel in the pot. I'll be back.' He kept the worry out of his eyes. Mary Ann was very sharp. He would have to have faith in his return, that was all, and not start thinking before he started what would happen if he didn't come back. He went out of the door. 'You have a nice house,' said Dualta to Mary Ann. Then he turned and followed Dominick. Mary Ann looked at Peter. He rose from his stool and they went to the door. They saw the two figures in the fading light heading down towards the lake. They stayed a long time looking after them.

'Does your father know?' Dominick asked.

'No,' said Dualta. 'Nobody knows. They think I am gone hunting. I don't know what it is about, just that you want to get to Inis Bo Finne and come back and there may be somebody with you.'

'It might be dangerous,' said Dominick.

'There are eleven sons in my family,' said Dualta. 'One won't be badly missed out of that.'

'Are you the eldest?' Dominick asked.

'I am the second,' said Dualta.

They stood for a moment on the hill. There was a wind blowing from the north-west. It drove their clothes against their bodies. The moon was big on their right.

'Is this wind bad?' Dominick asked.

'It's the wrong direction for going,' said Dualta, 'but it is good for coming back. I think it will ease.' There were black clouds scudding across the face of the moon.

They became circumspect as they approached the sea. They went to their knees twice when they saw the bodies of walking men silhouetted near the shore. Dualta led them. The ground was soggy in places. They crossed two streams that were in their way. They had to wade them. They were wet to their thighs. Then they came to the river that drained the two lakes. They followed along its bank until it debouched into the white sand near the sea.

It was quite dark. You couldn't distinguish rocks from the land. Dualta swung away to the right into a gully. Here Dominick could see the black bottom of the canvas boat turned up. Dualta got under the slanting bow and raised it on his shoulders. Dominick got under the stern of it. They walked it down to the river. Dualta went back and brought the oars. Dominick waited for him. When he came back, he held the boat while Dualta tied the oars to the thwarts. Then he whispered, 'Now,' and Dominick sat in behind him and they set the boat free. The current of the river took it towards the sea. They dapped with the oars to keep it off the sand, and then they had to row strongly where it met the force of the incoming tide. It was as well. The wind was cold. The waves were respectably high, but their tops weren't broken. They kept in the shadow of the land as long as they could and then they went to the south of the Bullóg Rocks that broke the force of the sea into the bay.

This was a rough land. The island outside had once been part of it, but the great seas had torn a twelve-mile gap between the land here and the island, and in between were many rocks and a few small grass-covered islands that had resisted the power and beating of the eternal seas.

They didn't talk. They saved their breath for what they wanted it for. Dominick was reassured by the way the boy in front of him was using his oars. Almost effortlessly, but with great power on the final jerky pull. He didn't want to think of where he was going. He didn't want to think that there was even a faint hope that when and if they returned Sebastian would be with them. His own hands were as hard as boards, so the shifting and grip on the oar-handles did nothing to them. He could hear the wood rubbing off their hard surface. They rowed for many hours. The wind wasn't high, but it was there, and you knew it. Sometimes a squall came from behind him, and almost made the boat stand still, and then released it again, so that their oars missed the waves. He could feel the salt water soaking his back and beginning to slop around his feet. The rhythm of continual rowing makes your mind become almost blank. The moon, higher in the sky, was shining to the left of them. It shone on the sea. The land was black, and when they left the point of the peninsula behind them, he could see a few flickering lights from Murdoc's group of buildings.

They were moving to the north of three great rocks into the passage between the rocks and a narrow island when out of the corner of his right eye he saw a movement. 'Stop,' he whispered. He crouched down. The boy in front of him did the same. The boat drifted, towards the rocks. Dualta thought that if they came down on those rocks they were dead. It wasn't the tall ones you could see, but the ones under the water with edges on them like sharp knives that would reef up their boat like a woman cutting cloth.

Dominick twisted his head.

He saw the bulk of a boat behind him. It was a boat with a sail. A squat one, slow moving. He could hear voices. Their own boat drifted towards the rocks. Soon they would be part of them. The sailing boat was tacking towards the moon. Blind them, O Lord, he thought, and a black cloud scudded and obscured the light. When Dualta saw the darkness, he jabbed his oars at the waves, backing the boat, and backing it again, and he held his breath as the clashing waves sped them between the tall rocks. Then they were through. The rocks were between them and the other boat, so they let it go and then started to ease round into the wind.

When the moon's face cleared again the boat had tacked, and was speeding towards the dark bulk of the island on their right. They followed after it.

It drew away from them fast. When it was a sight away, Dualta went almost due north and aimed to go round the small narrow island lying off from the main one. They rounded this and on the side wind came down towards the big island. There was no sign of the sailing boat. In another hour their boat eased silently into a dark cove that was shut off from the light of the moon by the high land all around it. Dominick said to Dualta: 'Judge the time for yourself by the passage of the moon. If I am not back in about one hour, go home, so that you will be landed before dawn. You hear. If I am not back, go!'

'Yes,' said Dualta. 'I hear.'

Dominick hoped he would heed it then as he climbed up to the top of the land. It was a rough craggy way, but not too high and not too hard to climb, and soon he lay on his belly on the top of it and looked. His vision was cut off by a higher bit of land ahead of him, so he rose and ran about fifty yards. It was rock-littered ground and it was only as he reached the top of this mount and threw himself flat that he heard the hoof of a horse knocking sparks from a stone. He buried his face in his arms. His heart was beating fast.

It had reason too, because he only escaped by a small margin. He saw the horseman almost within ten yards of him. When he came near, the horse shied. He got to his hands and knees ready to leap. The rider cursed the horse. He could almost hear the spurs cutting into the horse, who shied left and then right and went on protestingly. The rider cursed him. It was an English voice. The horse was cleverer than he, Dominick thought, as he relaxed. Soon he couldn't hear them any more.

He saw the sheen of the lake below him. He thought of this island. It had contained the monastery of a holy saint. His name was Coleman. There were other saints on it too, and sinners like Grainne Ni Mhaille had a fortress there for her raiding. And other men had weaned a hard living from it, but it had never been put to such use as now. Here they buried the popish priests, schoolteachers, and other dangerous persons. It was shut off from all sides, so that the tales of the terrible things that happened on it flew on the breeze. There was a bishop they had chained to a rock and watched him as the tide came up and took away his life.

He stopped thinking and started to make his way to the lake, heading for the south side. He thought that the message had been clear. Sebastian would be here every full moon for many months, waiting. Why should Sebastian have such faith in him? he wondered. He didn't want to be doing things like this. He wanted to salvage what he had saved, and build on what he had begun. Was it fair to his children to be putting his neck into danger like this when it had taken him so many years to get it out of danger? He felt a little resentful. Mainly because it was bad ground and his hands and legs were torn by the jagged rocks.

He closed on the moonlit lake. Bending close to the ground and putting the land against the horizon he finally spotted the tall black stone standing there, shaped almost like an abbot with a mitre, looking calmly on the waters.

He made the rock in a rush and lay there on the ground, breathing heavily. I will wait for one hour, he thought. One hour, looking desperately at the moon, which tonight seemed to be travelling like a fast horse.

'Dominick,' said the voice. 'Oh, Dominick.'

He jumped and turned and saw the face close to his own.

'It is you, Sebastian,' he whispered.

'It is me, Dominick,' said Sebastian. He was lying full length on the ground, with his face just showing, and then his face wasn't showing. It was buried in his arms. Dominick waited.

He sweated. He knew Sebastian was crying. This is a terrible thing. Waves of sweat went up and down his body. He sat on his legs, clenching his hands. He waited some time.

'Dominick,' said Sebastian, 'this is a fearful place. I am only human. I prayed, but I didn't really believe that you could come.'

'I am here,' said Dominick.

Sebastian was half laughing.

'Oh, my brave Dominick,' he said, 'how the Lord uses you as a reluctant hero!'

'Will we go now?' Dominick asked. 'Time is short.'

'Come with me first,' said Sebastian. He rose to his feet. Dominick faced him. He felt Sebastian's hands on his shoulders, pressing them. 'I should have known, Dominick,' he said. 'I should have known.' He kept one hand on Dominick's arm as they walked away from the lake. 'Being useless, seeing walking corpses in the hard wind, walking skeletons. These are eminent prelates, you have to remind yourself, as you see them sharing roots grubbed from the ground. Every day there are many who die, Dominick. If it goes on there will be none left. That is why the young ones of us, the still strong ones, have to get away and strengthen the people. It is better to die in the open if you have to die, than shut up here like a colony of starving animals. Ssh, here we are.' Dominick peered. In the light of the moon he saw a sort of rough place built from the twisted boughs of trees, not decent trees, but ones that will grow on the island, thorn trees and a few willows, stunted ones. It was a very rude shelter. The sides were made up of roughly banked sods. 'Come with me,' said Sebastian. Dominick bent low and went in after him. 'My Lords,' he heard Sebastian say, 'our helper has arrived.'

He moved aside. There were three men in the shelter. They were sitting on the ground. The moon shone on white hair and silver hair, shining eyes and cavernous faces. 'Dominick,' said Sebastian, 'my Lord Bishop of . . .' 'Better not names, Sebastian,' a soft voice said. 'In these days for the sake of the man himself it is better that we have no names. You are welcome to our humble abode, my son. God will reward you for your endeavours. Here is my hand on your head in token.' Dominick mumbled. He felt the hand resting lightly on his head. 'You are welcome to our home,' a deeper voice said then. He felt a hand resting lightly on his cheek, and a third hand touching him on the shoulder.

'My Lords,' said Sebastian, 'I will go and collect the other two men. I will leave Dominick under your care.'

'We will watch over him diligently,' the deep voice almost chuckled.

'Did you have trouble getting here, Dominick?' the soft voice asked.

'No, sir,' said Dominick. 'It only required brawn and cunning.'

He was smelling. The shelter was filled with this smell, and then he knew what it was. He had smelled the same when Sebastian had faced him. He had smelled the same before in the sieges and on their bitter wanderings. It was the breath that emanates from starving bodies. This is a smell essentially different from all other smells. An over-full belly can give off a smell, if it is overfull of wine or food, but the smell given off by a starving body is one that belongs only to itself. And this shelter was filled with the smell of starvation. What is becoming of us at all? he wondered. How low are we beaten into the earth, when here I am like this with three bishops, who are due to die with this smell on them?

'I am sorry, Dominick,' the soft voice said, 'that we can offer you no hospitality, but God is our Lord, and he will make up to you what is lacking in us.'

'I want for nothing but my helplessness, sir,' said Dominick.

'We run a very poor inn,' said the voice of the third man, suddenly. His breathing was hoarse. His breath was rattling in his chest. But he was chuckling. 'You heard that story of the man who called at an inn in a certain town.' He coughed again. 'In the morning when he was presented with the bill, he saw that he was being over-charged.' 'Like ourselves,' said the deep voice. There was laughter in it now. The others joined with him in the jest. Dominick wondered how in the name of God they could laugh. 'So he rated the innkeeper roundly, and went into the street, calling down the curse of heaven on his thieving head. In the street outside there was another inn across the way and in between the two of them there was a carved figure of the Crucified, so there the man stood and rated to the heavens, that it was no wonder they had this statue where it was and in the right place with Christ crucified between two thieves.' They laughed with him over this. Dominick could only wonder at them. 'Then the innkeeper across the way started to berate the traveller, saying that since he hadn't stopped at his inn, how could he call him a thief. So the traveller said: "Say no more now, and you can be the good thief." '

They really enjoyed this. Dominick could see the moon shining on their wrinkled faces, on the teeth in their sunken cheeks, on their long silvery hair. He thought he would never forget this.

And Sebastian was beside him again.

'We are ready now, my Lords,' he said.

'Then go with God,' said the soft voice, 'and don't be afraid. All over Ireland, the priests must come out of the woods and the caves and the cellars. This terrible oath that some are taking must be broken on the rock of faith. God be with you, Sebastian. Farewell, Dominick, we will not forget you where we are going.'

'God be with you, sir,' said Dominick. He felt for hands and he kissed three of them. They were thin hands. He could feel the loose skin moving on the bones, and then he backed and soon Sebastian joined him and they were moving back to the lake. There they were joined by two other tall figures. They didn't speak. Nobody spoke.

They got back to the boat. Sebastian and the other two men were squeezed into the boat between the legs of Dualta and Dominick. They had to sit there in the swilling water. The wind rose, but it was behind them and it drove them hard towards the land in the race between the moon and the dawn, and their own tense fear.

At the gully, to Dominick's surprise, there was the squat figure of Awley waiting for them.

There were no words spoken even there. Just a whisper between Sebastian and Awley and then Awley was gone and the two men were with him, and the first streaks of dawn were in the sky, so they put the boat back and raced the dawn over the hills, and not until they were near their own lake did they slow down. Dominick had to help Sebastian. He was not fit.

He said to Dualta: 'You are more than a boy. You are a man. You will forgive me for my first thought.'

'There is no need,' said Dualta. 'I have little time. I must get to my house soon. I am going now. I know nothing. What I have done I have forgotten. What I have seen was a dream. I wish you well.' And he was gone.

The nicest part of the whole night was going into the house, quite bright now inside from the dawn light, seeing Mary Ann near the fire with a wooden spoon in her hand, her head resting against the stones of the fireplace, dozing away, and Peter inside in the wide place asleep on the stool in danger of falling into the steaming pot, getting on his knees in front of them, shaking them gently and saying: 'Wake up! Wake up! Somebody has come to see you.'

Watching the sleep leaving their eyes, and their eyes focusing and intelligence coming into them; Sebastian kneeling in front of them smiling through his beard from a terribly thin face; to see the joy on the face of Mary Ann, and Peter's joy. Dominick felt that he was well rewarded.

CHAPTER TWENTY-THREE

HE LOOKED bleakly at the three dead sheep. Their throats had been cut. Neither wolves nor eagles nor yet grey crows carry knives.

It was raining steadily. He could smell the dampness off his heavy homespun clothes. The sky was leaden but there were patches of blue over the sea.

He looked at Peter. There was an anxious look on the boy's face. 'Bring the rest of them down,' he said. Peter nodded. He still looked anxious. 'It will be all right,' said Dominick. He jumped on to the back of the grey horse. They were on the high shoulder of the hill where his tenancy met Odo's. He could see his two fields, surrounded by the thorn thickets he had cut, showing green already under the gentler spring rains. There was smoke rising from the chimney of his house.

It had been too good to last, he thought, the peace they had found. You had to be always hoping that it was true, and holding your breath waiting for something to disperse it. He could let it go. Pretend that it hadn't happened. But he knew from his own life that you could not do that. If there was a fester you had to cut it out. You must never show fear.

He turned the horse and headed him down the other side of the hill. He was vicious with him. He dug his heels into him and hit him with his clenched fist. The horse was startled. He reared and tossed his head. So he had to soothe him, bring him to a halt and talk to him and then set him off again. I must not lose my temper, he thought. I must be firm but calm, that's all it requires. He gave the horse his head, cutting diagonally down the hill, over towards the right where Odo had built his house in a sheltered dip.

It had taken getting used to, the knowledge that your nearest neighbour lived about six miles away from you. You could travel for days through the surrounding mountains and not know that there was a soul living in them at all, but as you got to know them, you were conscious of where the houses were. Whenever you looked far away at the sun shining in a valley or when the heavy snow fell, you thought of the people you had come to know locked up in the mountains, so that the mountains ceased in a way to be cold lumps of nature and became rather personal things that you associated with hidden houses and hidden people.

Through Sebastian mainly he had got to know his neighbours. Sebastian would be gone for weeks at a time. Dominick had made two more trips with him out to the Island and four more shadowy men, with no faces, no voices, no names, had been sped into the land and had disappeared on their missions into the surrounding country. Once there had been Mass said in Dominick's house, and here he had come to know the people as people, not faces and names, joked with them, heard them laughing. He himself had journeyed into the mountains on other occasions to hear Mass in a strange place, with sentinels on the highest peaks watching the plains for the approach of the black men. He had eaten with them, and they had eaten with him. He thought all these things over now, to throw off the waves of mad anger which came into his brain when he thought of the three dead sheep thrown sprawling under the white rock.

. He stopped on the edge of the dip and looked down at the house of Odo. He preferred his own house. His own house was better built. The hounds spotted him and came towards him snarling and barking and showing white teeth. Dominick urged on the horse and came down on the approach towards the house. The doorway of the house was suddenly filled with children. They came there and stood looking at him. Behind them there appeared the form of a woman. She was rubbing her hands on a cloth.

He stopped the horse out from her. She was a buxom woman, with brown hair. She had intelligent eyes and a strong chin. She was tall. She would be about thirty, he judged. She smiled at him. A lot of teeth at the side of her mouth were missing.

'I am looking for your husband,' he said.

The smile left her face.

'He is not here,' she said. 'You are from over the hill.'

'I am MacMahon,' he said.

'I have heard of you,' she said. 'Will you come and rest yourself?'

'No,' he said. 'I called to see your husband. If he is not here could you tell me what has become of him?'

217

'He is gone into the castle,' she said. 'Today is the judgement. The brehon is sitting for the law. He is there.'

'Thank you,' he said. He was at a loss for words. He was glad Odo wasn't there with his woman. What could he have done or said? He looked at the children's faces. They were sturdy children. The youngest had a finger in his mouth sucking at it. They were all clean children, apart from the playing dirt that was on them.

'You have a fine family, God bless them,' he said.

'Odo is a hasty man,' she said. 'Sometimes he does not mean the things that he does. Have you a grudge on him?'

'What makes you say that?' he asked.

She was looking at him a bit sadly, he thought.

'I would like us to be good neighbours, MacMahon,' she said. 'I have brave accounts of your children.'

His face was bleak.

'Desires must be on both sides,' he said. 'I have never injured you.'

'Well, don't do it now either, without thinking,' she said.

He nodded his head at her and turned the horse out of the dip. The hounds followed after them, snarling at the heels of the little horse. He knew she was looking after him. She is a good woman, he thought. She is a likeable woman. She has given her niceness to Dualta.

He came down off the hill on to the rough track that led back towards the end of the peninsula. Once he paused on the road, wondering if he would turn back. But he decided against it and he passed on with determination. The rain had ended. He wiped the wet from his face. The sun came out. It was hot and sparkling. The land was beginning to take on a green flush. The streams were running mad off the hills towards the valleys. They filled the air with sound. The water was up to the belly of the horse as he waded through them. When he saw the buildings in the distance he increased the horse's speed.

Sebastian, who was in a cutting off the track, sheltering with his pupils in a rude hut of boughs and scraws where he was teaching them the rudiments of their religion, saw Dominick passing. He would have waved and shouted to him, but he was gone past too quickly. The tense look on his face, Sebastian saw, and the tightened jaw muscles, and knowing him as he did, his mind sighed, and he said : 'Oh, Dominick.' The children were looking at him. They were young, from six up to twelve, boys and girls from the buildings of Murdoc that men called the Castle. He thought it best not to gather them right in there, where Murdoc's ollamh who taught them profane things was not friendly towards him. Nor did he want to come particularly to the eye of Murdoc himself, so his classes were always held away from the place, under the sky where he could point his little homilies from the things about him.

'Today is done,' he said. 'We will give you the rest of it free. I will send you word when we are meeting again. God bless you. And don't forget what you have learned. It is more important than spelling or hunting or playing. Isn't it?' They assured him it was, ready to run.

'Go with you so,' he said, smiling.

And they flung themselves out and ran fast screaming, shouting, and tumbling on the rough track.

Sebastian was out of there in time to see the side of a small rise covering off Dominick from him. He wondered what had happened. His mind investigated the possibilities, but he could not find an answer. And not finding an answer he was worried and almost ran after the children.

Dominick came into the courtyard, and there was Odo facing him as if he was waiting for him, which he wasn't. The place was crowded. It was used as a little market on a day like this. And Odo had just happened to be facing towards him as he came into the place. His sons were with him, Dualta and the eldest, Cormac, a bulky, long-faced, big-limbed man like his father.

Odo had been laughing with the other men. They were standing in front of Murdoc's long house. Now he stopped laughing and looked at Dominick. Dominick got off the horse. Odo's silence had stopped the laughter. They looked at him and then at the figure of the small man whose clothes were steaming in the suddenly warm sun.

Even at that, it could have been all right, but Odo, grinning, put his hand into his belt and took out a knife. The knife hadn't even been cleaned. It was still stained with the blood, rust-coloured now. And Odo swaggered to meet him.

'I warned you about the mearing, MacMahon,' he said. 'You got the first lesson today. If that doesn't teach you, I will have to be after giving you more.'

Near Dominick there was a pile of wood, cut in six-foot lengths; branches of willow and sycamore piled to feed the fire in the long house. It was a pity it was convenient. Almost unconsciously Dominick placed his hand on the pile and his hand wrapped around a suitable one, and all his good intentions were lost and forgotten; his face white and his eyes blazing, one minute he was beside the pile and the next minute he was close to Odo and the wood swung and found Odo's knife-hand and he roared and felt his numbed arm. But he was fast too. The wood swung again, this time for his head. But he caught it and pulled, and very quickly broke it in two, and backswiped Dominick on the face with one of the broken bits. It brought blood to his cheek and sent him toppling in the mud of the yard, but he was up again as fast as he was down and snatching the broken wood from the ground he hit him with it.

Odo was roaring as he backed away, trying to defend himself with his own piece of club, but Dominick's blows were landing on him. Cormac, when the fight had passed him, was about to jump on Dominick when Dualta held him, firmly. 'Let me go,' said Cormac. 'Don't shame your father,' said Dualta, who didn't care that his father was taking a few thumps. Dualta thought his own father had a too heavy hand, and that was a fact. It pleased him to see a little man hardly half his size bringing a look of worry to the coarse bearded face.

But Dominick was small, and Odo was big. He reached a long arm and caught him by the clothes and brought him close to him and clouted him in the face, and Dominick fell again, but he was up once more and dodged under the groping hand and hit again and again, before another swing on the side of the face caught him and sent him into the muck of the yard. And he rose again and only the intervening figure of Sebastian stopped him.

'Dominick! Dominick!' said Sebastian. He was holding his arms. He felt them trembling under his hands. It was like holding a stallion. His eyes were misted over with anger. And then Sebastian saw them clearing and recognition coming into them, so he freed him. 'There are other ways, Dominick,' said Sebastian. 'There are always other ways.'

'Did you see what the little devil did to me?' Odo was asking in a loud voice. 'Amn't I entitled to kill him for what he did to me?'

'What is it? What is happening?' the commanding voice asked them as Murdoc came through the door.

He stood in the yard and looked at them; at the bloodied, dirtied Dominick, and the bleeding, blustering Odo.

'What happened, Dominick?' he asked. 'What's wrong?'

Dominick jerked a hand at Odo.

'He,' he said. 'The brave one. He cut the throats of three of my sheep.'

'I warned you,' Odo shouted. 'Time and again I sent word to you that they weren't to cross my mearing. I told you.'

'You are a braver man than you know,' said Murdoc to Odo, 'to do a thing like that to the little man. You are lucky to be alive. You could have come to me, Dominick. You didn't have to do this. This is the day of the judgement. It doesn't have to be settled in the yard. Let it be settled inside where is the place for it.'

'Am I to let him go free, Murdoc, after what he did to me?' Odo asked. 'Do you love the stranger better than your own? Can't I settle with him here and now? Put a sword in his hand and one in mine and I'll carve him. Who has done a thing like that to Odo and been freed from it?'

'You'll do it the right way I want it,' shouted Murdoc. 'You had plenty of land on your side of the mountain. You could have been a friend. Does three sheep eat your inheritance?'

'That whole valley, the mountain and the lake, all that was mine,' said Odo. 'You divided me, but there wasn't justice in the dividing. I was a man of peace. I made no motion on it. But there has to be a mearing. I keep my own. It's written down in the documents.'

'Go inside, Odo,' Murdoc shouted. 'You will get justice. You too, Dominick, go inside. That's where there is justice. You'll get it there.'

'I hope so, Murdoc,' said Dominick.

The whiteness was leaving his face. He walked past and went into the house.

It was then that Murdoc's eyes rested on Sebastian. They opened wide. Sebastian was looking calmly at him.

'Coote had you,' said Murdoc.

'He hasn't got me now,' said Sebastian.

'Have I been sheltering you, unknown to myself?' Murdoc asked.

'The hills have been sheltering me,' said Sebastian. 'The people have been sheltering me.'

'The hills and the people are mine,' said Murdoc. 'What they do, I do. I tell them what to do, and what not to do. So I could be faulted with sheltering you if you are found.'

'That's true,' said Sebastian. 'You are the leader of your people.'

'Hum,' said Murdoc. 'We will talk. Come inside first and see justice working. Could you not restrain Dominick? You were the only one who ever could.'

'This time I was a bit late,' said Sebastian.

Murdoc turned and walked in. Sebastian followed, and after him all the people in the yard; their business, their buying and selling suspended.

It was a warm, muggy, smoke-filled place now. The lower long table was placed against the wall and the upper table was occupied by the brehon O'Maoilfabhuil, flanked by Mac Cille Ceallaigh the poet-teacher who was writing in a book. Columba was also sitting at this raised table, and Murdoc sat beside her. From the misty memories of his youth Dominick could remember brehon courts that had more dignity and colour and ceremony about them than this one. But they had been on the decline for many years. They had been forbidden by the invaders, but since there was no justice to be found in the foreign courts they still had to resort to these. What was justice? he thought as he stood in front of the table with a grumbling Odo to the left of him, and feeling the heat and smelling the gathering behind his back. Does real justice exist for small people at all, English or Irish, except the justice that you exact with your own courage? The Lords-in-being appointed the judges. One time the brehons might have been powerful enough to defy even those who appointed them, in their just judgements, but looking now at the white-haired scraggly man with the thin face, plucking at his lips with dirty hands, with his blood-shot eyes and raddled alcoholic face, Dominick wondered if justice was to be found here.

Odo was stating his case. It was a good case to him, sound in law and justice. He was a wronged man who had acquiesced in the dividing of his holding to accommodate a stranger at the word of his chieftain Murdoc. But there was a line and this line had been violated after several warnings, when he had to take action, and for his pains he was assaulted and wounded by the stranger. He pointed out his wounds, he rubbed his hand over the still bleeding ones and showed the palms of his hands. He looked to the judge to uphold his virtue, that even though tempted he hadn't taken the life of the little stranger, which he could have done like he would crush a beetle under his boot.

Dominick in turn stated his case. He was a stranger, if being an Irishman was a stranger. He was peaceful. He had treated all with honour. He had no will to push himself against a stream. All he wanted was peace to build up a life that had been destroyed. Had Odo no tongue? Had he ever approached Dominick and asked him to keep his few sheep from the mearing on the rim of the hill? Was he a man or a beast? How could cutting the throats of three sheep prove that he was anything but a vengeful butcher? The one he had a right to attack was the owner of the sheep. That was all. He was a stranger, but that was all the more reason for justice being granted to him.

The case was simple, the judge said. It would not take up much time, seeing all the many cases that were to be decided. Odo had killed three sheep in his justifiable anger. That was nevertheless an offence and he must restore three live sheep in place of them. But Dominick had committed an offence by striking the first blow and he must give Odo three live sheep in compensation for the palpable injury done to him.

He showed them blackened teeth in a smile.

'And so,' he said, 'justice will have been served. One fine will cancel out the other, and after all, the stranger will be left with the mutton.'

He expected a laugh from this and he got it. Solomon has come to judgement, Dominick thought.

'I appeal to the chieftain,' Dominick shouted.

'It is your right,' said the judge, 'but is it wise?'

'Not wise,' said Murdoc. 'The judgement will stand. It is fair and equitable, but the chieftain will talk to the stranger in an empty room. The judgement will not be altered, but there will have to be proof that the same will not happen again. The court will sit again in one hour.'

Dominick just stood there. He heard the people behind him leaving. There was a hand placed on his shoulder. He didn't turn his head. 'You are only half a stranger,' a voice said in his ear. 'Belittle Odo a few more times like today and you will be a stranger no longer.' There was a laugh in the voice. It warmed him, but all the same he was seething. He didn't feel as lonely but still felt like a man from whom a throng of people had fallen away.

'Dominick,' said Murdoc, 'it was foolish of you to attack

him. If you had kept your head, something could have been done. But you lost your head and you lost your judgement at the same time.'

'You are afraid of them still, Murdoc, aren't you?' Dominick asked.

'I'm afraid of no man,' said Murdoc.

'You are new over them,' said Dominick, 'you are only feeling your way with them. You will not offend them, so you blind your eyes.'

'Dominick,' said Murdoc. 'These are difficult times. We will survive them, but only by cunning. I know what I am going to do to survive and how I am going to do it. Bit by bit. I want these people. I need them. I am going to make them survive with me.'

'But how can you make them survive with you,' said a voice from the smoke-filled room behind Dominick, 'if you do not show them good example?'

Murdoc was peering.

'I can't see the face but I know the voice. Come forward, Sebastian.'

'Here I am, chieftain,' said Sebastian, coming to stand beside Dominick.

'Have you more to say?' Murdoc asked.

'Yes,' said Sebastian, 'I have been wanting to say it for a time. These are hard times we live in. The leaders of the people have been killed, slandered, sent into exile. Few of them remain. Is that agreed, Murdoc?'

'Yes,' said Murdoc.

'So the ones that remain,' said Sebastian, 'must be examples of greatness to the people. They must honour justice and truth not only with their lips but with their lives. Can you say that?'

'What do you mean, now?' Murdoc's voice was very cold.

'I mean how can you show good example when you are living in sin with that woman by your side?' Sebastian asked calmly. 'Are you leading your people to survival by flaunting your adultery?'

It was a very heavy table, a long heavy table of solid oak, but Murdoc had grasped it with his hands, thrown it away from him, leaped over it and was facing the priest, with his hand raised.

It was only a scream from Columba that stopped him hitting Sebastian. She came from behind and caught his arm, made him lower it and held his clenched fist in her hand. 'No, no, Murdoc,' she said.

'You are alive,' said Murdoc to Sebastian. 'You should be dead.'

'We are in love, we are in love,' said Columba, looking into Sebastian's face. Dominick thought anybody could see that. Also that Columba was pregnant.

'We haven't come to where we are now,' said Sebastian, 'because we are all good people. We have been punished for our sins. If we expect to be resurrected from the low places to which we have been thrown we have to become better people, better than our enemies in every way. How can the people become really good if their leaders are bad?'

'You mealy-mouthed man,' said Murdoc. 'You have plenty to do, haven't you, without coming here insulting a girl, throwing things in her face, disgusting. You are supposed to have pity, sympathy, love.'

'And no fear,' said Sebastian. 'I pity her with all my heart. I sympathize with her with my mind, and I love her, but blame you. You were the strong one. You have been abroad. You have seen the murder of this land. Why didn't that put purity into your heart? Do you think you are bringing her happiness?'

'Oh, he is, he is,' said Columba. 'You don't understand. We have sent messages to France. My husband was an old man when he left before the siege. He is probably dead.'

'Mind your own business,' shouted Murdoc to him. 'You have plenty of it. You have old women dying and young men unconfessed and children who need to be preached to. Don't madden me, Sebastian. Do what you have to do but keep away from me, or you will be sorry.'

'My sorrow has nothing to do with it,' said Sebastian. 'Murdoc, can't you see what you have done to her? Can't you see what you are doing to yourself? How long a step is it from adultery to apostasy? Can you answer me that?'

'Look, Sebastian, I tell you this: you better go. Go now. Clear out of here. I don't want to see you any more. I don't ever want to see your face any more. I don't like you. I never did. If you were here for a hundred years I would never like you. Don't give me cause. Don't give me cause to really hurt you. Go away now.'

'All right,' said Sebastian. 'I will go, Murdoc. Columba, I

really love you. If I didn't I couldn't have faced this situation. Murdoc, I ask you with all my heart to examine yours. Unless you do you won't survive.'

'Go away, go away, go away when I tell you,' shouted Murdoc. He walked away from him, cracking a fist into his open palm.

Sebastian hesitated, then he bowed to Columba, who was looking at him with her forehead furrowed, anguish and indecision in her eyes, and turned and walked towards the door. Dominick looked at the two of them, then he too turned and followed the priest.

Murdoc saw him going.

'Dominick!' he called after him imperiously.

Dominick didn't turn. He walked through the haze and followed out of the door after the priest.

Murdoc put his hands on Columba's shoulders.

'Don't let him upset you,' he said. 'There is always one like him to spoil something beautiful.'

'But it is a sin, Murdoc,' she said, 'it is a sin.'

'Well, it is a sin, if you say so now,' said Murdoc, 'but we will find somebody to forgive it. He is only one man, a whey-faced, implacable letter-of-the-law man. Let him go to hell. How can he destroy beauty, something as tender as a flower he crushes in his ugly paw? Don't listen to him. Put what he said out of your head. You are mine and I know what is right. Don't let him spoil this thing between us. It is the first in my life, the very first, and I will hold on to it, and no ranting priest will destroy it, I promise you. You must trust in me, Columba. I am the one you must listen to. Everything will be all right.'

But she was downcast.

'I hope so, Murdoc,' she said, 'I hope so.'

'Believe in me, Columba,' he said, holding her shoulders. 'I will work your life for you.'

He was still raging. He walked to the doorway. He saw the crowd in the yard, and at the outskirts the tall figure walking with the short one beside him.

'Remember John the Baptist, Sebastian,' he roared after them. He saw the startled faces of the people. He saw the thin bearded face of the priest looking over his shoulder at him, with the wide deep sorrowful eyes. Then he went back to Columba.

Sebastian and Dominick walked on until they were alone.

226

'Three sheep are not so important after all,' said Dominick.

'There are more important things,' said Sebastian.

'Yes,' said Dominick with a sigh. 'I shouldn't have lost my temper.'

'We have seen a lot, Dominick,' said Sebastian. 'We have seen priests and men hanged and quartered. You saw noble men dying on that island out there. What good are the deaths of the innocent if we won't learn a lesson from them? If we don't apply the lessons how can we ever drag ourselves out of the ditch of despair? If the people don't get a lead, what are they to do?'

'I don't know,' said Dominick. 'Come home with me for the night. Can't you forget it for one night? Peter is panting to see you, and Mary Ann has learned to spin wool. She is proud, but what good if you won't see it?'

'I will,' said Sebastian. 'But just for tonight. There is so much to be done, Dominick, and so few of us to do it.'

'The sun will shine tomorrow,' said Dominick. 'God is good.'

'I am afraid for Murdoc,' said Sebastian. 'I am afraid for him.'

And he had cause to be.

227

CHAPTER TWENTY-FOUR

FOR COOTE came into the land.

There was a fairly wide and even patch of ground some several hundred yards from the castle of Rin Mhil. It was good drained ground and the grass on it was green and clipped very close by the sheep.

On a blazing June day, Dominick sat on a rocky hillock overlooking this field and watched the animated scene below him. It was the feast of St Jarlath, and the people had gathered from all their sheltered valleys and hills, and from many miles around. They sat or lounged around the field in groups, eating the prepared food they had brought with them. Off in the far corner of the field, he saw many hundreds of the small black mountain cattle. He could hear them lowing, and beside them there were many sheep and horses, jumping and neighing. There were pedlars from as far away as Dublin, peddling news and ballad sheets, and iron ploughshares, coulters and spades and hatchets and scythes, and net-twine and fish-hooks, and pieces of silk cloth, and dyed linens and tobacco and wine. Anything you could put a name on, they had it if you had the money to pay for it; ribbons and beads for decoration and rosary beads for praying, and little plaster models of saints.

There was a lot of noise down there near the fair. He could hear men singing, and see tumblers tumbling, and in another corner near-naked men were wrestling with one another, to shouts of encouragement or derision.

It was hot. It reminded him of the summer they had come here. How many years ago? Was it one or two? Two. It seemed so long ago. Here, where time had ceased to be measured by the work of the clocksmiths and was registered by the rising and setting of the sun. By what you had accomplished this year and by what you hoped to do next year. Last year they had spun and dyed their own wool. Wasn't that an accomplishment? To have climbed the mountain to the lake in the cup of it and dug deep for the grey black muck, bringing that down in wooden buckets and boiling it with the wool to dye it a sort of black for the heavy impervious cloth that would stop any wind or rain in the winter. There was the purple dye of the lichen moss, and the yellow-red of the roots from the bog. Warping the wool for the weaver's loom, a small dark taciturn little fellow who lived by the sea and shuttled away, day after day. Did he ever see the sunlight, Dominick wondered, or did he ever care if he saw the sunlight? He was like something that had been woven himself, he was impregnated with the smell of the wool, but it was good for a man to be silent if that was the way he wanted to be.

He lay back with his head in his arms, closing his eyes against the glare of the sunshine. He could picture in his mind the land he had reclaimed from the stony embrace of the mountain and the glutty pluck of the bog. He remembered the joy of reaping his first sheaf of corn. It was good and it would be better. His children looked well too. None of them had felt a touch of ill-health. They hadn't time. There was too much to do. And there still remained a lot to be done.

A great shout brought him sitting upright again.

The young men were playing hurling on the fields. There seemed to be a lot of them and there didn't seem to be any order in their playing. They were all naked to the waist, had linen about their loins and rawhide leather on their feet to save them from the sharpness of the protruding rocks. The soaked rawhide ball, now dried, made a sharp clucking noise as it was hit by the curving boss of the hurleys that were made from ash.

He could see the two champions in the middle of the field. They pressed shoulder to shoulder and thigh to thigh with their heavy hurleys waving, and mostly the ball was fed to them from the mêlée of players on either side of them, and when it reached them what a struggle they had! Dominick felt his own muscles tensing as he watched them. The sun was gleaming off their sunburned and sweating bodies. He knew the tall dark one was Dualta. He was well built. He had no spare flesh on him at all. The other was as tall as he, fair and very lithe, and his white teeth were gleaming in his face.

The struggle between the two of them took on all the signs of a good wrestling match as the ball came towards them and each one endeavoured to trap it, engage it, free himself from the attention of the other and send it sailing to the line of his opponent. The hurleys swung, and clashed, and the young champions dodged and twisted and threw themselves at one another, and out of their struggle the ball soared into the air towards Dualta's line, and they relaxed, and the fair-haired one's backers cheered for him.

Dominick wondered how they could be so energetic on such a hot day when they didn't have to be. I am getting old, he thought then. This made him think of Mary Ann and he looked for her.

He saw her on the edge of the field. She was sitting down in the midst of several other young girls. But you couldn't mistake Mary Ann's black curly hair and the profile of the round firm chin. He noticed that the girls were presenting an indifferent front to the struggle on the field. But they were watching the play of muscles in the sunlight. Wasn't that what most games were for? he thought with a grin – so that admiring females could see the prowess of the stretching muscles, like the bird he had heard of that arched a beautiful tail to attract the notice of the female. And the female always pretended not to notice.

Good God, he thought then, Mary Ann is growing up. What is she now? Sixteen. She was a young woman, he thought, as his heart missed a beat. No wonder she should be a young woman. She had seen enough and done enough since she was a child to have the wisdom of a woman twice her years.

All the same it was sad. He looked at Peter. He was with younger lads. They had pieces of sticks and an old rag ball and they were playing with those and to them their match was far more important than the one on the field.

Getting old, he thought, as he lay back again on the rock. Shortly my children will have grown from me, and I will end up an old man sitting over the fire of a lonely evening and spitting into the ashes. This picture of himself made him laugh; even if it was true or false, it showed from the thought itself that he was getting old.

'Don't move now, Dominick,' said the voice of Sebastian almost in his ear.

'I won't move,' said Dominick.

'Look over towards the mountain on your left,' said Sebastian.

Dominick shifted his head. He saw the mountain, ten, twelve miles away, enveloped in a blue heat haze, and from the very tip of it a black column of smoke was rising.

'Coote is coming,' said Sebastian. 'He will be here in a few hours.'

'What is that to us?' Dominick asked.

'I think it means a lot of things,' said Sebastian.

Dominick turned and lay on his belly. This way Sebastian's deep-sunken eyes were looking into his own. Sebastian's face was thin, but he looked healthy, tired but healthy.

'I have to do something for you,' said Dominick with a sigh.

'The word is that Murdoc is going to take the oath,' said Sebastian.

'Oh, no,' said Dominick, 'he wouldn't do that.'

'I am afraid he will,' said Sebastian. 'You must talk to him, Dominick. I cannot talk to him. There are very deep barriers between us. I could do more harm than good if I talked to him. He mustn't do this, Dominick. I have tried all I can. With him I can try no more. He would only do it to hurt me. Why doesn't he like me? Why am I so distasteful to him? I never hurt him.'

'The truth you talk is not palatable,' said Dominick.

'He is walking on the white stone shore,' said Sebastian. 'He will be such a lonely man, Dominick. But how many will follow him? Can you tell me that? As you know them, how many would follow him that far?'

'As many as you could put in your ear, I think,' said Dominick. He rose to his knees. 'You know their souls better than I do. It seems to me they are part of the mountains and their faith is part of them. I will go after him. Does he walk alone?'

'Yes,' said Sebastian. 'He is walking alone. Only say what you yourself have in your heart, you can say no more.'

Dominick got up, stretched himself and walked down from the hillock. The hurling game had ended in a shout of victory. His own side had converged on Dualta and had raised him on their shoulders, shouting and cheering. Dominick passed by.

The young men converged towards the place where the girls were sitting watching with an indifferent look on their faces. Some of them went and sat by the girls, joking with them, pulling at their plaits.

Mary Ann got to her feet and walked over to where Dualta was sitting on the ground. His hands were propping up his body, which was covered in sweat. 'Hello, Mary Ann,' he said.

'Hello,' said Mary Ann. 'Why do you work so hard on a hot day?'

'That wasn't work,' he said; 'that was pleasure.'

'You have little to do. What does it matter if one fellow is better than the other fellow?' she asked.

He looked at her serious intent face. He laughed, got to his feet.

'It means that the winner wins a prize if he is the champion,' said Dualta. 'Well, I must go,' he added. 'Tonight I will show you how to dance at the bonfires.' He walked away from her.

'And what prize did you win?' she called after him.

'Prize?' he asked, turning back. 'Oh, the prize. You were the prize,' he said indifferently, 'and I won you.'

He looked at the angry colour rising in her cheeks and laughed and walked on.

Mary Ann was really furious. She bent at her feet and scrabbled a clod of the soil with her digging hands and flung it after him. It was a lucky blow. It hit him on the back of the neck.

He said 'Ow,' and put his hand up to the hurt. He turned. The others had seen his discomfiture. They were laughing. They were calling to him. But Mary Ann was bending again for another clod. She gathered it and threw it. Dualta ducked.

'Do you think I am a sheep, a cow, an animal?' Mary Ann was asking in a high voice. And this time she took up a stone, and Dualta couldn't face it. He ran away with his hands over his head. And she ran a bit after him, and flung the stone. It missed him, but she had set something in train because all the girls were bending for clods and throwing them and the young men, laughing and calling and pretending great fear, were running in all directions over the field. But Mary Ann meant it!

Sebastian, smiling, watched them and wished his heart was as light as theirs.

Dominick worked his way through the gathering at the end of the field. He spoke to a few men, ducked his head at a few women. Soon he was clear of the crowds and he walked until he could see the sea, and when he had clambered over many rocks and rough places he saw the white stone shore, and he saw the figure of Murdoc standing tall near the shore and now and again bending and throwing a stone at the lapping water and all the time his eyes were directed towards the south. He looks like a man who is expecting a ship to come home, Dominick thought, as making up his mind he suddenly and determinedly made his way to the man on the beach.

Murdoc could see it all exactly as it happened.

A long trail of men would set out from the town, by midday on Tuesday, about fifty men, his watchful other eyes had told him. Since it was Coote they would be well armed and travelling light. He didn't think that the Commissioner, who was a stout man too fat and well fed for his arteries, would enjoy the journey because where they were going no carriage with wheels could go. It would have to be horses.

That night Coote would stay at the castle of Magh Uillinn while his men bivouacked in the inhospitable fields down near the rocky lands of the great lake.

From there that night the boats would softly put in with Morogh Dubh and their ten men. It was a moonless night, but not dark owing to the fine June weather.

The sentry would die swiftly and quietly, the lines of the horses would be cut, a shot would be fired and the horses scattered to the four corners of the land, and Morogh and his men would be away and collecting horses from their many relations before the black ones knew what was happening.

What would Coote say to the Master of Gnobeag? Murdoc wondered with a smile. He would not be very favourable to the Master of Gnobeag if all went well. That was as it should be. Murdoc did not think much of the Master of Gnobeag.

A half day lost collecting the horses. Some of them would have broken their legs on that rocky land. They would be shot, and the riders would be returned to the town.

Wednesday night Coote would rest at the castle of Acadh na n-Iubhar. The sentries would be doubled and trebled, but nobody would sleep with an easy head, and nothing at all would happen to them, and Coote would wonder if the Master of Gnomor knew anything about what had happened to them the night before at Gnobeag. He would be suspicious of the Master of Gnomor and that was as it should be.

But Coote would not leave the territory of Gnomor in peace. Some miles beyond Fuathaidh where the Abhann Roibh ran to the great lake and the land rose to the high bog plains and the thick woods, as their guide led them through the only bearable places, out of the woods would come ten horsemen on their mountain horses with their battleaxes and their swords swinging, and the rearguard would be chopped and disorganized, and bursting through them the ten men would let their able-footed horses guide them racing over the soft lands on the far side. He saw the column halting. He heard the shouts. He heard the shots being fired after the fleeing horsemen. He saw the troops detached for the pursuit, and he saw them and their horses, heavily loaded, big awkward animals, suddenly floundering to the bellies in the soft lands they couldn't negotiate, and the eyes of their riders white with fear as they felt the oozing bogs sliding up their thighs, the brown bog water pouring into their heavy cavalry boots.

They would have to be retrieved, and the dead above would have to be buried. He imagined Coote's frustration. He would look at the hills around him, search the plains. There were no peasants he could find to help them, even to kill them and make improvised pathways of their bodies. Coote would appear calm, his face as pale and undisturbed as ever, but Murdoc could feel the anger of his heart, the straining of his nerves, the desire for revenge in this barren land. And he would not feel good about the Master of Gnomor.

In Connmaicnemara they would wearily make their way into the holding of Baile na hInse. Coote would rest there in the castle on the lake. They would not be disturbed, but their nerves would be on edge. Coote would be suspicious of the Master of Baile na hInse, and the following day he would have cause to be, because as they passed close to the Beanna Beola – and the guide would see to that since Murdoc had instructed him personally – they would pass through a cutting, with sound ground under the horses' hooves, and from above Morogh and his men, at the right time, would loose a great fall of boulders and rocks that would cause confusion and maybe death or injury to the milling horsemen down below, and Morogh and his men would slip away and should soon be here, a comfortable time before Coote.

Murdoc laughed.

'Why are you laughing, Murdoc?' he heard the voice of Dominick asking him.

Murdoc turned.

'I am laughing because I am happy, Dominick,' he said. 'I am laughing at my dreams.'

'They must be good dreams,' said Dominick.

'Big,' said Murdoc. 'They are big, Dominick. I feel like an eagle looking down on a stretch of land between Loc Orbsen and the sea, who is saying: This is ours. Now this will be mine.'

He sat on the stones. He took up a round one. It was rounded from the action of the waves and was almost pure white quartz. He played with it.

Dominick sat beside him.

'Are you gaining all this to lose your soul?' Dominick asked.

Murdoc looked at him out of the sides of his eyes.

'Get thee behind me, Sebastian,' he said.

'Coote is coming?' Dominick asked.

Murdoc turned his head, let his eyes rest on the column of black smoke far away.

'Coote is coming,' he said.

'Coote would never come for nothing,' said Dominick. 'He must have a purpose.'

'He has a purpose,' said Murdoc. His eyes were gleaming.

'Tell me, Murdoc,' Dominick asked, 'are you going to take the oath?'

'Listen, Dominick,' said Murdoc. 'This is out of your life. You know nothing about these things. There are terrible forces moving in the land. They could grind us to powder or we could be cunning and fight against them. You are happy here. Tell me that? Aren't you happy here?'

'I have caught hold of the tail of happiness,' said Dominick cautiously.

'Be that way,' said Murdoc. 'But there must be a power to protect your happiness, to guard it. You and hundreds of people like you, every little house among the hills that sends smoke into the skies.'

'Would you trust a man like Coote?' Dominick asked.

'No,' said Murdoc, 'but there are other forces. Cromwell won't live for ever. Cromwell is going to die, and when he does there are going to be great changes. You know what will happen then?'

'Nothing good for us,' said Dominick. 'It will only be a change of masters.'

'I'll tell you,' said Murdoc. 'There will be changes. And the thing to do at that time is to have, and to hold. Possession will be the thing. What a man has then, nobody will be able to take from him.'

'If he has the right religion,' said Dominick. 'Is that it?'

'What religion is right?' Murdoc asked. 'What proof have we that ours is? You have seen what has happened to us. I have seen. Have I not felt for the raped virgins, for the broken-

235

skulled babies, for the hanged men, for the slaves of the sugar plantations? What is left of it all that was so flourishing? Nothing at all except the two islands out there where the last remnants of the old religion are dying with despair.'

'Not despair,' said Dominick. 'You don't know. There is no despair. There is only joy.'

'There shouldn't be,' said Murdoc fiercely. He got to his feet. He threw the stone he was playing with far out into the sea. It sank with a splash. 'If God favoured us, would the whole land be like it is now? Tell me that?'

'No,' said Dominick. 'It is the will of God that it be like this, to make better people out of the lot of us. To make us think so that some day we will be one. We have to fight for it.'

'I've thought a lot about it,' said Murdoc. 'God never intervened when thousands were slaughtered by the sword and by famine and pestilence. The stronger side won. We were defeated. If what we believed in had been right, wouldn't the Lord have been on the side of the righteous? The English God was on the side of the English. There is only one God, therefore He has pointed out unmistakably which side He favours. He favours them.'

'He only seems to do so,' said Dominick.

'You don't know what you are talking about, Dominick,' Murdoc suddenly shouted. 'It's important for the sake of the people that I be big and grow and protect them. I will grow and I will be big and I will protect them. If it is only the taking of an oath that is between all that I want to fulfil, then I will take an oath. What is it? What the hell does it mean to swear an oath on a Protestant Bible?'

'It means that you are throwing away the only thing that is worth anything at all to you,' said Dominick. 'It means taking the heart out of your body and throwing it into the sea like a stone. Do this and you will be a lonely man. Have you thought of that?'

'Of course I have,' said Murdoc. 'I just don't feel anything in here, Dominick!' He was hitting his great chest with his clenched fists. 'It seems nothing at all to me. I am looking at the future. What will happen in the future? Would it be better for me and my descendants to be over the people, than some proud Irish-hating man who will replace me and grind my people into the bogs?'

'No one will ever grind your people into the bogs,' said

Dominick. 'They can try. But they won't succeed. If they are ground in the stone mills there will always be one that will survive. You don't have to sell your soul for posterity, if that's what you mean.'

'I mean nothing. The things you believe don't seem to mean much to me,' said Murdoc. 'Maybe I'm sorry.'

'Then you will take the oath,' said Dominick.

'I don't know whether I will or not,' shouted Murdoc. 'It will depend. I have until tonight to decide. You go back to Sebastian. You get him to pray. If his God is right, let Him strike me dead before I take the oath. Maybe I will suddenly be filled in here with a strong belief. I don't know. Just that I know what I want, that's all. I know how I am going about to get it, that's all.'

'The price will be very high, Murdoc, believe me,' said Dominick.

'I will pay the price if I have to, Dominick,' said Murdoc. Then he looked out from him. He ran a little along the beach. Dominick looked after him. There was a sailing boat rounding the point. It seemed to be packed with men. There wasn't much wind, but they were helping it on with oars.

Murdoc was looking at the boat with shining eyes. He held his body straight, his hands on his hips.

Dominick looked at him.

He felt that Sebastian was standing beside him, even if he wasn't. It's no good, he told him, Murdoc is pregnant with dreams. I gave him no light.

Murdoc was waving at the men in the boat.

CHAPTER TWENTY-FIVE

'I INTENDED to be here last night,' said Coote. 'There was plenty of time to be here, but we were detained on the way.'

'It's a bad country for travelling,' said Murdoc.

'I don't think it need be that bad,' said Coote. 'We were attacked on three occasions. We lost men.'

'Iar-Connacht has always been a rough place,' said Murdoc. 'When I am travelling through it myself I have to travel well protected.'

The yellow-flecked eyes were looking at him calculatingly. Murdoc's face was bland and inscrutable. There was excitement in his stomach. It was always the same way when he was with Coote, as if he was engaged on a dangerous and exciting pastime, which he was.

'Where is Commissioner Bright?' Coote asked.

Murdoc's eyes looked at the vaulted stone ceiling. 'He is in the room upstairs,' he said, 'getting goose grease rubbed into his backside. He has a wonderful case of saddle-sore. The medical-ollamh is delighted with him.'

They were in the part of the buildings known as the castle. It was a three-storeyed stone building, thatched with straw. The walls were thick and the windows narrow and it was a cold place in the winter time. The walls were hung with plaited rushes and there were rushes strewn on the floor. Behind Coote there was a big wood fire burning in the open fireplace, because even in high summer this room had to be heated. Coote was sitting on the only wooden chair, which had carved side pieces and a carved back. It was fashioned from black bog oak. There was an oak table in front of him on which his arms were resting, and his white hands were kneading one another. Murdoc sat across the table from him on a bench, lighted torches guttered from brackets on the walls and a smoking fat-oil lamp was on the table between them. Sometimes as draughts blew down the stone stairway from the apartments above, the wick of the lamp swayed and threw thick smoke at their faces.

'I will make Iar-Connacht safe for travelling, I assure you,' said Coote.

'You will be doing a good day's work,' said Murdoc politely.

'There are many things about the place that don't please me,' said Coote. 'The people are wild. They seem to be uncontrolled by their masters.'

'Mountain people are difficult,' said Murdoc.

'Not when they are dead,' said Coote.

'You would want four armies to scour all the mountains,' said Murdoc, 'and even then you couldn't kill the wild ones.'

'I was thinking that there are too many masters,' said Coote.

Here it is, thought Murdoc. He waited.

'The loyalties are divided,' said Coote. 'How can they be taught to serve three masters and an overlord?'

'That's a problem,' said Murdoc.

'Once,' said Coote, 'it was all one from the lake to the sea from here to here.' He was drawing an imaginary map on the table with his fingers. 'I think it might be more malleable that way. Do you?'

'I don't know,' said Murdoc. 'They are a difficult people. You yourselves were responsible. You broke up the clans. When the clans were one a chieftain had a hand of iron over a wide area. He was obeyed. Now you have them broken up into so many small clanships that people don't know who they owe loyalty to. One claims this and the other claims that. There will always be disagreement and strife that way.'

'You have done well,' said Coote. Murdoc said nothing. 'Can you see my vision? One tight-knit area, however wild and broken, with one lord owing obedience to one overlord. Did you think of that?'

'Very little,' said Murdoc, lying. 'It has not been easy here. It has taken them a time to accept me. I think they do now.'

'Could you get the others over the vast area of Iar-Connacht to accept you in the same way?'

Murdoc thought about it. 'It might be done but it's a terrible burden,' he said. 'It would require time and force. But it could be done. But would it be good?'

'It would be good,' said Coote, 'I would see to that. If you gave me allegiance. It would have to be somebody I could trust. I think I can trust you, Murdoc, or can I?'

'I think you might be able to trust me,' said Murdoc, 'if by pleasing you I am pleasing myself, and also pleasing the people, who are my people.'

'You might be kinder to them than I will be,' said Coote. 'If I have to, I will banish them off the face of the earth. I won't leave one of them alive. I will grind them into their own rocks.'

There was a flush on his cheeks. His hand was clenched.

'I don't think you would live long enough to accomplish that,' said Murdoc.

Coote looked at him coldly.

'Will you take the oath?' he asked.

'You tell me what advantage there is to me in taking the oath.' Murdoc was leaning back. 'Is it going to make things easier for me, do you think?'

'There is no other way,' said Coote. 'I know you. You would go far along a road to better yourself, Murdoc. You have a grasping and ambitious nature. You are like myself. Make no mistake about it. We are here to stay, if it takes a thousand years, but no man will ever be a leader in this land any more unless he has the right religion. I promise you that. It's that or nothing. With it, everything. Power, wealth, influence, or poverty. There is no choice for you, except exile, or holing like a wolf in your mountains with a small band of men. You can live like a wolf or you can live like a king. You can go on or you can be obliterated. You can take your choice.'

The door behind them opened and Columba came in. She was carrying wine on a silver platter.

Murdoc kept his eyes on Coote. He saw him looking up casually and then he saw the widening of the eyes in recognition, and the hardening of the muscles around the thin lips. Murdoc was pleased. Why do I like this? he wondered. It was like taunting a tiger.

'Thank you, Columba,' he said then. 'You know Sir Charles.'

Columba was looking at Coote. Her face was stony. He had wiped all expression out of his face.

'Will you be staying the night with us, sir?' Columba asked. 'Will I prepare apartments for you?'

'No,' said Coote. 'I will be staying with my men, in the open.' Murdoc grinned. 'I am glad to see you safe, Mistress Dorsi. I myself am keeping your house warm for you.'

'You are beating the air,' said Columba. 'I no longer need my house.' She left the platter on the table in front of them. 'If you need me, Murdoc,' she said, 'I will be within call. We will sup in the long house.'

She closed the door softly after her. Coote was looking at

Murdoc who was pouring wine into the goblets.

'You like to play with fire?' he asked him. Murdoc looked up at him from under heavy eyebrows.

'If I am your man,' said Murdoc, 'I am your man for my own reasons. You cannot extinguish liberty. You can circumscribe freedom. Which is better for your purpose? A man who is a man, or a doll who is a lackey?'

'I find it hard to forgive insults,' said Coote. 'I have always found it hard to forgive. Don't play with the fire too often, or you might be burnt.'

The clattering footsteps came down the stairs behind him. The heavy form of the Commissioner came into view. He was a very fat man amply covered with flesh in all directions, puffing and blowing loudly like a seal on a rock. He was walking with his legs spread out. It was difficult for him to keep the flesh of his thighs apart, he was so fat.

'Ah,' he said as he came into the room. 'I am burning. I am on fire. Never again, Sir Charles, will you persuade me to saddle into this wild and barbarous land.'

The medical-ollamh came down behind him. He was a thin man with a big nose. He was rubbing his hands on his clothes.

'You fixed up our friend, Domhnall?' Murdoc asked in Irish.

'I rubbed all the skin off the fat fool,' said Domhnall. 'He is a mountain of flesh. The creature won't be able to sit down for a week.'

'You were pleased with the lotions, Commissioner?' Murdoc asked.

'Pleased! Far from it,' said the Commissioner. 'The fellow agonized my scald. But it is easing. It is easing. How will I get home, that's what I want to know?'

'You can go by sea,' said Coote shortly.

'Thank you, Domhnall,' said Murdoc.

'A pity it wasn't the other one,' said Domhnall, going. 'We could have rubbed poison into him.'

'Will you take the oath now?' Coote asked.

'What is your hurry?' Murdoc asked.

'I knew about the feast day,' said Coote. 'I wanted to be here in the light of the day. This must not be done in a corner. You must do it openly. It is my hope that what you do today, the rest of the people will do tomorrow.'

'How little you know them after all,' said Murdoc. 'The people are still here. There is a feast set for the long house tonight. If I do this thing, I do it with an understanding. Is that true? A wide understanding.'

'There are three others in Iar-Connacht,' said Coote. 'They will not conform. Their fate is on their own heads. We have an understanding. We both know what it is.'

Murdoc drank back the wine. He rubbed his mouth with the back of his hand.

'Come on then,' he said. 'Let us get on with it.'

Darkness had fallen outside, and seven bonfires were blazing in the field out from the courtyard. In the courtyard itself the meat was being roasted.

Around the bonfires the young people were dancing. It was a wild dancing. Around some of the fires the elbow pipes were squealing their fast dances and the young people were sweating and cavorting, some of them loudly hurrooing, turning and twisting and joining hands and separating and coming together again with nearly all their limbs in motion and their bare feet making no sound on the ragged short grass that was being danced and shuffled out of existence.

Around one of the fires there was a flute wailing plaintively and the people were seated on the ground and a man was standing, a tall man with his face to the sky. He was singing a very plaintive love song and his adam's apple was moving convulsively in his throat.

Some of the young people would fall out of the dance, and hand in hand pull themselves away from the light of the fire into the shadows, and they would lie on the ground facing one another, their breathing as fast as the dance that had exhausted them.

From one of these Servragh O'Feichin came, his hand clasping the hand of Mary Ann. He was breathing hard, and so was Mary Ann. She was very pleased with the abandon of the dancing. She thought it was good for people to abandon themselves like that. It took away the vapours and the labours of the house. She hoped that Dualta had seen her dancing with Servragh and that he took note of Servragh pulling her back into the shadows and sitting on the ground with her, because Servragh was the fair-haired young champion who had been opposing Dualta in the hurling game.

'You are a brave dancer, Mary Ann,' Servragh said. He was still holding her hand. He was lying on the ground on his hip, a

242

free hand supporting his head. Mary Ann was lying flat. Her chest was rising and falling.

'I'm really no good at it,' said Mary Ann practically. 'All I was doing was jumping.'

'You can jump like a young deer,' he said. Mary Ann giggled.

'Did I say something funny?' he asked.

'No,' said Mary Ann. 'It was the picture was funny.'

'Why are your hands stained?' he asked. He was examining the one he was holding.

'That's from dying wool,' said Mary Ann.

'Oh, lucky wool,' said Servragh.

That interested Mary Ann. She sat up.

'Why would the wool be lucky?' she said. 'I would say that it is the poor sheep who is unlucky to lose it.' He sighed.

'I was being poetic, Mary Ann,' he said. 'The thought of the lucky wool being handled by these beautiful soft hands moved me.'

'They are not soft,' said Mary Ann. 'They are damn hard from all the work I do.' She took her hand away from him, began to feel the callouses on the palms. He sat up too. He put his hand on her hair.

'Man,' he said, 'your hair is as soft as a mist.'

Mary Ann laughed.

'No, it's not. Be practical, Servragh. It's hard hair. It has to be. I haven't time to be doing things with it.'

'Have you no softness in you at all?' he asked her.

'I think so,' said Mary Ann. 'But all these things you are saying are second-hand. You got them from poems.'

'I didn't get this from poems,' said Servragh, and with his hard young hands he grasped her shoulders, turned her and bending her back to the ground, kissed her violently.

Mary Ann thought: This is the first time I have ever been kissed. Do I like it? No, I do not. He was hurting her lips, pressing them against her teeth, and he was leaning his full weight on her chest. So she pressed her hands against him and pushed him violently and he fell away from her. She stood up. She was wiping her lips with the back of her hand. She stamped her foot.

'You animal,' said Mary Ann. 'Why did you do that?'

He was indignant. 'If you don't want love,' he asked with reason, 'why did you seek me out and dance with me and come with me into the shadows?'

There was a loud blast of six trumpets. They swelled from the courtyard over all the feasting and dancing and singing. They brought down a silence over the land and stopped everybody from what they were doing at the moment. All you could hear was the sizzling and burning of the wood on the fires.

Suddenly the people realized that they were surrounded by horsemen. On all sides of them, closing them into a wide circle, herding them like cattle into a ring and gradually compressing them towards the courtyard. Sound ceased. Many hands moved to belts, to feel for weapons that weren't there, hovering a moment, feeling naked, and then moving where they were being moved, with a shrug of their shoulders. The soldiers had no weapons in their hands. They just sat tiredly and impassively, and dust-covered, on their big horses and used the bodies of the horses to get the people into the ring.

Dominick and Sebastian were lying behind the rocky mound where they had met before. They had been looking down at the colourful scene below them, at the blazing light of the fire that shone on the reds and blues and the white clothes of the women and girls; that illumined their teeth and their red lips and the flashing of their legs as they danced; on the bronzed and bearded faces of the men, and the clear skin of the young ones. It had been an odd wild view of a colourful, moving, ever moving and milling mass, against a crab-apple-green sky.

They had watched all this and then they had seen in the distance the reflected light on the buckles and the weapons of the horsemen who had gathered in a sinister ring far out and then had closed in at the call of the trumpets.

Sebastian's hand was hurting Dominick's arm.

'He is going to do it, Dominick,' he said. 'Coote has been with him over an hour.'

'Maybe he won't,' said Dominick. 'Maybe he won't.' Not having much hope, thinking of the change that had come over Murdoc, trying to remember the Murdoc they had sheltered from death in Drogheda so long ago. He wasn't the same man.

'Look at him now,' said Sebastian.

Murdoc was moving into the firelight of the courtyard out from the door of the long house. The place was lighted like day when the sun was red. Two men had placed a table in front and to this table came waddling the large fat Commissioner. A bench was placed for him and he sat painfully at it and arranged his documents and a thick book, and felt in his pocket and brought out small spectacles with wire frames which he fitted over his short nose.

Murdoc stood beside him. He was tall. He made Coote who stood beside him look small, if he wasn't. Murdoc has put on flesh, Dominick thought, noticing for the first time the swell of his waist and the beginning of jowls that were visible in the firelight. One of his eyebrows was cocked. That was Murdoc when he was going to do something daring, a sort of cynical twist of his face, as if he was laughing at his own foolishness.

'I'm afraid, Dominick,' said Sebastian.

Sebastian had his problem.

Was it his duty here and now to go down and address the people? To say : This man is turning his back on his fathers. He is turning his back on his God. He is opening the doors of hell for himself in eternity here and in the hereafter. Let him not be your master. Let none of you, for the love of Almighty God and the men who have died for you, follow his example. What would happen if he did this? He himself would die, almost straight away. That would be easy, but would it do any good? There was nobody at the moment to replace him. Who would baptize the children and bring comfort to the dying and the Holy Eucharist to the living if he gratified this handy desire for martyrdom?

No, he couldn't do that. He groaned and buried his face in the earth. Dominick left him alone, watching. Behind Murdoc was his household; his gallowglasses, the big fighting men, and his teachers and the people who subsisted on him. What would they do? Coote was looking coldly at the faces of the hostile people. He knew they were hostile because their faces were devoid of expression. At times like this he got a tingling in the nerves. They tingled right down to the tips of his fingers and his toes. When he felt this, he knew that he could satisfy it by violence. He would like to mount a horse and with his men behind him, he would swing a sword, because that was the only satisfying, personal way to impose death, to feel the sharp steel cutting into bone and sinew and having the red blood gush along the back of his hand.

He said now. 'Colonel Honnor of the Island tells me that priests have been escaping. Do you know about this?'

'No,' said Murdoc, 'I know nothing about this.'

'And yet in your own holding,' said Coote, 'there is a priest called Sebastian. He has started a renewed activity over all the land. I have heard about him. I thought they were gone, these priests, but they are raising their heads again in the wild places. I want this Sebastian.'

'I don't know him,' said Murdoc. 'If I could I would not give him to you. If I did a thing like that my usefulness to you would be gone for ever. You have to find somebody else to hunt your priests.'

'I will,' said Coote, and then he signalled with his hands and the trumpets called again.

In the silence the Commissioner rose, groaning. He read from a paper. Murdoc was grinning. It was in English. Not ten people present would know what he was saying.

Coote said: 'You will get one of your own to say all that in Irish.'

Murdoc thought over it. He shrugged. He signalled to his poet Mac Cille Ceallaigh. 'Tell them that,' said Murdoc in Irish. 'Twist it a bit so that it doesn't sound as bad.'

The tall thin teacher twisted it.

In order to preserve peace in the land, so that people might go their peaceful ways, serving their lord and saving their crops and keeping their bellies full, to save them from being ground into the dust by the black ones, Murdoc had decided to take the Protestant oath. The people would know what value to place on it.

The people, some of them, grinned. Murdoc saw that. Morogh Dubh and his soldiers. But others did not grin. The blank looks on their faces became even blanker. This sent a sharp sear through Murdoc's chest. What am I about to do? It is nothing to me. It is a jumble of words that don't mean anything. It is saying something I don't believe on oath, so that I will be able to preserve a measure of freedom for all this land; so that I will rise and bring the people on the rise with me. There is no other way. If this is the only way, why shouldn't I take it? What does it mean? It doesn't mean anything.

'Oh God,' said Sebastian in a whisper, 'the two things are not the same at all. Will the people be deceived?'

'No,' said Dominick hoarsely. 'They won't.'

The Commissioner was clearing his throat.

He handed the black Bible to Murdoc. Murdoc looked at it and held it in his hand.

The Commissioner handed him the long parchment.

Murdoc looked at it. It was in English. Then he recited it, in a colourless voice. But he had a deep voice. It boomed its way over the land until it seemed to hit off the mountains. Sebastian wondered that the mountains didn't fall.

'I, Murdoc O'Flaherty, detest and abjure the authority of the Pope, as well in regard of the Church in general, as in regard of myself in particular. I condemn and anathematize the tenet that any reward is due to good works. I firmly believe and avow that no reverence is due to the Virgin Mary or to any other saint in Heaven; and that no petition or adoration can be addressed to them without idolatry. I assent that no worship or reverence is due to the sacrament of the Lord's supper or the elements of bread and wine after con-secration by whomsoever that consecration may be made. I believe that there is no purgatory but that it is a Popish invention, so also is the tenet that the Pope can grant in-dulgences. I also firmly believe that neither the Pope nor any other priest can remit sins, as the priest raves, and all this, I swear...'

Going through his head as he said it, finding it a little difficult to work at the English with which he was not that familiar, what Murdoc was thinking was of his boyhood. These things he was saying were the negation of all the things he had lisped long ago at the knee of a priest. The years had clouded them over in his mind, but now they came back to him. He could hear the childish voice in his brain that was his own, reciting them. Had he recited them mechanically? What did they mean to a child? Wasn't it manhood that drove home the learned lessons of childhood? What had happened to him? In the welter of wars and blood and hunger and despair, why hadn't they been driven home into his intelligence? But he wondered at this boyhood memory. The thought came into his head: if all these things are truly true, that I am denying now, then surely I am in trouble.

'Say it in Irish now,' said Coote.

Dominick had felt the hair rising on his head as the firm voice spoke the heresies. Sebastian had his hands over his ears.

Murdoc started slowly and haltingly to translate the parch-ment into the Irish tongue. He had read two sentences of the oath when a strange thing happened in front of their eyes.

The people melted away.

They just silently turned and melted from the courtyard. If they were blocked by the bodies of the horses they went under their bellies and out beyond them. They sought the darkness in the awesome silence. One moment the courtyard was jammed with their bodies and the next moment it was emptied of them as if they had been carried away by a magic mist.

The soldiers were bewildered. What were they to do? They looked to Coote. Did he want to stop them by force? He made no sign so they stood where they were and let the people go.

Dominick was shaking Sebastian's shoulder.

'Look! Look!' he said.

Sebastian looked. He rose to his feet. Dominick stood beside him. In two minutes there was nobody at all in the courtyard but the group at the table and the few of Murdoc's household who stood behind him.

Murdoc raised his head.

He looked at the emptiness before him. He could hear sound all right, as men mounted their little horses and the hooves sounded on the sod. But no sound of a human voice arose to comfort him. He glanced sideways at Coote. Coote's face was deathly pale and taut.

Murdoc's voice trailed off into silence. Just the meat sizzling over the fires. Like I will be after this, he thought.

This brought his eyebrow up. It brought back the recklessness into his heart. He had known what would happen. But it was a game worth playing. He would come well out of it yet. The game was only beginning.

'We will go and eat now,' he said to Coote, 'even if most of the guests have departed.'

'It's that priest,' said Coote. 'I want that priest.'

Out of his sight, the priest watched him. He stood very tall on the mound. He felt tall. His face was turned to the clear sky. Dominick felt the relief that was in him, a surging gust of it, then he left him and went towards the fields where he had left the horses. He knew that his children would be there.

The bonfires, unfed, were dying under the stars.

CHAPTER TWENTY-SIX

IT WASN'T a very tall mountain. It was only about eleven hundred feet high. The side near the sea was almost inaccessible. The side going down towards the land with the lake below it was sloping and could be climbed even by the old people in an hour.

The top of the mountain was bowl-shaped, rock-littered, with good green grass holding a miniature lake with rushes around it like the pupil of a concave eye. It was an amphitheatre made by God and on this September day it was amply filled. Overhead the sky was blue and decorated with oddly shaped clouds that fled majestically before a moderate wind.

Father Sebastian, having wrapped the sacred vessels in linen and heavy canvas, and secreted them in the deep crevice behind the white rock on which he had celebrated Mass, turned, still in his vestments, and prepared to address his flock. The vestments he was wearing now were much better than the ones he had made long ago himself in that wood. If he had a church he could nearly have worn them there without exciting comment. If he had a church!

He said: 'Many of you here now, under the sky, have never seen Mass celebrated in a church. It is only God who knows when any of you at all will be able to attend the Mass when it is celebrated in a church. But the important thing is not the church, but the Mass and what it means.'

He listened to them clearing their throats. Some of them were kneeling on one knee with their hats between their knee and the damp ground. Some of them were squatting on stones. Some of the older women were sitting back on their legs, with the rosary beads in their hard hands. He could pick out their faces. He knew all of them. They were a hard-working people, with hard bodies. His eyes drifted over their faces. They were divided in the sense that on his left-hand side were the women and the girls and on his right-hand side were the men and the boys, and between them was the small calm lake, unruffled, and reflecting the blue of the sky and the scudding of the clouds. The O'Callanans, the O'Feichins, the O'Balbhains, the O'Colgans, the O'Dughans, and the MacMahons. He looked at Dominick who was standing with his legs spread and his hands held in front of him. What a different Dominick this was from the urgent, bitter and bewildered young man, so deadly intent on survival, his heart raw, his emotions ready to burst into flame like a prepared fire! He was controlled now. He had lost his litheness, the muscles and flesh had built up on his body. He still had an aura of quiet power about him. Always dependable if you needed help, Sebastian thought, almost indomitable, having made himself one of the people with whom he had cast his lot.

'The future depends on you,' he said. 'It is not an easy future. You will not hold your faith easily. Like a granite rock throws off the water you will have to throw off persecution. It is easy enough to fight and conquer persecution, but it is not as easy to conquer the inducements of the easy road. You will be offered these. Don't take them. They are for the weak and the wavering. It is not an easy thing to have to climb a mountain to hear Mass. God knows how long it will be before Mass can be taken from the desolate places into the heart of the towns and villages.

'They will kill your priests. They have killed many. They will kill many more. They have left not even a memory of them. They are gone like insects you would crush to extinction under your boot. But dead, they are not dead, and their blood and the blood of the people who died with them will win freedom for you in the end, whenever that will be.

'When they kill the priests they will be depriving you of many of the sacraments. You mustn't ever despair. You will hold rosary beads in your fingers when all else is gone, and you will be holding on to the hand of Our Lady; each of the five decades is a finger of the Blessed Virgin, whether the beads be made of gold or silver or horn or hardened bread. They can kill everything but the flame in your heart. That is something they must never put out, and they never will if you keep holding her hand.'

Dominick thought that Sebastian was very thin. He was very fine, very worn. There was no spare flesh at all on him. His face under the beard was thin and gaunt so that he seemed to consist of more teeth and eyes than he should. And his beard was grey. But he never stopped going. How many miles a day did he travel in this wild and mountainous land, mostly on foot, because a horseman was too conspicuous nowadays when more and more the soldiers had taken to patrolling from the Cliogain garrison? It was over a year since Mass had last been celebrated in a house. What Sebastian wanted was somebody to abduct him and lock him in a room and feed him like you would a cow in a byre.

'Since I have come to know you,' Sebastian went on, 'I have come to love you. You are part of your own land. Who can rip the heart out of a mountain? That's what you are and that's what you must remain, mountains of faith, strong, strong, no matter what your leaders may do; no matter what material compulsion makes them turn their backs on the real heritage and on the faith of you, their people; and when I am gone, I do not want you to weep for me, but to rejoice for me and pray that another will take my place who will be stronger and better than I.'

They were looking at one another.

Why did I say that? Sebastian wondered. I feel sad. I want a great church around me; to hear the voice of the people echoing off the vaulted roof. The sunshine seemed pale. The smell of the heather was not the smell of incense.

Dualta's brother Cormac was lying on the rim, looking down at the priest addressing the people. There always had to be somebody watching. But Cormac was careless. He hadn't seen the soldiers debouching at the bottom of the mountain for the last hour. He couldn't see the other side of the mountain where from the first light the boats had landed and the men had set out in the early light to assault the side of the mountain that was supposed to be inaccessible. Besides, even if Cormac had been looking towards the lake he mightn't have seen them, because they moved very cautiously, in a military operation, seeking every fold, of which there were many, in the smooth-looking deceptive side of the hill.

Cormac heard a scuffle, all right, but then it was too late. A bog-stained hand was clapped over his mouth and he was rolled from the rim and a soldier was kneeling on his chest. He had a knife in his hand and Cormac knew that he would use it if he moved. Cormac didn't move, but all the same the soldier feared the savage and despairing look that flashed in his eyes. He waved and was joined by two silent men who tied a dirty rag over the young man's face, turned him and tied his hands behind his back. Then one of them stood and waved, and the whole side of the hills seemed to suddenly come alive with soldiers who moved quietly and very cautiously towards the rim. On the other side, Coote himself led them. They had to scramble up steep gullies where the mountain streams ran as cold as ice, crawl on their bellies over wet moss-covered rocks where they sank to the elbows in the brown bog slime of the crevices. At one of two places they had to use ropes. They were wet from head to foot. Their faces were streaked with the brown bog dirt. They carried swords slung around their necks, hanging over their backs so that they would not ring against stone and cry out against them. Some of them wore muskets on their backs. Others of them had pistols in their belts.

If they faltered it was not for long, as the cold white-faced Coote looked towards the straggling ones.

Coote was the first to push his head over the rim between the two rocks. He gazed at the opposite side. The watcher was gone.

He allowed himself to feel satisfaction. It was a successful military operation. He took pride in it. He had been arranging it for over a year. If it was galling to think that he had to set up an operation like this to conquer over one priest, it was a great satisfaction to know that it was on the point of being successful. By his careful planning, the soldiers had come around by sea when he had received the final information. They had landed at the island and had struck out from there. The ones attacking the mountain from the land side rode the useful mountain horses instead of their own heavy and more cumbersome war steeds.

Yes, he told himself, as he got to his feet and waved his arm, it was an operation of which he could indeed be proud, and its culmination would be a lesson, one which those primitive savages would never forget. Did they think he could not conquer the mountains? Did they think that a man like him would not go down to hell itself if he had to?

Sebastian saw him, standing tall up there in front of his eyes. So that is why I felt sad, he thought. Is that why I could not shake off this numbing feeling?

The people saw his eyes and they turned to look. Suddenly the whole rim on that side was covered with standing soldiers with drawn swords or pointing muskets. It was the instinct of the young to run, and they ran, towards the other rim, but up from there rose the bodies of other soldiers, so they halted and turned back.

The men in the place moved instinctively into a circle encompassing in their swift movement the women and the girls and the priest at the altar. Any of them that had weapons drew them, but they were pitifully meagre – a few knives, a few swords – and the men without them bent to the littered ground and chose for themselves a heavy pointed rock.

But Sebastian was talking.

'You must not resist,' he said, in a clear calm voice. 'This has happened. If God had not wanted it to happen, it couldn't have done so. His purpose is in it. You hear. You must drop the stones. You must put away your weapons. You must give them no chance or reason to kill you. I ask you to do this!' It was an appeal.

Dominick dropped his stone. Other stones fell to the ground. The soldiers moved in from the rim and came down towards them. There was a great silence in the bowl of the mountain. Nothing you could hear except heavy breathing and the sound of the soldiers' sodden boots hitting on the rocks.

Sebastian moved through his protectors. He had to force his way first before they reluctantly opened to let him pass. He was wearing white vestments. He stood out from them and faced Coote. Coote was walking like an animal with ponderous grace. His clothes were stained and his hands and face were stained, but his eyes were glittering. He could have wished that the people would have resisted, but he didn't mind. He was in a good mood, this mood of eminent satisfaction. He stopped in front of Sebastian. He wondered that such a scrawny tall thin fellow could have caused him such trouble, but this bearded fanatic *had* caused him trouble, setting up waves of resistance like a stone thrown into a calm pond.

'You want me,' said Sebastian.

'I want you,' said Coote.

'You will let the people go free,' said Sebastian.

'You can make no terms,' said Coote. 'There are no terms. Their punishment will differ from yours, but you will all share it.'

'You won't reflect,' said Sebastian, 'that for what you do to a priest your sin is very great?'

'My reward is very great,' said Coote. 'In heaven and on earth.'

'I hope God will have mercy on you,' said Sebastian.

Coote felt the blood rising in his head. He clenched his teeth. The sweat glistened on his pale skin. He felt for a moment like putting an end to him here and now. He hated the sight of the wide deep eyes, with no fear in them; the miserable bones in his thin body. He could have stamped him out with his boots.

But he conquered himself. It would only disarrange the set-piece.

'Move,' he said.

Four soldiers came around Sebastian. He turned with them and moved towards the accessible way. He passed his people. They were looking at him with blank expressionless faces. A woman sobbed. He knew what they were feeling – not fear, but their own helplessness. He raised his hand in front of him and made the sign of the cross over them. Then he was on the rim and was walking down.

The soldiers closed in on the people, and they moved them after him.

When you are young it is a gay thing to climb a mountain. It makes going to church a high adventure. You have fun, if you are a boy teasing the sliding girls, helping them over the rough places. It is an opportunity to hold a hand or squeeze a waist. You listen to the groaning of the old ones whose bones are creaking in the ascent. You imitate them; maybe laugh at their striving, never reflecting that some day you will be the same. Anyhow you are under the sky and your heart is young, and the weather is mild and you don't know any different.

The procession down the mount was a very silent and awesome one. Dominick felt Mary Ann's hand slipping into his own. It was cold and it was trembling. He held it tightly.

Pedro was with them, and then he wasn't with them. He ran ahead of them. He broke through the ring of soldiers around the priest and he caught his hand. They were going to beat him away, but they were undecided. They left him.

'We have come a long way together, Pedro,' said Sebastian. 'You must not feel sad.' Pedro shook his head. His head was up to Sebastian's shoulder. He will be much taller than Dominick, Sebastian thought. 'This is the appointed time,' he went on. His thinness made it easier to walk. He had no fat to make him sweat. 'There is always a dangerous time when people are deprived of a prop. They become confused, like poor Murdoc is confused. He is blinded with ambition. Listen, Pedro, you must strengthen the young. You must strengthen the people. You'll find a way too, you'll see.' He glanced sideways at him. The tears were pouring down Pedro's face. 'You mustn't be sad, Pedro. This had to come some time. It was meant to be this way. You must pray that I will die well. God bless you. Leave me now, because I have little time to pray myself. God will bless you. Keep up your Latin. You are very good. Strengthen your Greek, and get somebody to help you with your mathematics. You're hopeless. Try Murdoc's ollamh. He's a good mathematician.'

He released Pedro's hand abruptly. Pedro stood still. He watched the back of the priest, so incongruous on the side of the hill in his vestments. The bottom of the white alb was being stained with the bog. He just stood there. He was engulfed by the people until he felt the strong arm of his father around his shoulder. Then he moved with them.

At the bottom of the hill the horses were waiting.

Coote mounted one. Half the other soldiers mounted theirs and one of them, a bulky man who was chewing tobacco and spitting on the ground, brought a strong rope and tied it tightly around the chest of the priest and under his arms. Then he mounted and tied the other end to the pommel of his saddle, and when Coote's arm dropped, the soldiers shouted and the horses jerked and ran, and the priest was pulled after the horse. He ran for a little, they saw that, and then he couldn't run. He fell and he was pulled over the ground. His hands were up trying to protect his face. They saw the blood on his hands and forehead before the twist of the hill took him out of their sight.

They were still herded by the walking soldiers. The lot of them felt drained with despair, devoid of power. They were walked about a mile to the little beach of the silver sand. The tide was out but it was on the turn. The beach was smiling under the sun. The waters were glinting green and blue. It was a happy day.

Dominick could follow the trail of the priest nearly all the way. Over the rocky ground, and through the thorns of the gorse bushes. He had left a little of himself along the way, a strip of vestment here, a little skin there, a drop of blood on a white stone, a little of his hair on the fruiting briars.

And on the beach they saw how he was going to die.

There was a stake out there driven into the sand. And all around it was piled dried pine wood and gorse bushes.

They were marched on to the sand. They were forced to stand in a ring around the stake.

Dominick had hoped that Sebastian would be dead, that a comforting blow on the head from a stone would have deprived him of his senses. But he wasn't dead. He was sagging a little in his bonds, and his mouth was open trying to breathe. The vestments were very tattered and bloodstained, and torn away from his body so that the white skin of his chest was exposed. But his eyes were open and looking at them. At times his lips moved. Sometimes he had to blink his eye as the blood from a cut over it blinded him.

Coote sat on his horse, looking at him. You could hear the lap of the waves. He wondered if the priest realized Coote's ingenuity. You must never make martyrs. Or if you do make them, there must be no bones, no bodies, no relics to remain. Here was the wonderful solution. He would burn him on the beach, hair, hide, and all, and the ashes that remained would be washed away by the sea. Sebastian would be obliterated; virtually obliterated.

Sebastian was in great pain. He found it hard to breathe. He thought that some of his ribs must be broken and piercing his lung. He saw the eyes of Coote and he read them, and if he could, he would have smiled. If he could have spoken to him he would have reminded him of the .desire of Ignatius of Antioch :

God's wheat I am and by the teeth of wild beasts I am to be ground that I may be Christ's pure bread. Better still coax the wild beast to become my tomb and to leave no part of my person behind once I have fallen asleep. I do not wish to be a burden to anyone. Then only shall I be a genuine disciple of Jesus Christ when the world will not even see my body.

Dear Coote, he would have told him, you can do nothing but the Lord let you.

Then he looked at the people. He tried to tell them with his eyes how much he loved them; his desire that they should know that what they were suffering having to watch him die would hasten the day of their own freedom. Then he was racked with terrible interior pains and had to close his eyes.

He opened them again to see Murdoc and his household coming down the beach on horseback. They hadn't come of their own will. There were many soldiers around them, and also the Colonel of the Island who was gazing at the battered body of the priest tied to the stake with some satisfaction. This man wasn't really cruel, Sebastian thought, he was just a good quartermaster, so many dead, so many alive. But why did they bring Murdoc? Then he was rent with pain again and he prayed: Lord, let me abide the fire before thy people.

Murdoc's face was rock-hard as he sat on his horse looking. He was away on the left with Columba, whose face was as white as a sheet as she looked at the drooping Sebastian. Behind him were Morogh Dubh and his people, all unarmed, all watching with blank faces. Coote was in the centre and on the other side of him were the people, who raised dull eyes to view Murdoc.

Coote's hand fell, and the torch was applied to the gorse. It flared, took light and swept upwards, and ignited the piled pine. They saw Sebastian's face, strained back from the smoke and the flame. But the fire was only beginning. Then the gorse spines crackled and held and burned with a white flame. They saw Sebastian's grey beard vanish, presenting for a moment the thin face of a stranger. Then his hair was gone, and then the remainder of his vestments departed. For a moment they saw his naked body through the flames. They were holding their breaths, clenching their hands, waiting for the pungent scent of scorching flesh, when out of the silence of themselves, and over the lap of the gentle waves there came the flat sound of a pistol shot. They saw the ball hit the breast of the priest and they saw the scarlet, and they saw his head bow as if in gratitude to the man who had fired the shot.

Murdoc's pistol was still smoking. He dropped it by his side. He looked at Coote. Murdoc's face was cold. Coote's face was colder. But he just looked and then turned away again, and the fire gained and grew and the shell that was Sebastian's disappeared.

They were kept there to the bitter end.

The sea was approaching, and when there was nothing left of the stake except a short burned stump, that was being consumed, the soldiers stoked and pushed the fire towards it so that none of that either would remain.

At this moment Coote reached into a pouch and took from

the pouch six brightly polished golden sovereigns. Then one by one he threw them, so that they lay glinting on the sand by the hooves of Murdoc's horse. One by one, and each one declaring: Here is payment for an informer. Here is the gold of Judas. Here is the price of the head of a he-wolf or the head of a priest.

Murdoc looked down at the glinting coins. His face became very pale. He looked at Coote. Coote was smiling. Coote was very pleased. By the Almighty God, Murdoc thought, what a wonderful revenge! What a wonderful beautifully timed revenge! He could almost admire it.

Until he looked around him at the faces of the people. He read doom in their eyes. How would they kill him, he wondered? Would they tear him to pieces?

Coote spoke. 'Nobody will put a foot on this beach for a month from now, under pain of death,' he said. Then he turned the head of his horse and walked him away.

Murdoc felt the hair rising on the back of his neck as the people moved towards him. There was nothing to stop them. The soldiers were gone. The four around the fire were grinning. They would not interfere.

But the people did a strange thing.

They left him alone.

They trudged silently past him up the beach, on to the soft ground leading up to the firm land.

Even his own people drew away from him. All except one or two, one or two. He was left there on the beach with Columba and Morogh Dubh. All the rest were gone so that he could muse at the ashes of the fire.

When the people got on a height overlooking the beach where there was a great stone that the sea could not undermine, they stood there for a moment looking at the scene below them, the blackened sand, the figures of the four soldiers, with the water beginning to swirl around their boots, the figure of Murdoc looking up at them.

Then they knelt on this place as if by an instinct and a young faltering voice started to recite the rosary.

'Our Father who art in Heaven,' Peter intoned.

That's right; Peter intoned.

He didn't know himself. He hardly knew. He didn't recognize the sounds that were coming from his own mouth, but they were coming and he was saying them. And his father heard them, and was looking at him. Dominick felt chills on the back of his neck. He knew Mary Ann knew when he felt her painfully gripping his arm, and he knew the people knew when he saw their eyes widening and their ears opening, and their voices swelling, and I'll tell you what was in Peter's mind as the words came out of him. He was thinking: why, words are round. They are round, like circles.

The last ashes of the fire on the beach succumbed to the obliterating waters of the sea.

And on this same day, far away, on a soft bed of down Oliver Cromwell died.

CHAPTER TWENTY-SEVEN

PETER MACMAHON was singing. He had rich lyrical notes in him but most times his voice was sadly out of tune.

This was what he was singing:

'The cat and the dog, they were singing together
With mee-ow and bow-wow that would deafen old leather.
The cat wanted mice,
And the dog wanted meat,
So neither got nought, for their song wasn't sweet.

The cow and the horse they were singing together
With moo-moo and nay-nay that was blasting the heather.
The cow wanted grass,
And the horse wanted oats,
So they died of their song and their master bought goats.

The lamb and the lion they were singing together,
Their maa-maa and urg-urg made the cock lose a feather.
The lamb wanted Mam,
And the lion wanted lamb,
So the devil took both in the shape of a ram.'

Dominick and Mary Ann were laughing at him, at the ways he would contort his mouth and his body to sing the sounds of the animals. He made it look convincing too, getting on all fours and shaking his head, his features almost taking on the looks of the animals he was sounding.

'Will I sing more?' he asked then. 'There are about another thirty verses.'

'No,' said Dominick, 'we have had enough. Let us continue with the hunt.'

'Get up on to your feet, you ass,' said Mary Ann.

He did so.

'And only kings have jesters,' he said, 'but they are paid. I amuse you for nothing at all, not even appreciation.'

Dominick wondered what they had to laugh about.

They were half way through the wood that clothed the side

of Benbreac mountain. It was spring but the ground was still soggy, even under the pine trees, after the very heavy snows.

'And you can't sing anyhow,' said Mary Ann. 'You sound like a female seal with a throat disease.'

'You are racked with jealousy,' said Peter. 'Oh, the years of enforced silence, when I had to listen to your croaking and couldn't protest. You have no notion the many times I wanted to comment upon your appearance, your thickness of intellect, your maddening egotistical stubbornness. If it wasn't for Sebastian —' He stopped. The name hung in the air as if it was suspended from the branches of the trees. The three of them stopped walking, holding their breaths as they thought about him, and the last time they had seen him. 'Sebastian,' said Peter firmly, 'who counselled me, many times, I could have lost my silent soul over you.'

'Father,' said Mary Ann.

'Yes,' he said.

'Think of the great days when he was dumb?'

Dominick sighed. 'Alas,' he said.

Peter laughed. 'I don't know how you existed,' he said, 'you poor people, without the counsel of my voice. It was like having a beautiful bird in a wicker cage and not being able to hear him sing.'

'We didn't know the beautiful bird was only a grey crow,' said Mary Ann.

They came clear of the wood. There was a thicket to the right of Mary Ann. It seemed to erupt, explode, as a red stag burst from it and ran ahead of them higher up the mountain.

Dominick aimed an arrow at him, but he knew he was too late before it left the bow.

'Run right, Mary Ann!' he called. 'Head him up. Don't let him run to the right.' He just waited to see her going right. The ends of her dress were tucked up to her waist to give her legs freedom. She had screamed when the stag ran from the thicket, but now she recovered and ran waving her arms and yelling.

Peter ran straight, waving his arms too and calling, the bow in his hand.

Dominick went left squeezing his eyes against the glare of the sun to distinguish the rising ground ahead of him. He could almost see the trail up, that the stag would take, and judged where he himself would go to stalk him. He hadn't expected to meet one so low down. He thought they would be higher. They always went higher up after the snow left the peaks. He threw a look over his shoulder as he ran. Mary Ann had succeeded. The startled stag had veered from the right and was heading up the mountain. He was an oldish stag with tall antlers and he looked as if he would have quite a bit of meat on him.

And they needed meat, Dominick thought grimly as he ran, a slow loping stride that covered a lot of ground without exhausting him. He thought that Mary Ann would never last the pace, the rate she was travelling. She was still yelling and waving her limbs. It was more to enjoy the fresh air than anything else that she was with them. 'I'm sick of the house. I'm sick of gruel. Sick of meal. Sick of silly hens.' That was Mary Ann when she decided that if they were going hunting she was going too. And they couldn't stop her, as she hitched her dress and covered her feet in the light leather pampooties.

For Coote hadn't been finished when he killed Sebastian. You would think that Heaven had been on his side with the wicked winter that had fallen on them, deep snows and heavy frosts so that the sea had been frozen at times, and the rivers and lakes were thick with ice.

All Dominick's sheep had been lost. When the first snowstorm had ceased after four days, all they had found was what remained of their carcases after the wolves had finished with them and left the rest for the scaul crows.

Then their grain had been requisitioned by the soldiers, as much of it as they could find; as much of it as couldn't be got under cover faster than the surprise raids. Milk, from their one cow, handfuls of grain from the hidden hoard, a few eggs, a rare fish from the sea. You find the fair land, Dominick thought grimly, but you don't find peace, and what you have to eat must be fought for. The thought of venison brought moisture from his teeth.

The land was rising more steeply now. He had to look up at it. His breath came in shorter gasps. He had to use his hands, and started to climb. In places there was a sort of track that he could walk precariously; at other places he had to dig with his fingers and haul himself up with his arms. He could see Peter starting to climb on his right. He was young and lissom and the climbing for him was an adventure. Of Mary Ann he could see no sign now at all. He hoped she was all right. She would be all right. When she got tired she would just sit and wait for their return.

Mary Ann was enjoying herself. She was breathless, but the paths she was following were not too bad. This side of the mountain led to the top in long slopes, some of them abrupt. You ran down one steep hill and had to run up another. The valleys between were soft bog in most places, but she ran lightly across them, so that they did not suck too badly at her feet, and her legs were splashed with the brown bog water.

She stopped and listened once as she heard dogs barking away to her right. They would be on the other side of this mountain. It's a good job they have me, she thought, and that's just the way they are using me – as a dog. There was a cold blue sky. She could see the very white clouds down near the horizon. She hoped the cold weather was finished. The land seemed locked in the grip of the bad winter. Nothing was shooting. Everything seemed dead.

She heard Peter's voice. He was singing again, an interrupted song, broken with explosive sounds as he climbed. She could see him clinging to a towering rock, like a fly on a wall. He waved to her. She could see the white teeth. She waved back to him before she went down another incline. The other path leading up was much steeper and rocky. Was it Sebastian that gave Peter back his voice? Or was it the horrible shock of a good man being burned to death just for being good? Peter himself didn't talk about it much. He would just say: 'The body is the body of Pedro, but the voice is the voice of Sebastian.' So she would have to say: 'Oh, no, Sebastian had a nice musical voice.' It was such a strange thing that you left it alone. You didn't talk about it, but it maddened her, the memories of Sebastian's last hour. She could tear with her hands. Oh, if only she was a man, what she wouldn't do to avenge him! That's just the thing that Sebastian wouldn't want, her father said. But she couldn't understand it. 'Are you sheep?' she would ask. 'Are you men? Why don't you kill somebody?'

She was on steeper ground now. She was walking on a narrow path. The ground fell away below her. She could see the lakes of the land and the islands of the sea spread at her feet. The air was crisp and fresh and clear so that you could see as far as the power of your eyes.

I should be a little frightened of where I am now, she thought, but it is so nice to be away from the skillets. There was a slithering sound above her head, and many small rocks fell towards her. She looked up and about ten yards away from her she saw the grey form of a big wolf bitch. She could see her dugs. The animal paused too and looked at her. Its jaws were open, its tongue hanging. It had been running hard. The eyes regarded her. Mary Ann felt afraid. They are like Coote's eyes, she thought. Then she held to her perch with one hand and bent for a stone with the other.

'Shoo,' she shouted and flung the stone. But that didn't send the wolf away but a sound coming from away behind her. She flashed out of vision, but the action of throwing the stone had unsettled Mary Ann. Her feet moved on the narrow track, and then slipped from under her. She scrabbled with her hands, but they failed to save her. She slithered down, her whole body stretched along the rock.

She was afraid and she would have screamed, but her feet landed on a grassy ledge. It was about two feet wide, a shelf of rock that had been seeded by the birds so that it became grass-covered.

Mary Ann's heart was beating very fast. She had to press her hand on her breast to ease it. Then she looked down. Below her there was a long drop. If she fell off the ledge, she would land among a lot of jagged stones, that had loosened and fallen from the mountain side. If she fell on to those, she would be injured. There was no way to climb down. The weathered face was too smooth, and to get up she would want to be about two feet taller than she was.

Well, she thought, when her heart stopped racing, it could be worse. She wondered if she would call. She called, cupping her hand around her mouth. She heard her call going out and echoing back to her.

No, she thought, they will be well up the mountain now. I am only wasting the air in my lungs. She went on her knees on the ledge and sat on her heels. There was just sufficient room to hold her. They will have to come back this way, she thought. It is very shameful, but there is nothing I can do.

Several times Dominick saw the stag above him. Once or twice he saw its antlers outlined against the sky. If we don't get him, he thought, there are bound to be more of them up there. Pity we didn't have some dogs. But they hadn't. We will have to get them. He kept climbing. Once when he paused for breath and looked upwards again, he saw the speck over his head in the sky, a black eagle with a great wing span, hovering in the air of the mountains as easily as a sparrow-hawk. The eagle had his eye on the stag too, a cold calculating eye. The tiny climbing figures of the humans labouring far below he could ignore, but he watched the stag closely, every turn and twist and laboured jump that brought him closer to the top of the mountain.

He coasted a bit lower as he saw him reaching the rocky ledge where he wanted him. This was a narrow ledge of hard granite that only the tiny hooves of a deer could negotiate. It curved around the head of the mountain like a winding staircase. It went around the back of the head and then led down into a saucer-shaped valley where the ground was firm and grazing good and where there would be plenty of time to flee with a choice of four other peaks to head for to get away from danger.

As the stag delicately set a hoof on this ledge the eagle swooped. A cloud covered the sky for the stag, but instinctively he knew and lowered and raised his antlers viciously. Easily the eagle avoided them, once, twice, with the stag at bay on the narrow ledge, and then he reached with his talons and gripped the antlers, and flapped his wings in front of the eyes of the stag.

It was like a black bag put over his head. The stag called. He tried to get back the way he had come, but the pull of the blinding wings would not permit him to retreat. So he tried to move his way forwards, lowering his head so that his eyes could see the trail under his feet, but the beat of the wings kept his head high. He roared and lunged and the eagle went with him and loosened his talons and turned to watch him fall. About three hundred feet the stag fell, oh, so ungracefully. And his body hit once, twice, on the way, against the steep rock sides before it struck the ground below and bounced and lay still.

On the rock over the valley into which the stag had fallen, Dominick had emerged. He had watched with awe. He had been conscious of Peter breathless on a stone away from him looking too. And when the stag fell and lay still he called excitedly: 'Did you see? Did you see?' And noticing Peter pointing into the sky he turned his head back. The eagle was dropping to his kill, and Dominick shouted and started to scramble down the steep slope. He took chances, dropped and ran, dropped and ran. He could see Peter doing the same thing. They reached the floor of the valley at the same time and started to run, and the eagle came to meet them, with widespread wings, and clawing talons and a vicious beak. Dominick waved his bow at the eagle. He was a brave eagle. He would soar and dive, soar and dive, but when the two of them came together and waved and shouted at him, he became bewildered. They could have killed him but they didn't want to, so he left them there walking towards his kill while he himself wound higher and higher into the sky, most indignant, and justly so, Peter said laughing, and hating those two-legged things that wouldn't be good to eat anyhow.

Dominick bent over the stag and felt his haunches, and they were good.

Peter was laughing.

'That eagle will never forgive us, never,' he said. 'For ever more he will hate the whole human race.'

Mary Ann was calling. She was answered only by the mocking echo of her voice. It was cold now on the ledge. She loosened her skirt and wrapped it around her legs.

I have been in worse places, she thought. I have been frightened before. It seems to me that I have always been frightened. Her memory of their house was dim. She remembered blood on Peter's head and she alone beside him, frightened that her father would never come back. He came back. He always did.

She remembered a day in the woods when she was very afraid. The shouting of men and the clashing of arms. That was the day she made her first Holy Communion, and her father was gone and Sebastian was gone. That was the worst time, she thought, and then she fingered the golden cross hanging around her neck from a silver chain, and remembered the tall fair soldier who had given her a silken kerchief. She still had that at home in a box. She wore it on big occasions. So her father always came when she needed him.

But suppose they followed the stag right over the mountain and into the valley on the other side! They would go back that way, thinking she had made her way home. She might be here all night. She looked at the sky. There were shafts of colour being thrown across it. The sun was low out in front of her, blinding off the far-away sea.

'Father! Father!' she called, and paused and called again and again so that when she stopped calling her voice was travelling the twelve bens.

'So that's what it is!' a voice said then over her head.

She looked up. The face of Dualta was looking down at her. And beside his face was the face of a shaggy wolfhound.

'I wondered what was screeching,' said Dualta. 'I thought it was a fairy woman. The hair was standing on my head.'

'I was not screeching,' said Mary Ann. 'I was calling. The face of the hound is far handsomer than yours.'

'Is that so?' asked Dualta.

'Yes,' said Mary Ann. 'And now would you mind please helping me out of here?'

'Let the dog do it,' said Dualta. 'He's handsomer than I am. He should be better at getting you out.'

'Well,' said Mary Ann, 'suppose I say that the face of the hound is not uglier than yours?'

'It would be a better saying, but not much,' said Dualta.

'Please, Dualta,' said Mary Ann, 'get me out of here.'

'That's a bit better,' said Dualta, 'but we mustn't rush these things. What are you doing down there?'

'I went hunting with Father and Pedro,' said Mary Ann patiently. 'I saw a wolf and I slipped. I don't know where Father is. He was following a stag.'

'So you are all alone,' said Dualta, 'and if I don't get you out you will be there until the cows come home, and that will be at the end of the coming summer. You realize the powerful position I am in?'

'It is only savages who would be mocking at a lady,' said Mary Ann.

'Ah,' said Dualta, 'savages. I see. That's the trouble about savages. They are very dull-witted. They see a lady in distress and for the life of them they can't work out a way of getting her free. May God remain with you!'

He had risen then and he was gone. She actually heard his footsteps. She couldn't believe her ears.

'Dualta! Dualta! Dualta!' she called

His face reappeared.

'Did you want me, Mary Ann?' he asked.

'Is this a time to be humorous?' Mary Ann asked plaintively.

'I am not a savage so?' he asked.

'No,' said Mary Ann. 'You are a cultured gentleman.'

'Is my Latin as good as yours?' he asked.

'It's better,' said Mary Ann.

'Do you admit that you are a self-willed and unpleasant girl at times?'

'No,' said Mary Ann.

'You don't?' he asked quizzically.

'Maybe independent,' said Mary Ann.

'How so?' he asked.

'Just,' said Mary Ann hotly, 'that if you think that I am just a one to sit around while men go to war, and walk ten paces behind them on the road, and be just an article to bear their children and cook for them and slave for them and have no freedom, even to open my gob when the lord and master is around, no.'

'Oh, look at the sparks,' said Dualta. 'And who would treat you like that?'

'Isn't that the way you all treat your wives?' she asked. 'Like ignorant chattels. They are just good enough to bear children and feed the animals and cook in big pots. I won't be like that.'

'Do you love me, Mary Ann?' he asked.

Mary Ann had been looking up at him, her face reddening from the fury of her thoughts. This stopped her dead. The anger went from her eyes. The ones looking down into her own were very soft. His chin was resting on the back of his hands.

'Because I love you,' he said. 'Apart from the fact that I won you in a hurling match and you're mine anyhow.' He saw her mouth tightening and hastened on. 'I love your eyes and your long lashes and your hair and your stout chin.'

'It's not stout,' said Mary Ann weakly.

'Firm,' amended Dualta. 'And I love you because you are stubborn and self-willed, and given to gusts of anger without cause, and if you don't love me the sun will be dark for me and I will have no reason to live. There are a lot of people in this world. I don't want to know anybody but you. I want to be fighting with you for the rest of life, and if you wish I will walk ten paces behind you and you need never cook. We will live on herbs and I will never open my gob unless you wish it.'

Mary Ann had retired. She was sitting on her legs again on the ledge, her head bent, but he could see the pulse in her neck throbbing. Quite a time passed like that. Dualta didn't mind. He got pleasure out of looking at her. Then Mary Ann stirred. She didn't look up, but she spoke.

'If I don't say I love you,' she asked. 'will you leave me on the ledge?'

He thought over that.

'No,' he said, 'since you agree I am not a savage, I will have to rescue you.'

'But if I say it,' said Mary Ann, 'in order to get free, wouldn't it be sort of forced out of me, and I might go back on it?'

'Other girls might,' he said, 'but not you. If you say it, then I know it.'

Mary Ann got to her feet then. She raised her face to his and stretched her hands up the rock face.

'I want to get out of here, Dualta,' she said. 'I love you.'

He had to smile as he reached down his arms. Even at the end it would have to be a compromise with her, but when his hands closed on hers he knew all right. They remained that way for a time. He had forced his spear into a crevice and his legs were wrapped around the handle of it, so he could stretch down far.

'Walk up the stone,' he said, 'holding on to me.'

She did so, and soon he had a grip around her body with his arms and he levered her off the ledge. They sat close to one another, face to face, and their breathing was fast.

She said : 'Wasn't it the lucky wolf that made me fall?'

He said : 'No, she was an unlucky wolf. I have her head.'

She sighed and said, turning her head reluctantly away from him : 'We have an awful long way to go home, Dualta.'

'Yes,' said Dualta, 'isn't that a great thing?'

'It is,' she said. 'It will take us hours. It'll be dark.'

'Yes,' said Dualta, 'what a happy day!'

They laughed.

They didn't know it, but they had been watched. Dominick walking back with the stag around his shoulders, blood-drained and relieved of its useless parts, had been called by Peter who had been ranging the ground, running up and down to find Mary Ann. He had come over this height and looked across the rock valley and had seen her on the ledge calling, and up above the figure of Dualta and his dog. He saw Dualta getting down on his belly to talk to her and Peter sank himself low so that only his eyes were over a rock. That was when he waved to his father. Dominick dropped the stag and came up to him and lay beside him.

They couldn't hear what was said, but they could guess at the actions. They saw her anger, and Dualta's mock walking away and his return and Mary Ann's sinking on the ledge.

Peter was delighted. He was chuckling. 'You are going to lose her,' he said.

Dominick was shocked.

'What are you talking about?' he asked. 'Mary Ann is only a child. She is only a child.'

'You mustn't have looked at her for a long time,' said Peter.

So Dominick looked at her now, and his heart sank. She wasn't a child. Even there, dusty and dishevelled on the ledge, she was no longer a child. She was a very pretty girl, and he knew with a great sinking of his heart that he was losing her. So he got angry.

'What kind of a fool is she?' he asked. 'She could have been killed. How did she know that we wouldn't go home and she'd be there all night?'

'She knew we would come back for her,' said Peter, 'but that's not the point. She would prefer to be where she is.'

They waited until they saw Dualta taking her safely from the ledge and then they pulled away.

Dominick was gloomy.

'Cheer up, Father,' said Peter. 'It has to happen to all fathers.'

'I can face up to it,' said Dominick. 'It's not that. Just she should be careful. She could have been killed.'

'Wouldn't that be a worse way to lose her?' Peter asked.

Dominick agreed a bit gruffly.

'What have you against Dualta?' Peter asked. 'He's good. He's all right.'

'His father,' said Dominick. 'That's what I have against him.'

'Well, cheer up,' said Peter. 'She's not marrying the father.'

This made him laugh, but Dominick's heart was heavy however much Peter tried to lighten it with chatter.

It was almost dark when they turned off to their own house with their burden, and as they approached the door the tall strong figure of a man seemed to emerge out of the ground.

He was a fair man, going grey, dressed in dark clothes, and Dominick thought: Where have I seen this one before?

'You are welcome,' said Dominick cautiously. The man had

clear grey eyes. The dying sun was glinting off the corners of them. 'Who are you looking for?'

'I am looking for you, Dominick,' said the man.

Dominick dropped the stag and went closer to him. The man towered over him. It brought a memory, a tag-end of a memory. He put his hand up to his head trying to capture it.

'A wood,' said the man, 'with a priest, and a troop of soldiers about to kill you. And they die and we talk.'

'Rory,' said Dominick, thinking of the tall soldier who had been kind, dressed in the uniform of a Cromwellian.

'You remembered,' the man said smiling. 'That pleases me.'

'You were going away,' said Dominick. 'Did you go away?'

'I went away,' said Rory. 'France, Spain, with a mercenary sword.'

'But Sebastian,' said Dominick. 'Sebastian is gone.'

'I know,' said Rory. 'I am here to replace him.'

'You are a priest?' Dominick asked.

'Yes,' said Rory with a sigh. 'I exchanged the sword for the breviary. Exiled soldiers are little use to their country. This is the better way. Do you agree?'

'Yes,' said Dominick, 'but it's so strange, so strange. This is my son.'

'Peter,' said Rory. 'I know. I have heard many things. Hello, Peter.'

'It's timing. Such good timing,' said Peter as he shook hands with him. 'We wanted a priest. We haven't seen one since Sebastian died. But we need one now for a *special cause*. I am not surprised but you had to come. You remember Mary Ann, do you?'

'I remember her,' said Rory. 'It was her first Communion and I gave her a kerchief.'

'Now you can give her a husband,' said Peter. 'Are you laughing, Father?' he asked of Dominick. 'You see how Mary Ann always gets her way, how all things always work for Mary Ann.'

'I'm not laughing now,' said Dominick. 'Maybe I'll laugh tomorrow.' He moved towards the closed door. 'Come into our house, Rory,' he said. 'All that we have is yours.'

CHAPTER TWENTY-EIGHT

ONE MORNING, before the summer, Murdoc finally came forth from his room, like a great bear awakening from hibernation. A shaft of light from the narrow window was blinding in his eyes. His mouth was dry and foul.

He sat up. There was a tankard of water beside him on a polished bronze platter. He took it up and drank greedily. The water ran down his bearded chin and down on to his naked hairy chest. He shivered under the impact of it. Then he poured some of the water into his palm and rubbed it on his face and over his hair.

He groaned.

He took up the bronze platter, rubbed it with his arm and looked at it. He saw a hairy devil glaring back at him with puffed eyes. He threw it from him. It rang as it hit the stone wall. He pulled on and belted his trousers. His head was aching but his brain seemed to him at last to be clear. He knew what he was going to do.

He went down the stone stairs in his bare feet with his shirt in his hand. A grey-haired woman in the room below who was talking to the little three-year-old boy, looked at him.

'Where is she?' he asked her.

She inclined her head towards the yard outside. Then he noticed his son. He went over to him. He held out his naked arms.

'Tadhg,' he said, 'come to your father.'

The small black-eyed little boy did not. He shrank back against the woman. 'I frighten him, Catriona,' said Murdoc.

'You would frighten the devil,' she said, 'with the cut of you.'

'I will change that,' he said.

He went into the courtyard.

The light hurt his eyes. He had to blink them many times before he could accustom them to the glare.

The courtyard was not as he had been accustomed to seeing it. It was empty. There was no smoke coming from the fires.

Some of the erected shelters had fallen in on themselves. In places there was grass beginning to grow where no grass had ever grown. He called : 'Columba ! Columba !'

He waited.

Then she appeared from one of the houses. Her sleeves were rolled up on her arms. There was white flour on them. She stood there looking at him. She was severely dressed. Her plaited hair was tightly bound to her head. He thought she looked thin. He walked over to her slowly.

'Why do you do that?' he asked her.

'There is no one else to do it,' she said.

'Is it that bad?' he asked.

'It is,' she said.

He looked around him.

'I have been sick,' he said.

'You have not been well,' she said.

He looked at her curiously.

'Why didn't you leave me too?' he asked. She didn't answer. These past months seemed like one long nightmare. He had tempered them with strong drink. 'I hope I didn't hurt you or say anything evil to you?' he asked.

She looked at him, and smiled.

'No,' she said, 'any evil you did was to yourself.'

'I am going to take you home,' he said.

'Where is home?' she asked.

'You have friends in Galway still?' he asked. 'It's not as bad in there since the evil one died. I am going there. I want you to come with me. We will find out how the land lies. I want you to be there in case I cannot come back. I want to give you time to be free of me, so that you will look at the future and decide on me.'

'What about my son?' she asked after a pause.

'I have talked to the Joyce,' he said. 'He will foster Tadgh for us. He will be safe with him. Nobody will hurt him.'

'You know what you are doing?' she asked.

'Yes,' he said. 'I know now.'

'I will get things ready,' she said and walked towards the house. Murdoc's heart was dreary as he looked after her. Then he went to the pool where they had trapped the mountain stream, blocked it with smooth stones so that the horses could drink here and the women could pound the washing. The water was icy cold. He washed his head and his body in it, and he shaved off the thick grey-black stubble from his chin and trimmed his moustache. Sometimes he could see his eyes in the water. They were red-rimmed, and red-veined. They looked sick. But he felt better for the wash.

He put on his shirt and high leather boots, then he went outside the courtyard and looked towards the stables. He called: 'Morogh! Morogh Dubh!' He called again. He didn't know if Morogh would appear, but he did. He came and looked and then walked slowly towards him.

Morogh examined him with his eyes.

'You are about?' he said.

'Yes,' said Murdoc. 'We haven't many left, Morogh?'

'About a fistful in all,' said Morogh.

'Where are they gone?' Murdoc asked.

'To their bits of land,' said Morogh. 'Some of them have gone to the one at Baile na hInse. Some to Gnomor. They are scattered.'

'Why did you stay?' Murdoc asked. Morogh just looked at him.

'You think I was not guilty, eh?' Murdoc asked.

'I stayed,' said Morogh.

'I am going,' said Murdoc. 'I should be back in six or seven days. Keep the place for me. I expect to come back. If I do not, everything will belong to you and the ones who remained with me, animals, horses, everything. You can strip this all bare. You understand?'

'Yes,' said Morogh frowning. 'I will go with you.'

'No,' said Murdoc. 'Somebody must stay. When I have acted I will be back, and I will accept the allegiance of the ones who turned their backs on me. But most, I will remember my friends. Get three horses ready.' He turned to go, then he looked back. 'There is nothing more precious in life, Morogh, than a faithful man. I won't forget.'

It didn't take them long to prepare. Weapons, food, and some extra clothes were all that they needed. Tadgh sat on the horse in front of Columba. They were seen away by Morogh Dubh and Catriona. Just two figures in that big courtyard. Murdoc couldn't help thinking how it had been before. The milling horses; the bleating sheep; the children playing; the waving hands; the good-humoured shouts, the accompanying on part of the way by the wild young men on the little horses, showing off their horsemanship, standing on the horses' backs and

274

hurrooing. You were conscious of leaving a thriving community that would be there to welcome you when you returned.

They were well on their way before he spoke again.

'If we find that Dorsi is dead, Columba,' he said, 'will you then marry me?'

'If I can be married to you by a priest,' she answered, 'I will marry you.'

'You know that can't be,' he said.

'It can be,' she said. 'It is for you to say.'

'But that is something I can't say,' he said. 'When you decide like I did, it's not something you do too lightly, and once you have done it, is it not easy to undo it. Do you love me?'

'I did,' she said.

'Or did you love something else, a sort of a dream of me?' he asked. 'Was that it?' He had turned off to the left.

'Where are you going?' she asked. 'This is not the way.'

'I am going to call on the little man,' he said. 'I have a reason.' The test of faith, that would be, and what he thought about him. During the last terrible months he had thought about Dominick, of the calm eyes that could become bright with anger, of the methodical incisive way of doing things. He would see. Was human nature altogether fallible?

'Suppose he doesn't want to see you?' Columba asked.

He looked at her. She thinks the worst of me, he thought, and who can blame her?

'Somehow I think he will,' said Murdoc, and spurred on the horse.

Rory was saying, standing tall with his back to the fire: 'No man knows what exactly is the value of his possessions until somebody tries to take them away from him. Do you agree with that?'

'Yes,' said Dominick thoughtfully.

'Then you wake up to the value of what you possess and you decide to fight for it, even if you are to be killed fighting. Then you find you are not alone. There are many thousands who have come to the same decision. So out of all the oppression and persecution a people is formed and then a nation.'

'What you are saying is that there won't be peace for us, even now, is that it?' Dominick asked.

'That's it,' said Rory. 'It will only mean a change of masters.

In fact there might be even worse to come for all we know. That's one of the reasons why I am here. Where you are an exile all the time you say : Maybe next year I will be going home. Once I was wounded. I was looking at my own blood flowing. When you are a soldier you expect that. But then you say : What cause am I bleeding for? You are bleeding for a foreign cause, on which your heart is not set, and you think : If I have to bleed would it not be better to be bleeding at home?'

The doorway was darkened. They hadn't heard the sound of the horses' hooves on the soft ground.

Murdoc stood there, his eyes searching. The light from the window was falling on Rory's face. Murdoc shifted his eyes and found Dominick who was sitting on a bench near the wooden table. Dominick rose to his feet.

Murdoc came towards him.

'Dominick,' he said, 'tell me something. Do you believe I did that thing?'

'No,' said Dominick immediately.

'What!' exclaimed Murdoc, almost shocked. 'But why didn't you tell me? Why did you leave me? I thought nobody on the face of the earth thought anything of me.'

'I tried to see you,' said Dominick patiently. 'Three or four times. You weren't there or...'

'Or I wasn't capable,' said Murdoc. He sat on a stool. He put his head in his hands. Then he raised his face. The light was shining on him now. His face seemed ravaged to Dominick. He didn't look well. 'Why didn't you think so? What made you doubt the evidence?'

'You are too big,' said Dominick, 'for a deed so small. That's all. I've known you longer than most people.'

'Coote is so cunning,' said Murdoc. 'I almost admired him for it. Would you believe that?'

'Who did it?' Dominick asked.

'One of ourselves did it,' said Murdoc. 'I don't know who. Sebastian's God will look after him. Somebody that was jealous of him. I suspect the *ollamh* who taught the children. He resented the way they loved Sebastian and abandoned him. It might have been the *breithim*. I don't know. There will always be one of us like that. I don't want to know. What's the use when it is all over?'

'It's not much use.'

276

'Will you come with me now, Dominick? I am going to the town. I am going to see Coote. He won't see me straight, so I have to find a way to see him by stealth and I will need help.'

'Why do you want to see him?' Dominick asked.

'I want to be straightened out,' said Murdoc. 'I want to find out if he is all bad; if he has even the wind of a word of truth left in him. I want you to come with me. I would have asked you even if you thought I was as evil as other people think. It's important to me.' He was on his feet. 'Aren't you the only man in the whole world of this moment who cares a straw for me?' He put his hand on his shoulder.

Dominick's stomach was falling. Caught in a cleft again I am, he thought. I don't want to go anywhere. I'm as happy now as ever I was or as ever I am likely to be. I am not as young as I was. I am over forty.

'Coote is dangerous, Murdoc,' he said. 'You ought to know that now. Let him be. Have nothing more to do with him.'

'He will crush me if I don't face him,' said Murdoc. 'I don't want to become a wanderer again. I paid too much for what I have. I want to hold it. I will build again even from the remnants of what's left to me.'

His eyes had drifted again towards the silent priest. He didn't look like a priest. He was dressed like a pedlar.

Dominick saw his look.

'Murdoc, this is . . .' Murdoc cut him short.

'Don't tell me,' said Murdoc grimly. 'I can guess. Just don't tell me his name or he'll end up the same way as Sebastian.'

'Can I help you, friend?' Rory asked.

'No, you can't,' said Murdoc. 'I am gone beyond you. Just don't let me know anything about you, or where you came from, or where you are going from here. That's all. Dominick, will you come with me?'

If he was even the same, Dominick thought. If he was the big, pulsating, laughing, reckless Murdoc I knew long ago, I would be able to resist him. But he wasn't the same. He was a giant with flesh hanging loosely on his face and his body, a sort of caricature of the big fellow he had known.

Peter and Mary Ann had come laughing across the hills. Peter was riding the horse and Mary Ann was holding on tightly to him. You get hiccups when you laugh on the back of a trotting horse, but Mary Ann got a cure for the hiccups when they came near their own house and saw the three horses at the side of it, and the woman sitting up on one, with the child in front of her.

'Look,' said Mary Ann. 'He must be with Father. What does he want him for? And Rory is there. Why should he come near our house?'

'He is the owner,' said Peter calmly. 'We are only his tenants. Why shouldn't he come near our house?'

'After what he did?' asked Mary Ann, sliding off the horse. 'After the terrible thing he did? What does he want of Father?'

'You don't know that he did anything,' said Peter. 'You have only the word of an enemy for that.'

'I know he did! I know he did! I know he did!' said Mary Ann. 'And he's not going to get Father into anything while I'm alive. He has done enough against him.' She ran past Columba. Columba said: 'God be with you, Mary Ann.' But Mary Ann just glared at her and headed for the house, running. Peter made up a little for it. He came close to her and said: 'Pay no attention to her. She didn't mean to be rude. She's getting married soon, and I suppose that upsets girls. Is this the little fellow?'

'Yes,' she said.

'Nice little fellow,' said Peter, catching the small hand. 'Good soldier, eh?' The child smiled at him.

So Mary Ann went in at the open door and went over to her father, talking. 'Father, I like Dualta's father. He's nice underneath. He has a bad temper. Very violent. But you're the same really, except that you control it better.'

'You are looking well, Mary Ann,' said Murdoc.

She ignored him.

'The pedlar will be at Cliogain tomorrow,' she said. 'We are going to go and buy the silk. Just a few yards, Father.'

She was displeasing her father, she saw. She didn't care.

'We will go now, so, Murdoc,' he said.

'Where are you going?' she asked.

'Murdoc and myself are going on a short journey,' he said.

'I am being married on Sunday and you are going away today,' she said. 'Is that a way to be a father? You mustn't go. He never brought you anything but trouble.'

'Mind your tongue, Mary Ann,' said Dominick.

'I don't care. It's true,' said Mary Ann. 'Don't go anywhere with him. Hasn't he done enough to us?'

'Stop talking,' said Dominick. 'Count what he has done for

us. You ought to know. You ought to know better than anyone.'

'You mustn't go with him,' said Mary Ann. 'I'm asking you not to go with him.'

'If you don't stop, Mary Ann,' said Dominick, 'I'll hit you!' He was getting mad with her.

'Do your own mean so little to you after all?' she asked.

He moved towards the door. He took his cloak from a peg, swung it on his arm. 'I'm ready now, Murdoc,' he said.

Murdoc was looking at her back.

'Don't feel bad, Mary Ann,' he said. 'He is helping somebody. He will be back to dance at your wedding.' She didn't turn to him. He made a gesture with his big hands and went out of the door.

'Mary Ann,' said Dominick. She looked, went over to him with her head down. 'Listen, I'll be back. Don't worry. Some day you'll find out too that there is more to life than ploughing your own furrow.'

'You can't fool me,' said Mary Ann. 'You like going with him. You hope it will lead to excitement. You like excitement. You were getting bored with the life here. You don't care about us.'

'Will you talk to her, Rory, for the love of God?' Dominick asked.

'I'll try,' said Rory.

'I'm going, Mary Ann,' said Dominick then.

She put her arms round his neck. She was as tall as he.

'You like it,' she said. 'I know you like it, and maybe you're not able for it. You are now over forty. Suppose anything happened to you.'

Dominick laughed.

'By the Lord!' he said. 'By the Lord! I'm harder now than ever I was. I am like a young oak tree. Make nothing of it, I say. Go on with your arrangements. You won't have time to think. I will be back.'

'You never left us alone before,' she said.

'Indeed I did,' he said. 'But let me remind you that you are grown up now. You have grown beyond your father, or I can tell you you wouldn't speak to anyone like you have done today.'

He left her. Rory came over to her. They walked out of the door. Murdoc was mounted. Dominick was swinging on to the back of the horse. He waved his hand and they were gone. Peter came over to them.

'Where is the old man off to?' he asked.

'There,' said Mary Ann, 'what did I tell you?'

'It seems Murdoc is going into a cage with a wild animal,' said Rory. 'And your father is gone with him to open it.'

'That's his trouble,' said Peter. 'He doesn't realize that he can't do the things that came easy to him ten years ago.'

'He is his own man,' said Rory.

'And he's our father,' said Peter, 'and something will have to be done about him.'

CHAPTER TWENTY-NINE

COLUMBA SAID to Diarmuid: 'You will love my son?'

He said: 'He will be the same as my own.'

Murdoc said from the boat, a bit impatiently: 'The time is running out, Columba.'

She was on the bank of the river. Murdoc and Dominick were in the boat. Diarmuid was holding the child in his arms. The child was upset, although he felt safe in the arms of the big Joyce man who was holding him. How can he leave him like this? Dominick thought. If he was my son, I would not leave him.

Columba, looking over her shoulder at Murdoc, said: 'The time is indeed running out, Murdoc.' Then to Joyce she said: 'I will be back for him. Keep him safe for me.'

Diarmuid laughed. 'Our lives run on wheels,' he said. 'Sometimes we come together and part again. I am pleased to foster a child of Murdoc. You must have no fear.'

'I will remember, Diarmuid,' said Murdoc. 'I will repay you.'

Columba kissed her son again and then turned and came into the boat. Dominick saw her looking at Murdoc curiously, and then looking at himself, and dropping her eyes when she met his own. She was a different woman from the one who had come with him before on what to her then was a great adventure.

Murdoc had three things on his mind. He wanted to get Dominick with him. He had done that. He wanted to hand over his son into safe keeping and his woman also. That was half done. Then he would see Coote. That would be the last thing, and until it was accomplished his mind would not be free.

The boat was loosed and went into the middle of the river that flowed to the lake. Dominick remembered this moment. The man on the bank holding the child in his arms, and his horse cropping the grass. It was a grey day. There was no colour in the sky or the clouds or the water or the mountains. He felt sad for the child. He felt sad for Columba. She waved once, and then they were in a wind of the river and cut off from the view of the two on the bank.

Dominick could feel the intensity of Murdoc's thought, could see it in the impulsion of the oars in his hands. He could feel Columba's sorrow. He knew it was the parting from her child. He wondered if part of her sorrow was for the shattering of her dreams. It would be partly her own fault, because her dreams had been too coloured. There was silence in the boat.

They travelled hard. There was little wind. It was the third night before they came drifting down the big river in the darkness. Dominick hadn't enjoyed it. Murdoc was brooding away. Columba was silent. He couldn't fathom the thoughts of either of them. He knew too little about their loneliness or their true feelings. Not until he had approached the Wood Quay in the darkness, feeling their way with Dominick in the bow dabbing in front of them with the oar. Here Columba landed. Her face was just a white blur in the darkness. Murdoc got out and stood beside her. Dominick held the boat. He could hear their voices.

'You know where to go?' Murdoc asked.

'Yes,' she said. 'I seek O'Fowda tonight and tomorrow I will go into the town.'

'If I can, I will meet you there,' Murdoc said. 'Then we will know. I don't know if I have hurt you badly. I care if I have.'

'We shared it all,' she said. 'I sought you.'

Murdoc put his hand on her arm. It was a soft arm, but it held no invitation for him.

'The future will release you,' he said. 'I won't ever forget you.'

'Your time is running out,' she said.

He left her then.

'God bless you, Dominick,' her voice said out of the darkness.

'And you too,' answered Dominick. He felt uncomfortable. They pushed out into the stream. They rested on their oars and let the drifting water carry them.

'She was born for soft beds and silk,' said Murdoc. 'She doesn't love me.'

'You don't know,' said Dominick. 'You had no fair road since she came.'

'I know,' said Murdoc. 'I am not very bright about people. You know that. Myself has always mattered more to me. But she matters more than myself now. That's why I give her choice, you see. If I was all bad I would give her no choice. You know what will happen?'

'No,' said Dominick.

'I can see it,' said Murdoc. 'Her husband will be alive. His kind always live. They get out when the trouble is coming and they find a soft place to equal what they have left, and then when the trouble is over they come back again. Like fleas seeking fat bodies. Oh, he will survive all right and she will go back to him. She feels that she is soiled, and she will expiate her sins in the arms of her aged husband. I know. And he will accept my son, and treat him as his own. But not if I am alive, by God. If I am alive, he is mine. Columba was never as big a sinner as I was.'

'Don't boast about your sins, Murdoc,' said Dominick harshly.

Murdoc laughed.

'All right, Dominick,' he said. 'She was never as great a lover as me, so. She wasn't for the hard places, in the hard lands, where you think big and act quickly.'

'Where are we going?' Dominick asked.

'We are going to slip into the town by the stream of the South Milinn,' said Murdoc, 'if they haven't the iron gate down. If they have, I will find another way. You let the boat drift then down under the arch of the bridge and wait for me. If I do not come back before daylight, cross over to the far side and go to the village of the fishermen. Wait there and I will send word to you.'

'Look, Murdoc,' said Dominick, 'can't you let it go? Can't you forget all you have lost? Can't you come back home and if you have to be small, be small? It is the small ones of the world, like me and mine, that survive the upheavals and the wars and the persecutions. When you are small they don't notice you. When you raise your head they notice you and chop it off. Long ago, when you were small, when we knew you, you were happy. Can't you see yourself that it is only since you became big that the freedom is gone out of your life?'

'It's easy to be small and become big, Dominick,' said Murdoc earnestly. 'But it is not easy to be big and become small. You don't know what I am talking about, but I do. Nobody can do it to me. Nobody will.'

'But what are you going to do?' Dominick asked. 'Even if

Coote promises you the moon, how can you believe him? Wouldn't you be better off tending a poor *creaght* in the hills, becoming old and dying?'

'No, no, no! You don't understand me, Dominick,' he almost shouted. 'Do you know, I am happier at this moment than I have been for a long time. My mind is alive. Now I am doing something. I would prefer to be dead than to be doing nothing. I would give the rest of my life for the moment when I step out of that panel and Coote sees me. Man, it will make me young again. But I wouldn't be able for it, if I didn't know that you will be waiting on the river for me. That makes it a fair chance, and if this fails, I promise you, I will go back with you and become a herder of sheep on Ben Gorm, as true as I am here. Watch it now. Guide her into the stream.'

They left the main river and drifted into the narrow mill stream by a groyne of loosely piled, seaweed-covered rocks. The tide was fairly high in the river but it was beginning to ebb as they closed on the walls of the town, and scraped down by them. The town smells came back to Dominick's nostrils, even sharper than he had ever remembered them. There was no sound to be heard except the sibilant retreat of the tide and the rising noise of the river water on the rough river bed.

Murdoc was crouched in front, feeling his way along by the wall. He checked their passage by rubbing his big palms against the stone walls. The dark arch of the opening to the South Milinn loomed in front of them.

'The gate is not down,' Murdoc whispered. 'Hold her here, Dominick.'

Dominick let the boat on a little, then stood and raised his arms and grasped the stones of the arch above his head with his hands. Murdoc was stripping off his top clothes. He threw them in the boat and then stood only in his trousers, with a knife stuck in his belt.

'I'm going now, Dominick,' he said. 'This is the way to live, eh?' He was nearly chuckling. If he could have seen his face, Dominick knew that the same recklessness would be back in his eyes, the quirk at the side of his mouth. It was the way he had nearly always seen him. Maybe it was the way he was at his best. Having something to overcome, somebody to fight. Not a priest burning at the stake. That would be hateful to Murdoc. That would drive Murdoc to drink. How could they have thought that Murdoc would be responsible for a thing like that?

Dominick felt his face close to his own, a naked arm around his neck.

'God be with you, Dominick,' said Murdoc. 'You were good to come with me. Nobody will defeat you, I know.'

'Only you, Murdoc,' said Dominick.

'I can't be fitted anywhere, Dominick,' said Murdoc. 'Because I don't know myself. I only know two things. People hurt me, or people are kind to me. I have always tried to repay both.'

'Coote is clever,' said Dominick. 'Don't forget!'

'He has the devil for his teacher,' said Murdoc, 'and maybe I'm working in the same school.'

'I hope not,' said Dominick.

'Wait for me,' said Murdoc. 'Don't forget to wait.'

'I'll be here,' said Dominick.

Murdoc slipped over the side into the fast stream, held the boat for a moment and let himself go. There was terrible suction in the water where it had been confined to put pressure on the wheel of the mill. Murdoc let it carry him, just keeping his head above the water, until his feet were swept out from him and his reaching hands felt the wooden blades of the wheel. It was stationary, so he swung himself up until he was free of the water, and then he walked along the slippery blade of the wheel, with the one he was grasping cutting into his belly, until his bare feet found the stone walk. The wheel was in the open. The shaft going from it led off into the mill. But here there was a walk past it leading to St John's Lane across a second stream. He let himself down into this. It was flowing slowly and the water of it only came to his chest. Across this he climbed and heaved himself on to the small pier and stood there for a moment, until a lot of the water had dripped from him. Then he headed for the arched opening into the lane.

It was very dark. Some houses he passed were dimly lighted. He had to close his nostrils to the stench that was assailing them, all kinds of smells; that always brought to his mind the smell of heather and the pine woods as if to compensate his nose.

There were no people abroad in the lane. He stood perfectly still at the archway leading into the street. Just as he put his face out the moon seemed to come over the top of the tall buildings to shine on it. He pulled back, but the street was deserted. A mounted soldier had just passed. He could hear the hooves on the stones. He ran across the street, fast and silently, ran through a very narrow lane with tall houses on either side. He came into the Bohar Cam, and didn't pause until, meeting the wall of the churchyard, he leaped at it and swarmed over it and dropped among the tombstones on the inside of it.

He was breathing fast. Too fat, he was thinking. I have put on fat. I will want to watch myself. I am not as fit as I should be. Even the thought of that, another obstacle to overcome, made him laugh. Coote mustn't know, he thought, that I am not fit.

He felt his way through the gravestones. The moon was shining clear now, as clear as it could through the grey overcast that had pursued them since they set out.

He remembered Columba's instructions, delivered in the calm way of hers. He found the place, and moved the stone, and went down into the musty depths, feeling with his feet, and pulled the stone after him. This was only an interior passage, Columba told him. There are six others which I don't know that lead out under the walls. It was the way the important members of the Tribes departed in times of trouble; either to flee with their possessions or else negotiate a bit of treachery with the besiegers.

He felt his way along. His outstretched hands touched the walls on either side, and his feet felt the slippery stones under them. It was very cold, very damp, and smelled of he knew not what. He went down and down and then the walk levelled off and he followed that for some time, and then as his feet met the steps that went up and up the muscles started to tighten in his belly.

Coote was feeling pleased with himself, as at the table in his room he signed his name to the parchment with a flourish. The bedroom was a comfortable place. There was a big bed with four carved and twisted pillars of polished oak holding a canopy. The furnishing of the bed and the room held traces of the feminine. It had belonged to Columba. There was a wood fire burning in a big open fireplace. The walls were panelled to half their height and the rest was covered with tapestries. He was sitting in a curved-back chair writing at a dark oak table. There was an oil lamp on the table, burning an aromatic oil, and thick candles were lighted in brackets on the walls.

Yes, I have done well, Coote thought. At this moment I am the most powerful man in the country. Just because he had the intelligence to anticipate the change that was coming. His moves had been swift. He had practically kidnapped the Governor of the town in order to make him declare with his troops for a Free Parliament. Securing the town he had ridden hard to Dublin. He had gathered the right people and there they had declared too for a Free Parliament. All these things had repercussions, but if they had, the name of Coote was always at the head or at the foot of the right documents. He was a good soldier who had obeyed his orders. He had obeyed the orders of the Protector and he would obey the orders of the King. Any orders issued to Coote under the name of the Government had been carried out to the letter however sanguinary they might be. That was not for him to judge. No man could ever say about him that he hadn't carried out his orders for God and the Government.

He smiled.

It had been a pleasing thing to become Mayor. Lord President of Connacht, Governor, and Mayor of the city, with faithful and frightened men in Dublin looking to him for a lead, his vast possessions tightened in a legal and unbreakable covenant with all the right parties. He could even settle down, he thought, as Lord-Lieutenant of the country. It was time for the right people to come back. It would be better to serve a king. Under a king the rewards were great too, and the dignity and honour of your position were discernible, and your investment with them had all the legality and sacredness of tradition.

He would rest now and take it easy. He would let the honours fall on him. He saw in the far years ahead a peaceful existence in palatial places which up to now he had no time to enjoy. Hunting, sporting. He would be a host at entertaining parties. This damned puritanism would die, colour would come back into the world, clothes, movement, enjoyment. All the damned drab years would be thrown away. There would be graceful living again for cultured people, music, poesy, the theatre, and one could hear the whisper as you passed by in great elegance: That is Sir Charles Coote, or Lord Cootehill, or the Earl of Galway. That would be pretty, what?

It took a few moments for his eyes to prove to him that he wasn't looking at an apparition. A naked, hairy-chested, grey-haired, big-faced, grimly smiling ghost, who had stepped from a panel directly facing him. The panel had clicked behind him, and that was the little noise that gave reality to his presence.

'God be with you, Coote,' said Murdoc softly. He enjoyed his moment.

Coote's hands were gripping the table as if he expected death. But as his panic-stricken eyes saw that there was no weapon in Murdoc's hands, he relaxed. He sat back on his chair but Murdoc was pleased to see that there was a sort of jumping tic at the side of his eye.

'You came an odd way,' said Coote.

'I came the way that Columba left,' said Murdoc. He saw the tightening of his face. 'It's a pity you didn't try harder to find how she left.'

Coote was in his shirt-sleeves.

'You could have come the front way,' said Coote. 'I would have seen you.'

'I tried to see you twice,' said Murdoc. 'I was refused. I sent you messages. They remained unanswered.'

'I have been busy,' said Coote. He realized that he was afraid. He had never before in his whole life been alone with fear. There had always been somebody else to carry the burden of it for him. 'What do you want from me?'

'You promised me something,' said Murdoc. 'You know that. It is far away from me. It is farther away than ever it was. You killed it, throwing coins on white sand. Why did you do that, Coote?'

'I like men to be obedient,' said Coote in a moment of honesty. 'You were insolent. You had taken the girl. You did nothing about finding that priest.'

'So you decided to destroy me,' said Murdoc. 'What did you think would happen to me when you left?'

'I thought they would kill you,' said Coote. 'I thought you deserved death for your defiance.'

'They didn't kill me physically,' said Murdoc. 'They just killed me with their feelings. I had given away a lot for you, Coote, but I thought the promised rewards were worth it. For a real reward you stripped me naked of everything I possessed, my people, my friends, my lover, my son, all.'

'You still had Rinn Mhil,' said Coote.

'I had,' said Murdoc, 'until you decided to sell that too. How much did the Blakes pay you for it?'

'How did you know that?' asked Coote.

'The walls and the winds have ears,' said Murdoc. 'I heard. So now where do we stand, Coote?'

Coote got to his feet slowly. He put his hands behind his back and walked to the fire. He was smiling grimly when his back was to Murdoc. He has no arms except a knife, he was thinking, and there is a loaded pistol under the pillow of my bed. So he could afford not to fear. Murdoc was convicted, found guilty, and would die. Coote felt his nerves tingling. He turned to face him.

Murdoc saw the change in his eyes and closed a little on him.

'Unless you can provide, and fulfil your promises, Coote,' said Murdoc, 'you are going to die. Think over that. After a few moments you will have no more life in you, no blood. You will be face to face with God who so commends you. He will pat you on the back for the children you have killed. He will praise you for the countless thousands you have sent into slavery, and he will kiss your hands for the bewildered ones you have hanged from many gibbets. Isn't that a pleasing thought, Coote?'

Coote's mouth was dry. He had to moisten his lips.

'Who has appointed you an executioner?' he asked.

'The people,' said Murdoc. 'All the voiceless ones. You made the law, therefore it is your law. It does not extend into the wild places because, as you have decreed, there live only beasts in those places who have no right to law, since they are the mere Irish. So they have commissioned me. All the voices of the dead.'

'And yet,' said Coote, 'you will bargain with their wishes?'

'Yes,' said Murdoc, 'because if you don't keep your promises, then I can always carry out the sentence.'

'I must sit down,' said Coote. 'I don't feel well. You have frightened me.'

'I am pleased that you have the courage to admit it,' said Murdoc.

He watched him closely.

Coote sat on the bed, his hands widely out from him, supporting his trembling body. Because he *was* trembling, and the fingers of his right hand were beside the pillow.

'All right,' said Coote then, 'I capitulate. I will make you the Lord of Iar-Connacht.'

'And what proof have I,' Murdoc asked, 'that this time you will really carry out your promise?'

'This is the proof,' said Coote, taking the pistol from under his pillow and pulling the trigger.

He should have waited, because his hand was not steady and Murdoc had been watching him closely. He jumped, the pistol boomed, and Murdoc felt the ball hitting his side, low down over his hip. It passed through the soft flesh and Coote saw the spurting blood, but by then it was too late for him because Murdoc was over on top of him with the knife bared. Coote had barely time to say 'No! No!' before the long moment that Murdoc had foretold for him arrived and he died on the bed, and already they were pounding on the room door, and Murdoc, trying to stem the flow of blood with his hand held to his side, was back at the panel.

But there he stopped, because he didn't know how to open it from this side. They were attacking the door now with axes, so he had no time.

He leaped over the dead Coote and the bed and got to the window behind. It was a narrow window with leaded panes. He reached for a chair and broke the panes outwards. He squeezed his body through. The remnants of the glass tore his flesh. He looked down. He was three storeys up, but twelve feet below the thatched roof of another house was built up against the wall of this one. He let himself down as far as he could go with his hands.

For a moment his eyes were on a level with the sloping sill and he could see the dead body of Coote on the bed, the mouth open and the eyes open, and could see the wood of the door behind bursting under the blows, then he dropped.

The straw was soft under his feet. He turned and walked down it and then felt with his feet for a window-sill, found it, transferred his arms to that and let his body down and dropped. He was in a lane. Up above there was a figure at the broken window. There was the loud sound of a shot and a voice calling 'Assassin! Assassin!' He ran from the lane and found himself in North Street. The moon was shining brightly in it. He fled down its length. It seemed to him that the whole town was coming awake. There were shots being fired and loud calling and lights were springing on in the houses. But he had run down the North Street into Lombard Street across the Shambles and into Kirwan's Lane before he heard the noise of boots on the cobbles and the sound of hooves. He paused here. He was very breathless.

He couldn't afford to wait. He was losing blood. They could trail him with it, and he ran down this lane into the lane of Martin's Mill, and pausing here he looked at the steps that led up to the ramparts.

They were unguarded.

So it would have to be this way. He ran up the steps and tried to think what depth of water there would be at this spot outside the walls. The tide had been ebbing when he left Dominick. Dominick, he thought. There is Dominick! He will be there. Dominick will set me free.

He reached the ramparts and climbed up and looked below him at the sea-flooded river. He could see the bridge to his right and he searched the arch under it through which the far stream flowed and he thought he could see the darker darkness of Dominick and the boat. He waved an arm.

It seemed to be a signal. From all sides muskets roared, from behind him and from the towers on the bridge, but they were aiming at a difficult target in the deceptive moonlight.

Murdoc only felt the ball that hit him in the back and hurled him off the ramparts into the water below. Nobody will ever see me die, he thought, as he fell and the water found him.

CHAPTER THIRTY

BUT DOMINICK saw him.

From under the bridge, where he had moved quietly and was holding on to the rough stones. He had heard the shots and the shouts in the town, and, his heart beating fast, he had remained there, looking behind him and ahead of him.

He had happened to be looking in the right direction because he had traced the sounds inside the town down towards Martin's Mill.

He had seen Murdoc on the ramparts, and when he had stood tall there and waved, Dominick had thought: Oh, you fool, you fool! and when the fusillade came, he had seen him fall as if he had been punched in the back.

And by this time Dominick and the boat were into the stream which was running fast on the ebbing tide, and he had pulled very hard, very hard, the fifteen yards that separated him from the Mill, and when the body of Murdoc rose from the water he was near him and reached a hand for him, but then decided and did what he had to do very quickly. For there were balls hitting the water around them, from the bridge behind and from the ramparts, so Dominick, still holding on to Murdoc, slipped over the side of the boat into the water, and held him close as both of them were taken by the cataracts that were formed just here by the great stones of the ragged bed of the stream. The boat drifted away lightly.

He didn't hear any more shots.

When his head emerged from the white flurry of water, or when his flailing feet hit the bed of the river he kicked away towards the far side. Between the ebb of the tide and the swift coarse flow of the river they were tossed like ships of wood on the power of the water, but the farther they got from the quays and the walls, the less chance there was of their being seen, and Dominick had no thought of how long it took or whether they were safe and sound, when he felt the rounded green-weeded rocks under his feet, and holding tightly to the body of his friend, falling and rising and falling again, but aided by the slimy dangerous rocks themselves, he dragged him as far

292

as he could from the grip of the river, on to the point of the land that was known as Rintinane, and he stretched him there on the stones and bent his face over him.

He had seen the hole in his back, but there was no blemish on his chest, so the ball was still in him. He put his hand on his face. It wasn't cold yet.

'Murdoc! Murdoc!' he called softly.

His heart was still beating. He could feel that when he put his hand on him, and then he saw the blood welling from his side.

'Murdoc! Murdoc!' he called again, and the eyes fluttered open and looked at him. His face was pale and looked green in the moonlight.

'Coote won,' he whispered. 'Go, Dominick. Go now. Save yourself.'

'What happened, Murdoc? Tell me what happened to you,' Dominick asked him.

'Coote clever,' said Murdoc. 'Pistol under the pillow.' He tried to laugh, but blood came out of his mouth. He knew this. 'But Coote is dead too,' said he. 'Dominick!'

'Yes,' said Dominick.

'Don't let them get me,' he said. 'Put me on the tide. They must not get me, Dominick. Now. Let me go now. On the tide. Hear, Dominick?'

'Yes,' said Dominick, 'all right, Murdoc.'

He closed his eyes. Dominick thought his face looked young in the light of the moon, all the grossness was wiped from it, as if it had been done by a healing hand.

'I didn't kill Sebastian,' Murdoc was whispering. 'I didn't kill Sebastian. Tell them.'

'Yes, Murdoc,' said Dominick. 'I'll tell them.'

'Sebastian knows,' said Murdoc. 'He knows, Dominick.'

'He knows,' said Dominick, and then Murdoc was dead. Dominick could hardly believe it, but Murdoc was dead; his tempestuous, confused, noble and ignoble life was snuffed out of him. Why, he should have a great wake, Dominick was thinking, so that people could say he did such a thing and such a thing and it was good, even if he did such another thing and such another thing and it was bad. Who is going to be the judge of Murdoc but God? And Sebastian would be there to speak for him.

Dominick was very sad. He felt very lonely, kneeling on the

wet rocks beside the body of his friend. Because he was my friend, he thought, he was indeed. There were feelings in us that were the same, for all the feelings in us that were different.

There was shouting behind him now, calling and more shots and the sound of horses. They would be pouring out over the bridge, he thought, and coming down this way by the reaches of the river.

He caught at Murdoc's shoulder and turned his head towards the water. He had to pull him over the rocks again. He hated doing this, but he felt too tired and exhausted to carry him. When the water was to his waist it was easier to manoeuvre the body; he turned with it and walked and swam with it until he could feel the pull of the river at his legs and the power of the ebbing tide. He went dangerously far out into the water before he let the body go. He didn't let it go until the pull of the water itself took it from his hands, and then he freed it and the tide took it from him and rolled it and turned it once or twice before it embedded it in the centre of itself and carried it away, into the bay, into the sea, to become part of it, maybe white bones on a Connmaicnemara shore.

Then he waded back himself and stood breathing heavily. He felt drained of strength and intelligence. He knew he should try to be getting away from where he was, so he moved along the rocky shore, stumbling and falling. There was little chance of his getting away, he thought. This point of Rintinane was a bleak place. It was flat. There was no place on the face of it where a man could hide and rest until he had recovered his strength. Anyhow, he thought, I have lived long enough. There isn't such a lot left for me. All the people I love are gone, Eibhlin and Sebastian and Murdoc. One time the thought of my children would have spurred me to new life and new endeavour, but even they no longer need me. Mary Ann would have her Dualta and she would live and survive, and Peter could match anyone in the world at whatever he wanted to do and make the name of this MacMahon survive.

So what in the name of God did it matter what became of him? Just that they would say when they caught him that he was the assassin of Coote. Such a thought nauseated him. He wouldn't touch Coote with a long stick, not to mention killing him. He would hate to be known as the assassin of Coote, and even if he was cut into little pieces he could never be got to say who was the assassin.

He walked along the shore. It gave way from rocks to sand. This reminded him of Sebastian. You will have to be kind to Murdoc, he thought. He did many good things in his life. You will have to speak up for him. He stood and turned.

He could see them, small figures in a line behind him. They were walking because no horse could travel this stony beach without a broken leg.

Then to his left down near the water he saw a crouched figure running. So he didn't run himself.

He stood. Might as well be now, he thought. Just as well.

Until this figure started talking.

'Run, Father, for the love of Almighty God,' the figure was calling, 'or they'll get you,' and the voice of this figure was the voice of his son, Peter. Dominick thought he was in the middle of a nightmare, until Peter was close to him, looking behind.

'This way, for God's sake, fast, Father,' he said, catching his arm and urging him. 'Dualta is at the end of the point with a boat. Please, Father, what's wrong with you? Run, for the love of God.'

Dominick couldn't say anything. Peter ran ahead of him, beckoning him. Is this a dream? he wondered, and then decided to go along with it. He ran and the figure was still ahead of him. There was a strong breeze blowing from the river.

'Keep low! Keep low!' Peter was saying. Peter? How could it be Peter? Was this the extension of a dream, like what poor Columba had felt for the dead Murdoc?

But whatever it was, it brought interest to him, if only to find out how such a thing could be. So he bent low and followed the crouching figure over sand, over rocks, over big boulders, to a place where the blunt black snout of a sailing boat was jammed on the shore.

He saw the man in the boat, and even as he saw him, heard the creaking of the sails. He felt the hand on his arm, the urgency of it, and he climbed into the boat and then the boat was free on the sea and the black sail rose over his head and the wind took the sail and the boat turned from it and silently and swiftly headed out on the water of the bay.

Behind them there were shouts and shots.

'Keep low! Keep low!' Dualta was calling. Dualta too? How could he be part of the dream? But he *was* part of it.

Dominick sat in the bottom of the boat. There was water in it and it swirled around his already wet clothes. He let his head drop into his hands. He was trembling, until he felt warm breath on his cheek and heard the voice of his son talking to his ear.

'Are you all right, Father?' Peter was asking. 'You're not hurt, are you?'

Dominick raised his head and felt for his son's shoulder with his hand. It was real, substantial.

'How, Peter? How?' he asked.

'Well, you are getting old, Father,' said Peter. There was a smile in his voice.

'Old?' Dominick asked.

'We decided when you left,' said Peter, 'Rory and Mary Ann and myself. He's not as young as he was, we decided. So Rory planned it, just like he was fighting a battle. Dualta and myself came by sea. You went by lake. We watched you. We got here first and I was watching the river, all the time. I saw your boat under the arch when the moon came out and all the rest. That's all. It was lucky we were here. Lucky the boat was hidden off the point. It was all luck.'

'Not luck,' said Dominick. 'Nothing like that is luck. So I'm an old man, hah? And what about Mary Ann? You left her alone?'

'No,' said the voice of Dualta. 'My father is with her.' He was laughing. 'He came over and brought three sheep for the wedding. You hear that. He says: Three sheep are just a gift for the wedding.'

'If you hadn't come I would have died,' said Dominick.

'That's right,' said Peter. 'Now you must know you are getting old and you must settle down to a quiet life.'

'Another thing I know,' said Dominick as he raised himself to look on the moonlit waters of the bay.

'If they send boats after us,' said Dualta, 'we will land and cut across to the mountains.'

'That would be best,' said Peter.

One time, Dominick thought, I would be doing all the planning.

'I know another thing,' said Dominick loudly.

'What's that?' Peter asked.

'It's this,' said Dominick. 'I really have a son. I am not alone.'

L'ENVOI

DOMINICK HAD his son until the following autumn.

Then one beautiful evening he said goodbye to him.

Dualta was holding the boat against the great wooden side of the anchored ship, and Peter had one foot on the rope-ladder and one foot in the small boat. There was a dark-complexioned seaman bending over the rails of the ship above, gesticulating madly, pointing to the setting sun.

'What's wrong with that fellow?' Dominick asked.

'He's doing a powerful lot of talking,' said Dualta.

Rory, who was looking down at them, said:

'It is time to go, Peter.'

'Well, God be with you, Father,' said Peter, looking at his apparently calm and unfeeling father; wishing that he himself could say all the things he wanted to say, but feeling tongue-tied.

'God be with you too, Pedro,' Dominick said. His son was seventeen. The wind was ruffling his fair hair. He was a well-set boy, taller than Dominick, but with his physical toughness, and his mother's delicacy of feature, Dominick thought. Rory was taking himself and three others to a seminary in France.

'This is as much working for our country as if I was going to be a farmer or a soldier, Father, said Peter. 'It's just in a different way.'

'Aye,' said Dominick, 'I know that, Pedro.'

'Only about seven years,' said Peter, 'and I will be back.'

Ah, but you will be different, so different, Dominick thought.

They heard the sound of the great rising sail as the blocks screamed.

'I'll have to go,' said Peter. 'I'll pray for you, Dualta, that you won't have too hard a time with Mary Ann.'

'I'll manage,' said Dualta with a laugh.

'Well,' said Peter, and then he climbed up the side of the ship and Dualta shoved away.

'I'll be back in a month, Dominick,' Rory was calling.

'Good! Good!' Dominick shouted, still looking at the face of his son who was leaning on the rail, trying not to look sad.

The anchor was weighed, and the sails filled, and the French ship moved away from them, leaving them looking very small on the great Atlantic.

Dualta set the sail on the boat and they headed in for the distant shore. There were no words between them. Dominick just sat on the seat there, staring before him, his hands dangling between his knees.

When they landed in the cove, Mary Ann was there waiting for them.

'He's gone all right?' she asked.

'He's gone,' said Dualta.

Dominick left them. He climbed out of the cove and up over the land until he came to a high spot where he could see the last rays of the sun shining on the white sails. It was well away. It was like a toy ship now. He sat on a stone and kept watching it.

That's that, he thought. All the striving and all the fighting and the building, and the anchoring in the fair land, there it all is now sailing away. For what has a man to work for if he is not to work for his son? For in the middle of all the working you are dreaming dreams, of your son and your son's son. You are dreaming stability. He had felt very calm when he was told. Indeed he had marvelled at his own calm all along, but now his eyelids were burning and there was a weight on his heart. There would never be a dynasty of the MacMahons in the fair land.

'Don't be sad,' said Mary Ann. She was standing beside him. She looked at him, the fair hair turning almost white at the temples, and the strongly lined face. 'You knew he would go like that.'

He shook his head. He didn't know.

'Well, everyone else knew,' said Mary Ann. 'Didn't he have Sebastian's mark on him?' I never knew, he thought. It was like a blow in the face when he told me.

'And you have me,' said Mary Ann. No, I haven't you, he thought. You have left me too, as is right, but you have left me. 'And you have Dualta,' said Mary Ann. 'He likes you very much, although I don't see how he could like an old gloomy one like you.'

Dominick grunted.

'Well, it's true,' said Mary Ann. 'And now you are going to have a grandson as well. What more can you want?'

Even that failed to shake him out of it.

'Aren't you coming home?' Mary Ann asked.

'Home after you,' he said, looking down, rubbing a fist in a palm.

Mary Ann looked helplessly at Dualta. He inclined his head and she went to him, and they walked slowly away.

He knew they were gone.

He dropped his head and rubbed his eyes fiercely with his knuckles. It shouldn't be, he thought. I don't deserve all this. I have been hit hard enough.

Strange, he thought, the places in yourself that you don't know about, the deep places inside you that can be weeping all the time that your mouth is talking or laughing.

The inside of you is like a well, a deep well about which you know very little. That must be your soul, where all the real things take place. And if it is a right deep place, and has been tended by your head, then he supposed that God would be deep down in there whispering to you always about the realities. So that would be the real fair land, deep down in yourself.

He turned on the rock and looked.

Not that this physical one wasn't fair too. The mountains were all purple-tinged and they ranged all around him protectingly, and below him was the white sand of the shore, and the heaving sea was stained with many colours.

Then he saw Mary Ann climbing the hill away from him, with Dualta walking beside her holding her hand. Mary Ann's head was bent. It was not usual, he thought, for Mary Ann's head to be bent. He grinned at the thought and rose to his feet.

He called out: 'Hey, Man! Wait there a minute!' and then as if he was a young goat, instead of an ageing (as they told him) forty-four-year-old man, he ran from his own rock down the hill into the valley and up to the top of the other hill where they waited and watched his running in surprise.

'What are we going to call him?' Dominick asked.

'Call who?' said Mary Ann, her mouth open.

'The new son,' said Dominick.

'Oh,' said Dualta, at once, 'we will call him Dominick, of course.'

He was winking at Mary Ann.

'Certainly we will,' said Mary Ann. 'Didn't you know that?'

'It's a sound name,' said Dominick judiciously, 'and let me tell you he is going to have a fine inheritance.'

They looked ahead of them. Around the corner of the hill in front of them they could see the long lake and behind it the deeply shadowed mountain, and on the slope of that they could see their house, which had been carved out of the hill, and they could see the pattern of the four wide fields that had been cleared; two of them were green and the other two were yellow with the stubble of the harvested corn.

'And we have only begun,' said Dominick. 'Eh, Dualta?'

'Only begun,' said Dualta.

'Then let us go home in the name of God,' said Dominick.

And they walked home.

All Pan Books are available at your local bookshop or newsagent, or can be ordered direct from the publisher. Indicate the number of copies required and fill in the form below.

Send to: Macmillan General Books C.S.
                    Book Service By Post
                    PO Box 29, Douglas I-O-M
                    IM99 1BQ

or phone: 01624 675137, quoting title, author and credit card number.

or fax: 01624 670923, quoting title, author, and credit card number.

or Internet: http://www.bookpost.co.uk

Please enclose a remittance* to the value of the cover price plus 75 pence per book for post and packing. Overseas customers please allow £1.00 per copy for post and packing.

*Payment may be made in sterling by UK personal cheque, Eurocheque, postal order, sterling draft or international money order, made payable to Book Service By Post.

Alternatively by Access/Visa/MasterCard

Card No.

Expiry Date

Signature

Applicable only in the UK and BFPO addresses.

While every effort is made to keep prices low, it is sometimes necessary to increase prices at short notice. Pan Books reserve the right to show on covers and charge new retail prices which may differ from those advertised in the text or elsewhere.

NAME AND ADDRESS IN BLOCK CAPITAL LETTERS PLEASE

Name

Address

8/95

Please allow 28 days for delivery.
Please tick box if you do not wish to receive any additional information. ☐